Y0-CZF-474

THE MASTERS CONNECTION

Also by David Chandler

THE MIDDLEMAN
THE APHRODITE
THE GANGSTERS
CAPTAIN HOLLISTER
HUELGA!
THE RAMSDEN CASE
FATHER O'BRIEN AND HIS GIRLS
THE GLASS TOTEM
A LITTLE MORE TIME

David Chandler

THE MASTERS CONNECTION

ARBOR HOUSE
New York

To Rita Chandler
with gratitude, admiration,
and more love than ever

Copyright © 1981 by David Chandler

All rights reserved, including the right of reproduction in whole or in part in any form. Published in the United States of America by Arbor House Publishing Company and in Canada by Fitzhenry & Whiteside, Ltd.

Library of Congress Catalog Card Number: 80-70213

ISBN: 0-87795-302-3

Manufactured in the United States of America

10 9 8 7 6 5 4 3 2 1

PART ONE

I.

HE EMERGED from the community center with the last two of the students who always flocked around his desk after every lecture. All the lights in the building went out as they descended the steps. "Can I drive you home, Mr. Glidden?" one of them asked. It was a fine night after a week of heavy rainstorms and he looked forward to the walk.

He was under orders not to let any members of his classes in the adult education program know where he lived, just as no one was aware of his real identity. The U.S. marshals had installed him in a smallish city under the Government Witness Protection Program; they had much experience in such matters, so he followed their instructions to the letter. The officials had not been so sure of his teaching activity, but the judge had made it a condition of his discharge from prison when he had reduced the sentence at their urging. "It would be better for this man, with his great knowledge and wide experience, to make amends to society by a socially constructive act such as teaching," the court said.

He was John Edward Ebersol. He was now a teacher in an adult education enterprise. Once he was known in financial communities around the world as more than a genius; he was also a peerless multinational corporation manipulator and executive. He was Number Two in the vast investment conglomerate that came to be known as the International People's Investment and Savings Fund; the set in the know said it was Jack Ebersol who actually made that billion-dollar dream happen.

He walked quickly. He was lean and hard—fifty-five months in prison had seen to that—and could jump with ease huge puddles left at every street corner by the recent storms. He considered himself exiled, like some Russian the Kremlin did not think worth the trouble of destroying outright. Exile in a grubby city was better than prison, where he had had an exceptionally difficult time, a violent world where he had begun life by taking a ten-inch gash across his face because some caged monster thought the new prisoner had not shown him sufficient respect. The marshals who protected him now told him they believed the violence directed against him had been bought and paid for outside prison walls.

He liked teaching, something he had often thought of back in the old days when he dealt with tens and hundreds of millions of dollars, francs, pounds, connected by telex to finance ministeries and banks all over the world. The students—older people, living on retirement incomes, some large, others modest—said he gave their lives meaning again. That made him feel good, as he had not in a very long time.

He was in love. Walking home, he felt an elation he had not known for years. Everywhere he saw signs of life reasserting itself after a vast disaster. It gave him proof life always offers hope and help for its victims. Mud could be swept away, fields restored, a small city's overburdened sewer system would begin to function again. In the soft, gentle night, the world seemed more beautiful to him than it had in a decade. In prison he had dreamed of a woman like Connie Martin. She had lived constantly in his imaginings; there were no inhibitions there of what the rest of the world would think of such a creature. Too large, too bold, too gaudily bedecked, too vulgar? Not there. He was a man who had known fashionable, worldly and sophisticated women the world over, but his prison masturbations were always with a lady in very high heels, silkily clad, big-busted, red-mouthed and softly and heavily fleshed. And here, in this city where he was hidden, his dreams had come to life.

The center was a mile from the old apartment court where a place had been found for him to live. Wisteria Gardens was a checkerboard of semidetached cottages with thin walls along a cracked cement walk that linked one to the other and to garages and garbage cans in the rear. Reasonable. Clean. There was even a swimming pool, token of the days when the neighborhood was not decayed and abandoned and the rent would have been three times more.

Ebersol could no more help observing material values than a bird could resist flying. He was capable of enjoying the Wisteria Gardens as a place of luxury after life in various prison cells, but he also assessed it as he did everything in the world, as a commodity, tradeable and worth money, taking in all the factors that could determine merit in the universal marketplace. Not that Jack Ebersol had ever been interested in real estate as such. Land and buildings were of marginal interest those days when Alan Masters, Larry Burns, Cal Trimborn and Bill Levi and he sat astride some two billion and three hundred million dollars of assets garnered from small investors the world over. Mere land and buildings were minor concerns to such a Fund's chief operating officer.

Prison hardens most men. It had not conferred that favor on Jack Ebersol. He did not like to think it broke him, but he knew it had changed him. He had believed Alan Masters. He wanted the Fund to become what Alan had promised—a source of profit for folk from Britain to South Africa, from Canada to Paraguay, a chance for ordinary men and women to put their money to work with the same advantages great investment houses reserved for their favored clientele.

When the Fund broke apart, when stockholders' lawyers and prosecutors and law enforcement agencies of a dozen countries fell on it, savaged it, destroyed it, Alan ran, and got away with nearly two hundred million of its assets. Alan Masters found one extradition-free fortress nation after another. The others had all gone to jail, died, one after the other, suicide, drugs and drink, auto accidents—Cal Trimborn by jumping off the Golden Gate Bridge, Bill Levi in a car off a cliff, Larry Burns with sleeping pills, dead now, all of them, except himself. And of course Alan Masters remained free, laughing at the French, German, Italian, Swiss and U.S. authorities who wanted to put him on trial.

Jack Ebersol was out of breath when he reached the old apartment complex. He had enjoyed tonight's class at the center. The questions from the old students showed verve, perspicacity; there was no fatuous one this evening about what to do with Aunt Wilma's telephone stock. Word was out that the classes at the community center given by the new man were worth attending, and some good people had found their way to it. This was also a token of life reasserting itself, he thought, like the world after the relentless storms.

He turned into Wisteria Gardens. Number One was Herb and Mary Jardine, he a retired mechanic, she working as a waitress at the breakfast shift at a Denny's down the road. Next to the Jardines', a recent widower, Lou Gabriel, still bore his loss heavily, comforted by the aged and yellowing miniature poodle which had been part of life with the dear departed. Mr. Gabriel's lights were always out by nine.

His heart leaped a little when he saw the glow in the front windows of Number Three. The shade was drawn almost to the sill; if he bent down a little he would see in. Connie Martin often had a girl friend over for supper or after work. She was very close to the hairdressers at the Salon de Beauté around the corner. They stopped in for a drink and a meal before heading for home and husband, she said.

In the first weeks out of prison, provided with a new identity, a job, a place to live where the chances were few that he would be recognized, his big problem was women. He was a tall, still handsome man; his hair was thinning but it covered every inch of his scalp. Women still flirted; chance encounters seemed to open conversations with strangers eager to know him.

But he had turned shy. It was not that he was afraid. At first he told the government men who supervised his activities that he had no need for sex. They teased him and said he was a burned-out case. But, nevertheless, they urged him to be careful. One day he would be helpful to them in finally nailing their number one target, Alan Masters, which was all they cared about.

When Connie Martin had moved into the Wisteria Gardens the month before, he trembled when he first saw her walk around the place. A big silver blonde wig topped a face that was like a child's, big innocent eyes over a full, eager mouth. Low-cut dresses showed expanses of a soft, tender chest. Too much makeup. Her rump waved as she went about in towering heels.

Connie was gentle, understanding of his shyness as they chatted around the pool; he took her to dinner several times. One night she held his hand in hers, kissed the trembling fingers, laid them on the breast that always swelled out of the too-snug dresses she wore, and said, "I'm lonely too, honey, you don't haveta be afraida me. You can spend the night here, baby, just so long as you leave me have my privacy and don't take no advantage. I wouldn't want people to think some man just knocks on my door whenever he wants to, ya understand what I'm trying' to tellya?"

He had not known how much he would come to cherish her, to need her. Home, he hoped before this night was over that she would open his door as she did so often, kept unlocked for her, she in a street coat against the chill, over nothing but that lovely, soft nakedness in which, whether Jack Ebersol or Raymond Glidden, he found manhood again.

"That's him getting home," Connie Martin said. "He leaves me know by moving around the joint."

"Good." Her caller wore a ski sweater with reindeer across the chest. He pulled a stocking cap low on his forehead as he prepared to leave. "Now you got it all straight?"

"I gotta tell you this," she parried. "He's a real nice guy."

"I'm a nice guy. Everybody's a nice guy. I got a job. You got a job." He turned toward the door. "You'll stick around here for a month. Take it real hard. Cry a lot."

"That'll be easy." Connie sighed and put a finger to an eyelid, where she pressed the fake lashes. "I like him. Poor shnook. Who is he? Why they doin' this to him?"

"Never mind. A month," the man in the ski sweater said. "Everything goes okay, I'll see you get a bonus."

"He says he loves me," she mused aloud. "I think the guy means it."

"Congratulations," the reindeer sweater said.

She let herself into his place a half hour later. Soft, silky dress with nothing under it except the push-up bra she needed and the tiniest bikini panties. He came at her hungrily, but she turned her lips from his. "You'll roon the makeup, lover," she pleaded.

"I always want you so," he whispered into the softness at her neck. "I'll never get enough of you."

"Later, sweetie, later. Take it easy. I'm not made of stone." She let his hot breath course to the show of bosom over the dress. "Oh,

God," she said, pushing him from her, "I want you too, you got me so hot you make me twitch, baby. It ain't going nowhere withoutcha. Please." She was free of him and saw he was embarrassed by his ardor. "I wanna go out tonight. I'm restless."

"Of course, my darling," he said. "Anything."

"It's my birthday, I'm not gonna tell you which. Let's just say it's not twenty and it's not thirty."

"We'll celebrate," he said happily.

"Later—" she reached his mouth and brushed it with soft, glossy lips, "I'm gonna eatcha alive, I'm gonna make you ball me four times."

She paused just as they were ready to leave. She remembered a row earlier that day with the neighbors. She'd brought a Coke bottle and a glass to the pool, against the rules, and had left the garbage cans uncovered the night before so dogs had got into them and turned them over. "They got me dead to rights and I lost my temper. I wanna write a note and apologize." Her writing was lousy. Could he help her, please? He took a sheet from a pile on his writing table and wrote in large capitals what she dictated:

> TO ALL CONCERNED: I'M SORRY FOR
> WHAT I DID. I HOPE EVERYBODY
> WILL FORGIVE ME.

Connie said "done," but he fixed it for her without comment. She said she'd sign it when she put it up over the garbage cans.

They went to the Red Wagon just off the Barstow cutoff, sat in a back booth near the jukebox and laughed over the funny things that were always happening to her. It was dark in the Red Wagon and there were not many customers and Connie didn't care about her smudging her lipstick here and they drank brandy and champagne which Connie said was called a French thirty-four and a half which meant it was only half as good as the real thing and she said she wanted to get real high tonight, so high she'd fly when they hit the sack.

"I adore you. You make me feel alive after being dead for a long time." He trembled when he spoke to her.

"Don't talk like that, Ray-baby," Connie declared and pushed him away.

He found her hand and pressed it to his mouth. "My darling, forgive me. I wouldn't do anything to offend you."

She called for more brandy and champagne and put her face to his chest and whispered that she was beginning to feel real horny, she would make him beg for mercy. Did he ever come with amyl nitrate? Wow! What a kick. People saw them kissing and groping and drinking in the back booth until closing time. The man was visibly staggering when they left the Red Wagon.

He drove her car home. He had to fight sleep most of the way, even though her hand kept reaching for his member. He pulled into her garage and let his head fall back; he closed his eyes wearily. Each of the apartments had its own narrow, wholly enclosed space in the row of garages behind the Wisteria Gardens. She put her hand over his when he moved to cut off the engine; it was cold and the heater was going; that was to be the explanation in case he asked, but she did not need it. She unzipped his trousers and quickly engulfed his member in her mouth. He looked in the rear-view mirror only briefly at the open garage door behind them; he took her head and held it tight between his hands.

"I gotta have you here and now," Connie moaned.

"Let's go in," he pleaded half heartedly. She lapped at his erection, bit at it with sheathed teeth, giggled, made obscene, ecstatic noises, begged him to wait, to wait. Time came to a stop. She pulled away after his orgasm, her hands reached to his eyes to be sure they were shut. His whole being was spent. She whispered how fine it had been and how strong and wonderful he was as she made sure he slept. Carefully she closed his trousers, her head still snuggled in his lap. She even pulled together the belt around his waist. "Take it real easy, baby," she whispered. "Let's sleep here a while." She began to hear his steady, rhythmic, heavy breathing. She made sure he was asleep and dropped the note she had had him write on the seat beside him. She pulled down the garage door and went to her apartment, making sure no one saw her. She had not turned off the TV; Bette Davis was wearing a silver-fox coat, *Dark Victory*, one of her favorites. She watched it for an hour before deciding to turn in for the night.

2.

FEAR, ALAN MASTERS had learned to live with; it was the boredom he could not manage. Boredom was life in a banana country with favorable extradition laws until the local politicos caved in to Washington's pressures, dreary towns behind high walls, strict upper-class Hispanic morality and a language he was too old to master. Or life in one of the money-short new nations strung like a necklace of fake pearls in the Caribbean. Grand Cayman, Granada, the Bahamas had banks, and that was good. But they too were vulnerable to pressure from their financial masters in New York, London, Paris, Frankfurt and Zurich.

Protection now accompanied him wherever his flight took him. Tall, powerfully constructed men were always at his side in public. When he moved from one country to another, he was passed from agency to agency. Private-security people had their own network, just like the official American, French and German ones. The bodyguards were all business, cold-eyed, efficient; he knew he was safe as long as he moved with them. He knew he had good reason to live always on the defensive.

He did not let his financial skills grow rusty. In fact, in the years since the collapse of the Fund, he thought he had grown sharper, more perceptive. To keep what he salvaged from the wreck of the International People's Investment and Savings Fund, he had to be shrewder and smarter than ever. Batteries of brilliant lawyers and advisers like Jack Ebersol were no longer available to him. He was managing without them. The others had ended in prison, or dead. They had taken their chances with courts, every one of them. Not Alan Masters. He knew what had to happen there. He remembered what he had told them: "Money buys freedom." He alone proved it could be done.

All the others—nailed. Spilled their guts. They said the Fund was always meant to be a scam. (They knew better.) They said they themselves took enormous profits for their own accounts. (They did well, but they did not speak of the profits the Fund showed all its investors in the go-go markets of the time.) He heard of threats to his life. Bill Levi: "I'll get that son of a bitch, that's my promise." Larry Burns to the reporters as he was led from the courtroom: "He betrayed me. He swindled thousands of people. One of us somewhere, somehow, will get even with him, as God is my judge."

Larry was a suicide. Bill Levi, dead. All of them caved in, gone, quiet. Good riddance.

But he was alive. He and Jack Ebersol.

Masters heard Jack was out of prison, sequestered somewhere by the U.S. marshals, filling their ears with the lies and half-truths they wanted to hear, preparing them for the day when Alan Masters stood before a U.S. court. Jack Ebersol was the most dangerous to him of all.

Remembering Jack Ebersol tore the fabric of his restless sleep. He tossed the blanket aside, gazed at the inky mass of black hair on the pink pillow next to his own, groaned a little and made his way from the drape-darkened bedroom to the sitting room. He looked out to what promised to be another sunny, smog-hazed day.

Outside the door, a Lebanese bodyguard sat, immobile, unsmiling. Reassured, Masters returned to the scene of last night's inevitable conquest. Mansour Bredi, general manager of the Hotel Saint-Georges, was more than a boniface, he was a good friend and had a staff who knew how to manage these things. The visits to Beirut were always filled with dangerous possibilities, but necessary. The banks here had numbered accounts, more protected than the Swiss. Several had gone bust but Alan Masters's bankers were wholly protective of their customer, not like certain gentlemen he had encountered in the Grand Cayman or the Bahamas, or even, truth to tell, in Panama or Liberia. But, of course, he had to keep in mind that Lebanon was a client state of Washington and could succumb to pressure from there at any time. And, also, for some time now he did not like what he observed in the Lebanese political scene. He saw conflicts which seriously threatened his financial holdings. Masters made his way to the telephone, past the battlefield of empty Veuve Cliquot bottles, the silver bucket now filled with water, overturned wine glasses, wilted flowers, barely touched patés and hors d'oeuvres, the ravaged supper table. He ordered the room cleaned up at once.

In the bedroom he pulled the draperies. The hair on the pillow stirred and a face was revealed to him, young, last night's makeup blurred; nothing could diminish its loveliness. It touched him; he had not known how beautiful the face was in daylight because he had known it only in nightclub light. "Gotta go. Right now."

The smeared eyelids opened, a sweet smile greeted him. "Hello, luv." A touch of Midlands in both words. She was part of a four-girl act working the hotel cabaret. It had taken him three nights to bring her to the penthouse. She held out bare arms above the coverlet. "Let's have another go at it, what do you say?" she teased, but half in earnest, he thought.

For a moment, he felt good. Cash had not been discussed, so this was a real victory. He settled for a kiss and an affectionate pull that got her out of bed. "I've got a very important meeting, my love. Please hurry."

While she was in the bathroom, he put several large notes of currency in her bag. He hoped she would not be offended when she found them. When he had first laid siege to her in the nightclub, she had pointed to the play-for-pay girls at the bar. "I think they're what you're looking for, sir," she said. She did not know this made the hunt a million times more interesting to a bored man.

When he finally managed to be rid of her and the cleaning biddies had erased yesterday in the sitting room, he made his phone calls. He called his people at the Beirut banks. He put in calls to Zurich and London, which was like praying for rain, local service being what it was. He worked on the papers that went everywhere with him.

At 11:30, precisely, Abu ben-Sandriquen was at the door. Sadriquen had come a long way from the day he had sought Alan Masters out at the Fund's head office in Geneva years before. Then he was a recent graduate of the Harvard School of Business Administration who'd made up his mind to work with what he called "the great financial genius, Alan Masters." He was a tall, exotically dark-complected young man who dressed himself in sound Ivy League tailoring. He was not ever going back to his country, he said. It was a vicious and corrupt state, he said. His life was to be devoted to the Fund.

But when the General overthrew the ancient and corrupt hierarchy, Sadriquen came to his boss and said it was his duty to return. His nation would need the financial skills he had learned with Alan Masters. Could he understand? There was at that time known to be only a little oil under the vast Sarumnan desert; not so much as to excite patriotic approval in Alan Masters for such a profitless move. But he could not stand in the way of his young assistant's love of country.

In a few years the Fund was destroyed, Masters was fighting for his fortune and his freedom, seeking safe havens in a series of rickety, poverty-stricken republics with assets less large than his own. And Sarumna discovered that it sat astride the largest and finest pool of sulphur-free crude oil in the world, enough, it was said, to last for a century.

Sadriquen had found Masters incognito with a forged Canadian passport here in dying Lebanon. "Tell your boss to take all your assets out of this place, as I'm doing," Masters had advised him. The other oil states were hesitating. "It's going down the drain."

Sadriquen strongly urged the General to follows Masters's advice. The leader was at first reluctant to do so; the other Arab leaders felt it a duty to stand beside the beleaguered state. But, finally, he allowed himself to be persuaded. The national deposits in the Beiruti banks had been largely withdrawn in time as the banks broke apart. "The nation could use such a man," the General told Abu ben-Sadriquen. "I need Masters here with us."

Sadriquen stood before Masters and grinned broadly. "I am so glad to see you. This is a great day for you and for me. We will leave this miserable, dying country. I have a plane waiting. You won't need those fellows at your door, you'll have our people to protect you, night and day."

"What are you talking about?" Masters said. The proposition had been laid before him weeks before. Citizenship. Immunity from extradition, no matter what existing treaties said. A guarantee of personal safety, new identity papers which would enable discreet foreign travel. Total freedom to join his personal assets to those of the General and a few trusted others. It had one vast disadvantage: Jack Ebersol was alive and working with the authorities back home.

"Look what good news I have brought you, dear friend," Sadriquen beamed as if he could read Alan Masters's thoughts. He gave him a copy of the *International Herald Tribune*, which had just arrived in Beirut.

The suicide of Jack Ebersol was page one. A picture showed him standing beside the Cézanne he had just bought at auction at Christie's in London for £100,000, before scandal and prison had broken him, handsome, smiling. He was found dead of carbon monoxide poisoning in an obscure town in California. He had been living under an assumed name with the help of the federal government, just as Alan Masters had been informed. It was now revealed that he was to be the prosecution's ace in the hole the day the wily Masters would misstep and be returned to the jurisdiction of the American courts, but he had taken his life in a friend's car.

The story went over the old ground: The Fund was described again as an international swindle which began by selling shares to American GIs abroad and used the money to seize control of banks and corporations and to expand its operations in a dozen countries in Europe and the Far East. It spoke of financial interests that once stretched from San Francisco to Kuwait, from Luxembourg to Hong Kong. All the old stuff that Alan Masters preferred not to read again, for, as usual, they had got it wrong, and it was tiresome for him to recall the banks that went sour on the Fund, the securities that failed to keep their promise. The fall of the stock markets—well, they weren't the only ones who couldn't predict that. They had never registered with the Securities and Exchange Commission. In the Unites States, after the fall, this had been made to look like a very sinister move, but the Fund could never have operated as successfully as it did, when it did, under those misbegotten rules.

Jack dead: dangerous as the man had become to his own survival, it was a stab in the guts. Masters put down the newspaper. He once had cherished Jack Ebersol, as a friend, as an adviser; he admired his style, his flair, the way he handled victory and defeat.

At his first trial Jack had stood up to all of them, admitted only to the prosecuting lawyers he was a buccaneer whose business it was to sail dangerous corporate waters. Risk was the nature of the game they all played, he insisted, no matter how hard the faceless men of Wall Street tried to conceal the character of all financial speculation. Conviction and denial of appeal and the agony of prison had ultimately broken Jack Ebersol. Masters knew all about everything after the fall. Ebersol's betrayal had become an obsession. Masters paid large sums of money to find out everything being done against him by the man he was once pleased to call his dearest friend, his good right arm, his better self. Now that Masters was free of Jack Ebersol he shuddered a little. Was he himself free now? How could he be? The whole world was conspiring against him. He faced police of half a dozen sovereign states, open and covert agencies, at every turn.

He looked up and saw Abu ben-Sadriquen staring at him as if he were some kind of statue. "Are you all right, Alan?"

It took Masters a moment to reply. He recalled their last meeting here in this very hotel.

"I'm fighting for my life, Sad. I have enemies."
"Come to us. You'll have all the protection you need. The General wants you at his right hand. You'd be his éminence grise. *His financial Kissinger. He says he'll see to it you'll get anything you want. Name it, Alan."*
A strange light burned in Masters's eyes. "My former number two."
"Jack Ebersol you mean, Alan?"
"He could destroy me. As long as he lives, I'm in danger."
"We could help you."
"I've heard that before, Sad. In the banana republics and in the golden Caribbean. My money was very attractive to the local politicos. But push comes to shove, Washington has a lot of power. And I'm out. Who's the biggest customer for your fine sulphur-free oil? That's what counts, not the rhetoric. I know they hate you guys and you hate them but that seven billion dollars a year they spend with you..."
"Twenty now," Sadriquen corrected him softly. "And growing."

"Means I'm a hostage to your oil and their money."

"No, dear friend. They are the hostage. You will sit astride a golden flood we don't know what to do with. I'm not speaking of the public side, you understand. We're spending for hopsitals, schools and all the rest of it. But there are critical financial needs outside our country. What you once did for thousands, I now suggest you do for us and for yourself. Tell me what you want done to this man you fear so much."

"I want Jack Ebersol dead."

Masters kept looking up at Sadriquen and let the newspaper fall to the floor.

"It says he died by his own hand." His voice was barren. "There was a suicide note."

"And so he did. And so there was. Welcome to Sarumna, Alan."

Alan Masters came back to see himself in a safe harbor at long last. A grin formed slowly on his face as he realized how reluctantly he had come to this decision, how obtuse he had been in understanding what price his own survival demanded. His life had to be tied to this nation, their leader, General Abdullah, that nation's vast fortune. How stupid he'd been! The West had not taken well to General Abdullah. *Their problem, not mine,* Masters thought. Abdullah, too, was a man surrounded by those who wished to destroy him. And could not. *Exile is over.*

PART TWO

3.

"**I**F YOU go out that door, I don't want you ever to come back." Amanda Miller knew her mother meant every word. Bitterness, disappointment and endless defeat had tightened the mouth and fired the light in her eyes with grim anger. "He was my father," Amanda Miller offered.

"He abandoned you when you were five years old."

"He didn't abandon me, mother, he left you."

"He didn't leave me. I threw him out," Marva Miller wailed. It was a distinction she always was sure to make when the subject came up. Amanda was too young a child at the time to understand the pain, the humiliation. She was even too young to comprehend the newspaper stories when the scheming with Alan Masters first came tumbling down. Thank God she had moved here with the child after the divorce and started a new life. Thank God for Clarence Miller. Clarence was, despite the inevitable disappointment later, a good man, adopting Amanda as his daughter, giving her his name, *hiding* them. When scandal came for Jack Ebersol, at least Marva Miller had done *that* for her little girl.

At twelve, Amanda Miller had somehow found out who her father was, papers Marva had been careless about. The girl ran away from home, the first of several times. Marva thought the child felt disgraced. Amanda even made her way to Dallas, where the much delayed case was finally being tried when she was fifteen. She managed there the first reunion with her father. "I'm glad I went," she announced when she came back to Arizona.

Despite all Marva Miller could do, the connection had not been severed. Amanda was a shy girl, torn by doubts and uncertainties. Her mother had seen to that. Life, Marva believed, had treated herself badly, so she made sure her daughter knew what agony was in store around every corner. Amanda managed to see her father at least once a year while the long legal proceedings were under way. When he was serving time in prison, Amanda Miller came to maturity, a grave, withdrawn young woman who somehow felt herself imprisoned too. The convict Jack Ebersol was considered a troublemaker and was forced to serve his time in hard establishments. Their meetings were carefully monitored; they talked behind glass screens, their words transmitted through microphones and amplifiers. Every asset Ebersol possessed had been stripped from him, so he was careful what he said to his daughter. Nevertheless, she often heard him say: "I have a wonderful friend in Amsterdam, Holland." He made her repeat the name. George van Leeuwen. "Go to see him." He would not tell her why; he could not. Visitors inside the walls did not know the snares and traps everywhere.

So now, her father dead, she was going to Amsterdam, no matter how her mother pleaded. She felt a strange and new electricity within her like nothing she had ever felt. A sense of independence. She was frightened still, but she was no longer immobilized. Shyness and fear still held her, but she dared. This trip, for example. A standby on a charter to Amsterdam. She had been working, since graduating from college, in a gift shop. Managed to save $270 without mother knowing about it. This Dutchman her father wanted her to see—why? Who was he? It could only mean something her father had not wanted the prison authorities to know about; that much she had since figured out for herself. Before his death she would have been afraid to have any contact with such a stranger. Now she felt under an obligation to her father to go.

She wanted, if nothing else, to have this friend tell her what he thought of the suicide. Would he agree that Jack Ebersol was not the kind of man to kill himself after what he had already been through? Mother said her father lived on thin ice. His end was foretold. She said such a man killed everything he ever came to know and cherish. So he could kill himself. That was mother, at fifty bitter and sour with disappointment.

Amanda knew better. Tortured and distorted as their meetings were, Amanda saw in her father a proud and stylish man, destroyed by his need for accomplishment and by the total trust he gave his friend and associate. He made mistakes with the Fund, he told his daughter, but never to defraud anybody. If events over which he had no control had worked out fractionally different, he insisted, he'd be enshrined as a benefactor instead of imprisoned. He had no hesitation in saying that the real culprit when things began to go bad was Alan Masters. When Masters ran away with 200 million the government could not touch, it persuaded everyone that all the rest of them had criminal intentions. Masters's defection abroad was why he rotted in prison. The pain, the suffering, the agony of the guys who ran the Fund—it ended in death for all of them, except for him and Masters. Masters took all the chips and was buying his freedom wherever he could or had to. "I dream of him all the time," he told her once, "and when I get out . . ." His voice drifted away.

"What, father?"

"I'll see he faces the fire I had to." Through the glass pane she could see the set of his jaw, the teeth clenched, the eyes burning with a low, unquenchable flame.

Now that he was dead, these meetings of theirs came back to her in a rush. Life in a gift shop was not anything to cling to, nor mother, though she still felt intimidated by her.

"I don't care if you threw him out, mother," Amanda heard herself say now. "Or if he simply walked out. I'm all he had, I owe him this."

"What's going to happen to you without me?" her mother keened. "You're too plain, men don't fall for you the way they did for me. I could have had any man I wanted just by waving my pinkie. Even your father, when he was the glamorous figure in the financial world, he could have had any girl. He fell for me."

"I'll wear makeup and have my hair done," Amanda said with an irony that was lost on her mother. "Tell me it's all right to go, mama."

"I hate him. I hate you," her mother said. "If you leave me now I never want to see you again."

"Good-bye, mother," Amanda said.

4.

SHE STOOD before a brick house in the early evening where the dark waters of the Prinsengracht meet the narrower Egelantiersgracht in the Jordaan neighborhood near the Westertoren. A trim lady in her early fifties answered the door. "I am Bep van Leeuwen, his wife, may I tell him who you are and why you have come, please?" Her father's name elicited a tiny gasp of surprise and an invitation to come inside. The house was warm, richly paneled. She was brought into a big room, one wall of which was lined with books. There was a long, narrow table, two chairs on one side, a single chair at the other. After a long time, George van Leeuwen came in, both arms extended. He was tall but very frail, his hands when they took her shoulders were as bony as a bird's feet. "Mary Louise Ebersol"—he knew her only by the name she had been given at birth—"I am so glad you have come!"

"Where are you staying, my dear?" his wife asked.

"Send for her things, Bep, dear," the old man said. "You will stay here, we have much to talk about."

She had found a room in the old Schiller Hotel. "I'll go there myself and fetch your things," Mrs. van Leeuwen said. She knew how much her husband wanted to talk to the young lady.

When they were alone, the old man said: "What do you know about me?"

"Only what my father told me."

"Which is?"

"Your name. And that you live in this city. And he wanted me to see you."

The old man smiled. "Where shall I begin?" He had been a

diamond dealer with an office in Antwerp when he met her father. He was closing his business there for good when John Ebersol came in one morning and said he was a collector who had lately got fascinated by diamonds and was looking for a curator-teacher-partner. He had finished a private survey of various names given him and had decided that that person was to be George van Leeuwen. The old man had not known who John Ebersol was until his visitor made mention of the Fund.

Ebersol told him he wanted to create a collection of the finest, rarest diamonds, not only as a hedge against inflation (he was a financier, so considerations like this always came to his mind, he confessed), but also because no such great private collection existed apart from that which belonged to the British Crown. Could a private individual, he asked soberly, with unlimited resources, match such a trove?

The old man doubted it, but he confessed that a brilliant collector could come close. It was an intriguing project but, alas, Ebersol had come to the wrong place. Van Leeuwen was retiring from the diamond world; he had made his fortune, he was getting along in years, he wanted to spend his remaining years in his native country and not make these endless trips to the diamond capital of the world.

"This is my proposal," the old man recalled Jack Ebersol saying. "I want to learn about gem diamonds, I want the best advice in the world. I require a partner of total honesty and integrity. Only a handshake will bind us. My partner will have total custody of the collection. I will depend wholly on his word. I do this to avoid legal complications not for any other reason. I pay my taxes wherever I have to but I also have large amounts of Euro- and petrodollars in my personal accounts, just sitting there. I buy art, but art has become everybody's in-game. I like to combine business with pleasure and I want to use my resources elsewhere, privately. Why privately? I can foresee an occasion when two dozen lawyers would give two dozen different opinions on the correctness—even the legality, if there should be trouble—of everything I've done from the first day I went into business."

The old man paused. He looked out to the canal and turned to face his visitor. Had his friend perhaps foreseen the fate that would overtake the People's Fund? He thought not, he suggested, coming closer to Amanda Miller. "He dealt constantly with lawyers, and he often could anticipate what they would think, friendly or unfriendly," the old man offered.

"He persuaded me to be his diamond amanuensis. Front man, if you prefer." George van Leeuwen's watery eyes glistened at the remembering. "These were to be special gems, not your everyday diamonds, the meat and potatoes, as you people say, of the trade." He challenged Ebersol's naivete in entrusting an entire collection to a stranger. "You are no stranger to me, sir," the old man recalled Ebersol saying. "I trust you completely, why should you not trust me?"

They heard the front door open. Bep van Leeuwen came in with a cab driver who was carrying Amanda's luggage.

He came to his wife and embraced her. Amanda could not resist a smile, for the gesture was so plainly that of an ardent lover who ached when they were not together. "Let us talk no more of the past or the future," he said to Amanda. "We shall take up such things again tomorrow. This evening let us three be happy that we have finally come together in a noble cause."

Jet-tired, Amanda could not sleep. So this was why her father had spoken of George van Leeuwen. Diamonds. Among women of her age, they had lost their lure. They represented naked, unabashed wealth, that was all, ugly symbols of dead or dying upper classes, the sterile rich. She knew about her father's art collecting, Postimpressionists, New York School, de Kooning, Pollock, Hoffman. *That* she could understand and honor him for. But status-proclaiming baubles, self-adornments—what good were they?

She was not her father's daughter for nothing. Van Leeuwen held title, that was clear. Father had been careful there. Look what happened to every work of art he owned. Taken away. Was it legal? Proper? The old man was right, not two dozen, a hundred lawyers would give a hundred different opinions, each opinion dependent on the source of the fee. What was van Leeuwen leading up to?

When sleep finally overwhelmed her, she did not return to consciousness until late the next afternoon. The day was cloudy; when she awoke, for a time she thought it was early morning. The house was quiet. The housemaid heard her stir in her room and brought her a breakfast of roggebrood, roomboter, vitsmyter, snykoek and rookworst. Amanda Miller consumed it all.

Downstairs, she found van Leeuwen in a shade-drawn room. He took her hand and led her to the long table. A black velvet cloth had been spread across its length. An array of necklaces, brooches, bracelets, tiaras, pins and unset stones gleamed in the half-light.

". . . Marlborough necklace," he was saying. "Each has its own story. This one's interesting. Emeralds and diamonds, you see. As fine a choker as anything in the collection. Bought in New Delhi in 1942 by an American film star during a USO trip she made to entertain the troops. Tossed it into her barracks bag so Customs never even knew she brought it into the States. She bought it for a good price. So did we from her. It would fetch twenty times what we paid." He moved his hand to touch a huge necklace. "Alfonso of Spain acquired this from the Romanoffs, gave it to his wife two years before his abdication. We have quite a few things from royal collections. That one is Russian, but made in Paris." He picked up an unset stone. "This is called the Dibrugarh. The Nizam of Hyderabad held it secretly all his long, miserly life. Thirty carats. I'd rather have it than the great Koh-i-noor, the prize stone in the queen's crown, despite its hint of yellow."

A sense of revulsion overwhelmed Amanda Miller. "Why do you show me all this now?"

The old man smiled sympathetically. "At your father's wish, I own them. But you command them."

"I don't understand."

"There is nothing to stop me from disposing of his property in any way I choose. And these things await your orders."

"I still don't understand."

His hand waved the length of the table. "Your father often spoke of his family. Your mother did not approve of him?"

"My mother does not approve of anyone."

"He was not an emotional man, but the longing when he spoke of you was clear."

"It never failed to touch me. My mother married again, almost immediately. She moved as far away as she could from her old life, I was taught to call her next husband *father* and *daddy*. It should have come easily to me, I was that young. And yet I knew, some deep instinct within me forced me to look for the man who had become a dim memory. Luckily for me, my mother hated him so much that she kept every letter, every shred of her past with him. But when his troubles began, I couldn't stand it any longer. I ran away from home and went to see him."

"He would not make a move that could hurt you," the old man mused aloud. "I know after the indictment he never again made contact with me. Of course, I always understood there were unacceptable risks there."

"I saw him whenever I could," she went on. "The case dragged on for years. I was in college when all the appeals had been taken and he was finally sent to prison. I visited him there, difficult as it was for me. I saw with my own eyes how brutally they treated him. He refused to protest."

Van Leeuwen sighed. He began to return his display into their cases, snapped them shut and stacked them like so many volumes that had to be returned to the shelves. "Nor did he call for my help then," he said sadly. "I could have found a way to help. But, of course, the terrible risk was still there. And I had certain orders."

Amanda Miller went to a window when she found herself alone in the room. She looked out on the dark waters of the canal. Never before had she felt so close to her father. John Edward Ebersol knew what he was doing when he entrusted those priceless gems to George van Leeuwen. He knew what he was doing when he urged her to go to Amsterdam. She shuddered a little, crossed her hands and embraced herself, as if the weather had suddenly turned cold. Or, she wondered, was it a sense of personal power she had never known or felt before? All her life, timidity or second thought had short-circuited every big move she ever contemplated. Mother, of course. She had long ago given up fighting her mother and the heritage she had laid upon her; what was left was pity and compassion for a lady endlessly enamored of her own self. Still, Amanda knew she had never entirely freed herself of the hobbling her mother had bequeathed her. But she felt the presence now, for the first time, of a sea change: the collection in van Leeuwen's safe.

When the old man returned, her manner was crisp. "How much is the collection worth?" she asked.

He smiled slightly. "How do you mean? What did we pay? What if we had to sell everything at one time at auction in London or New York? Or dispose of it a piece at a time? I always bought and sold from a position of power. Big cash when someone was forced to sell; big cash behind me when someone offered to buy, so an offer had to be doubly attractive. I am an old man, so there is a consideration of time, but I have taught Bep many things, so there is no need for you to worry there. Let me say this, there is enough here for all your worldly needs for a very, very long time."

She found herself in the old man's embrace. "I'm still afraid."

He stroked her head. "I know what you are thinking, my dear."

She looked closely at him. "Do you? Let me tell you. I am certain my father did not kill himself."

"I am certain of that too."

She sighed and clung closer to him. "After all he'd been through he would never quit."

"Of course, my dear."

"Who wanted him dead? Who in all the world pursued this broken man in defeat and degradation? Am I being crazy, Mr. van Leeuwen?"

"No," he said. "He would be proud of you."

He could feel her fill her lungs, her shoulders pull back, her whole body go rigid. "Will you help me?"

George van Leeuwen said: "Have I not told you, my dear? Everything in my safe is yours to command."

5.

ROGER PHILLIPS moved with a feline wariness, searching for prey among the knots of people gathered for cocktails on the terrace and garden of Colette O'Brien's home just outside Palm Springs on a golden afternoon. The champagne was Mumm's, the bourbon, Jack Daniel's, the Scotch, J & B or Glenlivet. He did not drink. Four musicians colored the desert air with old pop tunes which he neither remembered affectionately nor liked particularly. A decade later, he still had a vaguely undergraduate air about him, loose-limbed, casual and uncommitted. A striking appearance caused some to regard him as little more than an amiable fellow, though he was once a serious classical scholar and a rebel of the early Seventies who had seen his share of conflict with the authorities. Today his dress was unexceptionable, yet among Colette O'Brien's guests, he still managed to appear something of a misfit.

His eyes came to rest on the quarry he had been seeking. She wore a pale pink sheath loose from a pair of tiny strings over her shoulders, flowing from a delicately carved décolletage to the rippling curves of her body. Her skin was already taking on nut brown from the desert sun and honey hair flowed softly around her face. "They are looking for a house, darling," Colette had said. "Try to be civil."

"You must be Joan Alexander," Roger Phillips began. "I understand you're in the market for a house. I build them. Really great and unusual ones. Can I show one to you?"

"And of course you're Roger!" she exclaimed in a burst of bell-like laughter. "You sure know how to cozy up to a prospective buyer, don't you? The soft approach."

"But aren't you—?"

"Yes, we are, but usually it's done more subtly. Obviously you're no supersalesman." She showed him her tseth in a smile. "But on the other hand you're far too beautiful for that to matter. I understand you were once a college professor, isn't that just about as incredible as your being a salesman?"

"An assistant professor with no tenure. I found out teaching wasn't the life for me. That's why I'm building houses in the desert. I mean, really fine ones, Mrs. Alexander, using the terrain and the sun—may I show you one?" His voice dropped. "I've got five."

The bell-like laugh again. "And no buyers. Poor baby." She touched his bare forearm and ran fingertips to his elbow. "I'd love to see one." Something in a stand of oleander bushes at one side of the garden seized her eyes and would not let them move. She watched the bushes quiver as a live object pushed its way through the tangle of low-hanging branches.

"Shall we go right now, Mrs. Alexander?"

The lady seemed to have lost interest in him. He said: "I'm not an architect. I was a student of classical cultures, you understand, specializing in Roman colonization in the Mediterranean. As I said, it didn't work out—"

She turned to him briefly. "Do you have many enemies?"

"Not really anymore." He grinned. "Used to, I guess. Got into a little college-protest trouble, jumped bail, hid out from the cops for a while, but now we're all friends. Forgiven and forgotten. Everybody decided we were all a little wrong. Now about my houses—"

"You may still have an enemy or two, Roger," Joan Alexander said darkly.

"Hardly. Now, as a matter of fact, I could show you my own house, Mrs. Alexander. Built it right into a hillside. Cool in summer, warm in winter."

"Don't look now, my dear." Joan Alexander watched the figure in the shrubbery part thick branches for a better look—shot?—at them and her voice began to quaver. "Someone's either trying to find a vantage point to kill you, or maybe it's me, jealousy, perhaps. Someone jumping to conclusions. After all, I've not seen your house and already I've got to pay the price for your philandering. Perhaps she's the local talent when there are no parties, someone you've already seduced and abandoned, who's tracked you here with the swells, who's come to make a scene, tell you what a rat you are and all that. Do you think she's got a gun? In any case, it's very damned distracting."

Joan Alexander's hand pointed to the bushes and he saw it plainly there: a figure scooting for deep cover in the dense underbrush where the branches were thickest. "Don't go away," he said over his shoulder.

He must have been spotted, because as he ran to the oleanders the figure took flight across the fairway in front of two golf carts, sliding to the sandtrap that guarded the fourteenth green. The girl ran well, shifting her course, ever reversing her field to avoid him, sprinting in a wide curve toward the O'Briens' again. When he finally seized her wrist, she fell to the grass like a dropped doll. "You've been stalking me," he told her. "Why? Do I know you?" He certainly did not, of that he was at once certain. She wore a peasanty dress, faded in color, too long, her legs covered to the calf by its big skirt. Her hair was short, dark in color. The face showed no makeup and the eyes were pale and unaccented except for heavy eyebrows.

"No," she moaned, freeing herself. "I'm terribly sorry, Mr. Phillips."

"What do you want? Why've you been tailing me?"

The girl got to her feet. "I—forgive me—I wanted to be sure—I don't know what I was doing," she stammered.

"Don't know? Followed me while I'm with a lady, hide in the bushes, run? Who are you? What're you trying to do? Get lost!"

"I've ruined everything," Amanda Miller wailed and took off toward Colette's, remarkably fleet and graceful, he thought. He shrugged and reminded himself of the prospect he had left a moment ago.

At the driveway to his home Mrs. Alexander offered the usual giggle. "Where's the roof? It looks like a cave with windows."

He'd built it for himself, he said. His sample case, so to speak. Happy to sell it. All the features to show his houses' uniqueness. Years ago he'd spent a lot of time in a real desert and he'd played with ideas like this. He pointed to solar panels and the rocky hillside he'd actually brought into the house. Mrs. Alexander was much impressed. "You're something, Roger," she took his hand and brought him to a sofa. "Tell me, you don't seem like a building contractor. What's a nice boy like you doing in a house like this?"

"Want to know the truth? I'm stuck here. I'm up to my rump in construction loans and mortgages. Thought I was getting back to basics. Away from academies and libraries. No more conflicts with authority. Work with the hands. Me and plasterers and plumbers, masons, rough carpenters and pourers of cement."

"You have five places like this? Why don't they sell?"

"People ooh and ah but at the moment of truth they go with wall-to-wall conformity, white and gold, trick kitchens, fancy johns. Palm Springs chic. So my business stinks."

"I love your house. The problem is Randall wouldn't."

"Your husband?"

She got to her feet. "Still, it's fascinating. I suppose there's a wild bachelor bedroom with an outsize bed, mirrored ceiling and quadrophonic sound," she teased.

"Mrs. Alexander, it's a beautifully thought-out bedroom. You'd love it."

"Show me." She found his hand and pulled him to his feet.

The bedroom had a wall that was also part of the rocky hillside; a trickle of water streamed to an indoor hot pool. The bed was large enough for two but inadequate for a decent orgy. No mirror anywhere. Light sifted below from an apex window thirty feet above them.

"It's really very lovely," Joan Alexander whispered.

"Twenty percent down would handle it. Less than half of what a conventional joint like Colette's would cost. Let me show you the patio."

"I don't care about the patio. I would like to see you with your shirt off for starters," the lady said without warning.

"Mrs. Alexander," he began.

"It only takes *me* a second, you see." She pulled a string at the top of her dress and it fell in a silken pool at her ankles. She stood, entrancingly nude except for tiny panties, on high heels.

Roger Phillips came to her, took her warm shoulders at arm's length, admired what he saw, held her close for a moment as various alternatives became evident to both of them. Finally he bent to retrieve her dress and put it decisively into her hands. "Why has game-playing sex come to bore me?" he asked glumly. "We don't have to prove anything, you and I, do we?"

"You mean there's to be no more fucking just for the hell of it, angel? Or, is it, no sale, no fuck?"

"I'm trying to give the fuck back to true love, whatever the hell that is. I often have a hard time of it, as you must surely have noticed."

His visitor laughed loud, as if a practical joke she only now appreciated had been worked on her. "Let's go back to Colette's," she offered without resentment.

In his old XKE, as it raced down Palm Canyon, she put her hand on his knee. "You're marvelous," she said. "Mad. A true romantic. I thought you guys were an extinct species."

"I *am* extinct," he said.

"And what happened to you?" Colette O'Brien found him hunched over her caterer's Stroganoff alone at one of the tables set for four. "Ah, I know," she went on irritably. He had brought his hostess to the house at the beginning of the season. Things had gone rather differently then. Naturally, Colette O'Brien had fixed ideas of what happened whenever Roger showed it. "Why isn't Joan here with you?"

"I think I failed her," he replied with a full mouth.

"I can tell you this. You failed someone with a lot more money than the Alexanders."

"What are you talking about?"

"Amanda Miller. A young lady Mr. Henderson at the bank brought to me. Was Roger Phillips going to be here today? Yes, I told him. Would I invite her, please? Wanted to meet you. Told me she got him to draw a cashier's check in your name for $100,000. And, he says, the letter of credit allows for considerably more. She tried to get up the nerve to talk to you. She's terribly shy, she said. Found you very intimidating. While she's trying to find courage to talk to you, what do you do? You tell her to get lost."

He gulped the ball of paste inside his mouth. "I thought it was some kind of nut." He stared moodily at the still full plate before him and pushed it away. "Why didn't you tell me about her beforehand?"

"You didn't do more than wave to me when you arrived."

"She stalked me like a goddam Indian. I didn't know what was going on." He threw down his napkin. "Where is she? For a sale I'm prepared to apologize abjectly."

"She's at the Tennis Club." He was on his way. "Hold it a minute, Roger, my sweet," Colette brought him to a stop with evident delight. She took her time coming to his side. "Miss Miller asked me to tell you not to call on her until noon tomorrow. I guess you've upset her so much she needs time to compose herself. So you might as well relax here." She took his hand and led him back to his table and cold noodles.

6.

THREE AIRPLANES hung across the sky like a silver necklace. They flew over General Mohammed Abdullah International Airport in single file, so low the colors they bore could be seen, orange and black, the same as the Sarumnan flag; they passed over the stand filled with high functionaries and their assistants and a few diplomats who had been persuaded that their absence would be regarded as an affront.

The General always wanted a first-class international airline. He had spoken of it when he had taken power. Air Sarumna, the old airline, flew the Mahgreb but wwas not much favored; its equipment was out of date, not well kept, and there were stories about its personnel. He wanted none of that from now on. In the distance he watched the 747s turn as they moved to descend. He filled his chest. There had been some difficulties but he had prevailed. Three new 747s, cost: $70 million each: No problem. Spare parts had to come along, although the Boeing people had a system in which they could deliver any spare not in stock within twenty-four hours. Still, $60 million for necessary spare parts. Crews were the problem. Air and ground. The General was impatient. He wanted it all now. And here it was, the planes, the parts, the ground crews, ticketing personnel—all at once.

He turned to Ābu ben-Sadriquen and smiled. "This is a glorious day," he said.

"A tribute to your genius, Mr. President," Sadriquen replied.

When the first Boeing touched down, a cheer rose from the grandstand and from behind the fence before the old air terminal where students and populace had been gathered. The band struck up the national anthem and people began to sing the words, as they always did, because the song, first offered almost fifty years ago during the days of the now-hated oligarchy, touched the people's hearts:

> *O land of golden light,*
> *Home of my father and my father's father,*
> *How dear, how beautiful you are ...*

On this occasion, many who sang were prouder than ever. Even the General, impatient with sentiment and detail, felt his throat constrict. As the planes drew up in a line, a hundred flags were unfurled along the runway. The General was pleased at the spectacle that had been arranged. The national television had of course deployed every camera it could lay its hands on to cover the event.

Two hundred seventy million dollars was easily managed; all the crews were contracted for; delivery had been a serious difficulty. After all, the Seattle company had outstanding orders, and when cancellations came along, they had every right to assign prior delivery elsewhere. There was no alternative, company officials insisted.

Alan Masters was, as was proper for the author of this splendid coup, the first out, changed from the Arab dress he had worn during his incognito three-day visit to his native land into the French-tailored worsteds he preferred. He waved to the General.

"I'll go, General," he'd said.
"That is very brave of you," the General had countered. "But I would not permit such a risk."
"You'll send a party, sir. I'll be lost among them in Arab dress."
"Someone could recognize you. After all, they know you're here." The General was not always given to understatement. There had been numerous requests for information about the status of Alan Masters. Ambassadors or their assistants were instructed to respond that no one by that name was known. Masters had been given an Arabic name, hence they were correct.
"If we're to have an airline operating as quickly as you'd like, General, I'd better go, risk or not."

"I'll have four of my personal security men with you. I'm prepared to create a serious international incident if there is any attempt on the body of my personal representative. Is that understood? And they are to be at your side at every moment."

"I understand."

The General grinned as he rarely did; he was young enough to think a smile unbecoming in a great national leader. "Even in the bedroom, dear friend. They know how to turn their backs, I assure you. That's an order."

And there his airline was, a daring, dramatic coup only a few people knew about. Three big airplanes, filled with parts and over two hundred Danes, Swedes and Norwegians to fly and service them, scooped up when the planes made a stop in Copenhagen.

> O land of desert sands,
> Beloved from ancient days
> Touched by Allah's grace
> Beautiful beyond imagining . . .

American planes. A finger went to a corner of the General's eye and found a tear. The beautiful song had been written by an American, words he put to an old Arabic tune. The General hated the Americans now, though he dealt with their contractors and their hard-faced oilmen, but sometimes he felt close to them, as he did at this moment.

He descended the wooden steps from the temporary grandstand and, followed by his bodyguards and his uniformed ministers, made his way to where Alan Masters waited for the General to be in position on the ground. At a signal, he ran down the steps to a presidential embrace.

"You accomplished it!" the General exclaimed.

"It is your achievement, General. I was a mere mouthpiece for your vision and your tenacity." Masters felt the hug grow tighter. There were other formalities the General was forced to attend, so Masters drifted to the background. Sadriquen found him and touched his forearm.

"Good work," he whispered. "What'd you have to give besides dollars?"

"Advice. Luckily for us, engineers are not too knowledgeable in international financial matters, so they listen."

"Customers all over the world and they don't know what to do?"

"Let's say they don't always understand what's available to money. Or it could be pointed out more forcefully by an outsider than their own people could manage. What matters is that we got his toys for him."

"And he's got a surprise for you."

"Tell me."

"He's asked me to report to him personally how you react, so let's do it his way."

"He is a goddam kid," Alan Masters muttered, "his own airline overnight and now we have to play childish games."

"That's what makes him a charismatic leader."

They were soon on the new, black road that led from the airport to Zarplis. It crossed a salt marsh and connected with the highway to the capital, the old road once named after the tyrannical oligarchy now bearing the General's name. Masters sank low in back of a stretched-out Mercedes, his feet on the jump seat before him. He glowed, recalling what had been provided him during his three nights in the northwest of his former country. "Tell the General he's got a marvelous man running his embassy in Washington." Each of the ladies who had visited him had proved to be more thrilling than the last. There had been seasoned ladies and gee-whiz, holy-whillikers girls in jeans and funny T-shirts, big ones, small ones, oral artists and acrobats and bedroom actresses who could almost convince a man it was the real thing. Yes, Masters said, the trip was worth the risk. He dozed off—the nine-hour time difference was a physical fact as real as the nine visitors.

When Abu ben-Sadriquen woke him up, it took a moment for Masters to place himself half a world away from where he had been a few hours earlier. He looked up to a white marble edifice on a slight rise of ground, the sea beside it, tall colonnades and a gleaming terrace. "Had it fixed up just for you," Sadriquen said.

"Was built by an Italian a long time ago. They've been wondering what to do with it. He knows you've been unhappy where you've been." Austerity was the keynote the General always sounded, despite the flood of money that overwhelmed the treasury every day. He and all the ministers maintained discreet and plain dwellings. But, of course, Alan Masters was not a member of any Revolutionary Council and it had been decided it was unfair to deprive him of his style of living.

"He's brought in a couple of young men from Rome to advise you on furnishing. They're out scouring other expropriated villas for stuff you might need."

Sadriquen seemed put off by Masters's lack of enthusiasm. "I'm supposed to tell him how you reacted. You don't seem especially thrilled," he complained.

"I just wish the hell it was outside of Paris, what else can I say?"

"I'll make up something he'd like to hear."

"No, be honest, tell him it's tough for an infidel who's got to cheat on him just to have women since he's so strict about them."

"He tries to look the other way," Sad interrupted. "He's really done an extraordinary thing—this is a better house than most ambassadors have. And he knows you need your women. He even lets you have alcohol, which he won't permit the embassies—so tell me what to say, please."

"Tell him I regard it as another sign of his greatness, tell him I don't deserve it, that I was at a loss for words."

Inside, the Roman decorators had already begun to gather a few things. "I'm dead tired," Masters said. Sadriquen led him to the bedroom suite that would be his, white marble and silken walls.

"I'll see you in a day or two when you're over your jet lag." He started to go. "By the way, Alan, I heard from the Swiss consortium. They've conceded, just as you insisted."

"I always said they would."

The details of that deal were fuzzy in his head, but he remembered the Swiss were firm the last he had seen them, that if he didn't accede they'd walk away from the deal. So they hadn't. How many tens of millions were involved he did not now remember. God, he was sleepy.

7.

COOL. "IT'S ME, Miss Miller. Roger Phillips. Good morning. Or should I say good afternoon? May I begin by apologizing? I'm really very sorry about what happened yesterday." Calm. Under stress always be calm, he'd learned that the hard way, the longer the odds, the more detachment. This was a lady come to do business and he'd blown it. "I was very rude, I hope you can forgive me. Thank you, no, it's a little early in the day for a drink." She was a client, remember that. People did not throw money at some dude who got himself loaded before lunch, no matter how much they thought of his houses.

What the hell. Business was business. God knows his was bad. When it wanted to be good, the clients were cash-short. "I thought your house would be cheaper than the conventional kind." Up yours, Charley. Cheaper, for Chrissake, these are prototypes. Here is a lady with c.o.l., cash on the line. So bend low from the waist, pal. You need the money.

"Forgive me, Miss Miller, I'm talking too much. It's because I'm sorry, really, truly sorry." Still, don't overdo it. Get to the subject. Remember that cashier's check. Be assured. Remember what Colette said. She's very shy.

The damned minute hand didn't want to move. It was still twenty minutes before noon. He stood outside the Tennis Club. Too hot to sit in the car. Too early to go inside. He'd gone over it a dozen times. Cool. Skip all the stuff about *why* he was so rude. A supersalesman told him once to stress the positive. Not the negative. Apologize, but be light about it.

He walked into the lobby ten minutes before high noon. At the desk, the clerk took a long time to lift his eyes. Calm, remember. Also, what the hell was the rush? He didn't want to be too early, right?

He waited for the clerk to bring him into focus. "Amanda Miller. I'm expected. What's the room number, please?"

"The lady checked out," the room clerk said without hesitation.

Roger Phillips thought he felt something suddenly snap. His neck, he hoped. He shook his head in tight little movements, as if to make sure it still worked. "Checked out?. What do you mean?"

"Left town. Early this morning."

He forced a smile. "Did she leave a forwarding address?"

"Not to be given out, sir."

Calm. Cool. Roger Phillips had played with crazies before, everybody was a little crazy, so keep the eye on the target. Smile for the man again. "What do you know?" Scratch the scalp. See, now maybe he'll think it's a lovers bust-up. "Listen, pal, I've got to see her again, you know how that is."

The clerk shrugged and offered a cynical smile. "Told us not to give any information to anyone. Tough, pal," he offered, a man who knew the pain of seeing a live, rich one get away.

Henderson at the bank had set her up. *He'd* know. Roger Phillips ran to his XKE.

"It's impossible, Phillips," the banker told him firmly. "She left explicit instructions with me. I'm sorry. She seemed quite set in her mind about you, I'm afraid."

"I'm inquiring about her socially, Mr. Henderson," he pleaded shamelessly. "I'm interested in dating her."

"Sure you are, Phillips. And why not? But you seem to have offended her." The bank manager looked among other papers to shuffle. He had no trouble finding what he was looking for. "By the way, Phillips, what are we going to do about these overdue notes of yours? On all of your properties? I can't carry you any longer."

Roger Phillips got to his feet unsteadily. "Please," he muttered, "not today, not now, Mr. Henderson."

"I'm afraid we're going to start foreclosure proceedings."

When he got back to the Jag, this time it wouldn't start. Battery checked okay. But nothing happened. His trusty Jag. He could always count on it to quit when he needed it, so he wasn't surprised.

It was late afternoon before the car could move.

He sat Colette O'Brien down with firm hands and pulled a chair so close their knees touched. Something very strange was going on and though he had lived in the desert long enough to take curious doings by its visitors for granted, there had never been anything like this. A woman—young, damned young, Colette saw that—arrives with cashier's check made out to him in her timorous little hand, not to mention a lot more funds in the Palm Springs branch of the bank. Arranges to get asked to a party to meet him. Plays cat-and-mouse games rather than just get Colette to bring them together, and what's more, it's the mouse that stalks the cat. With all that money, remember. Then she runs. Leaves town. What's even more, without a forwarding address and with explicit instructions no one's to tell where she can be reached. "What is going on?" he asked wanly.

Colette O'Brien knew nothing that could be helpful. The girl had arrived by cab. They spent an hour chatting while Colette was seeing to last-minute details about the party and putting her face on. Seemed a sweet, if plain, thing. How did she even know about Roger Phillips? Colette never thought to ask. She assumed, from what Henderson had told her, the young lady wanted to buy a house. What else? She was a dear little thing but terribly drab, not Roger's type at all. His type was more like Joan Al—

"Never mind all that," he broke in to keep her on the track. "What about the girl? What'd she talk about? What'd she tell you about herself?"

Colette recalled that the girl said she'd played a lot of tennis with the pro at the hotel while getting up the courage to see him. Amanda Miller said the pro there was very good. Amanda Miller also said she was not so bad herself on the tennis court, Colette remembered her saying that she'd played varsity tennis at Arizona State; she'd showed how her right arm was bigger than her left from all the years on the court.

"Well, that narrows it down a little," Roger Phillips said disconsolately. "A girl who plays so much tennis her right arm's bigger than her left. There're probably only two or three who fit that description there. Thousand."

"Big-right-armed girls with all that money. That ought to narrow it down a bit more for you," Colette offered. "I wish I could help you, my dear."

"I need fifty-four thousand dollars right this minute to meet delinquent notes," he said glumly. "Outside of that, there's no way anybody can help." He kissed her cheek and went out to his car. It started without incident.

One last shot.

The pro had a tanned-leather face. He was working with one of those teenybopper girls who make strong men want to burn their tennis rackets. The kid kept the old champ busy earning his money. When the session was over, he wiped his forehead and talked freely about Miss Miller. Nice little thing. Hell of a serve. Tendency to come in too quickly. She'd come to say good-bye when she had to leave suddenly. Damned classy of her. Very generous too. Yes, she had told him where she was going. No, she hadn't said anything about not telling anyone. Roger Phillips smiled as innocently as he could manage. They'd been dating, he confessed shyly, and well—they'd had a little spat.

"That's why she split so unexpectedly?" the pro asked.

Roger Phillips was glad there was no mirror to reflect to himself the demure expression he managed to put on. "I want to make up to my girl, you know how that is," he whispered. The all-too-evident anguish touched the old pro's heart.

8.

Two hours, seventeen minutes later, the 55-mile speed law a mockery for all but fourteen minutes of that time, Roger Phillips knocked on a door in the new wing of the Beverly Wilshire Hotel in Beverly Hills.

"Come in, I've been expecting you," Amanda Miller said as she pulled open the door. His eyes burned fiercely. On the way in, he'd planned his tactics: he'd be gentle, the suave salesman, but he could not hide his annoyance, his bewilderment at the game he was being forced to play. "I was absolutely sure you'd search me out, Mr. Phillips," Amanda Miller said. "Still, I had to make sure. You did what I hoped you'd do. You're splendid." He regarded her, more puzzled than ever. What happened to the wee tim'rous mousie too shy to come out of the shrubbery to talk to him?

"Would you mind telling me what the hell gives?" he demanded.

"If you promise not to tell me to get lost. Would you like a drink? Ah, yes, I know that you don't drink alcohol. I've found that out. You take apple juice, unfiltered, fresh, I know that too. I know a lot about you, Mr. Roger Phillips."

"I'm delighted to hear that," he broke in. "Then you know I build fine houses, not very popular at the moment, not yet, but when the energy crunch really starts hitting people, my houses will double, even triple in value. I'm prepared to give you a deal beyond your expectations. I'm wide open to any proposition."

"I know all about your problems, Mr. Phillips. You're in a lot of trouble. I told you, I know everything." She let the words hang in the air, pausing like a judge about to pronounce sentence. "I've employed computers, private investigators, the whole baggage of modern science to find out and to reach you."

"Why?" he said in a small voice.

"I have a special kind of job for you."

"Not building?" His head went from side to side unconsciously. From the look in her eyes, he knew the answer was not the one he wanted.

"The job carries a retainer. I've already had a check drawn to your order, as I made it my business to have you told about. There's more once you're ready to go to work."

It was time to end the whole business, he decided suddenly. Some rich people had strange ways of getting their kicks. He looked again at Miss Miller, more carefully. Didn't seem the rich-girl-gone-whacko, but appearances were deceiving. Plain, all right. Drab, as Colette said. Good nose. Pretty lips, looked like the bow you see airborne cherubs carry in Renaissance paintings. No lipstick, of course. Thick, aggressive eyebrows, lost eyes, hair like it didn't know what a brush was. Good legs, though, lousy shoes, clodhoppers. He got to his feet. "I don't know what smoke you're into, Miss Miller, but I build and sell houses, I'm not looking for a job. So thanks a lot and good-bye. Keep out of bushes next time."

She raced to stop him at the door. "Please don't go."

"They get seventy-five cents every twenty minutes for parking at this place, and, as you said, things are a little tight with me."

"You can keep the check even if you turn me down, Mr. Phillips. Won't you just listen to me?"

A hundred thousand? Enough to get Henderson and the bank off his back. "You *are* nuts," he heard himself declare. Still, he turned from the door like a man in a hypnotic trance.

He returned to the world when he felt the check being put into his hand. It had his middle name on it, Roger *Augustus* Phillips; how in hell had she found *that* out? He looked at it for a very long time.

"What do you say now?"

His throat was filled with sand; when he found his voice, "May I have that apple juice, Miss Miller?" came out.

He studied the check. There it was, all a near-bankrupt builder could ask for. A hundred thousand, not a personal check, the bank's check made out to his order, signed by good old Henderson, the very signature which would have appeared on the foreclosure notice.

He took a glass from her hand. Unfiltered, as he preferred apple juice. How did she know *that*? And the *Augustus*? "You know a good deal abut me."

"It's our times. No privacy. Everything part of a record. I know all about your schooling, job experience, travels, even your language ability. You might call what I did detective work by computer. Amazing what footprints in the sand we all leave. You practically ran this historical dig in Sarumna, then threw it over, left your university job. Everybody was all for this thing you were doing during that campus protest, but there was this judge—have I got it right?"

"Eight million years ago, I've forgotten."

"There was a run-in with the police and you were supposed to've been rather clever in avoiding them for a time. Just what I want!"

He held out the glass. "Miss Miller, you pour an excellent juice, thank you, but really, what the hell are you up to?"

"I told these people with the computer what sort of individual I need and they did the rest. I wanted a man who knew Sarumna, how to live in it." She filled the glass again and held it out to him. He seemed unable to resist it. "He had to be a man who wouldn't be afraid to confront authority. You were that man. He'd know how to manage if things went wrong. He'd be physically—well, capable. Decisive. Wouldn't stop at mere legality when higher considerations were involved."

"Anybody I know?" he teased her. He put down a half-filled glass.

"When you managed that historical project in the desert, the reports said you overcame 'local and bureaucratic hindrances of whatever nature so the work was never impeded.' "

"What they meant is that I did a little light smuggling in the line of duty."

"Exactly! And never for personal gain."

"Which shows what an idiot I was. Most of the oher scholars were sending out a few choice antiquities for their own collections."

"And then of course, look how you changed careers. What flexibility that shows! And how you found me here after I deliberately left all sorts of obstacles in the way. Oh, Mr. Phillips, yo're the man I've been looking for."

"For precisely what, Miss Miller? What is it you have in mind?"

"You know Arabic even!" she parried.

"Very damned little. And I've become quite rusty."

"And you know the desert—"

"The tamed and gardened desert," he said sourly. "From Cabazon to Indio, from Rancho Mirage to Joshua Tree. I know *that* desert."

"The Sahara. The desert in Sarumna. That's the desert I'm talking about."

"Would you stop all this and please tell me what in the hell this is all about, why you throw a hundred thousand at me?"

"A half million for your share." She let that sink in and resumed in a quieter voice than any he had heard her use. "More, if it has to be. You'll need help from others. I leave all that to you. Money's no object, you'll be authorized to spend whatever you like."

"For?"

"Does the name Alan Masters mean anything to you?"

"You tell me what it should."

"He engineered an escape with hundreds of millions in corporate assets after a scandal that involved a lot of ruined lives, suicides, prison, even murder. He alone got away."

"I'd tell the cops."

"The police of five countries are looking for him, maybe more. And he's been getting along fine for years. Still working, still maneuvering. I want him brought back to this country."

"Against his will of course."

"I'm afraid so."

"That's what is called kidnapping."

"He's wanted by all kinds of authorities. Any of them would be grateful to us."

"It's still kidnapping. About the gratitude, well, maybe. All over the world, though, you take someone who doesn't want to go with you, it's against the law. Except, of course, if you *are* the police and have your own badge." He reached for his wallet. "So, I'm going to return your check, Miss Miller. Want to know why? Because even talking about kidnapping, as we've been doing, is against the law. Taking your money cinches it. I'm a flop academic and a flop builder, but my guilt feelings don't extend to inflicting prison on myself."

She laid her hand against his as he reached to retrieve the check. "Wait. I also had the computer people work up all the charges, ours, the British, the French, the Italian, the Swiss, everything. The whole story. The persons involved. The financial manipulations since he got away with all that money. Read it, I beg you."

"It wouldn't make any difference."

"Just read it," she insisted, withdrawing her hand. "Then you've earned the money for your advice and you're in the clear."

"Okay," he said at last.

She brought a fat ring-bound book to him. "I'll leave you alone."

"I won't be here when you get back," he said.

"It's a gamble I'll take."

He watched her go from the room, a short, mousy kind of girl. He did not know such women cosld be dangerous too.

9.

THE REPORT was written in that curious lingo that machines and their operators use, computer all-caps, the words gone gray, washed clean of color, love and hate, anger and pride. Alan Masters was SUBJECT MAN and the Sarumnan name were all mispelled or confused with each other.

But he could not put the book down.

He remembered reading about Alan Masters and the collapse of the Fund. Probably in one of the newsweeklies. It happened back when he was working in the desert with Professor Carver. In those days he was not much interested in what was going on in the world after the fourth century A.D., but he used to look at the news magazines when there was nothing else to take into the john.

Alan Masters reminded him of Roman traders who coud steal whole treasuries and set up shop, or new colonies along the Mediterranean and soon find Rome sending the protection they needed. The report located Alan Masters in Sarumna. That, of course, was why the mousy lady had sought him out. Surely, she knew it was all over for him and all the American researchers there since the General took over. He hated us, she had to know that, we wee Satanic, we were loathsome unbelievers, agents of sin and destruction. Everybody said the General was dangerous. Some Arab leeders called him a maniac. For his part, Roger Phillips, aware of Abdullah's dubious enterprises, regarded him doubtfully; however, he was consistent. Compromise with his religious beliefs would have been easier, but at least here was a politician who did not have two lives, public and private. Roger's own existence in Sarumna had given him a deep respect for the Koran and the Arab people. There was, of course, also that business about the General and the terrorist groups the General financed in Germany, Italy, Japan and Ireland, but perhaps those were only unproved charges. The report averred that since Masters had been granted Sarumnan citizenship the financing of subversive groups around the world had grown more discreet than when the oil money had to be funneled through government sources. This, too, Roger Phillips decided, was only surmise and a wild and general charge. His university training had made him a careful and always skeptical reader. Besides, he did not want to be involved.

The report went at some length into the rise and fall of the International People's Investment and Savings Fund and the sorry aftermath. Amanda Miller's connection to all this was obscure until he came across several underlinings in the text which connected her to John Edward Ebersol. It described him as a sincere man who spent years insisting the executives of the Fund did all they could to bring high returns to their investors in very risky enterprises. He always contended they may have failed but they did nothing deliberately criminal. Finally, Ebersol broke; perhaps it could be said he became convinced he was wrong. No matter. He felt tricked by Alan Masters and in prison began at last to cooperate with the authorities, who badly needed him as a corroborative witness for the time when they would finally get their hands on Alan Masters.

Prison had not gone easy for Ebersol. The report believed that Masters was responsible for Ebersol's prison problems. Usually, corporate felons such as Ebersol find their terms limited to a few years in one of the country-club establishments of the federal prison system. The report averred that Masters had paid certain persons in Corsica with international connections large sums of money. From the very first day of Ebersol's imprisonment, this resulted in all sorts of attacks, fracases and affrays in prison yards made to look like the new prisoner's doing; these led to his being declared a dangerous and antisocial prisoner. For this he was sent to a series of very tough establishments. There were savage attempts on his person.

An extraordinary man, Roger Phillips decided, because he fought his own battles behind prison walls and never ratted on his tormentors. Thus, he proved himself to be, at least to the other inmates, a model prisoner, and all the money in the world could not destroy him after that.

The report went into detail about the relationship between Ebersol and Alan Masters. There was no question that during the Fund's successful years both men began by believing they were creating something marvelous for investors around the world. They were closer than brothers. They became rich but not out of proportion to the wealth they brought to the Fund. Their closeness ended when Masters ran and Ebersol elected to stay behind and plead his cause before the courts.

Yes, Roger Phillips decided, John Edward Ebersol was the link to Miss Miller. He reserved his opinion about murder by proxy; yet the possibility seemed impressive. Still, it all came down to kidnapping, and returning to General Abdullah's Sarumna. Roger Phillips closed the notebook, brought it to a table at one end of the room and put it down. For a moment he debated with himself about the check. He was no lawyer, but he decided he had turned down her proposal hard enough and so could keep the check. He didn't like taking the lady's money. For what was he engaging in this shabby self-justification? To get back to Palm Springs? To build houses nobody wanted? He thought of Sarumna, the great, lovely, frightening country, the hard, yellow light, the real desert, not the one he had come to rest in, swimming pools and green fairways and cocktails and all those bored ladies and their dull husbands. He wished he had the guts to wait for Miss Miller. Nevertheless, he left.

10.

THE HATEFUL, loathsome Americans, personification of everything vile and sinful, the eternal godless enemy, sponsors of Zionists, supporters of the Jordanian and Saudi puppets, masters of dubious client states on all sides of his own beloved nation's boundaries, shameless materialists, their painted women, flaunting harlots all, a government of conspirators against the true God, alcohol-swilling infidels who do not even obey the precepts of their own prophets—the General dealt amiably if privately with them every day.

The Borchard Corporation had contracts with his government for various projects which came to something in the area of $2 billion every year. *Moore* was a name most people in the United States did not know; thousands of automobiles passed its vast, opaque-windowed building on the busy freeway everyday, saw only the name before it, and had no idea of what the name meant, signified or what business it covered. Moore was also a contractor aiding in Sarumnan development and building. It earned something like $3 billion per annum.

Borchard and Moore had once been small potatoes compared to Western and Alliance Petroleum. WAP, as it was called, explored and developed the first oilfields during the days of the hated predecessors. Fifty-fifty had been the arrangement then. WAP would pay all the expenses, take all the risks. The revenues were split down the middle, the company bearing all the expense, past and current. Conventional wisdom regarded the arrangement as unfavorable to WAP, but the man who drew it up knew better. In ten years the company became as large as any of the Six Sisters, Royal Dutch Shell, Texaco and the others who controlled the oil world.

Marcus Raskoff, the author of the arrangement, was a born survivor, a capitalist beloved by Bolsheviks and the Islamic fundamentalists as well as by Labour, Tory, and Republicans and Democrats at home, both conservative and liberal.

The General regarded him as a friend, though it was often pointed out to him that Raskoff had been born a Jew; however, no evidence could be adduced to prove him a contributor to Israeli causes. When he broke the contract set up by the tyrants who preceded him, then Major Mohammed Abdullah privately urged Raskoff to accept the new terms quickly. Since Western and Alliance had long since retrieved its seed investment money and reaped enormous profit as well, Raskoff allowed himself to be persuaded to stay and run the oil fields for 10 percent and expenses. Since the world market was growing geometrically, it was not hard for the old man to accept several billion a year and to remain the oil world's principal source of fine crude oil.

Marcus Raskoff and Alan Masters had something else in common besides being held in affection by General Mohammed Abdullah. They shared a mutual loathing. This tended to make them suspicious and very polite to one another when they found themselves together. It also made each anxious to prove to the other that he bore no malice. Favors passed between them easily. Respect for each other's access to the mercurial President-for-Life cemented their eagerness to prove amiability.

Raskoff would have liked to bring back Alan Masters to Washington as a free man. He did his best, but the government had batteries of obscure, civil-service-protected lawyers trying to win recognition for themselves by nailing a figure still newsworthy. He offered campaign contributions discreetly, he made calls, he hired lawyers, all to intercede in Masters's behalf, directly or indirectly.

"I'm afraid it's hopeless right now," he reported on his annual visit to Zarplis. "You're still a hot potato."

Masters sighed. The two of them had dined alone in his big new house. Raskoff had brought fresh pork from London and the cook that went everywhere with him. The wine was a superb Montrachet. Hard booze Masters was able to find in good supply. The only wine available in Sarumna was homemade, and horrible.

"Then I'm to be a latter-day Philip Nolan," Masters said. "A man without a country."

"You've got citizenship in this one," Raskoff said. "In time it will be as powerful as any in the world."

"On paper." Masters sighed again. "Until the oil gives out."

"That's the problem down the line. Right now they want Sarumnan crude."

"How badly do you think Washington wants me?" Masters reached for the wine.

"In my view they'll be content to let the matter quietly die just to keep the General happy. Also, there's this—if they bring you home they know you'd raise a powerful stink about who helped and supported the Fund in the highest government circles. I often wonder why your Number Two never went into that."

Masters put down the bottle. "He was self-destructive."

"His end certainly proves it," Raskoff said. He waved away a proffered tray of patisserie. Masters did the same. "Is there anything else I can do for you?"

"You're fairly sure about Washington wanting the thing to die?"

"I'd still be careful, of course, and wait here. There're always middle and lower echelon people in government anxious to make a name for themselves in the papers."

"Will you keep me posted?"

"I have people on it routinely," Raskoff assured him. He leaned forward. He knew when to press a point for himself. "About our own contract renewal. Have you spoken to the General about it?"

"Naturally." There was a pause. "I urged him to renew."

"Thank you, Alan." The old man sighed gratefully.

Masters knew when to press a point of his own. "There are some things we'd like done. Privately, of course."

"You must understand, I've had some nasty problems with Senate committees and such rather recently."

"I know, Marcus, I know," Masters reassured him. "We want to acquire certain real estate. Our London firm. If you bought the property and we acquired it from you it would be nicely shielded. I'll see you get the shopping list. About twenty properties, one in Houston and another on Fifth Avenue we especially want. It would be well regarded here, I assure you."

The old man took the paper from Alan Masters's hand. He

studied it, his face the mask it always was when he found himself in a bargaining position. Masters was asking the difficult but not the impossible.

"The buyers and the money come through London?" Raskoff folded the list and put it away.

"Or Switzerland, if you like. We've got a consortium there too."

"London's okay." Raskoff started to go.

"The next request's more ticklish, Marcus." He saw the old man's bushy eyebrows rise as he sat back again. "I hear Italia Motors is in trouble. Very cash-short."

"That is true."

"I can raise all the cash they need."

"A takeover?"

"I wouldn't want that, Marcus. I mean, under different circumstances that would have happened."

"As when you ran the Fund in the old days?" the old man teased.

"Of course. But even then Italia would have been one hell of a big bite to swallow. Third, or is it second, largest automotive company in the world? No, we'd just like to buy into it in a big way. Maybe 1.2 billion. I figure that would give us about 10 percent of the company stock. They needn't be frightened. We haven't got the manpower to run the company. We'd be open about our purpose. We have surplus cash to invest. That's all."

"There'd be international ramifications."

"In the financial community. For a few days. It'll die down. Always does. You know them, don't you?"

"I know them." He was on his feet. On the way to the car, Raskoff said cheerfully, "By the way, I've acquired two Renoirs your former partner Ebersol once owned. He was a remarkable collector. Had a chance to buy several others years ago and went after these two very superior ones. And got them. Dynamic, unusual sort of man, wasn't he?"

"I don't remember anything about him," Alan Masters said crisply.

II.

Roger Philips returned home and found pasted to the door a lengthy document he had not the stomach to read beyond its announcement of liens, attachments and the like. He pulled it down irritably, turned around and headed his Jaguar bankward.

Amanda Miller was not entirely surprised to find that Roger Philips had left her in the lurch. She was somewhat comforted by the fact that the man proved realistic enough to have finally accepted the hundred thousand. That told her that at least he was human.

Her usual shyness and reserve came back to her in a flood. She had pushed hard and it had come to nothing. Could she go back to him? She did not think of the money. Van Leeuwen had spoken of larger amounts that might be necessary. "You are declaring a limited war against a sovereign state. That can be very expensive, but do not worry about that part of it," he had said.

She had nowhere else to go, no one else could help. People who knew Sarumna well enough to pull off what she wanted, who spoke at least some Arabic, who had some experience in eluding police pursuit—how many such people were there? Here was Roger Phillips—even his run-in with the authorities proved he had style. He himself hadn't been charged with anything. They wanted him as a witness against his best friend, and Roger had simply disappeared. Made some prosecutors damned anxious to get at him, so they escalated the search; still he managed to remain lost until the friend had cleared himself and signaled for Roger to come out, come out, wherever you are. She needed this man.

Still, she could not bring herself to go back to Palm Springs.

She hated herself for coming to a dead end. She thought of her mother and could see the self-satisfied, smug grin, the turned-down corners of the embittered smile when the details of failure were spelled out. "I could have told you what would happen." All her life there had been those words. Or: "Perhaps if you'd been different," meaning a finer-looking lady, one whose looks and body would have challenged, drawn and persuaded a man to dare the impossible . . .

It was late; her stomach began to rumble. The room, handsome as it was, began to oppress her. She had set up a final test and he had refused it, that was plain. What did they used to say? "Every man has his price." Well, this one's crazy enough not to have one. She sighed and decided she did not want to eat in the room; she did not want to stay in Beverly Hills another day; she did not want anything but to be buried somewhere. She went down to Wilshire Boulevard, saw the Brown Derby across the street and decided to relieve her pangs there. Waiting for the light, she heard behind her, "Listen."

Roger Phillips, his hair blown out of shape, was in an old sweater with no shirt under it. He glowered at her even when he must have seen her smile. "I've got to talk to you. Come on."

He took her elbow and walked her to the street called El Camino with such long strides that she had to jog to keep up with him. He did not speak until they reached the top-down XKE. "Let's go somewhere better." He U-turned and headed south to Olympic, muttered, "Damned traffic," headed west and made it his business to get to the ocean as quickly as traffic lights allowed. He had a favorite place. In the dark at this time of year they were the only car in a vast black area. He leaned over, pushed open the door for her and climbed out of his side. "Over here," he said. The ground rose to a little clump of ice plant and grass. He sat; in the moonless dark she could see his hand pat a space beside him.

"I cashed your check."

"It was yours, so why not?"

"A lot of money for damned little. So I think I ought to tell you why what you want to do is impossible."

"That's exactly what I don't want to hear."

"When I say impossible," he went on like a man talking aloud to himself, "I don't mean it can't be done. Hell, I suppose someone could kidnap the chairman of the Joint Chiefs of Staff from his offices in the Pentagon. Highly unlikely, but it theoretically could be pulled off."

"Tell me how it would be possible," Amanda Miller urged quietly.

"No, I'll tell you what you'd be up against. First, getting in." In the dark night he found magisterial poise and detachment; she felt like a student being lectured by a professor on the problems that beset a historic military campaign. *Terrain of battle.* Sarumnans traditionally consider themselves a big family; outsiders were either intruders or honored guests. What would they be? Self-invited meddlers invading a privacy they neither understood nor appreciated. Since the takeover by General Abdullah and his Revolutionary Council, things had grown massively worse. People thought of Abdullah as a crazy, but crazy can be merely eccentric and harmless. Abdullah's madness was that he regarded his power as limitless. His judgments were Allah-given. He was the ultimate religious-political zealot. In all countries, in all religions those people were dangerous when they had political leverage. Abdullah felt duty-bound to support dissident and terrorist groups all over the world so long as they fought his enemies, real or imagined, potential or present. At home he knew he had potential domestic enemies, hence his security measures were horrendous in their thoroughness.

Problem of supply. Getting in the right people simply to kidnap an important counselor like Alan Masters would prove difficult. Very well, assume they got in, Roger Phillips conceded. They'd need equipment. How do you bring in the necessary hardware? They search every inch of baggage, hand carried and stowed, for alcohol, for weapons, for Israeli and Zionist manifestations, for Western seditiousness, for fellow-Arab betrayal. So it'd have to be done without guns.

There was a very long silence between them.

"Okay," he resumed gravely, "suppose I know a way to get the party in. And suppose I could move fast enough to steal a beat on his Iron Curtain-trained police. Grab your Mr. Masters. Then what?" Amanda Miller found her hands engaged under her chin as if she were praying. Roger Phillips sighed deeply and rubbed his chin. "Where do I go? What do I do with him?"

"We'd be stuck." Roger Phillips seemed to be thinking aloud, his voice was so soft. "Which means dead." He let that sink in. "The whole country's only a strip of fertile soil along the Mediterranean coast. The rest is desert, vast, naked desert without a rock a scorpion can hide behind. That's where the oil is, but what good is that if you're running? So tell me—We're in. I've got your man. What do I do now? How do I get him out?"

He sat quietly as if he had proved his case and was ready to rest it.

Amanda Miller felt herself shiver; she heard the rumbling in her stomach, but apparently Roger Phillips did not. "Please tell me how it might be done," she said eagerly, as if she knew he really wanted that question.

There are a lot of Americans in Sarumna, he continued; they work the oil fields. Did she ever see how Americans live abroad? What they do is recreate their vision of their good old U.S.A. wherever they are, set up their own schools, commissaries, their own cable television with the usual sitcoms and game shows, hamburgers and the YMCA, little suburbia in the outlands. Would they, could they be of help? No. First of all, they all had good, well-paying jobs they would not want to jeopardize. Second, why should they?

So who could help? The plain fact was, No one. Unequipped people would find unfriendly terrain and uncooperative countrymen.

"I hope that doesn't destroy you," he said finally, his voice more gentle than she had ever heard it. "You seem a rather fine person. I take it John Edward Ebersol is somehow related to you."

"He was my father. I got to know him only after he was in trouble. A rare man."

"Don't try to play God and exact retribution. I remember learning in Sunday school that's a sin."

"If I were looking for retribution, I'd go there myself and

somehow find a pistol. I don't want revenge. I want Alan Masters brought before the bar of justice, that's all."

The silence between them stretched to a long moment. Far away they could hear the surf crash on the shore. Amanda's stomach rumbled as well. "How would you do it," she asked, adding in a voice smooth as cream, "if you could do it?"

She saw his teeth flash in the dark. "My old professor, a wonderful, sweet character, must be a million years old by now. He's regarded as a saint there, knows the country better than any of them, speaks flawless Arabic; it happens he wrote the national anthem, how's that for a kick?" He offered a few bars. "Was declared an honorary citizen. They wouldn't turn him down if he wanted to come in."

She watched Roger Phillips thoughtfully rest his chin on cupped palms, elbows on upraised knees. "And if you got in with him?" she said softly. He swiveled his head toward her.

"Have to move fast. Do it. Get out. Probably by sea." She saw him grin again. "A fast boat. You know there are a lot of little islands in the Mediterranean people never think of, Pantelleria, Isole di Pelagie, Lampedusa, Lampione. I guess you've never heard of any of them?"

"Never."

"Malta. Sicily. Those you know, right?"

"They're none of them all that far away, you say?"

"Mussolini called the Mediterranean 'our lake.' I mean, it's a sea, it raises hell often enough, the bottom's full of ships whose captains thought they could challenge it, but if the timing was right and the boat fast enough . . . One of those islands . . ." His voice dwindled away.

"It could be done," she said, not a question.

"It'd be too tough. Couldn't count on everything falling into place." The spell was over. He got to his feet. "You'd need a backup."

She rose beside him and dusted sand from her jeans. "Something always goes wrong," she offered, to beat him to the point.

He stared briefly at her. "You'd better believe it."

"What about all those Americans?" she pursued. "If they're into recreating the U.S.A. and all that, wouldn't there be macho types weekend-flying Cessnas and Piper Cubs?"

"The oil fields are far apart," he mused, almost as if he were alone. "We can assume the contractors have got substantial air traffic between them too. DC-3s, executive jets, carrying spare parts, people and supplies from one field to another."

"So?"

"You'd want to bring someone who could fly an airplane." He saw her smile. "Still—where would a guy like that go?" His voice assumed an icy edge, like a man shaking off a dream. "Assuming he wasn't shot down before he even got off the runway. They've got a very damned good air force trained by Poles, Roumanians, Czechs, the people who also run the new hospitals they've built now that they're so rich."

"But there *are* planes for what you'd need for a backup, right?" she persisted. "One could be stolen . . ."

"Let's get you home," he broke off crisply.

"I'm starved." She was sure a seed had been planted.

"We'll find a hamburger joint on the way."

"Not that starved." She was fighting for time to be with him.

"You like fish chowder?"

"I'm crazy about it."

"They call it bouillabaisse but it's a chowder."

Very precise, careful guy, she thought admiringly. "I don't care what they call it."

The place was a big barnlike structure in Venice. They ate in silence for a considerable time. Roger Phillips eyed the lady across the table and noted that in a well-lit room she would not, perhaps could not, return his gaze. Somewhere, in the tangle of hair and eyebrows, a pretty face struggled to be found. She was, he decided, a curious mix all right, shyness and aggressiveness, plainness and fieriness. Hell of an appetite, too, he observed.

After her third helping, she pushed away her plate and saw how intensely she was being observed. She averted her eyes quickly.

"Have you really got the kind of money you've been talking about?"

She nodded. "That's no problem."

"Where's it come from? Your report said the Internal Revenue people took every dime Ebersol had in the world. Even sold off his art collection."

"That's true."

"Maybe you're not his daughter. Maybe that's a cover story. You're CIA and they're looking for some shnook on the outside to cover the dirty work for them."

"If you ran the CIA would you hire me?"

"Where else would anybody get so much money?"

"I told you: that's not the problem. I'm not the CIA."

"That's what they'd tell you to say, of course."

"Does it matter who I am and where the money's from?"

"Not really." He called for the check with a raised hand. "The whole thing's a pipe dream anyway."

On the drive back to the hotel he was silent until they reached Wilshire Boulevard. "I've already spent your money, you know. I think there's about a dollar ninety-eight left, after paying what I owed, late charges, assorted penalties and the bank's legal fees."

"Do you need any more?"

"Money," he grumbled. "When I was teaching I never made much yet had all I needed. Lived well, dates, books, theaters, trips. Once I started with a big line of credit at the banks and the savings and loans, it became a struggle. I must say, I put up some damned fine houses. Problem is no one wants to buy them. To the untrained eye they look funny. Where's the mansard roof? The sliding glass windows? Know what I'm saying?"

He pulled up in the cobblestone alley between the old and the new part of the hotel. "Why don't you come up and tell me about it?" Amanda Miller suggested.

In the room, she pointed to a chair but found he had already put himself into it. Some instinct told her not to speak, to listen, to let his mood sail its own course. She had the feeling he was not even aware she was in the room once he'd stretched himself in the chair.

"There was one guy who offered to buy them all," he went on dreamily. "No kidding. Said he was crazy about my houses, called them kooky and nutty. This big, hairy character with a voice that rattled windows. Wore white polyester slacks, white kidskin shoes and a maroon blazer, also synthetic. Built more than a thousand houses, he told me. Two-car garages and all the built-in gimmicks. Said I'd never sell mine, except at a loss. He told me ten years down the way they'd be worth five times what I was asking. He offered to buy them for half of what I wanted. Meant I walked away broke after I turned him down. I was dead. Until you came along."

Amanda Miller had found a place on the floor not far from Roger Phillips's feet. She noticed that her guest was talking with his eyes closed.

"So, thanks to you, I'm saved," he went on again. "But for what? The polyester crowd still won't buy my houses. They want fairways on the patio, not mountains in the living room." He emitted a slight self-deprecatory laugh. "Those who like my houses can't afford them, and, besides, they're a minority. Does all this bore you, Miss Miller?"

"Not at all. Why don't you call me Amanda?"

"To me you will always be Miss Miller, the young lady in the bushes. Now why did you do that?"

"Can't we forget about it? I wanted to observe you."

"No," he said, shifting himself somewhat, "you're not CIA. Couldn't be. Again, unless they're so fiendishly clever they chose someone deliberately clumsy . . ." He broke into a harsh laughing. "So you could be one of them."

The room grew silent. She thought for a moment he might have fallen asleep on her, but he hadn't; she found his eyes fixed on the ceiling. "If I sold the houses, at a good profit, what then? Build other houses? *Their* kind of houses? Then it's just a job, who needs that, right?"

"Right." She began to like what she was hearing.

"I could make a ton, what I've learned about people. Give them sunken tubs, lots of glass, marble veneer, walk-in closets. Oh, shit." He lapsed into silence again.

After a long time, he said, "A lady the other day called me a romantic. Do you think I'm a romantic?"

"A romantic would jump at this chance."

"It's late," he broke off without warning, getting to his feet and stumbling over her in the process. "I'd better get going. I'll see you tomorrow."

She sensed a small triumph for her dreams. "You could spend the night here." She caught the baleful glare. "The couch there is a bed."

"No need to impose. May I use your phone?"

"Of course."

He had a little black book and he knew what page he wanted. Amanda Miller tried not to listen to what he said on the telephone: "Hi . . . It's me . . . Yes, I know. I've been busy . . . Look, why don't we talk about that in person? . . Oh, you are? . . That serious? . . Well, good luck to both of you and all that, Cindy." He turned to Amanda Miller and grinned sheepishly. "One more, if I may." She thought to go into the bathroom and turn on the water so she couldn't hear, but she let her baser impulses prevail. "Hi, it's Roger . . . Yes, I know it's late, but . . ." (*Thank God,* Amanda Miller thought, *that some women have character.*) "Yes, I have, Cathy, I really have . . . I've been so damned involved . . . Very much . . . And you, me? . . I can be there in ten minutes, ciao." Amanda Miller retreated to the bathroom.

"Look, I want to talk to you tomorrow," he ordered brusquely through the half-open door and over the rush of water in the tub. "Early. Be here."

Amanda Miller did not reply. She knew she had won some kind of victory, but she wasn't happy at all.

12.

SIXTY-FOUR of them in camouflage battle gear and German-style helmets drove all night in ten fully armed weapons carriers, three of which hauled mobile antitank guns. When the sun began to rise over the northern Sahara, they rendezvoused, exactly as planned, with twenty others already positioned two miles from the border fort once named after a distinguished French general.

Surprise being the essence of what the men were taught, they waited under the trees in a nearby oasis for high noon, when they would attack. At ten they turned from the equipment; some of them were readying for battle and faced east for prayers.

When the plan was broached, the attack on the neighbor's sovereignty called for four hundred of the neighbor's nationals in training at the General's special liberation-training area near El Guettar to storm the frontier station. Four hundred ardent freedom-fighters, not Sarumnans, to raise the flag of Islamic fundamentalism and once and for all create a true Arab republic on Sarumna's eastern flank. No one at the desert training base found the courage to inform the General there were not four hundred of those nationals at El Guettar. Japanese, yes. Their Red Brigade held about that number at the camp. West Germans of various groups, a smaller number. There were Italians, Egyptians, Irish, Palestinians so militant they loathed and detested Arafat for his timid and accommodating style against the hated enemy, South Americans of various nationalities, even a few trainees from the monstrous United States itself. But only sixty-four of *them*.

This was to be a bold attack designed to draw to its own

number some eight hundred new recruits said to be stationed at the border, who, everyone was assured, would rush forward at the opportunity to free their nation from its Westernized whoremasters. This, in turn, would trigger rebellion everywhere and achieve liberation. No one in command had the courage to inform Zarplis that sixty-four only were mustered for the attack and the fort could not house eight hundred recruits. Such a message would mean instant demotion, or worse.

The commander of the revolutionaries was said to be a poet, a teacher of English for some two of his twenty-six years. He himself had not proved an outstanding student of the military arts, either in the classroom or on the training ground at El Guettar, but he had zeal. He spoke a gloriously resonant Arabic. His instructors deemed him a natural leader.

Shortly before noon, an emissary sent in civilian garb to scout the fort reported that just two days before four hundred raw recruits had arrived for basic training. Their top officers had departed the night before for a political celebration at a small city some four hours away.

"The ripe fruit awaits a tender plucking," the poet-revolutionist said.

At twelve precisely his men crossed the border, killing three sleeping guards in their cots. The gates to the old fortress having long since been dismantled, the raiding party stormed the parade ground, firing in the air to create confusion and fear. Shouting proclaimed a new era, a return to Islam and the death of the Westernized republic and all its corrupt leaders.

Opposition developed and twelve of the raiders were soon dead or wounded. A number of them stormed into a barracks where the recruits were kept. They were found still bedded in two vast dormitories when the doors were broken down; it was an hour after high noon. "Arise, youth, this is the day of your liberation!" the poet proclaimed. Youth did not arise from their sacks. It turned out that on the day before they had been given all their immunizing shots, every one from smallpox to yellow fever, eight in all, administered in one package so the medical officers could join their brother officers at the national celebration. Youth could only groan painfully at the call to freedom.

Within the hour all firing ceased. The poet ordered a wireless to his headquarters. It was long, suitably couched and proclaimed a total victory. A sergeant of the overwhelmed national forces also managed to reach a telephone. By the time the poet's message was processed at El Guettar for transmission to General Abdullah, the Defense Ministry in the capital of the invaded nation had been alerted, as were the ambassadors in the French and American embassies. Paris and Washington were informed, naval units of both countries were given new orders and alerted to stand by. By nightfall airborne troops of the violated nation reached the fort, killed all but twenty-two of the invaders. The survivors were captured, bound and flown to a military prison.

At Zarplis General Mohammed Abdullah proclaimed a glorious victory. "Young men of great courage and faith and true patriotism," he said, "have died gloriously in a struggle against corrupt betrayers of the true faith." He denied complicity.

In Alan Masters's residence, the telex clattered intermittently all day. Marcus Raskoff kept repeatedly urging Masters to call him on the scrambler telephone. His secretary, at the other end of the telex, was told each time that Alan Masters was not available and would be given the message as soon as possible.

Alan Masters was spending the day visiting Roman ruins, an activity which had always bored him from his first hour in Sarumna. He suffered as gracefully as he could because he was playing guide to a Kentucky girl he had seen walking along the Corniche in a swirling skirt and a very naked backless top. She was being followed by a pack of young men keening the air around her with moans of sexual arousal, darting in and out after her merely to touch the flesh of a woman's arms and shoulders. He got out of his Rolls, said his name quickly and urged the young lady to take refuge in the car.

She was newly arrived and was leaving on the morrow. Her brother worked the oil fields and she had been given permission to come into the country for two days. However, the message to her brother had not been delivered and she was stuck in the Strand Hotel. She had decided "to take a little sun" before she left, little knowing what bare shoulders and naked backs did to the young manhood of Zarplis.

When they finally reached his house after the sightseeing, the sun had set. The messages from Raskoff lay on top of each other. "Urgent." "Please." "Most important." He paid them no attention.

"Is this your house?" the Kentucky girl said somewhat hoarsely. "It's so beautiful!" He poured champagne and let her take in the splendid view.

"Would you like to see the rest of the place?" he suggested a little later, taking along a third cold bottle.

He showed her what the Roman decorators had done and what had been collected in his behalf. He led her up the marble staircase to his bedroom, turned on the hi-fi and brought her to the balcony. She said, "It's heavenly," and he said, "It was fated for you to be here, my dear. May I refill your glass?"

Some time later there was a rapping on his door. Marco, a combination secretary-butler, who had some English, ran the house and reported on him to the General's personal police, kept saying behind it, "Is important, sir."

"Go away." Masters was equally insistent.

"Is Mr. Raskoff in Milan. He begs me to inform you is most urgent, sir."

When Alan Masters got to the scrambler phone, Marcus Raskoff was waiting for him. "What the hell is going on there?" he demanded.

It took a moment for Alan Masters to realize the old man was not talking about the events inside the house. "I've got the deal with Italia almost set for you and your man starts a war? It's war, you know, when one country invades the other."

The facts emerged from the sputtering voice at the other end. It was all over the newspapers up there and certainly around the world by this time. When was the General going to grow up? Whom did he think he was kidding? Training all those harebrained terrorists, and for what? He was the richest of all, why did he need bomb throwers and airplane hijackers? And now this. A few damned subversives trained in his country, sent back with his equipment to start a goddam revolution—really, Alan. He'd done business with Sarumnans since the General was a boy and he'd kept his mouth shut at many of the things that had happened since he'd taken power, but how far would the General go?

"Tell me, Marcus." Masters's voice was unperturbed. He stood barefoot on the marble floor in the tiny room that held the special telephone, Marco gazing at him and two inquisitive house servants behind Marco. "Tell me how the Italia deal stands."

"Why the hell do you think I've been trying to get to you. It's almost set."

"I'm ready to transfer funds tomorrow. A few more hundred thousand if you need it to spread around where it can help close the deal today."

"They're nervous here about the possibility of war."

"If the General said he had nothing to do with it, I assure you he had nothing to do with it." Alan Masters glanced significantly at Marco but did not turn full-face toward him. "He doesn't need to apologize for his convictions. The world calls them training grounds. All he's doing is to provide rest and recreation for people whose ideals he respects. My God, every country in the world does that, don't they?"

"He makes doing business very difficult outside of his country," Raskoff grumbled.

"The point is, he's got the capital, and lots of companies need it, Marcus. Does Italia want our money or should I draw up another shopping list? Remember, I wouldn't like to fight my man if he's of a mind to cancel any contracts."

"Discreet." Marcus Raskoff was plainly ready to concede. "Can't you urge him to be discreet?"

"I need some good news if what you tell me is true. Close the deal right away, today if possible, and call me back."

Alan Masters stood by the dead telephone for a long time, unaware of staring eyes. He even forgot about the girl in the bed. "Has anybody else wanted to talk to me?" he asked Marco. There was a shaking of the head. "Good. My guest. Apologize to her in my behalf. Have the car bring her to the hotel and wait for her there until she's ready to go to the airport. Help her in any way she needs. See she takes a suitable souvenir. Got all that, Marco?"

"Yes, sir."

"And leave word for the General I've got very good news for him and am at his disposal at once."

"Anything else, sir?"

"Yes. Have the young lady sign the Guest Book before she leaves." Often—quite often—he had little to comfort him but memories, and names helped . . .

The General always wore military dress, as did his staff, even those with civilian responsibilities like running the national television or the new hospital services. When Alan Masters was brought into the presence it was after midnight, the fate of the intruders abroad had been sealed in a hastily convened court-martial in that country's capital. The General carried sidearms and a steel hat was on a nearby table. He seemed exhilarated by combat, even when an engagement had turned out less well than he liked. Masters met with him in one of six or seven dwellings maintained for his security around the city. He had a home where a wife dwelt and where, it was said, he frequently rested, but Masters had never seen it or her.

"I bring you good news," Masters said. "A glorious day for you and your people, General. I am not a military or political person, as you know, sir, but for my part this is a day to celebrate. Part of the nation's resources has been put to work. The nation will now receive income from a source other than oil, sir. You will recall, General, I have been speaking to you of the necessity of diversifying."

The General approached Alan Masters as if he had never seen him before. "Tell me the good news, Masters."

"Italia Motors, second or third largest in the world, passenger cars, trucks, buses, railroad cars, everything that moves on the ground, from motorbikes to ten-ton tractors—you, sir, now own one fifth of that company. If you cannot have such a company here, why should you not have one abroad?"

Alan Masters was surprised by an embrace. The General muttered something in Arabic, but the hug told the story, the words did not matter.

The General called for coffee and sat across from Alan Masters. He wanted to know everything about Italia. Specifics: where the factories were located; how many they employed; their factories abroad; which countries; the size and value of the company's exports; did they make any military equipment; could they; would they; what sort of people were in top management; did they export to the occupiers of Palestine; were Zionists in its management; did they build a car suitable for a head of state? Mohammed Abdullah was doubly exhilarated.

"They are businessmen first, last and always."

"And what do they think of me?"

"You have power, sir. They respect it."

"Some of the people around me say we ought not invest in an enterprise so closely identified with the West."

"They are businessmen, as I said, General. They link up where they have to make sales."

The General sighed. "You are a good man, Masters." He rose to indicate he had other duties and obligations. "We must take better care of your person. Enemies. My enemies are everywhere. I am redoubling your security."

"I'm a mere financial counselor, sir." His houseman's presence alone Masters found oppressive. There were guards on the grounds of the new house.

"A personal bodyguard, responsible to my own security people. He will be with you all the time."

"All the time, General?" Masters protested wanly.

"He does not see what he sees or give tongue to what he knows. You will get used to him and soon take no notice, dear friend and counselor."

They knew everything he did and said anyway, so what could he say? But he would never get used to it, and for some reason he felt very homesick.

13.

AMANDA MILLER greeted him frostily, did not wait for him to come in but returned to the table where she had been taking breakfast and refilled her cup from the silver carafe without asking if Roger Phillips would like coffee. He did not seem to take notice of any of the tokens of disapproval she laid so pointedly before him.

"An office," he began. "It would be wise to rent impressive space in an office building." She regarded him briefly. The man's face was smooth shaven, the hair still wet from a shower. *Smug sexist rat*, she thought, *I really hate him. I hate his women too.* "Stationery. Very important. Must be ready no later than tomorrow. They'll say it can't be done, but offer enough money."

All the loathing deliquesced, like sugar in hot water, as she realized he was moving ahead in her direction. She could not bring herself to press for an affirmative commitment for fear he was still daydreaming among the pro's and con's. "Why so quickly?" she murmured.

"Everything will have to go very fast. I'll come to that. On the stationery, a list of names. Make them up. Long list, small type, under a heading, *Sponsors*. Dr. Amos Robert This and Professor Cornelius T. That. Remember, they're paranoid about Israel, so nothing south of Barnhardt. It will need a name. How about Friends of Archaeological—no, friends of anything sounds trendy, do-goodish and too Left. The Society for the Resumption of Historical Research. Got it? Can you handle all that?"

No coldness now; nothing was left in her but an urge to fall to the ground and embrace his knees. She contented herself with a whisper, "Does this mean you're going to do it?"

"It's got to be done before they discover what the hell is going on." He rattled on as if the question was rhetorical. "I mean *fast*. They've got sharp intelligence people in their Washington embassy. It won't take them long to find our Society for the Resumption is a phony. That all the names are phony. That we rented the office space today and the phones have just been put in, and that there's no one up there except a secretary. Oh, yes, hire one who believes what she's told, preferably an old lady with a speech impediment, nobody sharp, for God's sake."

"What else do you want me to do?"

"Money. Cash. This is going to be more tricky. Gold. I'll want enough to raise a fever. I think there are restrictions about getting it out of the country."

"I can manage it."

He frowned as if to say he had not expected agreement. "We'll need more cash to work with."

"The money's no problem, as I've always said. But who are the people you're—"

"Does it matter?" he broke off, but softened somewhat with, "Sorry, I can't tell you."

"How many people will it all need?"

"At the most, four. More than that would be suspect from the word go. I'll tell you whom I've got in mind. My old professor, Walter Evans Carver, Ph.D. and four L.L.D.'s from places like Harvard and Cambridge. He's a beloved figure in Sarumna. Has worked there almost all his life. He didn't let the great museums loot the ruins; he was a pillar of righteousness during the old corruption that led to the new corruption. He even wrote the words to a song that became the national anthem. They made him an honorary and perpetual master citizen, whatever that means. If he says he wants to return to the beloved country with a few associates in behalf of our society, they won't be able to say no."

"And will he?"

"I haven't seen him since he retired. He's getting old. I keep thinking he'll be glad of the chance to go back for a last look."

"Even when he finds out what it's all about?"

"He's not going to find out. When I was in charge of digging operations for him in the desert, he was dead-concentrated on what he was doing. What I did was to make it possible for him to work without interruption. Maybe your computer detective told you I tripped the light fantastic with bribable officials and ask-no-question types who could bring in the goods we needed. I don't think the professor ever knew what I was doing. He's crazy enough to have thrown me off the project. If he finds out what we're trying to do there now, he'd blow the whole deal sky-high. So I'm playing games with an old guy who always loved me and helped me, being the shit I am." He pulled in a deep breath as if he had to overcome something distasteful, but resumed quietly and quickly. "Then there are the Boardmans. This couple I know. Used to know, should say. The golden pair we all envied. Have done, can do everything. Sail a yawl from here to Tahiti, fly airplanes to Patagonia, weld a rudder at sea, navigate by the stars, ski, sky-dive, and they used to be what were called swingers. I mean, the lady knows how to use sex to get what she wants, and from what I've been able to find out about your man, we could use someone like that."

"And the fourth person on the team?"

"That's me, of course."

"I mean the fourth one you're bringing along," Amanda Miller pursued.

"Those three and me, that's it."

"What about me?"

"What about you?"

"I don't get to go with you?"

"Why in the world would you go with us?"

"Because—well, because . . ."

"What would you do there?"

"Whatever has to be done."

"I think you regard this venture as a kind of cookout," he snapped. "Nothing to do except take in custody a man who won't want to go and get him out of a very hostile environment. Mrs. Boardman not only has got a very sexy way about her, but she can fly an airplane. So can her husband. He can also make it fly in case it doesn't want to for one reason for another. The professor gets us in and knows where we can hide or where there's a road that isn't on the maps, or a cove—you get my drift, don't you, Miss Miller? It's a team of specialists, carefully chosen."

"You don't know me. I'm very capable."

77

"I do know you, Miss Miller. You were only pretty fair at hiding in oleanders, but you run fast as hell. You're the money we need, what's wrong with that?"

"If I'm the money, I insist I come along."

Roger Phillips got to his feet and turned to the door. "Then you take over. You now know what has to be done. I'm out."

"Please." She seized a sleeve. "I don't mean that."

"What do you mean?"

"I only want to go," she pleaded.

"It isn't a game, Amanda," he said gently, for it came through to him at last; it was a job, an adventure to him, but to her it was a personal fulfillment. Yet reason conquered emotion within him. "It's going to be a very tricky business. Right now I'd guess our chances of pulling it off are not fifty-fifty. Everybody except us has to function without knowing what's going on and be able to function efficiently, professionally. The less they know what's going on, the better for them, if it falls apart. You can't pretend to be duped if you're in on it. Today's police are too good at uncovering that sort of thing. So my professor and the Boardmans won't know a damn thing about what I'm going to do. They may hate me for it in the morning, but I'm trying to protect them. Because if anything, *anything* goes wrong, it can get very, very painful unless some kind of innocence can be convincingly established. So they'll be doing what has to be done without knowing what they're doing."

"That leaves you very vulnerable."

"Never mind that. If it's to work, I'm the boss, the only boss. What I say goes, who, what, when—never mind why. If you don't agree to that, the deal's off. Is that understood?"

"Yes," she said softly. "But I'm really better than you think," she persisted. "I'm strong. I know how to survive in the desert."

"This desert's a relentless adversary, Amanda. Maybe that's made me buy your deal. Sure, I need the money. Sure, my life's come to a dead end again. But what's bringing me back to the Sahara may not be just money and nostalgia. Maybe I have to test myself again, to see if what I once had is still there, can you understand that?"

"Yes, Roger," she said, but she did not understand.

PART THREE

14.

THE FIGURE knifed down the Olympic-size pool on its fourth turn, the arms reaching out with powerful strokes, the legs churning the water hard enough to leave a wake. From a small gallery above the deck Roger Phillips watched the swimmer make his last turn, find from somewhere within himself a spurt of power to make a sprint to the finish in classic style.

He pulled himself up and sat, feet dangling in the blue water, mouth wide open as he gasped for air. His hand went up to his head to pull off a little yellow swimmer's cap. The head was almost bald; there were very gray hairs on the chest, but for the rest the man looked like a varsity team swimmer at his daily workout, not like Walter Evans Carver, emeritus regius professor of classical and Islamic history. Roger Phillips waited until the old man got to his feet, found a towel, threw it over his shoulders and started for the lockers. The old man had to be approaching eighty, Roger Phillips knew; the years seemed hardly to have touched him. He was a lanky figure, certainly six inches over six feet; the legs were still like a water bird's, spindly, so long as to be out of proportion with the rest of him. He walked, as he always did, quickly, as if he might fall down at any moment. He did not raise his eyes to the gallery above the pool; if he saw Roger Phillips, Carver offered no sign of recognition, which would not have surprised his visitor anyway.

Roger Phillips waited outside for the old man to be dressed. He emerged into the bright, ocean-scoured sunlight, tweedy as ever, scanned the world before him and finally caught sight of his old pupil and associate.

"Ah, Roger," he greeted him, as if he had seen him the day before.

"Morning, sir. Beautiful day." They had not seen each other or communicated for three years.

The old professor grunted and started to walk like a man already very late for his next engagement. Roger Phillips tagged along. He knew his man better than to force a conversation. They crossed the campus of the University of California at San Diego, which is located in the suitably named town of La Jolla, the jewel, and did not stop until, some blocks later, they came to a small park and an available bench. Professor Carver glanced at his watch, made a little smile of approval, and sat.

"You said you'd never come back to *la vie académique*," Carver began.

"Didn't you always say life's an adventure or it's nothing?"

"A teacher finds himself saying many things he's not quite sure he believes. Are you rich? Did you strike that golden chord? Have you found a satisfaction deeper than you knew before? I believe those were some of the words you used."

"Was I that pretentious?"

"Worse. You abandoned a promising academic career in mid-passage."

"A product of my times, sir. I plead guilty."

"And I thought I'd brought you through safely. Our discipline has always been beset by philistine enemies. 'What's the relevance of that?' 'Who cares what those ancient people did?' 'What's that got to do with today's problems?' And you fell for it."

"Hard to resist the pressure of one's peers."

"*Peers*. A word I loathe in that context. Look it up, please, in Webster's Second before you use it again." Carver studied him closely. "Don't tell me you want to come back to the ancient world and the rise of Islam."

"Not quite."

"Good. Along with many, many activities, like the study of Greek, Homeric and Attic, Aramaic and Arabic, our discipline is dying. Baseball players make a million a year batting .248 and managing a mere thirty-eight R.B.I.'s and I know of some so-called universities that don't have a single Latinist in the whole faculty. You'd have made it, however, Roger. You were very nearly my prize student, in the field you chose. My favorite. Do you know I found your undergraduate translation of Catullus's Fifth, '*Vivamus, mea Lesbia, atque amemus,*' the other day? You did it in your first year at Berkeley. Knocked me off my feet. I still consider it as fine a rendering as any in English verse, which goes back a long way and takes in some poetic giants who had a go at it. Why've you come down here to see me?" he concluded without shifting gears.

The story Roger Phillips offered was remarkable for its simplicity and plausibility. He began it in a world so affluent that any extravagance was possible. Someone had approached him, back there in the manicured desert where the rich fight boredom and a sense of disassociation from life. Wanted to know about the work along the Mediterranean that had once been done by the university. Hadn't he once been part of it? What had stopped it? Wasn't it time to resume? Offered—here Roger Phillips did his very best to wreathe his face in a surprised and innocent smile—to finance a survey group after Phillips had told him how and why they'd left. All the money they needed to see for themselves what it would take to start over again. "I said I'd do it, sir."

"Why?"

Roger Phillips went into the failure of his own enterprises. Here he was as straightforward as he could be. Yes, he had grown weary of the academic groves, the fakery, the politics; he felt impelled to go forward after the self-destruction of his generation's hopes and aspirations. So he'd wanted to make money, lots of it. He'd failed there too, learned the making of money was a crock. The pursuit finally destroyed you. So he'd jumped at the chance to go back to Sarumna. They *had* left in a hurry. Surely Professor Carver remembered that?

"What makes you think they'll let you in?" Carver asked.

"I need *you* to lead the team in, sir."

"I don't have any intention of seeing what's happening there with my own eyes."

"I didn't either, sir, until I started thinking about it. All the work we'd done. A lot of it's still there. The next generation of scholars—"

"Damn you, Roger," the old man said through tightened lips.

"Sorry, sir. I felt the same way. A week, I'd say, is all we'd need. Just to assess the problems. No more. Just you, me, and this man I know who's very good on supply, maintenance of new equipment. From here on out we're going to find digging teams using sophisticated techniques, helicopters, aircraft and the like. And his wife, she's a pilot too."

The old man eyed him curiously for a time. Finally he broke off:

"You're with the CIA, right, Roger?"

"No, sir."

"Come now. All the money it would take. If you knew the begging and pleading I used to do—and now out of the blue someone wants to breathe life back into a moribund project . . . ?"

"As I said, these people have money to throw around and they're always looking for something their friends haven't thought of first."

"The CIA has come to me before," Carver said dreamily. "Do I have the mean rainfall figures in Cyrenaica, and just where did the Phoenicians land? Of course, they could have found all that in a good library, assuming they can read, which I doubt. I've never had anything to do with them. So now they send you."

"No, sir, they haven't. I give you my word."

"Of course they'd have you say that. And, of course, you would."

Roger Phillips suppressed a bitter grin, recalling what he'd said just the day before to Amanda Miller. "Maybe not. If I did, I'd be duty-bound to assure them of your passionate commitment to Jeffersonian democracy."

"Why do they think it so important to resume now?"

"For tax reasons, the sponsor wants it done right away. Then there's the publicity. Fame. Maybe wants to see the name in the papers."

"Who is that person?"

"You wouldn't know the name, sir. Wants out of it for now."

"An individual then, not a foundation?"

"The Society for the Resumption of Historical Research. Based in Beverly Hills."

"Why come to me? Why not just go on your own?"

"If you called the embassy in Washington they'd let us in at once. Without you, there'd be weeks and weeks of letters and frustration. As I said, time's important to the sponsors for tax reasons. You know how discouraging some Arab states can be about visitors, sir."

Carver sighed wearily. "I'm late for an appointment. Can you come to my place later for a drink, say, at six?"

"Like to, very much, sir."

It doesn't look good for me, Roger Phillips thought. *The old guy's spent a lifetime doubting, questioning, impugning, suspecting, and he knows I'm playing fast and easy with him.* He watched the old man hurry away on absurd flamingo legs, always late, still trying to beat the rush of time behind him.

In retirement, Professor Walter Evans Carver inhabited a condominium town house about four blocks from the university library. It was furnished in classics-scholar disorder, chairs and tables Roger Phillips remembered from the house the professor had when he was teaching up north in Berkeley; books and scholarly journals still littered the floor. Unwashed dishes in the sink and an unmade bed were visible as his visitor was led into a book-lined room. Carver moved about in stockinged feet. "Look what I've found, professor," Roger held a dark bottle aloft. "Ricard, true Marseillaise *pastis*, not that stuff you used to call *pisse de chat Americane*, remember, sir?" The old man's favorite aperitif even when some liquor was available on the site in the old days. He could never find Ricard but Roger Phillips always somehow managed. Carver smiled in spite of himself. He waited until the former student put a prepared drink into his hands.

"Look about you and observe a dismal success story," Carver mused as he drank. "Came down here after they'd really got tired of my excuses for staying on another and another year and threw me out. Near the ocean, which I like, easy weather, which I wanted, hard by a good library with access to the university collection—and these digs at a good price. I understand they now sell for three times what I paid. The weather's superb. I have friends who need help reefing sails, so I'm out on the water whenever I like. The library's all I could want, and, as you saw, I even swim every day. All my creature needs, even my intellectual interests are fulfilled. But I'm bored to death in retirement, Roger, it's pushing me to the Styx, I tell you that." He took a long sip from the cloudy liquid and sighed gratefully. "Damned good stuff, still."

Roger Phillips sipped apple juice.

"I've been considering your story," Carver resumed. "It was wrong of me to put you on the spot. Foolish. Your"—he coughed slightly—"sponsors know more than they want me to know, perhaps even you. Very well. After all, that is the business of central intelligence, right? I must know one thing. Did they ask you to seek me out?"

Some things Roger Phillips was not going to fight with a surprise victory in hand. What harm to let the old man think what he liked? That would cheer a vigorous man driven into retirement simply because he was approaching his eightieth year? "Yes, sir, I said it would depend on you."

The old man glowed. "It's good to hear one's still wanted. I'd need more particulars before I accepted, of course."

"I couldn't make a move until I was sure I had you." Roger Phillips felt good not having to lie for once.

"I am inclined to go but would like a day or so before I give you a firm reply, Roger." The old man held up his glass. As an undergraduate, he'd been told to call him Walter and was honored by being called by his own first name, a privilege not even fellow senior faculty members were vouchsafed. He loved the old man. He hoped all the lying he was putting him through wouldn't alter the old man's affection when the truth came out...

Roger Phillips fixed another drink and began thinking about Ted and Tracy Boardman and wondered whether they still lived in Bolinas. He'd find them all right, people like the Boardmans were visible wherever they nested.

Professor Carver held his glass high again. "To the very last adventure I shall make in this life."

"To the one after it," Roger Phillips responded. He found himself shuddering a little, to his own surprise.

15.

THE WIND snarled and howled. The clouds were heavy and low, blurring the sun at midday. He inched along the road near the Pacific shore north of San Francisco in his rented car. Roger Phillips remembered Bolinas for its crisp sunlight, the clarity of the air, the long, empty beaches, the wind-swept hills. This wasn't the place he once loved.

Maybe Tracy and Ted Boardman had changed too, he mused as he moved carefully forward. *The years have forged many of us in a way no one could have predicted. Hadn't the classics scholar become a home-builder-contractor-salesman?*

No, he decided, *he hadn't changed, the Boardmans won't have changed. We remain the same; the scenery changes, that's all.*

Tracy Boardman was the golden girl. She was beautiful, anywhere and everywhere and always. In dirty work clothes, in jeans, in skirts, in overalls, her hair pinned up on her head or falling uncombed to her shoulders; morning, afternoon, evening, her natural beauty brightened the world. She loved to laugh, she was bright; she was modest, or at least sweet about the gift of physical perfection fate had bestowed on her. Women, young and old, liked her, sometimes loved her because she cared about *them*, because she refused to threaten them in any way, because she was outgoing, frank and loving. As for men, they all fell for her, and even their women, if they were attached, understood why it was inevitable. Tracy knew how to turn back those ardent approaches—long experience by the time she was eighteen—in a way that offended no one, not the ladies, not the swains.

And Ted? The Ted he remembered? Being captain of the

University of California at Berkeley Golden Bears didn't mean much when it came to winning games on the football field or achieving a championship, but this jock won a Rhodes scholarship, fought the good fight with students when struggle was called for, and he cared more about doing the right thing than going to bed with all the girls who threw themselves at him.

When they married, everybody said it was inevitable. They got into films, not in a serious way, commercials mainly, they earned tons of money, and when Roger Phillips met them sometime later he was not a little surprised at what he saw. She was painted, bedecked in braless, see-through clothes; he was playing the macho game and trying to make time with someone else's wife. Tracy didn't care. They were into grass and cocaine and playing switchees at parties with other peoples' mates and they made fun of Roger, called him square and tangled in old-fashioned moralities.

Then one day, Roger heard, it was split time. They were gone, left the swinging scene, had moved to remote Bolinas, gone into living off the land. Ted had always flown, so now he was doing a lot of that; she had turned herself into an accomplished pilot as well. They'd fly airplanes on contract; they delivered new ones; they'd bring planes to remote places where the owners wanted them, or back to the States for overhaul and repair. In any event, that is what people were supposed to believe. They now lived a quiet, almost secret life. Dropped the old friends.

Roger Phillips had visited them in Bolinas when he decided to quit academe. They'd changed course in mid-stream, hadn't they? They could tell him how it was out there in the real world, encourage him.

It was different from what he expected. Tracy came into his bed in the middle of the first night. "My God, if nothing else, what about Ted?" He tried to whisper some sense into her. "He doesn't care. Good balling's all over between us." Still, he hated himself in the morning. Later, he found out Tracy hadn't misled him. Ted had a couple of girls on the string, confessed he wasn't making it with Tracy anymore—well, hardly anymore.

Roger Phillips also figured out that what the Boardmans were doing to support themselves was flying grass and snow from countries below the border. They weren't your average hungry pilots making trips on equipment that fell apart or was easily intercepted. Something Ted said told Roger Phillips they were acknowledged the best in that dirty business. They didn't do it often, but there it was.

He found an excuse and left.

Now Roger Phillips was going back.

He could use that kind of talent.

Tracy Boardman was in khaki jeans and a turtleneck; Roger Phillips had forgotten how damned beautiful she was. She rushed to embrace him. "Do you believe in fate?" she demanded. "The galactic flow has brought you back into my life-tide right now. It's our Kismet." Such talk made him uncomfortable. Ted was cool as ever; time had stood still for him too. Roger told them what he wanted and there were no questions about who and why such as he'd had to face from Carver. They appeared to buy the story about resuming work in Sarumna. The money he offered was good, not so much as to excite their suspicions, but good. Ten thousand for a week. Each. Ten more if they had to do any flying. Might have to fly out, even though they'd go in by commercial airline.

"Split without filing a flight plan, that what you're trying to say?" Ted asked with controlled irony.

"You know how they are there, lots of rules and regulations."

"Just asking," Ted said mildly. "I figured something like that's what the other ten thousand's for."

"Mainly we'll want to know about chartering non-military equipment available at various drilling fields, how ready any of it is, that sort of thing," Roger Phillips said, he hoped with conviction.

"Can I let you know in the morning?" Ted got to his feet like a man who has almost forgotten an important appointment. "You'll stay the night." He knew what had happened with Roger and Tracy the last time. Roger Phillips tried not to look at Tracy when her husband left.

When he heard the car's engine come to life, he said, "Wow."

"Don't trouble your pretty head," Tracy said. "It's all over for good this time between us. Just a little financial arranging to do."

"Why didn't he say yes?" Roger Phillips asked as they heard the car race away from the house.

"The money's not all that much."

"Not all that much?" he echoed. "For one week?"

"Surely you've figured out we're into bigger things. Now and then, it's true. But the payoffs are ten, twenty times that. We've been waiting for a last big one and then it's the end between us, no tears, no regrets on either side."

"I need you and Ted," Roger Phillips said earnestly. "You've both got to do this for me. If it's more money, it can be managed."

"He suspects your story's a scam. Or maybe he doesn't care. You know what he'll really be thinking about—in between fuckin' around with his girl, of course?"

"Tell me."

"Sarumnan hashish. Best in the world. Everybody in the business knows that."

"A tough country, Tracy. The police are on your ass every minute of the day. No way he could make a score and get away with it."

"He knows that too. But he'll be intrigued enough to want to explore on the spot."

"If that's what'll bring him in, okay," Roger Phillips conceded.

"And me? You make my coming along sound important."

"I'll level with you. You're the bait."

"I've played that role more than once down there in macho-land," she offered drily.

"Then you know how it goes."

"I do it very well. Am I supposed to ball anybody in particular?"

"Christ, Tracy, you make me sound like a pimp."

"You didn't answer the question," she insisted.

"I just want someone strung along." *Sure, I do,* he thought bitterly. *A web of deceit for a man who'd done so much for you in life, that was acceptable because it didn't involve sexual tricks and games? But this you gave a dirty word to and found distasteful? It was all pretty scummy and you knew it from the very beginning when Miss Amanda Miller gave you a shot at busting out of a life that wasn't working very well, so what the hell?* "Did you have to go to bed with those guys below the border?"

"Why, darling," she said, and smiled, "I love my work, you know that."

He caught a hardness around the corners of her mouth he'd never seen before. "You're putting me on."

"Maybe I've been kidding myself. I wasn't making it up about fate when you showed up, you know."

And she wasn't, Roger Phillips discovered. She was much into life essences and extraterrestrial forces, auras and karma and webs of destiny, a new turn to her worldly existence; it turned out that Roger had been much inside her head, as she put it. And here he was.

They sat around a big fire and watched the room grow dark as they talked of the slow death of dreams and the sharp memories of ten years ago. She drank chablis and he made do with grapefruit juice from concentrate. They remembered old friends, the promising ones who'd never made it and the dull ones who'd grown older and famous, the hot rebels who'd married rich girls and were boosting themselves high in the world of business and politics, and the nice ones who'd died, disappeared or dissolved into thin air. She let the fire grow low, adjusted the screen before it and took his hand.

"I'm taking you to bed, my sweet. Do I sense a certain shyness?"

"Tracy," he began.

"I tell you it's over with Ted," she assured him. "He's already promised to marry this girl he's with tonight. We're all friendly, it's awfully goddamned civilized. He's over there every other night. It's just a matter of time and money with us, that's all."

"Not only that, Trace. I'm—well, afraid . . ."

"Don't tell me you're another case of women's-lib-induced impotence? That it's no good unless you're the aggressor?"

She pulled hard enough to bring him to his feet. "The other night I went to see a girl there couldn't be a problem with," he said as he resisted her tug. "I mean, all we ever meant to each other was two bodies humping for the sheer pleasure of it whenever I was in L.A. It was like playing tennis with a pro." (*Why did he suddenly think of Amanda Miller? Ah, yes, of course.*) "It's not a question of winning or losing, it's the game, nothing to be tangled in the emotions, all she wanted, all I wanted was a good, lusty ball, nothing more, thank you darling, let's do it soon again. It's been happening to me in the desert as well. All the available ladies. Who wants unadorned fucking, who needs it, what do I still have to prove? Groucho used to answer the question, 'Are you a man or a mouse?' with 'Put a piece of cheese down there and you'll find out.' I know I'm a man."

"We're back to bait, huh?" Tracy smiled and pulled at his hand again. "You'd better be nice to me if you want Ted and me, baby," she teased.

"Yes, ma'am." He made a shrug to show he would now offer no resistance. "I sure will, ma'am."

"That's my good boy. Now—shall we go upstairs?"

Look at it this way, he said to himself as they climbed the steps, *I've got my team, so what the hell? How great she looks, in front, in back, early or late, downstairs, and for a fact at the top of the staircase as well, hands extended to me.* "Tell me more about our fate," Roger Phillips said.

Ted Boardman wouldn't hear of him leaving the next day. "You've got to meet my Lynne. I suppose Trace has told you all about us."

"Congratulations."

"Lynne's a wonderful girl. It's too bad about Trace but it's just one of those things. I'll bring her over for dinner. I'll stay at Lynne's again tonight so I won't be in the way."

He already had won Ted's consent, and there was much to do down south, so he was not anxious for another night despite, or perhaps because of, his current wife's unquestionably magical ministrations. Roger Phililps pleaded the pressure of time.

"Want you here for at least another day," Ted insisted. "I've got to know precisely what it is you want me to do."

Lynne Fielding turned out to be everything that Tracy Boardman was not. That was perhaps Ted's revenge. Dark, a bit broad-beamed and fuzzy-haired; she talked too much and everything she said was a rich blend of psychobabble, *relate* and *acknowledge* and *share, organic, meaningful, creative* and *constructive, fulfilling, positive* and *supportive* flowed from her endlessly.

After dinner, Ted took him for a walk on the beach. Was there anything Roger wanted to tell him that he could be assured would never go beyond this moment and this place? "I guess you know what we've been doing. I figure it's what brought you here. Level with me."

"You're right, Ted."

"These airplanes you want me to look at. We going to have to steal one?"

"Only as a last resort."

"What's your first resort?"

"Can't tell you."

"Why?"

"To save your ass in case anything goes wrong. The less you know the better. Very rough people to deal with."

"If anything goes wrong for you, you mean? Maybe I'll have to hijack a plane to save the ass after all."

"There's always that."

"You going to off anybody? What do they call it? 'Terminate with extreme prejudice?' You're working for the CIA, right?"

"No, and I'm not. On my word."

"Why should I believe you?"

"I wouldn't involve Professor Carver in a killing, no matter what I had to do."

"Why not? Please, no bromides."

"I just love that old guy. No—it's not murder, I assure you."

"Have it your own way." He'd formed his own opinion, it was clear. "When do I get the bread?"

"Half before we leave. Or all, if you want. I know you won't let me down, Ted."

"Wouldn't do that to an old friend. The money when we're there. And I promise not to try to bring out any dopey goodies. And I won't disappoint you. I can fly Connies, Super-Connies, DC-4s, 6s, 6Bs and Lockheed Electra-jets, all of which the oil companies use over there. How's that for being helpful? I made some inquiries today, just to find out. And, of course, I'm qualified for jets. In a pinch I can even fly a chopper. You'll get your money's worth."

"Don't be disappointed if you don't do more than just get to look at old airplanes," Roger Phillips said.

"You know why I knew you were fated to come back into my life?" A cold sliver of moonlight lay across the bedroom like a limp, ghostly knife. Tracy Boardman's skin was icy; she had left him for the usual ablutions after another heroic coupling and had been gone so long he had almost fallen asleep. "Something I wrote about our destiny years ago. Our Kismet. I thought I had it in my desk but I can't find it. Can I tell you what it said?"

"Please don't, I embarrass very easily." He resisted telling her those words made him restless and itchy.

"It said," she went on without pause, "that you, Roger Phillips, were the kindest, gentlest man I'll ever know." She held him close, her fingers like icicles against his spine. "I can't stand being alone. That's why I've stayed on with Ted after it's been over. I need a man. My karma tells me our rivers flow together into the universal sea."

"I'm not kind and I'm not gentle and I bet I'm not the most athletic or expert lover you've met, Tracy, so don't settle for me. There are better prospects out there."

"I know I could love you, it's meant to be."

He pretended to snore so she wouldn't say more. In a moment, he slept, really slept.

In the morning he collected their passports. Amanda Miller would be in touch about the arrangements.

"Are we going there together?"

"I've got a stop to make on the way. I'll meet you in Zarplis."

She clutched at him. "I'm afraid. Not of North Africa. Of being alone. I'll do whatever you want but afterward you'll be kind and gentle, won't you?"

He put his lips to her cheek. "You can always count on me." His whole life was lies, what did one more matter?

16.

These same days were busy ones for the President-for-Life, chairman of the Revolutionary Council, General Mohammed Abdullah. He had to preside at a massive protest meeting in the central square of Zarplis to honor the insurgents taken prisoner by the whore state to his west, summarily court-martialed and executed. He threatened dire reprisals, although he did not spell them out, and taunted the neighbor as a pawn of Paris and Washington. He called on people around the globe to rise against the Satanic powers which had corrupted an Islamic nation, such as the neighbor pretended to be. The protest meeting required a lot of effort on the part of government departments. Schools had to be let out, hundreds of buses had to be taken off usual schedules and commandeered so that sufficient mobs of protesters could be brought into the capital to be shown on television in Sarumna and abroad waving fists at the lenses and shouting *"Al Fatah! Al Fatah!"* Students could be counted on to be enthusiastically demonstrative just to be e out of class, but the busloads of workers had first to be assured a full day's pay despite the holiday to work up a pr er head of steamy indignation at the executions.

At the same time the General had been asked by his neighbor to the south for support against a rebellion mounted by a former defense minister whose popular forces were on the verge of capturing its capital. The General did not like being called an international bandit and a demented outlaw, although he pretended contempt, so he was anxious to show he could support a legitimate government against subversion. Although the former defense minister was a Muslim and was in fact trying to overthrow a corrupt and inefficient tyranny, General Abdullah rushed to support his neighbor. There were Muslims in the north; Christians and blacks

95

who followed tribal religions in the south were controlled by the government. The General's decision was not easy. It meant sending tanks, Mirage fighters and 3,000 Sarumnan infantrymen to fight Islamic brothers. He did what he had to.

At the same time, the gentlemen from Italia Motors were brought to the capital for ceremonials attendant on receiving more than a billion dollars and the usual pay-offs in Swiss accounts to express their gratitude to their new partners, the people of Sarumna.

And then there was the matter of a trusted and old friend, turned traitor.

After seeing the succored capitalists off, Alan Masters returned to his villa by the sea to find Abu ben-Sadriquen waiting for him, face pale, its muscles tight; he was out of the army uniform which was standard dress for him. "Please, will you come with me?" He was plainly worried but he refused to divulge its source. Masters saw the government Cadillac turn into the new government compound, move past the presidential offices, directly to the building which housed the Revolutionary Council.

"What's going on, Sad?" he asked.

"I am sworn not to discuss it with you," Sad replied in a monotone. He was as good as his word.

Before the council building four junior officers, grim faced and glowering, reached for the doors before the car came to a full stop. No word was spoken. Sadriquen was escorted fore and aft and walked swiftly to the entrance. Alan Masters had all he could do to catch up with them.

They were brought to a conference room where sat the General and four men Masters had not met. Although he had exchanged courtesies with all the members of the council at one time or another, these sat frozen like figures in a wax museum. General Abdullah offered him no sign of recognition.

The proceedings being in Arabic, Alan Masters could only guess what it was all about, but if he lacked specifics, there was no doubt these four growled like men who wanted blood. Sadriquen's? Yes! They thrust out arms and pointed accusing fingers at the man beside him. When Sadriquen tried to speak they cut him off. They turned to the General, as if the facts were above and beyond proof and all that remained was the General's order to execute.

Masters felt like a man ensnared in chains and caught in a whirlpool. What could he do? Say? Why had Sadriquen brought him? What was it all about? He knew Sad for as honest and decent a patriot as he ever met in this place. He had not even included himself in many of the consortiums where the General and so many of his ministers and brothers in the council protected themselves. What could Sad be accused of? Why were they screaming at him in a way that showed only his death could appease their rage?

The General raised his hand. The chamber became still as a tomb. He said a few words, none of which Alan Masters could even take for a hint as to their intention. The junior officers came forward and took Abu ben-Sadriquen in custody. There seemed to be a murmurous approval and the meeting broke up. "Stay," the General said to Alan Masters without rising. A wave of his hand emptied the council chamber but for him and Masters.

"I want a warning sounded. His execution is to be a signal. Our way of passing the message to all—Do bad things and you too will be stung to death."

"What's he accused of? What'd he do, sir?"

"A public display for everybody to learn from! Crowds everywhere, hanging from windows and atop trucks the better to see an official execution. Women, children, babies in front, the bigger ones atop their fathers to get a better view."

"What'd he do?" Masters pleaded again. "He's never shown anything to me except total loyalty to you and to his country."

There was no answer as to what Sadriquen had been accused of, let alone what he had done.

The General seemed to be musing aloud: "To be put to death in the public square, machine guns firing at point-blank range, so close his bloody flesh spatters the women and children in front—"

"Sir," Masters broke in, "I oversee everything he does, he confides totally in me. Never—"

The General raised his hand for silence. After a time, he said: "You know him only for business and economic affairs. This was politics."

"He's devoted to you!" He could not tell the General how many times Sad had defended his President when Masters had echoed the usual international opinions. Sad had never wavered. Others had. Indeed they had. Made faces to show disapproval or contempt as they quoted him or obeyed an order. Others also, ranging from cabinet ministers to schoolboys called out to storm the streets with clenched fists and cries of *"Al Fatah!"* But never Sadriquen. And he was to die . . . What gesture of protest could Masters offer? Resign? And go where? And if he found a safe haven, what about the pooled investments he was part of? He began to feel very dizzy.

Whether he fainted or simply became so befuddled that he lost his balance, Alan Masters never knew. He came to and found himself lifted by the President-for-Life, supported by strong hands. He thought he heard General Abdullah confide: "They tell me he spoke seditiously."

Masters could only shake his head weakly, hopelessly. "Never."

"You swear, Masters? You swear on the prophets you and we share? On their honored names?"

"I swear," he heard himself mutter.

Suddenly he was free, standing alone, swaying a little, watching the General walk thoughtfully to the window. "I will send him to his father's home in the desert at Gorbah. Let him consider there how to control his mind and his tongue. I do this only because of my regard for you, Masters."

"He's told me about it. A desolate village."

"Where he will have time to consider his mistakes."

"Cut off from the world."

"He could have been cast out of the world, Masters," the General said sternly.

"He is a most valued assistant—" he began hopelessly.

But General Abdullah's mind was set; he moved like a man who had other, more important, duties, as indeed he had. Word from the southern neighbor was that the former defense minister's forces had given a signal to retreat and the commanders on the scene wanted to know whether to pursue and destroy the traitor. The time might come, however, when General Abdullah could use that former defense minister. So it was a decision he had to give some time to. "To his father's home," he said again. "But let it be a lesson to you and to all," he added darkly, and quit the room. *Now why would he say a thing like that to me?* Masters wondered. He still felt dizzy.

17.

LIKE ROGER PHILLIPS, Amanda Miller was always uncomfortable when confronted with the word *fate*. Her own life had not conditioned her to believe things happened in some preordained sequence. When she was a little girl she confirmed what she had always felt in her bones. The man she called papa was not her father. Still a child, she ran away and felt the touch of her father's arms around her. Leaving girlhood, she came to his side when the courts were savaging him. In young womanhood she visited him in prisons thousands of miles from her home. In death, he had changed her whole life. As for *destiny*, what about the break with her mother? She still bore scars and infirmities but she hadn't floated along helplessly there either.

So when the young man, gold chains around his neck, in sleek pants and shirt, said, "Don't be shy, ma'am. It's your destiny to come here and for me to find you," her eyes looked about restlessly for a way to escape.

It happened at the door to the beauty salon in the Beverly Wilshire. The fact was that she had never been in such an establishment in all her life. She washed her own hair, never had it set by a professional. Mother used to say it was a waste of time and money. The only time her nails had known color was when she was a very little girl and had got into her mother's things and tried Revlon Savage Cat. As mother said at the time, she wasn't the type.

Amanda Miller had paused more than once at the door to the salon in the hotel. Walking down Rodeo Drive, she had paused also at the door of Georgette Klinger, where they were supposed to do magical things with makeup and facials. She also paused at the red door of Elizabeth Arden, not to mention the glass portal of Vidal

99

Sassoon, across the street. But the salon in the hotel was one she found herself passing whenever she left the hotel. More than once she almost went all the way in.

Then this young man came up from behind her and said here was her destiny. He'd seen her uncertainty at the door more than once and brought her in for tea and talk. He told her about himself. Drew Mercer. Ran a high-style boutique on Rodeo and had a recent falling out with his Paris-based bosses, so it was back to hairdressing where he'd started out until he could make another connection. He could tell she'd never had her hair done and she didn't believe in makeup, lip color, eye liner and shadow, anything like that, right?

At the beginning, Amanda felt foolish. She really did not believe in all that stuff, she confessed. It had nothing to do with being liberated, it just—well, self-adornment didn't ever seem important. Phoney.

"I bet the man you think about," Mercer said, "has his hair done at a stylist's and not a barber's."

She'd never thought about Roger Phillips's hair, but Mercer was probably right about that.

Maybe not about Roger's hair, but she'd thought a good deal about other things. Like his refusal to share not a bed but even a room with her for a night, what about *that*? She wasn't that bad-looking, was she? She'd had her share of awful, groping experiences back there when she went to college at Tempe. She wasn't even a technical virgin, there was that cab driver and that assistant manager in that hotel, maybe it wasn't Romeo and Juliet or Héloïse and Abelard but it was sex, wasn't it, so why did Roger Phillips take her as some kind of untouchable?

Well, she'd seen him operate at that party in Palm Springs and that handsome painted sex object he was ritually courting. Maybe that was the answer, men being easily tricked by ancient and obvious arts and devices. Hence, the pauses before the salons on Rodeo and the repeated hesitating before the beauty shop in the hotel.

"You're really quite attractive," Mercer said. "A mess, but there's an enchanting, vulnerable quality. The shyness doesn't hurt one bit, but you must learn how to use what you have, my dear." He stood beside her chair, running expert fingers through her hair. "Your head's an absolute disaster area. You look like you're practicing to be a nun. What do you wash it with, fudge sauce? Your eyebrows have *got* to be civilized before it's too late and they go back to jungle. Your eyes are good but why are you hiding them?"

So it went for several days and, as often happens, they became instant friends; he took her to dine at Le Bistro, at her expense, of course; they went for clothes to Giorgio's, and as long as they were on Rodeo they stopped at Ted Lapidus and Celine and Jerry Magnin's and he had her buy a crazy jumpsuit at Courrèges and properly absurd shoes at the Right Bank.

There was, of course, a method in her madness. If the old Amanda Miller couldn't persuade Roger Phillips to spend a night, maybe the transformed woman could persuade him to permit her to go to North Africa. That was all she wanted now. Desperation drove her.

He was bound to see how efficient she was, too. The Society for the Resumption of Historical Research was already in quarters in the Wells Fargo Bank Building in Beverly Hills. The stationery had been delivered, per orders. A Mrs. Crimmins was in place, waiting for the phone to ring or someone to dictate a letter for the fake letterhead.

What Amanda hadn't expected was how expansive her soul felt all because of a haircut, blusher, liner and eye shadow. "Would *you* sleep in my room if I asked you?" They share a laugh at the thought because that would be out of the question, Mercer being much in love with a man he had known for almost a whole year. He assured her no straight would turn her down after she learned the final lesson: "Being beautiful isn't just makeup or clothes," he told her, "it's feeling inside you're beautiful too, knowing it so surely it colors everything you do. Then you'll be irresistible."

"That's got to take me a lot longer," Amanda declared dejectedly.

On the day that Alan Masters learned his friend and sponsor was believed to harbor thoughts traitorous to General Mohammed Abdullah, Professor Walter Evans Carver entered the Wells Fargo

Bank Building in Beverly Hills, California, scanned the tenant directory and took the elevator to the top floor.

Over carved oaken doors at the end of a long corridor he saw the legend emblazoned on a wooden shield: Society for the Resumption of Historical Research. He grumbled an unintelligible vocable and pushed his way inside. He found a softly lit reception room carpeted in white and furnished in the aseptic modern he detested. The walls were bare but for two posters for films the professor had never heard of.

A lady of uncertain age seemed to be the whole office staff. In time she brought him into the presence of a shining, and he thought pretty, young thing in a spectacular-view office. She knew his name and performed a ballet of nervousness, shyness and pleasure at his presence with an almost convincing sincerity. Amanda Miller told Professor Carver she had heard much about him from Roger Phillips and was sorry she did not know his whereabouts at the moment.

The old man frankly showed his disapproval at the lavish surroundings. "What is all this? Why have I not heard of this society?" he demanded. "I'm delighted Roger is not here. Perhaps you will be more direct with me than he has been. Who are you? What is all this about? Who is behind this lavish display? Be forthcoming, if you please!"

The blunt attack had the effect of steadying Amanda Miller's nerves. She knew how vital Carver's presence on the team was to Roger Phillips. "I have come into a considerable fortune," she began in a firm, unwavering voice, though when she spoke she found it difficult to look directly into her visitor's eyes. "The truth is I want to do something different with my money—and this is what I've come up with."

"So you begin with all this wasteful splendor?" An upraised hand had the effect of stopping apology or explanation before it began. "Thank you, I've seen grosser examples of administrative self-indulgence among foundations, so save your breath. But with the Ford Foundation at least one knew where their funds came from."

"You ask me for straight answers. Very well. These offices belonged to an independent film company. They made two films which died at the box office and they went bust. I took over the lease last week. It's all me. Extravagant, perhaps, professor, but money doesn't matter, I've enough to waste a lot, but I want to make a start, now, at once. And Roger says we need you desperately."

"'Almost thou persuadest me,' as Milton has God say to Lucifer," the professor muttered, "but I happen to be an old hand at this sort of thing. Why the hurry? The work in Sarumna has been stopped for a long time and no one's been particularly anxious to resume. Why the urgency now?"

"Why not?" Amanda Miller heard herself say. She was even surprised at what sounded like a giggle a rich and eccentric girl would make.

"May I tell you why not? Because the present leadership in Zarplis is more anxious for international adventures than for researching its history. Because they're paranoid, to say the least. Because they prefer to make themselves a danger to their people and to the world. Why don't you tell me straight out, Miss Miller, that you are fronting for the Central Intelligence Agency? That this is some part, whether large or small, of a design Roger would not reveal to me? Admit it."

"It's all me, I swear," she insisted. "I tracked Roger Phillips down with the use of computers and such to lead the survey. I thought it would be too much for older people. He told me you were vital to the enterprise. Going in, there was a good deal I was ignorant about."

He seemed taken aback at her candor and directness. "You *are* CIA, however?"

"No, sir."

"I give you my word, it will go not a step from these offices," he persisted.

"It has nothing to do with spying, conspiracies, political upheavals, anything like that. It's all just me. Maybe I'm crazy, but it's not what you think at all."

"The CIA never concedes, even when it doesn't matter. And it doesn't to me, Miss Miller. The fact is, you don't have to appeal to my patriotism. I am bored, bored with retirement, bored with my good life, hungry for some excitement. I want to go, Miss Miller, even if the CIA chooses not to inform me. When do we all leave?"

Amanda Miller's eyes went shut quickly, as if to remind herself to take a moment to consider where she stood.

"When do we all leave, Miss Miller?" she heard him say again.

"I'm not to go. Roger has already decided that I'd be of no help there."

"Not to them, given their reluctance to deal with the female sex, but to me you'd be of considerable help. I insist you come along. I make it a condition of my acceptance."

She found herself helpless to resist rushing to embrace the old man. "I won't be a burden, I promise, thank you, thank you!"

Professor Carver quivered at the impact and looked down at her with the same dismay he might have shown if he found he had unwittingly snared a bird. "Good heavens," he said.

PART FOUR

PART FOUR

18.

WHAT BROKE apart and forever ruined the career of Julian Christopher was never revealed; the cause was not even known to his immediate superiors or to his associates. For more than two decades he was one of the most promising members of what was called the intelligence community. He rose from a very junior status in the Central Intelligence Agency to a position where the chief or the president was often asked to consider him for positions of the most sensitive and highly demanding character. If he was passed over it was because he was still so young that there was no question that in good time his loyalty, character and skill as an intelligence operative would be suitably rewarded. Hardware was his specialty; persuasiveness, the art of selling ideas, especially those dear to him, his genius.

Was it drink? In fact, his indiscretions were no more frequent or embarrassing than those of other highly rated members of the Company, as it was known to those who made a business of public reticence. He was married and was, as an old encyclopedia describes the Bengal tiger, "absolutely faithful to his mate but for occasional infidelities." Under different covers he had served in stations as various as Afghanistan and Zaire. He was an expert in fitting the hardware to the situation and to the native skills available to handle sophisticated weaponry.

After his sudden disappearance from the Company rolls, it was said he had undergone some kind of male climacteric. People recalled wild changes in mood, flashes of red-hot anger, an uncontrolled temper. Yet, the more they thought about it, the more those very people regarded these aberrations as transitory, if in fact they were true.

But he *was* gone.

Some time later his name began to appear in company transmissions. He was reported to be working for the beset government of Ian Smith in Rhodesia. He was also located among Kurdistan nationalists seeking autonomy from the Shah's regime in Iran.

By the mid-1970's, Julian Christopher dropped out of sight for good. A short, stubby beard, a weekly application of Clairol hair dye and a new, if illegally obtained, Canadian passport now identified him as Michael Kelly. Kelly became known as a mercenary who served effectively in various trouble spots. He was brought to the attention of foreign intelligence agencies working in the District of Columbia. SAVAK, the Iranian covert intelligence agency, regarded his previous work for the Kurds as only professional, detached from personal feelings. It gave him frequent, well-paid assignments among dissident anti-Shah students in America. The Chilean regime after Allende required an assassination; the Somoza regime had enemies inside Nicaragua and elsewhere who needed handling.

When the FBI, the Office of Naval Intelligence and the CIA itself began to be aware of Mike Kelly's activities in the United States, Kelly decided it was time to move on. He had friends in the emirates along the Persian Gulf but he saw no profitable future for himself there. He found warehouses stocked with arms but, what is more, he discovered he knew more about this equipment than the salesmen who marketed these marvelous tools, not to mention the establishments which received them. One night in Dubai he met a trader in the gold *souk*; one thing led to another; this, in turn, led to a meeting in a suite of the Dubai Hilton. There Kelly made certain promises which were regarded skeptically as typically brash-American.

Not a month later, a cable was received by one of the people Kelly had met in the Dubai Hilton. The next day Mike Kelly and a pair of Sarumnan diplomatic couriers were aboard a chartered cargo plane in Milan bound for Zarplis.

General Mohammed Abdullah had illegally acquired U.S. Redeye missiles, shoulder-launched, heat-seeking weapons capable of bringing down an airliner, not to mention a variety of other possible uses.

Beside himself with ecstasy, General Abdullah and three members of the Revolutionary Council who dealt with sensitive military matters met with Mike Kelly. Under orders to maintain the strictest intelligence security, Kelly was given a handsome contract. He was placed in charge of final training of foreign and Sarumnan agents designated for high-level work in espionage, sabotage and general psychological warfare as well as the design, manufacture, implementation and teaching in their own countries and elsewhere the detonation of explosive devices. All this was to be disguised in the budget which foreign embassies studied so carefully as training by Sarumnan coast-guard forces in the clearing of mines from waterways and possible enemy landing areas. Kelly was authorized to recruit a teaching team of American clandestine operatives, paramilitary specialists, professional killers and explosive experts, not to mention hit men with connections to Mafia chieftains knowledgeable in less politically connected means of murder.

Kelly's Americans, when seen coming and going at General Abdullah International Airport, were always taken to be involved in the oil business. They wore point-toed Lucchese cowboy boots, battered Stetsons, work-stained jeans and jackets, smoked, swore, and walked through life with the air of studied contempt for mere humanity common to the men who worked the oil fields. They used the code name Camptown to identify themselves and their operation. They included Dutch and German mercenaries as well as skilled ex-sergeants formerly with the Special Forces of the United States.

They were housed in the palace built during the final years of the oligarchy for the last ruler of the old regime, a marble pile that outclassed in size, ugliness and vulgarity that of Farouk of Egypt found when he was unhorsed by Naguib in 1956. It suited the men of Camptown perfectly, although for a time the Revolutionary Council had considered opening the place as a showcase of oligarchical corruption. In marble and mirrored halls, in ballrooms and regal game rooms, the Americans taught students the arts of constructing, maintaining and using such devices as flashlights, attaché cases, transistor radios, hand-held calculators and refrigerators—all made into death-dealing bombs.

Mike Kelly found all the United States firms he needed to

supply him with sophisticated timing devices, radio control apparatus and sensitive surveillance and communications equipment. Since most of this material was strictly guarded as to sale and dissemination by government regulation, special arrangements had to be made for delivery to unauthorized representatives. Mike Kelly had no difficulty finding cooperative parties who even helped him in billing General Abdullah's emissaries in amounts reflecting the extent of his and their labors. Everybody in the process knew there was overcharging up the line until the diabolical contrivances reached Sarumnan harbors, but money did not matter. The secret operation was one dear to the General's heart; better a thousand-times overcharge than to report a stalled program.

Mike Kelly arranged for Alan Masters to be brought to Camptown headquarters. Masters for some time had suspected the existence of some such detachment but knew nothing of its size and scope. He lived a mile down the Corniche from the old palace; he had never suspected it was even open. *No question*, he thought, *a brilliantly managed operation.*

The tour was quickly over. Kelly brought Masters to his own quarters in what was once the private regal apartment. He pulled out a bottle of Glenlivet (which sold four bottles £200 sterling in the Zarplis black market; of course Kelly did not have to go there for his) and got down to business at once.

"I didn't know where to turn, Masters, until it came to me you're the one to help." Kelly had money problems, he explained. He spoke for himself and a small number of his top associates in Camptown. They worked in a dull, lonely and puritan world; they made a lot of money; nowhere to spend it except in poker games and they were boring no matter how high the stakes. Send it home and there were tax problems. "We want to get in on the real action too," he said flatly.

Masters knew these were floodgates of financial special advantage that had to be kept rigidly locked. He pretended to be mystified at what Kelly was driving at and gave out hints that his own duties were strictly limited to aiding the government and a few General-designated individuals. "I know all that," Kelly said, reaching for the Scotch. "I'm ready to join that select company."

"I'm afraid I'd need authorization from the Man himself,"

Masters begged off. "I'd be happy to oblige, even though it would present a few problems."

"Were there any problems for you?" Kelly asked blandly. "We're both professionals and outcasts, so we needn't pretend. Surely you're not trying to tell me you're different?"

"Perhaps we are, at that. You're military or at least paramilitary. When word gets out that we're into some venture in the West, difficult as it is, we say we're just businessmen looking to put money to work like business brothers all over the world. If there were a military tie-in—"

"Hold the bullshit, Masters." His voice was steel hard. "Everything in this country has a military tie-in."

"I don't have to tell you how the outside world reacts to the General's ventures."

"I don't give a damn about the outside world. Just as you don't. I go my way, just as you go yours."

"Me?" Masters seemed surprised at the personal turn the conversation took.

"Seems to me you've been fighting your war without regard to being liked. And as for military tie-ins, I'll do better than that, sir. I'll go so far as to say you wouldn't be here but for Mike Kelly."

"I don't know what you mean." His voice was unsteady, like a man who suddenly is aware a weapon is aimed at him.

"Like all of us, you had enemies. It's an art getting rid of them, especially when there's no hardware to be used."

Masters forced a smile; it emerged weak and aborted. "I hadn't known you—"

"I never met John Edward Ebersol. Never wanted to. Never had to. Luckily, I have friends. But you better know this, Masters, we are people who remember the good things done for us. And being only human, we like to be remembered for the good things we've done."

"How much money are we talking about?" Masters said at length.

"This room is totally secure, you understand," Kelly said without hesitation. "What's said here, dies here." He laughed a little. "Hell, if we couldn't do that to one room, what good would we be? The answer to your question is: a hell of a lot of money.

Everybody makes a profit that finds its way here before it reaches the Man's training camps—and we're no different except we get the most. What's a two-hundred-dollar walkie-talkie in Schenectady will cost two thousand here, and be a bargain, do you get my drift? Takes a lot of know-how to get it this far and everybody's picked up his dollar on the way. We'd like to put some of our well-gotten gains to work, just like you do and the favored others around here."

"And the General? Does he know? Does he know everything you do, Masters?"

"No."

"This is also private, you might say. And you might also say, Masters, it protects you, personally, officially, every which way. Your well-being your security is our concern. When we need you, baby, you can be sure nothing's going to harm you. Will you drink to you needing us as much as we need you?"

Alan Masters always knew how to concede graciously. He held out his glass without hesitation. "There's a Swiss group," he began, "a consortium going into resort real estate and construction of a tourist complex. We are talking not about immediate income but big money five years from now. In Swiss accounts. How does that sound, Kelly?"

"Welcome to Camptown, brother," Mike Kelly said, putting more Scotch into a glass than a man could drink in an hour.

19.

ROGER PHILLIPS stood in the square that serves Catania as bus depot and found no sign of a taxi or a taxi station. A couple of cars speeded off with arrived friends or relatives. A small, untidy park held three grizzled old men warming themselves in a thin broth of Sicilian sunlight. Across the square, the exterior of a municipal building—Mussolini-classical with statues of fascist soldiery instead of deities under the eaves—celebrated Italian wounded in the Ethiopian conquest. Glory had grown as shabby as the victory in the intervening decades. Since it was Sunday, it was also closed, so there was no hope there either. Roger Phillips started to walk with the small bag which contained a change of linen, toilet things, packets of hundred-dollar bills, and a certain amount of gold.

In Los Angeles he had begun to feel things were running out of his control. Professor Carver wanted Amanda Miller to come along; he had to concede. *He'll know how to get out when he has to. If she stays close to him, she'll manage too*, he thought again. The professor was indispensable. In Washington they ran into the expected difficulties. The professor was superb before the chief of mission. He was a brother, he spoke a beautiful Arabic, he was a son, he was a father, an old man returning for the last time to the land and desert he loved. He would pass on to younger colleagues some measure of the work to which he had devoted a lifetime. Let the world know the depth of the nation's commitment to its ancient past, he said. He could not be resisted.

The old man fussed and fluttered around Amanda Miller. *My-dear* this and *dear-girl* that. Roger Phillips had never seen him so fetched. *So much the better for you, Miss M.* You would have thought all Catania such devout Christians they took the Sabbath as strictly as Trappists; there was not a soul on the streets. A lonely bus raced past him on its way to the center but would not stop at his waving. Amanda Miller was playing a game, too, just like the professor. It seemed ridiculous at first, a little girl pretending to be what she is not, putting on her mother's lipstick and rouge and trying to walk in high heels. Ted Boardman, married to one lady, committed to another, gave her all his *macho*-charm full blast. Even Tracy took notice. "You didn't tell me about *her*," she muttered like an accusal. He replied that there was nothing to tell.

In Washington, waiting for their visas, he got them down to business. He and the professor did the necessary briefing. Carver filled them in on what they could expect. No one knew or respected the Arabs and Arabic culture more. The typical Western view was not only vulgar and inaccurate, it was also a disservice to ourselves. Nor were Arabs all rich, spendthrift and materialistic. In Sarumna, it was to be remembered, they were in a revolutionary process. A charismatic and mad leader had them in thrall. We knew what mischief such men could manage, he reminded them; in the West there had been more than one or two, political and religious. History was long. And they had to take a long view here as well. He reminded the two ladies about public display.

Roger hastened to amend this injunction. He made light of the professor's observations. When he'd been there, there had been not a few girls along the seafront drive they called the Corniche who shunned the veil; he saw them in jeans, he saw them listening to the Beatles and Elvis. Yes, Sarumnan young men were horny beyond belief, but at least they were open and uninhibited about it. The General did not permit wat he called "mixed bathing," but that did not mean Miss Miller and Mrs. Boardman were to go about like nuns. He suggested that it would be condescending to their hosts to dress and comport themselves differently there. He was thinking of Alan Masters. He was thinking of that lazy, easy walk of Tracy Boardman, that body that keened a mating song wherever those legs went.

The professor began to raise an objection, but some instinct told him to keep quiet. Amanda Miller seemed to smile, although Roger Phillips was not sure she knew what he was talking about. *Perhaps she does not understand*, he thought, still unable to find a taxi in all downtown Catania. There was not even a snack bar open on a Sunday. On the airplane, the old man had slept. Amanda Miller found Roger Phillips sitting alone.

"Do you want me to make sure the lady turns it all on while you're away?"

"She knows what she's there for. Besides, she can't help doing that, whether I'm there or not."

"I thought she was supposed to know about airplanes."

"She knows that too. I told you she was unusual."

"The lady has eyes for you. It could spell trouble if the husband suspects."

"He wants to get rid of her, that's how much he cares. What'd you do to your hair?" Roger broke off without warning.

"I cut it, I bleached it." She pushed her fingers through it carelessly. "What the hell."

"It doesn't suit you."

"You sound like my mother. I did a number to get you to take me along."

"The professor decided that for me, didn't he?"

"He thinks I'm sweet. He's old-fashioned, but a dear man, just a little out of date."

"What's happened to you anyway?" Roger Phillips said with a frown. "I still think of you hiding in those oleander bushes."

A figure loomed over them, Tracy Boardman, her long, silken hair half-hiding her face, her breasts visibly free under a silken blouse. "May I join you?" Her teeth shone like stars.

"I was just leaving," Amanda said.

"She digs you," Tracy said, sinking low in the seat that had just been vacated.

"Please," he begged off.

"You're not going to fall for all that money, are you? Why've you been avoiding me?"

"No, and I haven't been. This is a job, Tracy, a damned serious and dangerous job."

"So why are you leaving us?"

He wasn't about to tell her about Colin Hume and the high-speed boat with dual gas tanks that would get Masters out. The more they were duped, the better for them if they ever had to face Sarumnan police. "I have business in Holland." He did not mention Sicily.

"Some chick, I bet."

Women! he thought. *The most gorgeous hunk of stuff that flesh could manage to be and she talks like a clod who can't get a man to take her to dinner.* His head turned to Amanda Miller across the aisle and two rows down. She was being made up to by the regius professor emeritus and Ted Boardman, dangling both men with flirtatious smiles and pretty murmurings as if she were the Great Catherine herself being amused by two beautiful lieutenants. *What incomprehensible creatures women are.* "Yes, a woman," he teased Tracy Boardman. "In fact, two."

"Don't forget me, that's all I ask," she said grimly. "Or to put it another way, you damned well better not fight the terrestrial tide."

"Save all that for later. You've got a job to do."

"Yes, I know. I'm the bait now. But I'm telling you. Warning you, dig?"

At Leonardo da Vinci Airport it was good-bye. Amanda Miller made the call to Amsterdam and was reminded what had to be done once she got the party to Zarplis. "Tracy knows what's expected of her. The point is to get Alan Masters to see her and not let the cops close down on her. And don't tell her too much, she can't be counted on."

"I understand. I'll manage."

"Just don't go getting moralistic on me. It's dirty pool using sex as a come-on but I don't know a better way to bring him into the trap. But remember, Boardman's got to see to an airplane. Make sure he gets out to visit American oil fields."

"Don't worry about me getting an attack of morality." He found himself staring at her; sometimes she did not sound like the Amanda Miller he knew. "You take care of yourself, Roger, we'll never make it without you."

He discovered her hand held out for his. He took it but found himself shyly avoiding her gaze. He grimaced a little at the reversal of positions. "Thanks. I'll be all right. By the way, I like what you did to your hair, no matter what your mother would think."

"Thanks for letting me come along. I won't let you down. I promise."

Unusual lady, he thought in Catania. In front of the hotel he saw a taxi at last. "The Englishman by the sea," he said. Everybody knew about the crazy Englishman who built a glass cage for himself, a house on an escarpment that overlooked the Ionian Sea. Its own funicular, its own beach, even a road to connect to the highway that went to Taormina. The wild, impulsive, happy Englishman they all knew and loved.

"You *Inghlese?*" the cab driver asked in his own English as the car threaded its way to the hills that curtained the sea from the town.

"Yes." *Interesting*, he thought. *Now I lie even when I don't have to.*

Still, he hadn't lied to the old Dutchman. "I need a lot of gold and fifty thousand in hundred-dollar bills."

"I can manage whatever you say," van Leeuwen said.

"My problem is the damned security procedures they use against hijacking. That'd pick up the metal if I try to take it on the plane, won't it?"

"You mustn't take the chance. I have a dealer in Palmero. You will receive it there."

"Can we trust your man?"

"I have, all my life. The Sicilians are marvelously dependable when it comes to circumventing the law."

"How does it get to him?"

"Leave all that to me."

When van Leeuwen came to his room later that day at the Amsterdam Hotel, the old man said, "It is arranged. He will find you in a little hotel on the Via Cerda, the Méditerranée, second class. I guess he knows it and can trust it. That's to make absolutely sure there is no connection between you. Saturday night, he says. That means you will have to take a bus the next morning to Catania. He says it would be safer for you to use public conveyance—just in case."

There were many things he would have liked to speak to the old man about—this man Ebersol, was he a crook; his daughter, what kind of person to do all this for a dead father?—but he held back. "I honor you for your work here, Mr. Phillips," van Leeuwen said. "You are doing what the official police forces of five major nations can't or won't do."

"Don't strike any medals just yet," Roger Phillips offered.

Colin Hume's house was in Acitrezza, farther out of town than he remembered.

"It's the life I've always wanted, Roger. How many men do you know who can say they've managed that? I've got it all worked out. The airlines bring in the girls by the dozen. They're down there." They stood among the wild grasses blown by the sea breeze a hundred feet below them. "I'm up here. They'll be curious, bored after a couple of days on the package tour. 'Won't you come in?' I'll say. They'll want to, don't you see? They get to assume their natural role, the pursuer. I'm too old for the chase. Besides, I don't like going to bed if I have to play seducer."

He had a World World II British Navy MTB, the hull was old, of course, but he had overhauled the Rolls-Royce engine so much it was better than it ever was. His torpedo boat could outrun a destroyer, he always said. "The Midnight Import-Export Company," he used to call himself. Ran qot, that hedgelike dope Arabs chewed, wads of it in the cheek like baseball players with a bulging chaw; hash, the fine Sarumnan stuff he himself had tried once and foresworn forever after it had lifted him so high he did not know where he was or what he was doing; American cigarettes; booze; tires; liquor; the scared rich; revolutionaries, in; about-to-be-made-dead politicians, out. Everybody knew about Colin Hume but could never catch him at it.

"I'm rich now. I don't need to work."

They were good friends though more than twenty years separated them. Women liked Roger Phillips; that made him attractive to the wild Britisher to begin with. Roger Phillips was blunt and without cant, never explained, never apologized, did what had to be done, let others justify, rationalize or point the finger later. Colin Hume brought in stuff the digging crew had to have right away, couldn't wait for. "You're an odd chap. There's always one of your people after me to spirit out some archeological treasure and there you are, the number two, and you've never asked the same favor."

"Peerless character, just like my Number One," Roger Phillips said. "Don't do it for them, Colin."

"Petty thievery," Colin Hume said. "I have an inflexible rule: Never steal small."

Did he really retire? Roger Phillips paid off the taxi and walked to where the glass house sat against an embankment. The wind was kicking up; behind patchy clouds, the sun was trying not to give up the struggle and peter out in midday. Down below, he saw a sailboat at anchor. On the beach small boats were lined, keels up. From around the house, he heard the laughter of young women. What else would Colin Hume have in his home but crystal voices? He was troubled when he saw no sign of the old torpedo boat.

"I'll never need to smuggle again."

Had he scrapped the Midnight Import-Export Company at last?

A nut brown maiden in a string monokini answered the door. She had tiny, perfectly formed breasts, long, straight Scandinavian dirty blonde hair and a smile that could warm an igloo. "Sorry, I thought it was Collie," she said but made no effort to hide her loveliness. "Is he expecting you?"

"Do you know where he is?"

"He went out with Inga to fetch someone at Taormina. My name's Kristin."

"I'm an old friend of Colin's. Name's Roger."

"Won't you join us in back? There isn't much sun but the pool's heated."

Colin Hume's house on this day contained six guests besides the girl who brought him in. There was a Shoshana, a Patrizia, an Anke, a Lucienne, a Mei Ling and a tall willow of a brown-skinned girl named Charlene with a New York accent and a laugh that gusted quickly and came to sudden stops. Roger Phillips did his best not to let his eyes rest however briefly at any of them below the neck lest he be thought some kind of hopeless square, but it was not easy. For some reason he felt as shy as a new kid in a schoolroom or a stranger at a party. He thought of Amanda Miller hiding in the oleanders.

"What time do you think Colin'll be back?" he asked the brown girl who had found a chaise next to hers for him.

"Colin says time doesn't exist here." Charlene gusted one of her laughs again.

"Does it?"

"*Vogue* wants me in Rome when they shoot the new Missoni collection, so I guess it does. But I'll be back, baby. I love it here." She got to her feet and stood like a bronze goddess before him, a *V* over the pubis all she wore. "Can I get you something?"

"Anything wet if it's fruit juice," Roger Phillips managed, his eyes entrapped in spite of his efforts.

"Collie'd never approve, but I'll see what there is." Her breasts quivered as she gusted another of her laughs, perfect, half-circles, with tiny, erect pink aureoles and nipples. "Don't go away, baby."

Would I risk this if I were Colin? he thought, watching Charlene walk away, stately as a queen, her beautiful cocoa brown haunches wholly naked.

20.

THE AIR-SARUMNA flight to Zarplis was called one hour and fifty minutes later than scheduled. No substantial food was served during the almost three hours the trip required from Leonardo da Vinci Airport in Rome, and of course, nothing alcoholic. Arabic music on the headsets. There was no movie. The Danish stewardesses offered sweets, cookies, fruit and trays of orange juice and cola beverages.

Fatigue caught up with Professor Walter Evans Carver shortly after they boarded the 747. There were so few passengers that Amanda Miller was able to find a row of seats he could stretch out on. Ted Boardman joined her not long after.

"I hope you don't mind."

Ted Boardman filled her with an obscure, indefinable fear and uncertainty; the way he looked at her, his possessive grin, as if in search of something that could give her away; she did not know quite how to handle him. "I was trying to doze."

"I'll be boring so it'll help." After a moment, he sank down lower in the seat so their heads would be on a line. "How long've you known Roger?"

"Not long."

That gave him all the excuse he needed to dilate on the Roger Phillips he knew. Boardman was one of those storytellers who prefer to tell more about themselves than the tale they have in mind. He himself was a restless soul, he saw that now, perhaps even more so than Roger. That brought him to tell Amanda Miller about Tracy and their supposedly made-in-heaven marriage. That was over, he told her, though he said nothing about the girl in Bolinas named Lynne he was already engaged to marry.

"Why don't you tell me something about yourself?" he suggested some time later when it became apparent that Amanda Miller had not uttered a word.

"Nothing to tell, really."

"You're financing this venture?" he pursued. "You personally? Why?"

"A whim."

"An expensive one."

She shrugged. "I think I'd like to see if I can sleep now."

Ted Boardman lifted himself a little in the seat, looked about to make sure they would not be overheard before he sank down again. "There's something very appealing about you, Amanda. May I call you Amanda? Mine is not to question why, mine is just to do and lie, know what I'm saying? I'll be of great help. If it has wings I can fly it or make it fly. I don't even care to know what it's all about so long as we'll be getting out in one piece. But I do like a more—how shall I put it, a more friendly ambience."

She smiled wanly. "I don't want to be unfriendly, Ted."

"That's better." He sank even lower next to her. "Tracy has got a thing for Roger. Did you know that?"

"No."

"She's an incredible woman. Don't you think so?"

"Yes, I do." She really did not want all the details but was at a loss to stop Ted Boardman.

"I mean this girl can do it all."

"Wonderful, isn't it?" she agreed helplessly.

"You're extraordinary too. I mean, putting this venture together. Forget about the money. You have this quiet, almost timid way about you and, boom—here we are, four people on the way to Nowhereland. From what the professor and Roger have been telling us, I figure it's going to get very hairy before we get out. May I make a suggestion, my dear?"

"Please," she acceded, mostly to close him down.

"Stay close to me, I'll take care of you. You'll find I'm invaluable."

It came to her she was letting personal feelings overcome a cool appraisal of what she ought to be doing to insure the success of the mission. "I will, Ted," she said gently. "I feel better already."

"I've been on deals like this before, Mandy. Something always goes wrong, you can count on that. Then it's helter-skelter time, run for your life. Know what I'm saying?"

"I'll remember that."

"I'll take care of you, Mandy-girl. You can rely on Boardman, Theodore Morrison." He laid a hand on her knee and smiled paternally as he awaited her response to the touch.

"Thank you, Boardman, Theodore Morrison," she said, offering none; she let her eyes close, as if in sleep. Later, she heard him move and opened an eye enough to catch a glimpse of him working on one of the Danish stewardesses. Amanda smiled a little and must have dozed off. When her eyes opened again, she found Tracy Boardman beside her.

"You and I ought to talk, woman to woman," Tracy began. "Which is to say *sans* horseshit. Roger's told me I'm to be the bait. Maybe it's time for me to be told what the hell this is all about."

"What we've said all along." Her voice was buttery smooth, even though it was clear Tracy was not of a mind to be easily reassured. "We're here to—"

"I've heard all that. Isn't all this going to a lot of trouble to start something the world isn't exactly holding its breath for? What gives? What's this all about? Who has to be hooked? Why? Let's talk like sisters, not idiot-girls. I'll do what has to be done but level with me, Mandy."

Amanda Miller remembered what Roger had told her about this lady. Tough, but not to be wholly trusted. In fact, he'd said, no one, not the professor himself, could be told everything.

"This man we need sits at the right hand of the big man in this country—"

"And he can make or break you? Get you the permission? It's that simple?"

It seemed absurd to hold to this, but Amanda Miller knew she had no alternative. "Exactly."

Tracy could not restrain a laugh. "That's *it*? You swear?"

"That's it," Amanda repeated gravely.

"What his name?"

Roger Phillips had ducked this one several times. An hour or two out of Sarumna evasion seemed pointless. "Alan Masters. Does it mean anything to you?"

"Should it? No."

Amanda Miller sighed nearly imperceptibly.

"What's he doing there?"

"Right hand of the big man, as I said."

"That's a big deal? Sits at the right hand of some guy no one ever heard of?"

"The country's one of the richest in the world. So he's making himself richer too. And he can help us."

"How do we get to him?"

"The idea is that he approaches us."

"You think he will?"

"He's one hell of a superactive chaser."

"Sounds like you know an awful lot about him. Is he also an *ex* of yours, husband or boyfriend?"

"Why would you say a thing like that?" Amanda Miller exclaimed.

"I get these hateful vibes about him from you."

"I never even met the man." She caught herself; demure now.

"I'm absolutely infallible about auras," Tracy insisted. "I wonder why all that malice spills out about a stranger."

"Maybe I hate all men." Amanda Miller grinned, hoping she had found a road to retreat down.

"No, my dear. I saw the way Wonder-Boy Teddy Boardman was making a play for you. Men sense manhaters, and you're not one anyway. You're too—well, too vulnerable. Sometimes these self-styled cocksmen dig little helpless creatures—not that you're anything like that—but that wouldn't stop guys like that from thinking it's true, and tumbling."

"May I make a confession? It's never happened to me."

"Stick around, Mand. Knocking off guys is easy. I'll show you how."

The General Mohammed Abdullah International Airport was either two or fifty years old, depending on what criteria were employed. Professor Walter Evans Carver felt at home in it; he remembered it from the old Military Air Transport days. Ted Boardman liked it for its simplicity; he was at the 747's window trying to make what he could of its runways and hangars as the plane landed. Deplaning was done on the field; immediately the aircraft doors opened, glowering police burst into the passenger compartment like a raiding party. They shouted orders in an angry and impatient way. In Arabic.

"They want us to leave the carry-on luggage," Carver said in a quiet voice. "They also want us off the plane at once. We're to follow a man at the foot of the steps. Do not panic," he continued, not translating now. "Everything will be all right. Remember, please, this is a military state and runs on a war footing."

It had been told them many times. They now had occasion to see how it worked for themselves. Everybody was in army green, even the children. Airline counters, directional signs, various legends and rules posted on the pillars holding up the structure—everything was in Arabic. Black paint obliterated renderings under the script in other languages. At the Customs gates men stood armed with heavy weapons.

They were brought to a room and ordered to wait. A small wooden table with a chair behind it stood at one end; benches lined the wall; a picture of the General was the only decoration. "Please be patient and do not take any of this as some kind of personal insult," Carver urged them. Amanda Miller and Tracy Boardman felt chilled, suddenly somewhat naked, despite decorous travelers' cottons. They had seen no woman since landing, not even one covered in that all-enveloping garment the professor called the *barican*.

"I guess they open the rest of our luggage without even giving us the courtesy of standing by," Ted Boardman said to the professor.

"Guns and whiskey in any form, as I've told you, that's the first thing they search for," he replied mildly. "I trust we've all followed instructions literally."

"How long will it take?"

Carver shrugged. "That should tell us a good deal."

Two hours.

"Could've been a good deal worse." Professor Carver watched the luggage being brought into the room. A soldier with two pips took the rickety chair; two enlisted men stood beside him, carelessly leaning on rifle barrels while they rested on one haunch and

125

riveted their eyes on the ladies. None of the others knew what the professor and the officer were talking about.

"What is the purpose of your visit? . . . Why have we not been informed earlier of this visit? . . . Yes, we know of you, but who are these people, why have you chosen them to join you? . . . Who are these women, why have they been brought with you? . . . Where is the other gentleman who was supposed to come with you? . . . Why is he not here? . . . How long do you plan to stay? . . . When do you expect to leave? . . . Where will you be staying? . . . What individuals do you plan to see during your visit here? . . . Do these ladies understand that they must be suitably garbed when in public? Bare arms are strictly forbidden in the streets, do they understand that? . . . All telephone calls and cable messages must be approved beforehand, have you told them that? . . ."

The professor's replies were polite and prompt. He did not raise his voice nor reject any implied slurs. He was courteous and graceful.

All this took another hour.

When they emerged from the terminal, the sun was going down slowly. They could see it on the flat horizon, a great glowing ball sinking into the desert. It was steamy hot outside but it was good to take in fresh air again. A new but battered Fiat wagon with the front right fender off and a growling transmission received them and their luggage. No one spoke all the way into town.

Marco had three jobs. He not only functioned for Alan Masters as secretary-butler and worked for Special Intelligence as informant on the domestic activities of his boss; he also worked for himself. Foreigners who lived in Zarplis frequently used his services in the manufacture of beer. The materials necessary for its making were readily at hand in many food shops, not to mention the bottles and the tools necessary for capping tops and so on; but the preparation and handling of the finished product were often beyond beginners' capabilities.

Three automobiles were at his disposal; his duties took him all over the capital. His boss was wise enough to be discreet in Marco's presence about governmental or financial matters. Marco did not even know of the liaison formed between Masters and Mike Kelly.

What he did make it his business to know was the arrival of every Western female at the Strand Hotel. He paid the clerk there for such information. In turn, he was rewarded with a handsome bonus by Alan Masters for such information, the size depending on the extent of detail about the arriving ladies, which is to say, age, appearance and general attitude. Visiting aunts, older sisters, mothers and other family members—the only people generally granted tourist visas—were thus carefully sifted out before reaching his boss's attention.

So it was, while the party rested in three rooms of the spartan Strand Hotel, the most *luxe* hotel in the nation, a grim, five-story, prisonlike structure, that the phone rang in Alan Masters's home. Marco's informant was, like himself, a product of a Sarumnan father and a half-Italian daughter from another historical era, a social outcast forced to make ends meet as best he could, which was not very often. "Two of them," he said in an Italianate pidgin those boys learn in their vile alleys.

"Good ones?"

"*Ma'mia,*" the clerk uttered breathlessly. "I would gladly die for either one."

"I must see for myself."

"I want double this time. After all, there are two."

"Are they Ingleezi?" To Marco anyone who spoke English was English.

"*Mahdi.*" Marco heard the sigh over the telephone line. *Touched by God*—you had to have infidel blood to use such a word to describe mere female flesh, but Marco knew what the clerk was driving at.

"Half of what he gives me I'll give you."

Marco smiled as he put down the phone.

Colin Hume's Fiat was identical to the one which brought the party to the Hotel Strand in Zarplis, a Diesel Panorama 131, but its white paint glistened, there was not a scratch on it and the transmission was creamy smooth. He had left Ingrid at the Holiday Inn in Taormina and returned with an English girl named Gillian. They had stopped to talk to friends on the beach at Naxos so they were late. Gillian was a tall young woman, a natural redhead dotted with coppery freckles across her chest, her reddish green eyes like tiny flames behind mascara-darkened lashes.

Colin embraced his old friend as if Roger Phillips had returned from the dead. "I thought I'd lost you forever! Have you met everybody? Have they made you comfortable? You must stay here! You *will* stay, of course."

"Of course," Roger Phillips acceded. "I've come to talk to you."

Colin Hume held up his hands as if in dismay. "One of those old friends with new propositions. Spare me, dear friend. The answer is no, sight unseen, or is it voice unheard?, but you'll stay anyway, I insist."

They had dinner in a glass-encased solarium, the young ladies now discreetly and beautifully garbed. They drank a table wine, and not much of that. Colin still favored Scotch on the rocks in amounts staggering just to observe. He regaled them around the table with old tales Roger Phillips had forgotten about: A one-inch cable for a tractor the old government would not allow in the country for some forgotten, dumb-bureaucrat reason and how he and Roger had dumped it on the beach near the dig only to find they left it in twenty feet of water at low tide. "I bet it's still there, Roger!" he roared, reaching for what was left of a bottle of Teacher's and emptying it in a crystal beaker.

Roger Phillips did not know what to expect. The afternoon nakedness elicited expectations of fleshly pleasures, but it turned out that evenings the girls read, studied Italian from cassettes or looked at dubbed American TV shows.

"It's not a playboy's harem, dear boy," Colin Hume said. "We are friends here, dear, warm, friends, no one owes anything to anyone, no one is obliged to offer more than understanding and kindness, we are grateful for each other's company and the depth of the warmth among us is not a matter of obligation. It's heaven and it's yours if you want it. I told you when I left I was going to create a happy life here, and I have." He sighed. "Except of course we've got the real world out there always intruding. Charlene's got to go to Rome and Milan to work and Shoshana misses her mother in Haifa, things like that."

"And I've got a real-world proposition for you," Roger Phillips said. "Let me tell you about it."

"Don't want to hear it, old boy," he cut him off. "I love you, I want you to stay here as long as you can or will, but please, no propositions. I'm through with all that."

"I need you desperately, Colin," he pleaded shamelessly.

"They always say that," Colin Hume pulled another bottle of whiskey from his stock. "And I always say no."

21.

By the time Hafir Azziz turned up at the office where he functioned as minister of cultural affairs, Professor Walter Evans Carver had walked from his hotel to the Boulevard Mohammed Abdullah, its whole length to the larger-than-life equestrian statue on a pedestal seventy feet high, to the ancient mosque, to the old city, to the awakening *souks* in the alleys rebuilt after the earthquake of 1938—when he himself had been cited for heroic work among the poor—to the old harbor, to the new harbor where mile-long tankers waited to be connected to the arteries pumping the nation's blood to the world. He was neither elated nor depressed; he had long before learned to accommodate himself to the onrush of time.

Azziz he knew as a student in the old days. He was a man of fifty, a graduate of Haverford College and a failed candidate for a doctorate at Berkeley. They shared a secret not mentioned in any of the biographical literature about the leaders of the revolutionary state. Azziz had been married to an American girl; Carver knew because he had been asked to be best man. He supposed they were divorced, one way or another, by now.

Azziz greeted him correctly if somewhat more coolly than the old professor would have liked. He had of course been notified by telex from Washington about the party's arrival. "I do not know any of the other names, except of course, Phillips's."

"They are technical, Mr. Minister," Carver urged gently, careful to be eminently polite. "Two of them are concerned wholly with transportation matters. We believe that with modern technology we will be able in the future to go ahead with our work without being held up by supply problems, as we were so often in the past."

Azziz looked at his desk. "And Miss Miller?"

"My secretary," he responded without hesitation. "I loathe detail, as you know."

"And Phillips? What are his duties?"

"My executive officer. I'm getting too old for trivialities."

"Not you, professor," Azziz said. "You know, of course, this is a bad time to think of resuming the work."

"It was always a bad time, Mr. Minister. When I first came here, I was told it was a bad time."

Azziz coughed discreetly. "We are surrounded by enemies."

"From what I see, you have nothing to fear. These new buildings, all the uniforms on the streets, the vessels in the new harbor. Who would dare challenge such power, sir?"

"Ah, yes, thank you. But you know what I'm talking of, professor."

"My whole life is what is buried in this ground, this nation's glorious history. I loved it when it was weak and poor, I guess I have to admit I love it even more when it has grown rich and strong."

"What can I do for you, professor?" the minister said at length.

"May we travel freely?"

"That will be difficult to arrange."

"But it can be done?"

"For how long, professor?"

"One week."

"Limited to the old digging site and this city?"

"One of our people would like to make contact with civilian contractors using aircraft in their work," he suggested smoothly. "We want to look into buying surplus aircraft, or at least to get the benefit of their experience. Nothing fancy, you understand. Old transports, perhaps nonmilitary small craft."

"Difficult. That comes under security, internal and external."

"We understand." Carver knew when not to press; he knew his people well enough to approach them through the generous spirit with which they embraced their guests, at home or in their land.

"I will see what I can do."

"I am grateful to you, Mr. Minister. May an old teacher also add that he is proud of his student?"

"You are very kind." He rang a bell and ordered coffee. "How many cars will you require?"

"Three. Two to use, one to stand by."

"And three drivers?"

"May Phillips and I do our own driving? It would be an added pleasure for us, knowing the country as well as we do."

"As you like."

"And you will permit our transportation man to visit several major drilling sites of American companies? I would be most grateful."

"Professor Carver." Azziz held out a small cup filled with dark brown liquid. "Do I have your solemn word you are here as a private individual? Alas, we do not have friendly relations with your government."

"Mr. Minister," he began severely, "I have not ever, I do not now have any connection with my government. I give you my word of honor I am here as a private individual."

"You shall get whatever you need, my dear old professor," the Minister of Cultural Affairs replied.

In the morning he looked like the Colin Hume Roger Phillips used to know: grizzled, slightly hung over, garbed in wrinkled poplin pants and a workshirt that did not quite make it inside the belt. They had coffee on the terrace; the sun, lifting over the sea, was going to come through today bright and clear. Down below two yawls were testing the Ionian winds.

"Like it?" Colin Hume grumbled over his second cup of black coffee, his first words.

"What's not to like?"

Colin Hume grumbled approval. "It's changed me. Came here, all I wanted was girls. Lots of girls, all shapes, sizes, new bedmate every night, that was my dream."

"Still a lot of them."

"I love 'em, more than ever. I've learned not to use them. Don't mind being used by them. It turns out we've been awful shits there, we've got a lot to make up for, just like you with your blacks. Anyway, how stupid we've been about the fuck, old boy. It's not one body plugged into another after all, it's two souls colliding in heaven or it's nothing."

"You *have* changed, Collie."

"Only there. I'm still your basic buccaneer."

"I need that guy for a trip, Collie," Roger Phillips broke off.

"He's not available."

"I can make him available, Collie. One job, one shot, one day, very tricky, but very damned important to me."

"I misled you, old friend." Colin Hume shouted for a servant to bring hot coffee. He got up from the table and walked around the sun-drenched terrace. "I'm not wholly retired, Roger. I've got one client."

"Then you can take on another, for one day. I'm going to make it very damned worth your while, Collie."

"On your way here you notice anything about this town? You happen to notice, for example, there are no Chinese restaurants? No Milanese restaurants? Lots of things aren't available down here, even more important than chow mein or *osso buco*. Know why? My client won't let them in. Yes, Virginia, there is a Mafia, and it runs Sicily, family by family, in the towns around this island. My guy runs Catania. Everything that happens, even the littlest fast-food snack bar or my doing a turn for an old friend has got to have his approval. The laundries, the whores, the hotels, the taxis, name it, my client says yes or no. That's why Sicilian kids leave the island—if they're not in with my client, they've got no future here. That's why things don't change much down here."

"And why you've got this way of life."

"Exactly. I told you: nothing happens here without his approval."

"What do you do for him?"

Colin Hume put his index finger upright before his closed lips, the classic *omerta* sign. "Odd jobs."

"What would he—" Roger Phillips turned from the table, bent to a small bag on the tile deck and laid a felt-encased object between them. "What would your client think of this? I've one for you too. Or, if you can, you may keep them both." He caught Colin Hume's hesitation. "Open it, Collie, I'd never seen one, maybe you have." His own, somewhat nervous fingers were trying to pull the drawstring above a velvet envelope that encased the object on the table. "It has a serial number, the mark of the maker, and a certificate of assay." It lay there, gleaming between them, a small brick with the legend:

> ONE KILO
> FINE GOLD
> 999.9
> ENGLEHARD

irresistibly asking to be picked up.

"You barstid," Colin Hume muttered, his eyes riveted to the metal.

"I think we paid 650 an ounce. You figure what it's worth—and add that it's here and only you and I know. By the way, remember it's got a sister here too. You can keep it or give one to your client if you have to, as I said."

"What do I have to do for them?"

"Pick me up."

"And?"

"Drop me off somewhere else. You've still got the old boat?"

"Hell, no."

"You're putting me on."

"Got a better one. Faster. Bigger tanks. Longer range. My client needs one now and then."

Roger Phillips sighed visibly. "Christ, don't scare me like that."

"Where do I have to pick you up?"

"Sarumna."

"No can do," he said quickly.

"A simple, clean operation. I'll be waiting for you. I'll fill in the details when you say yes."

"You know what goes on there these days? Bad enough in the old days. It's worse now. The madman's got hot-pursuit patrol boats all over those coastal waters. Besides playing tag with the American Fifth Fleet in the Mediterranean, the Russians are working with the general—the oddest political marriage in the world today."

"No one could stop you in the old days, Colin," Roger Phillips offered gently.

"The Russkies have been coaching them on how to patrol the shoreline, giving them high-speed boats, radar, even guns. When the local boys aren't good enough, they man the Coast Guard with Iron Curtain proxies."

"I fly in," Roger Phillips pretended to be uninterested in specifics. "We set a time and place here and now. Maybe a one hour spread for you to come in, pick me up, and split. I've even checked the tides. Put me off on any island, long as it's Italian. Or Malta. Good-bye. There's another bonus. My client has got all the damned money you need."

"You're asking a lot," Colin Hume said after a very long silence.

"I'm paying a lot."

Roger Phillips brought up the second sack and let it fall with a thud on the table. "Two kilos—you tell me how you want it split."

"I'd keep the gold. But I might like to give the client ten thousand."

"And there'd be ten thousand more for you when it's over," Roger Phillips said.

Colin Hume's hand reached to the two bars. "Heavy darlings, aren't they?"

He found Roger Phillips's hand rigid over his own. "I've got to count on you. You'd be there?" The words came out like rocks falling hard.

Colin shook off the hand as if a fly had touched his own. "Have I ever failed? In twenty years have you heard of Colin Hume not getting through, ever letting a friend down, not doing what he was being paid to do? I've had some bad moments, there've been some hairy encounters, but I was there, old boy. I'd be there for you if I had to make it in a dinghy."

Roger Phillips squeezed the hand appreciatively. "I know you would."

"Do I get to know what it is I bring out with you?"

"No."

Colin Hume grimaced a little. "Don't like to fuck around with political figures. Those guys never forget."

"It's not political."

Colin Hume grinned. "Then it begins to sound possible."

"I've some maps in the room. Then you can help me out of here right away, they're waiting for me in Sarumna. Have we a deal?"

"You're on, old man," Colin Hume said, finding out how heavy four and four-tenths pounds can be.

The Strand Hotel was five floors of dark corridors, dusty windows and mops standing, wet heads against the corner walls. Every floor had a man on a straight-backed chair near the stairs to observe the comings and goings of the guests. He was always black, a boy from the southern neighbor, without question, Ted Boardman surmised, shy in his ill-fitting, probably recently acquired, army greens.

Ted Boardman was up and out early, though not as early as the professor. Zarplis reminded him of some coastal city in Colombia where the drug people owned everything and had to know what everybody was doing. Not that it looked as colorful; the cocaine coast was prettier. Zarplis was drab and shabby; the main avenues were well paved and the cars racing up and down were big and new, but when he turned down a side street, the pavement broke apart and there was the stink of sewage in the rivulets that ran along the curb. As in Colombia, he observed with an experienced eye, he was followed here too.

The boy at the head of his floor also marked his return. He found Tracy in bed. She was awake, propped against two pillows. "I called for breakfast an hour ago. I don't think they understood me," she said drily. "I know I didn't understand *them*."

Ted Boardman found the small radio in his bag he always traveled with. The back of the set was loose; that told him they had taken it apart when they searched the baggage. He smiled. Clicked it on. A female singer was hung on a couple of notes in an Arab song; he made it louder. "The place may be bugged," he said close to Tracy's ear. "Be careful."

"What's it like out there?"

He turned his thumb down and made a face of deep distaste as he cut down the volume. "Beautiful town. Terrific people." That was to tell whoever might be at the other end of a microphone there was nothing sinister in turning on a radio and jamming his reception, and, anyway, what they were saying was innocent.

Tracy grinned. She went into the bathroom, turned on the faucets in the sink and a listless shower. When her husband joined her, she asked him: "How heavy is the *policia*?"

"You don't see 'em, you feel 'em."

"You're not trying to connect with dopers here, Ted? You promised Roger."

"Looking, that's all."

There was a timid rapping at the door. When Ted opened it, a black boy came in with a tray: a drab silver carafe and an upturned cup over a saucer sitting on a tiny napkin. The toast was curled and burnt. The Arab woman's song went on and on. When Tracy emerged from the shower she held up a small, wholly soggy towel. "How do I dry the bottom half?" They both laughed, then seemed suddenly embarrassed by the moment of affectionate intimacy.

Shortly before noon, Tracy Boardman left her room and joined Amanda Miller in the lobby. Only a clerk stood behind the counter. There were signs on the posts but they were all in Arabic. The sun was bright outside and streamed across the floor like a golden sash. The central air conditioning was not very effective here. Tracy wore a simple cotton frock, sleeved to the elbows. They had gone into all this at home and on the airplane. "Simple yet provocative," Amanda Miller had said. The blue dress was fitted close around the bodice and she did not wear a slip. For her part, Amanda Miller wore a white eyelet blouse, a square neckline and a skirt that barely reached her knees.

When they walked from the hotel grounds they saw the usual expensive cars. In a dark-windowed Mercedes SEL, whose interior was blacked out to them, two eyes followed their progress from the steps to the street. "Oh, yes," Alan Masters moaned. When the ladies crossed the street to walk under the palms that lined the Corniche, he gave the order to the driver to go home.

Colin Hume was unpredictable, as impossible to grasp as mercury, larger than life, contradictory, changeable. "He's the ultimate hedonist," people used to say. "Everything exists for his pleasure." Even his new pose as a liberated man, so unlike the old Hume who thought women existed only for his taking—even that Colin Hume was shot through with elements that just did not ring true to Roger Phillips. Women were now his friends, his equals, not objects to be wooed, seduced and reduced to statistics to prove his virility. Yet he surrounded himself only with girls of utmost loveliness, and they disported themselves nakedly in his private world.

Roger Phillips could not make up his mind about that side of Colin Hume on their way to Fontana Rossa, the Catania airport, but one thing about Colin had plainly not changed. He was a doer. They discussed the problems they would face. Roger had gone into them in detail: place, timing, signals, everything. The moon would be almost full. They would meet at the same place they had used countless times in the old days, a rock formation a few kilometers from town called Eagle Rock because, when the GIs had used it as a recreation point for diving and ocean play during the war, someone had decided it looked like an eagle's beak with the rocks behind it resembling outstretched wings.

Colin would approach on the windward side because Eagle Rock formed a wind-protected cove where he said small-boat crews frequently put in for the night. Besides, with the backup of oil tankers waiting to fill up, the great ships frequently stretched to a point abeam of that cove. It would be a bit tricky boarding from the open, windward side, but perhaps safer. Roger said he could handle his part of it.

Roger Phillips's last stroke was arranging the rendezvous on a Friday, the holy day. Strict fundamentalists as they were in Sarumna, Colin Hume could count on a certain laxity in security procedures on the water. On land? Well, they would have to see...

They would maintain radio silence, of course, Roger pointed out. Colin Hume was astonished at the care with which every detail had been worked out. The charter from the Catania airport could make Valletta in a little over an hour, Colin Hume pointed out, and Malta was a lot closer to Zarplis than Rome, but Roger did not want any questions about why he had chosen to come in from the island when the others had flown the national airline.

"Very well," Colin Hume said. "I pick up two of you."

"Now comes something I haven't told you about," Roger Phillips offered.

"Tell me now."

"I've needed help, nailing my man, getting into the country. You remember my old boss, Professor Carver."

"So we have to take him along..."

"And three others."

"Good heavens, a ruddy package tour. Why not make it an even dozen?"

"Absolute minimum plus one, I assure you."

"Five of you in all, plus your whoever, have I got it right, nothing else I have to be told about?"

"Can you handle six?"

"Can they hang on the deck by their fingernails if they have to?"

"Not very likely."

"You're the boss. You tell me what to do."

"One of the people is seeing to getting an airplane—in case we need a backup, so don't worry about the others."

"You won't need it for your passenger and yourself," Colin Hume said. "Is there any reason you and your passenger won't be there? Let's discuss it now. I don't want to chance a trip like that and find myself playing moving target for Russkie deck guns."

"Then it's settled. You know the time and place, Colin. See you there."

At the door to a chartered executive jet, they paused. Colin Hume took a hitch in his pants, wiped his mouth the back of a hairy arm and said, "Listen, you miserable Yankee. I see you've a lot on your mind. Maybe you think now I've got your gold, I'm prepared to leave you in the lurch. I want to show you how you can set your mind at rest." He thrust something at his friend. "Me sainted mother guv me this." He mocked a workingman's accent. Roger Phillips looked down at an impressive ruby set in a man's ring. "I want it back the minute you come aboard."

"You son of a bitch, you never had a mother," Roger teased.

"It was a real honest to God maharanee guv it me, one I met at the Aga Khan's pleasure dome. She said two nights on the percales with Colin Hume was more than the bauble was worth. Called me the finest lay in the Western world."

"It's probably glass."

"I've no doubt, but the sentiment that went with it means a lot to me. This lady knew the best studs from Beverly Hills to Bombay. It's a compliment I cherish more than life. See you at Eagle Rock. Don't keep me waiting."

When the two men locked in an embrace, Colin Hume planted a fat, wet, brotherly kiss on his friend's cheek. "I love you, dear boy," he murmured.

How could you not love back a man like that?

22.

"INCREDIBLE!" PROFESSOR Walter Evans Carver exclaimed. The four of them had managed to struggle through the lunch provided by the kitchen of the Strand Hotel. Cold coffee arrived at the same time as a messenger with a big envelope stuffed with documents which required Carver's signature. He signed, exchanged Arabic words with the messenger incomprehensible to Amanda Miller and Mr. and Mrs. Ted Boardman, went to the window to see for himself. "I can't believe it!" A calmer Professor Carver would never have allowed himself such a redundancy. "I've never known them to be so prompt! Let's go outside!"

They found two sedans and a Land Rover, all new, all unbattered. The documents gave the professor the right to proceed to the Roman ruins he had done so much to restore as well as to examine such caches of material necessary to his work which may still be in existence.

The old man seemed to wipe a tear from the corner of his eye with a knuckle. "We mock them, we look down on them from our Western cultural snob heights, but look how gracious they can be, how prompt, how trusting! I'd almost forgotten."

Amanda Miller found herself looking at the dashboard of an Audi sedan. One of the drivers in the usual army green appeared and offered her a smile with very stained teeth.

"He asks if we'll need them. I told him we could manage by ourselves," the professor told her. "They've seen to everything." He pulled a document from the envelope and gave it to Ted Boardman. "Here are the scheduled noncommercial flights in and out of the area. Western and Alliance has got three. WAP, they're the biggest. You can go there right now if you like."

"If they're that on the ball, hold one driver. I'm on my way."

"I'll go with you," Tracy Boardman said.

"You'd better stay here." Amanda Miller's voice was gentle enough to soothe a baby but the authority in it gave them all pause.

"Tell the driver I'll be down soon as I can," Ted Boardman, breaking the silence, said to Professor Carver.

"I'll give you a tip, Mandy," Tracy said when they were alone. "Never make yourself too available for any man. Let him come to you."

"I'm going to visit my beloved old city," Professor Carver returned to say. "Will you ladies come with me?"

"I'd love it," Amanda said.

"I hate ruins," Tracy said.

"Drive around town in the Land Rover, Tracy," Amanda Miller suggested. "Real slow. And remember what you said about being too available."

"I've a better notion," Tracy said with a mischievous smile. "I'll let this man take me with Ted to his plane. Then I'll go swimming in the ocean."

"I'll have him stand by to make sure you're not molested on the beach," Carver said. "Please do not wear a bikini."

"Good hunting, Tracy," Amanda Miller said.

The return call was not from the President-for-Life's office but from his Minister of Cultural Affairs. Alan Masters knew Hafir Azziz very well, having provided space for him in a group he set up in an English-banked front which bought property adjacent to the George V in Paris, two new office buildings on the Adolph Max in Brussels and a stretch along the beach at Marbella on a twenty-year leaseback deal. Azziz was cordial, grateful but somewhat reserved, knowing well that in political relationships descents are often as dizzying as ascents. He always accorded Alan Masters every courtesy possible so long as it could contain no bitter aftertaste in case of a fall.

Hafir Azziz returning his call meant, Alan Masters knew, that the General and his staff were out of Zarplis, either at one of his many retreats where he nourished his desert-born soul or at a residence he was said to maintain close to the eastern border. Abdullah's absence could not have come at a better time."I called about those Americans who have just come," Alan Masters began.

"An archeological survey team, headed by Professor Walter Evans Carver," Azziz replied. "One of the ladies is accompanied by her husband." Azziz knew his man.

"How long are they here for?"

"A week."

"I would like to give them a party. Any objection?"

"You know how the General feels about alcohol."

"Nothing official or indiscreet, Azziz, I promise. I'll have everybody chauffered both ways."

"No objection here but I'd prefer that I know nothing about it officially."

"I need all the names for the invitations, that's all. I'd like to lay it on a bit."

"I understand, Masters."

"Thanks very much. By the way, an interesting situation is developing in Hong Kong. Shall I keep you in mind for it?"

"I would be very much obliged. Do you have a pen? I'll give you the details you need."

"Very kind of you. Why don't you stop by too? Just a small group, I'm sure they'd like to see you in an unofficial capacity. I could fill you in about Hong Kong."

His trips abroad were fewer these days and more difficult to manage. Masters looked forward to the sound of American voices, the careless diction, the sing-song of some, the slangy informality of others. It would be good to have these American guests. And the women. He knew about the married one, as Azziz briefed him now over the phone; seeing her, he knew ladies like this well, he was acquainted with the manhunting bitch, the pretend-tease whose game was to be maneuvered into bed. And the other one, whom Azziz described as the professor's personal secretary, she was like a pretty bird wheeling gracefully in the sky, waiting for that one shot from a well-aimed barrel . . . The husband, surveying oil-field transportation problems. *Sometimes everything works*, Masters thought. *A good party, should he ask other Americans, Mike Kelly? Why not? They're mine, in my house. Come over and look, Mike, see what I've got, Mike.*

One hour twenty minutes from General Abdullah International by an old Lockheed Electra-jet bearing a cargo of pipe and drilling equipment and Ted Boardman was back in the United States of America.

The maps designated the site "Kitr" but the dominant residents dubbed it "Enema Point" and were proud of isolation so complete they could not tell among the native fellow residents Arab from Berber or, for that matter, Christian from Muslim. Those who were not Americans were foreigners there.

They were glad to see an American visitor and were soon sharing alcohol they distilled and cut themselves and made potable with canned grapefruit juice. Some of the younger men had a supply of hashish which Ted Boardman pronounced of superb quality.

"If there was only some way . . ." he mused aloud.

"Yeah," he heard, "if elephants could fly . . ."

He spent the afternoon taking note of the aircraft on the ground at the Enema Point airstrip and asking questions about possible equipment which management might be willing to call surplus. He thought about going back to Abdullah but the afternoon was pleasant, the hash was plentiful and there was going to be a real Texas-style barbecue with "the best damned chili this side of San Angelo," and he thought of that hotel room in Zarplis, and there was a bold-winking chick who said her husband was troubleshooting for the company all the way the hell over in Algeria and barbecue was no fun alone, so Ted said he'd stay.

The old man's energy astounded Amanda Miller. He was like a child returned to a familiar room he thought he had lost forever. "This is Punic!" he called. "Cenotaph of a Numidian chief!" He ran across a flagstone street. "The baths!" His hand waved wildly. "We'd only just begun work there." She sat on a grassy knoll surrounded by a semicircle of decapitated columns, dead-tired, and saw what love could do to an old man.

He was a very long time coming back to her. "It's as though we left it yesterday. Nothing's changed."

Something broke inside her, something so tiny she never knew it existed, something with no name. A sense of shame that she had exploited this fine old gentleman overwhelmed her. She uttered a little gasp, struggled to find her voice again and ran away from Professor Carver's side.

"Amanda." She turned from the column she was leaning against to find he had quietly come to her side. "Talk to me."

She felt his bony hand take hers firmly. "I'm sorry," she said.

He took her across a marble-littered square to a high point that overlooked a green, cultivated valley. "Feel the breeze," he said. "They used to give names to their winds, you know. The winds were old friends, known to them and to their fathers. What we feel now used to be called 'the rose of winds.' We have a carving somewhere." After a moment he resumed: "Amanda, what are we really doing here?"

Half of her wanted to surrender, the good half, she suspected, the part that believed in honesty and decency and loving trust between people. This was the half she had learned to struggle against, the submissive daughter, the shy young woman. It took a moment to bring back the part of her that had seen her father in prison, seen him destroyed by forces he could not resist and which somehow forged in her a steel she had not known she was capable of.

"You're going to pick up this work where you left off, professor."

"I am an old man, I see things with wise old eyes, Amanda. Whatever you're trying to accomplish—what an unlikely crew you are! How could it have been formed? They'll never let us in this country again, don't you see?"

"You'll have all the money you need, I promise," she insisted to change the subject.

"You refuse to tell me?" he said. "Just you, me and the rose of winds?"

"There's nothing to tell," she said, glad she had found the strength to conquer her good half.

Roger Phillips descended from his charter at Ciampino Est. He took a cab to the international section of Leonardo da Vinci Airport and found that he could make a Swissair flight that was an hour late for Luanda which made a stop at Zarplis. "But we never take anybody for Zarplis because the papers are never completed to their satisfaction," he was told.

"Mine are," he said. "Look."

In California, where the sun rises almost half a day after it has begun its passage over the Sahara, the morning mail brought a Mailgram from a valued and well-paying client of the Henning Security Agency, a detective and industrial protective agency headed by a once well-known local chief of police.

Usually the Embassy of the Worker's Republic of Sarumna, as it was officially known, made inquiries about Sarumnan nationals resident in the United States. Since the General had many times publicly proclaimed he would not permit the youth of his nation to be contaminated by the educational system of the "most corrupting and disgusting materialist, godless state in the world," most of the Sarumnans he asked the Henning Security people about were prerevolution residents, citizens, or in the process of becoming American citizens.

John Henning, the chief, held the self-justifying, solid and profitable American view in dealing with foreigners that he was paid to perform a task immediately at hand and not required to weigh himself down with considerations of moral or political implications. Thus, he was used, in recent years, to filing very detailed reports for the Sarumnan embassy which he gleaned even from such supposedly legally protected credit agencies as TRW, which keeps detailed computerized financial records of Americans from paycheck to how and when they pay their bills. Henning had access as well to similar records from auto and life insurance files. Somehow he was even privy to records of charitable contributions made by private citizens. The secret police, posing as diplomats in the Washington embassy, found this invaluable because it revealed to to them what they called "Zionist agents," that is to say, people who contributed money to one or another Israeli cause, not to mention individuals who made statements unfriendly to the General, thus becoming enemies to be variously dealt with.

The Mailgram of this morning asked for information to be developed as quickly as possible on the Society for the Resumption of Historical Research in Beverly Hills and five individuals whose home addresses were thus listed on the submitted passports. Henning was asked to note that Carver and Phillips were known to them but might require updating. Mr. and Mrs. Theodore Boardman claimed to reside in a town in northern California and Miss Amanda Miller gave her home address in a place called Tempe, Arizona. This Miss Miller also stated her religion as "Unitarian," a device frequently used by Zionist sympathizers and agents seeking entry to the country, which Henning was to take into consideration along with the possibly Jewish surname as making this woman and her background worth a very complete and careful workup. Authorization was given for any expenses involved in a visit to Arizona by an agent to interview such friends, neighbors and family members who could be able to help complete the dossier on this woman.

23.

SWISSAIR'S PILOT put down the big airplane as gently as a mother returns a baby to its basinette. The plane did not refuel there; the stop was routinely made to maintain the airline's landing privileges.

Roger Phillips was the only passenger to deplane. He was greeted on the tarmac by two surly soldiers who ignored his Arabic words of greeting and gestured him into a waiting jeep. The Swissair steward who had accompanied him to the ground shook his head hopelessly, mounted the steps and closed the door as the jeep spun away. The airplane, which had not shut down its engines, began its move to the end of the runway.

Roger Phillips had mixed emotions on returning to a country which had once been so important to his life and his career. The day was still young enough so there was a coolness in the air as the jeep sped across the airport, a touch of sea perhaps. Still, he felt an oppressiveness he had never known. Sarumnans used to be regarded as easygoing; the first two he encountered seemed to go out of their way to be surly. He had to take into account that they already knew more about him than they were supposed to. Could someone already have goofed? Or was it simply the new revolutionary bad manners, the usual wise-guy anti-Americanism?

At a building some distance from the terminal itself the jeep came to a stop. His passport was returned to him. He was gestured to a small waiting room and ordered to wait.

The sun was directly overhead hours later; the waiting room had grown oppressively hot. Later, when he opened a door to go outside to relieve himself, he found it locked from the outside.

O land of golden light, he chanted softly and decided to stretch out on a bench along the wall. He knew they were doing this deliberately to him; God knows they had little else to engage them. He closed his eyes and decided it would be better to play his own game. He managed to doze off.

The grass widow whose husband was in Algeria slept in full makeup. She had had too much to drink the night before. Ted Boardman wondered whether her sleeping kids in the next room had heard mom during the exertions on the Beautyrest. The lady was okay, just okay. Not a Lynne, certainly not a Tracy. He let himself outside, looked at his wristwatch, found he was there at the appointed hour and saw a station wagon headed toward him down the street of lawns and tricycles in the driveways and drawn draperies.

His caller's name was Stubby and he was an amateur flyer and he was taking the day off to go with the visitor to meet the guys of the Desert Rat Air Club about buying or renting an airplane.

"Hi. Sleep good?" Stubby winked knowingly.

Ted Boardman let himself in the wagon. "What the hell."

"Life's tough on the little ladies out here," Stubby said. He had the car up to eighty as soon as they cleared the last bungalow.

"Not tough on you guys?"

"We got work and hobbies. They got nothin' but time on their hands."

It took something less than a half hour to get to the Desert Rat location. It had been a landing strip during World War II and was still well paved and in good shape, even to the old wooden Air Force tower.

"Here's the AT-5 I was tellin' you about," Stubby said.

They took it up and he played with it. The owner had been transferred home and Stubby could accept any deal. The airplane was not bad. Souped-up.

"Only one problem, Stubby," Ted Boardman said when they came down. "Need more room."

Stubby scratched his head. Nothing much he could do about that.

On the way back to Enema Point, Stubby remembered a twin-engine Cessna at Wap Three. That was an old drill site two hundred kilometers west. Why didn't he see for himself?

"What else they got?"

"Lots of good stuff. Company owned. Could put you down there. You could hitch back to Zarp."

"What's to lose?" Ted Boardman said.

The invitations were done by a calligrapher whose flowing Arabic was superb, but when the cards came they were all wrong, so Alan Masters decided to scrap them and do the job in person.

It was somewhat embarrassing, but he had no alternative. He had a rundown on the background of the people in the party; these were no kid sisters visiting big brother, out of the good old U.S.A. for the first time. He had seen them for himself. They looked like women who knew what they were doing every moment. He liked that. He preferred a fair hunt. That was why he began with the formal invite to all of them, a businesslike cocktail party. So he would do it himself.

He chose the time carefully. Late morning, before the sun was too oppressive. He was dressing to go when Marco announced an emissary from the oil minister. The message was brief:

"May I have the honor of an urgent personal meeting at once?"

Alan Masters had no responsibilities in that department but the request was unusual and strong enough to be unrefusable. He would go from the ministry to the hotel and in a government car. He ordered Marco to stand by in the house all day.

The oil minister had his orders, he told Masters. The General was insisting on a price ten dollars a barrel over the agreed OPEC price; it meant offending all his opposite numbers. The oil minister had assured them repeatedly that Sarumna would not break the line. He had to do what he had to do, of course, but he needed a statement that would justify the break: something about the oil and the Western economies that would strike a different note, something to rationalize the General's posture.

It was a fascinating problem to a man driven by the exquisite pains and gratifications of finance as strongly as he was by sex, and a chance for a stab at his own oppressors as well. Also there was this: One day, perhaps not so far off, the American government would need a friend—himself—someone in the counsels of the General or the Revolutionary Council. The Americans would want something. He was the one man who could manage it for them, at least speak for them. As Marcus Raskoff had told him, there was always the chance some junior bureaucrat in Washington looking to make a name for himself was out there trying to work an extradition. Ten dollars a barrel over the Saudi clients would hit them between the eyes. Next year another hit. Yes, one day they would look for—and need—him.

Alan Masters took off his coat and rolled up his sleeves.

He had a six-day growth of stubble, a service revolver dangled loosely from a web belt, and he wore an army cap perched dead center on his head just as the General did.

"What is the purpose of your visit?"

Roger Phillips sighed but restrained any show of impatience. He mentioned Professor Carver and the rest of the survey group from the Society for the Resumption of Historical Research. He recalled his own credentials. Six-Day was not much impressed. "What is the purpose of your visit?" he repeated. Roger Phillips mentioned Professor Carver again.

"Why did you not come with the party? Why did you come later? Why did you come on a foreign carrier?"

He pleaded business in Rome. There was the matter of transfer of funds. He had to make certain arrangements there. As for the flight in, it was the first available. He was anxious not to waste another day so he took Swissair.

"Whom do you plan to see here? Where do you plan to visit? Have you any connection with any government other than that of your own? Do you use alcohol?"

He remained polite and responsive. Six-Day remained vexed and surly, rejecting Roger's gestures of amiability until the very end. A grunt of disapproval seemed to end the interview.

"When can I anticipate leaving here, sir?" Roger Phillips asked.

"One of our people was detained by your people in New York for fourteen hours, did you know that?" Six-Day snapped.

"I know now exactly how your man felt." Roger attempted a

smile, but none was returned for his effort. He also knew now he would be set free after fourteen hours.

He had never found a stay in this city pleasant. Professor Walter Evans Carver preferred the desert. He often told his hosts this proved that he was Bedu at heart, at least an Arab. Zarplis had not changed from the scruffy, shabby place it always was. There was the so-called Corniche; all over the African littoral the new masters felt they had to copy the original. Two or three thoroughfares were smoothly blacktopped. At one end of the city a magnificent new hospital now stood. Not far from it another was being completed, long, low-lying buildings designed by master architects in Rome and Berlin and staffed by Polish and Roumanian and Bulgarian doctors on contract. At the other side of town two apartment towers stood, the tallest buildings he had ever seen in the Mahgreb outside of Tunis or Casablanca. They were iron skeletons, wind whistling through them, the harsh sunlight playing strange games through the naked beams. They had been under construction by an Egyptian contractor with Egyptian labor when the Great Betrayal occurred. The General had unhesitatingly expelled every last one of them to show his anger. Carver had heard many times since his arrival about the luxury housing the new wealth would bring the Sarumnan people, but the skeleton was all the luxury housing he saw.

Except for tiny homes being built in clusters on the back streets, occupied by squatters even before they were completed, the city had not changed much for its usual residents. He knew he might be shadowed wherever he went, so he did not pause to chat with the dwellers in the unfinished homes.

He had succeeded in tracking down the inventory hastily prepared on the departure. Three crates were marked for shipment to Berkeley; they never arrived. The Department of Antiquities was somnolent or terrified, he could not tell which. It was housed in a rabbit warren of wooden buildings behind a large building always crowded by job-hunting foreign laborers come to Sarumna for its high wages. The highest official available in the Department of Antiquities was an old man who stuttered and stammered before the distinguished visitor. The department's own files and indexes were in more dreadful shape than ever, Carver observed. He wondered what would have happened had he himself not persuaded them years ago that history did not end with the Romans, that the rise of Islam itself was documented in the earth here, and must be preserved.

Preserved it was, in the original crates, grown cracker-dry after endless hours in the hot-boxes that were the department's buildings. His own memory was faultless. He remembered those last frantic days after the collapse of the old regime, the hurried inventorying which he himself supervised. One man had a metal trunk for his personal belongings. Professor Carver had ordered it emptied and filled it with material he now sought.

He could not tell if it had ever been opened. It had a lock, of course, but he had been careful not to use it. It was marked HARDWARE, in English and Arabic, and it was surrounded by enough of the other crates containing everything from shoes to picks and shovels to be boring to the nondigger.

Carver lifted the metal lid, put aside a tray filled with labeling devices. Below it were chains for winching cars out of sand, chains for tires, bicycle chains, and, his hand felt among them, the barrel of a wartime Sten gun his security man had once felt he needed, as well as boxes of clips for the Sten. The groping hand felt other armament, but of those he had no memory except to know they had once been cached. He took off the cotton coat he wore and pulled at the hardware until the Sten was free.

It was forbidden for ladies to take the sunshine at the pool. Tracy Boardman returned from a venture into the *souks*, where she found little to intrigue her. A Berber bracelet, a primitive jade necklace. She found Amanda Miller in her room, staring pensively from the window.

"I'm beginning to be a bit concerned," Amanda said without turning her head. "What's happened to Roger?"

"I'm not afraid, I'm just bored to tears. What happened to the man I'm supposed to bait?" Tracy threw herself on the bed. "I've done everything permissible in this woman-hating place. Maybe I ought to try a striptease on the front lawn. Do you think your bad vibes have scared him away?"

Amanda stared at the vast ball of fire the sun turned to as it almost touched the sea. "I'm really worried about Roger. Where is he?"

"What's Roger to you?" Tracy said casually.

Amanda turned from the window. "Why do you ask that? Nothing."

"Nothing?" she teased. "I get vibes there too."

"The Society has retained him to run this trip, that's all."

"Meaning you? You don't have to pretend, my dear." She got to her feet and kicked off her shoes. "He's going to be mine, you know. The mistake Ted and I made was to get married. Locking it up chokes love to death, I've found that out. But I can't stand being without a man. So I've put a hold on Roger. Did he tell you?"

"Why should he tell me anything?" she asked irritably.

"Your vibes about him. So I'm informing you up front."

A knocking on the door froze the moment. They stared at each other, their eyes showing panic. This was not the rapping of someone announcing a presence or seeking entrance. It sounded like a hammer or rifle butt looking to break it down. Then, as suddenly as it began, the hammering stopped. Amanda saw an envelope slipped under the door. She turned the latch, looked down the corridor, and saw one of the hotel cleaning boys racing down the hall.

She turned to find Tracy reading the note. Tracy looked up and smiled serenely. "The great fish has taken the bait." She was reaching for her shoes. "It's time to pull and make sure the hook's in deep. It's your Alan Masters. Come on. He's downstairs and begs the privilege of speaking to us."

"Now?" Amanda's voice was two octaves higher than normal. The old diffidence and shyness sought to cripple her again; even she knew it. "Like this?"

"Of course *now*. Later he'll see what miracles makeup can do. Let's go."

"I can't. Not now," Amanda protested.

"It says he would be honored to see us both. If you don't go, madam, I don't go."

"Help me," Amanda said, breathing deep. "I'm scared to death."

Tracy saw a tall, slim man who looked younger than his years. He wore Italian-cut trousers, tight across the hips, a white Lacoste shirt, tennis shoes. He moved toward her with the measured assurance of a winner. "Hi. I'm Alan Masters. I've come to welcome you here and to ask you to a party tomorrow I'm giving for some fellow Americans, meaning you." He held out his hand.

Amanda saw a man untouched by life, a contemporary of her father's, who was even cheating life of its exactions of age, too young-looking, too assured, too easy. He was dressed, she thought, too dandyish, like the clerks in those high-style stores along Rodeo Drive. It had never come to her before that she might have to face him; she felt her knees shake a little.

"And you must be Miss Miller." His hand was extended for her to take now. "You see, I know about all of you. One gets very lonely here, I must confess. You will come, won't you? I'll have cars for all of you both ways."

"Do you have a pool?" Tracy Boardman asked.

"Indeed I do."

"Could we swim there? They won't let us here, you know."

"My house is my castle, I am allowed anything." He grinned. "It is America."

Amanda looked about shyly. The words betrayed something to her, the pain of his exile; they meant nothing to Tracy. "Can we swim now, right now?" she heard Tracy say.

"But of course."

"Then let's go," Tracy exclaimed.

"But we can't—we haven't—" Amanda began.

"Suits? Mandy's quaint, Mr. Masters," Tracy said. "She has no reason to be, believe me. Come, this heat's unbearable, I'd love a swim and so will you." Amanda was certain she caught a sly wink of Tracy's eye.

He'd brought the El Dorado convertible. "Now I feel I'm beginning to live again," Tracy said, the wind blowing her hair in a silken plume behind her. "We've been o bored!"

Amanda felt her thigh being pinched. "Yes, we have," she added as convincingly as she could manage.

"All that's over." Masters pressed down harder on the accelerator. "If you like you can all move into my house—you'd find it a lot more comfortable than that hotel."

"We've heard of you, you know," Tracy said boldly. "Haven't

we?" she asked Amanda. "What do you do here? I don't think we know that for sure. We know you're important!"

"I'm a special adviser to General Abdullah for business affairs."

"You live here all the time?"

"Why not?" Amanda caught a discordant note there. They were coming to his house, a white marble pile in *Il Duce-classico*, very grand. "This isn't a bad place to call home."

"I love it already!" Tracy exclaimed.

He led them to the pool area, larger than the off-limits play area of their hotel. "It's all yours." Amanda was sure that she sensed a nervousness in his manner, a larger-than-necessary push of assurance. "I'll make certain arrangements."

Tracy touched his shoulder. "Don't on my account, angel. Nothing to hide."

"It wouldn't be good for them to peek. I'll only be a minute."

When they were alone, Amanda turned to Tracy. "You clever bitch," she said amiably, smiling a little.

"We'll own him, baby. He's a woman-user. They're *easy*." She was getting out of her shoes at the pool's edge.

"You're really going in?"

"Listen to me, you want to own him, do what I say. The guy's putty, he's used to being the aggressor. Outmaneuver him, I know his kind, the happy cocksman on the hunt." Tracy stood stark naked at the pool's edge, a figure so superb Amanda Miller could understand its delight in its own nudity. "The trick is to make him run faster than ever. Do what I tell you. Get out of those clothes."

"Are you crazy?"

"Do what I tell you. Please, no little-girl modesty. I've handled these cats before." She was in the pool. "He'll be ours, baby!" she called.

Masters came bounding to them as quickly as he could. Amanda got out of her frock and leaped into the pool after Tracy. "Mind if I join you?" Masters called out eagerly.

Tracy swam past, her hair flowing behind her. When he dove in, she was half a pool away. Amanda was making for the opposite side under the water when he came up. He was left hanging on to the edge of the pool, not a quarter the swimmer either of them was, Amanda observed.

They swam, they laughed, Tracy dived from the surface of the water, her handsome rump and naked thighs all Masters could see, the flash of skin above water gleaming like a tawny jewel. She came close to him as he clung to the side. "Do you still want us for your party tomorrow?" Tracy asked breathlessly.

"Not tomorrow. Stay for dinner, please."

She knew the pleading in his voice. "Love to, my dear. But we have work tonight."

"But surely—" he began.

"Wait, darling. Tomorrow will be wonderful too. *This* has been marvelous." Later, she could command him: "Do you think you can get us some towels? We must be getting home."

"... so soon?" he begged.

"... tomorrow." She was sliding down the pool again, her arms reaching forward powerfully, the kick steady and strong.

Amanda found him staring at her body in the water. She smiled a little for she had taken it all in. "Tomorrow." She tried the same vague air of assurance she'd seen Tracy use.

He pulled himself from the water. When he came back he was encased in a terry robe and held out two for them. Amanda watched Tracy get into hers. This free woman was practiced in all the bitch arts they were supposed to hate these days, doing it all magnificently. *He's hooked,* she thought, remembering how Tracy had put it, *and the hook is going deep into the flesh.* She let the man see her quite naked as she came into the robe he held out for her, and didn't give a damn.

HENNING SECURITY AGENCY
111 W. 8th Street
Los Angeles, California

Reference: File 312

FROM: JOHN HENNING
TO: MR. AZEIRI

1. In accordance with your instructions received at this office, the above File has been opened.

2. I have taken personal charge of this matter and offer a preliminary report herewith.

3. The Society for the Resumption of Historical Research has offices on the eighth floor of a building in Beverly Hills, California, known as "the Wells Fargo Bank Building." These offices comprise 2400 square feet and were taken over by the Society from a lease formerly held by Grandview Film Production Company, now defunct. The lease was signed by Amanda Miller, named in your Mailgram as a visa applicant, and paid for with funds on deposit with the Bank of America, Main Branch, Beverly Hills. Said funds were deposited out of Amanda Miller's personal account. As far as can be determined aforesaid Society has received no backing from any other source and appears to be the creature wholly of the aforesaid Amanda Miller, described by bank and lessor as a very wealthy heiress.

Preliminary investigation shows that to this date aforesaid Society has not applied for incorporation in this state, nor tendered any claim as a charitable or educational foundation, entitling it to tax exempt status.

We would point out that in previous similar matters covered by this office, official and quasi-official organizations have always gone through the process of making such application to cover secret activities. This may indicate a new tactic on the part of the former organizers or may be employed here for purposes not yet publicly disclosed.

4. We are proceeding with investigations as to background and other connections of all individuals named in your letter.

5. May we respectfully call your attention to outstanding account, our File 271, involving two weeks' work covering activities of club, since disbanded, called Students for a Democratic Sarumna, copy of which is once again herewith transmitted.

Yours truly,
John Henning, Chief Officer

24.

WHEN ROGER PHILLIPS finally opened his eyes, it took him a long time to piece together where he was and how he had come there. He had slept deeply and had dreamed wildly about a dinner party where nobody got to sit down and people he did not know were grinning at things he was supposed to grin at too, but couldn't. He staggered when he got to his feet and made it to the window and looked out to the activity in back of the Strand Hotel. The sun was too bright for early morning. When he found his wristwatch, he did not want to believe the hour could be so late.

He had reached the hotel in the evening; he remembered it now as he decided he would feel better in bed. They did not know him, they did not expect him, they had no room, they had no record of a reservation, they did not know Professor Carver or anyone else. He reached into his pocket and found a big note, a fifty, and put it before the clerk, with a few gracious words in his best academic Arabic, followed by a very slow and careful English: "I am quite sure there is a reservation for me here and that my friends are here too. Please look more carefully. I don't feel well. I've got to lie down."

Petty corruption was the Sarumnan way; he accepted that without rancor; the man had other things on his mind and did not want the intrusion. The fifty brought a smile, a search, apology, and a room. "It is not much but all we have. We can change you perhaps tomorrow."

All night he felt progressively more sick. When he fell asleep, it was a drugged, dead sleep. It was only when he woke that he had a feeling of control, and that was very feeble. He stood over the sink, saw how yellow his face was and refused to believe what his eyes saw. He found the litter of his clothes on a chair and saw testimony to his haste. *I have been drugged.*

Why? His stomach heaved. He bent over the bowl. It was terrible but when it was over he felt a little better. *Why?* He thought back to two terrible trays which had been brought him during the fourteen hours at the airport, endless cups of black coffee in tiny cups. He refused to believe it. *Why? But why else would I feel so lousy?*

You could have the flu, he told himself, *dengue fever. Remember dengue? You had it here once. My God, the second, or is it first, richest country in the world and they still have bugs that can knock you out with breakbone fever?*

"Maybe they're wise to you," he said aloud. It came to him that this was the first time he had been alone, truly alone, that the engine of abduction was going, gathering speed, and he did not know where it stood, or what kind of speed it was driving at, nor even what was his position now, nor what he could do about any of it. "Maybe it wasn't poison, maybe it's fear," he said to himself. *I don't know which is worse.*

It glistened, it broke the searing desert sun into a trillion pieces and threw it at Ted Boardman's eyes like diamonds, it was the most beautiful plane he knew, had ever known, one he loved, a delight to fly, fast, smooth, twelve passengers and lots of room for . . .

"That's for sale?" He tried to hide the excitement in his voice.

"Hell, no."

They were at Khorfa, the number one drill site in the Sahara, where the first big strike was made years ago. The plane was reserved for the use of the very top echelon. It was a Jet Commander, specially equipped from engine mounts to rudder. Ted had flown this airplane. It wasn't your usual patched-up smuggler job, dirty, creased, begging to be questioned by the D.E.S. and their dope-smelling dogs. This was strictly top-executive class. Yes, sir, no sir. Have you something to declare this time, sir? You haven't, sir? Thank you, sir, good to see you again, sir. If there was a payoff it wasn't on a lonely airstrip in rural Georgia. Not with this airplane, baby.

He flew it out of Miami, more than a few times, its owner a political refugee who made speeches about tyranny and was quoted in the papers at certain times. Peru. And don't forget the east coast of Colombia. The Jet Commander had that kind of range. Whatever Roger had in mind, this plane could do it. Tracy and the big cat she was bait for, Roger, the fast getaway which was Roger's plan: this was the vehicle. And . . .

"How about a charter?" He looked at his man. Eddie Parker and he had hit it off from the beginning. Both men could fly anything and had similar flying histories. Parker landed with WAP five years before and was in charge here. Had to be a hard dollar. The company used native pilots, trained them, all in behalf of showing the government it wasn't anti anything. This made it tough on Eddie Parker because those fellows needed help. Eddie was restless, Ted saw that. They were also serious about booze in this country, booze and women. "What the hell else was life about, you get my drift?" he complained to Ted more than once. Trouble was, the pay was so good.

"They want a lot of money for a charter," Parker said.

"If a guy had a lot of money?"

"We charter quite often to the big political guys, when they've got to go somewhere fast, to make an impression on some of those gulf sheikhs with plush jobs of their own. This one's small but classy. Got range too, as you know. We go nonstop to the gulf, to Rome, even to Madrid. Where would *you* get a lot of money?"

"I'd score hash."

Eddie looked around. "That'd take nerve," he said.

"I've also got a lot of nerve."

"And more cash than we've been talking about."

"Got that too. You know where I can find hash?"

"Used to carry some in the old days. Rome. Madrid. No more. They cut your head off now for dealing."

"You didn't answer my question, Eddie."

"I mean, no trial, no delay, you got hash, they find it, you suddenly got no head."

"Where would you go if you had a lot of hash today, Eddie? Not Rome, huh, not Spain, right?"

"Beirut's too chancy these days. Valletta would be better. Malta's an independent country."

"I'd go one-third with you. No risk to you. I'm here with a copilot who gets a share, and is worth it, take it from me. The plane's recovered in perfect shape in Malta."

"How much would my take come to?"

"How much dope could you get?"

"I still know these Bedouins . . . Enough to fill ten planes."

Ted whistled soundlessly. "Jesus."

"You can't handle one full planeload?"

"I've got passengers to think of."

"They've got to be hip to what's going on?"

"They could figure it out."

"So?"

"So it's a deal."

"I'll need ten thousand up front, Ted, to show the bookkeepers it's a real charter."

"I just happen to have it on me, Eddie," Ted Boardman said.

Amanda Miller was downstairs early. Professor Carver had bluntly refused to go to the cocktail party, but had acceded to her plea that it was very important that he be there. She looked out the window. The black Rolls-Royce looked like it was waiting for a film queen to proceed to an opera ball.

Where was the professor? Tracy planned to be late. She wanted Amanda to go on alone and send back the car. "Infantile games," Amanda blurted out.

"They work with infantile men," Tracy said.

In the lobby, waiting for the professor, Amanda Miller grew nervous, assailed by doubts and a terrible sense of events running out of control. She went to the desk and asked a junior clerk for the number of the professor's room.

When she found it, some time later, she did not get an answer. She called the guard at the end of the corridor, or whatever he was sitting for hours in his straight-back chair. She gestured for him to open the door. He would not. She persisted, making a pantomime of an old man sleeping, and finally prevailed.

She found the clerk had given her the wrong room. Roger Phillips sprawled on the floor of the bathroom, arm draped around an unspeakable bowl. His torso was covered with sweat, his face was stubbled, and deathly pale. She found a rag of a clean towel, wet it and brought it to the back of his head and gently around to his forehead. She helped him make it to his feet and to the bed.

"I think someone doesn't like me," he jested. His eyes closed briefly but soon opened. "I think I got all the poison up . . . I feel like a curtain's been raised . . .How'd you get in, Amanda?"

"Never mind, what happened to you?"

"Not sure. Maybe the food." He studied her for a long time. "Good to see you . . . You're all dressed up."

"Alan Masters is giving a party for all of us."

"Good work."

"Your girlfriend's got the man slavering. She's something."

"Told you. And her old man?"

"Out in the toolies. Looking for airplanes, like he's supposed to. You going to be all right, Roger?"

"I may live. And the professor, what's with him?"

"My God!" she exclaimed, and stood up as if pulled to her feed by an invisible giant. "I'm supposed to meet him right now. He was late and I got worried so I asked the desk and they goofed and gave me your room, thank the Lord. Let me bring him here."

"No," he said, and then had a second thought. "Why not? He doesn't know anything, does he?"

"I have a hunch he's got a few theories by now."

Waiting alone, he knew the retching and the vomiting were over. His body was beginning to feel cool again. What would not go away was doubt, uncertainty, a small cancer of fear, of himself, of already being exposed.

He looked up to see Carver above him. Long bony fingers touched his forehead. Roger Phillips went over what had happened at the airport, the long detention.

"It was deliberate, no question," Professor Carver said. "A message. They couldn't refuse you entry but . . . It's a very ancient trick to work on someone whose visit you don't relish, Roger."

"They suspect me of something?"

"Not exactly. They don't deal in precisions, as you know. Maybe it's a message for all of us. To be very very careful."

"They didn't have to go to all that trouble. I thought I was doing just that."

"I shouldn't think so. Not, that is, until you fully inform me what is going on here. I may be able to help after all."

"Tomorrow will be time enough, sir. You're going to a party now, I'm told."

The old man looked from him to Amanda, a slight, knowing smile creasing the old, weathered skin around his cheeks. "As you like," he acceded at length.

They watched him leave first. "See what I mean?" Amanda Miller said.

"It all goes tomorrow night," Roger Phillips announced as soon as the door closed behind him.

"So fast?"

"What they did to me proves they're suspicious even before they know what the hell to be suspicious about. It's all set. Make a deal to be with Masters tomorrow. All day, if possible. See if he can't tell his people he'll be out of touch so they won't miss him for a while."

"Do you want to see Tracy?"

"Tomorrow morning will do. Or if she wants to, let her stay with the guy. You come alone after the party and fill me in. Remember, we want him after dark tomorrow."

"Can you tell me how we're getting out?"

"I can, but I won't."

She moved to see if he was comfortable. "The man's hooked, Roger. He's ours."

"Don't get overconfident."

". . . waiting to be pulled in, that's all."

"Don't underestimate him."

"When I saw him, can you imagine what it did to me?"

It wasn't anything he wanted to deal with. Not here. Not now. "Later. The professor's downstairs."

"I went dead inside." She had to tell him; she had to tell someone. "I even forgot what I was here for."

"Don't waste your hate. Right now, he's a thing, a package we've got to get out, that's all. I'll see you in the morning."

She filled her lungs and kept them filled for a time. "I'm trying, but it's not going to be easy." She leaned over and for some reason, some impulse, kissed his forehead.

He stared at her as she went to the door. "Miss Miller . . ." It stopped her.

"Yes?"

"I never really noticed before. You've got very good legs," he said.

"Hell, it turns out I've got a good body, which I never realized." Amanda offered a smile he had never seen on her before. He fell onto the pillow and closed his eyes; he knew he would be all right in the morning; he was glad he understood the message about the poisoning.

Ted Boardman saw the professor in the lobby; he was glad the professor did not see him. Ted walked swiftly to the steps and took them two at a time. In the room he found Tracy in her simple, knock-'em-dead pale silk sheath, the one that never failed. Sleeves to the wrist, a turtleneck over the throat, the length discreet, all the wrong things for a lead-on dress. It was a proven little number more provocative than nakedness; it rippled over every curve on that fabulous body. Ted found himself staring at it in mute admiration, as if he'd never before seen it, or the body it covered.

"You dating the old prof? Saw him waiting in the lobby."

"My man's giving a party for us. You ought to come. They're sending the car back for me.There's plenty of time for you to dress."

"Trace," he began with ill-concealed eagerness. "I've found the deal we've been waiting for."

"Jesus," she muttered. "You promised Roger."

"I won't screw up his deal, whatever the hell it is. This goes right along with it."

"You told him you wouldn't try to score here."

"I fell into this one."

"Yeah, and you didn't happen to be looking to connect, right?"

"We'll make a ton! It comes in on the East Coast. New York. Boston. Not one of those hot ports of entry we've had to use. A freighter out of Malta—cool, baby, cool. This'll be it."

He found himself holding her in his arms.They both seemed surprised, as if a spark they had both seen die flared to life again. After surprise came embarrassment. There were no words. She smoothed the silken skin that lay over her own. "You'll come to the party."

"Yes, baby," her husband said, and found he could grin.

25.

IT WAS routine. Whenever Alan Masters gave a party, a small detachment of Revolutionary Council Special Forces, as they were called, was dispatched to the big marble house on the Corniche. They were positioned at the entrance, both to check guests and to frighten away any residents of the city of Zarplis who might be curious about the revelries infidels engage in.

Within the house, the Italian decorators had succeeded in creating a setting for this occupant's delight. These occasions were what Alan Masters lived for, the rest was dull, dull, dull, as he told them repeatedly. He wanted an intimate, seductive atmosphere. He got a somewhat-less-than-intimate drawing room which was softly lit, and a high-style ambience befitting a man on the make. Marco provided young men from the tribal south in flowing traditional gowns who discreetly served canapés and silver trays of drinks. In one corner of the room, three blacks whose forebears were slave-traded from the south generations before wove intricate, lyric patterns on woodwinds to the beat of a brilliant drummer.

"Does the Man offer any objections to such wild goings-on?" Mike Kelly asked.

"A few grumbles now and then. He knows how corrupt we infidels are."

Alan Masters saw some of his guests arrive. Two Polish nurses from the General Abdullah Hospital, very lovely blonde young ladies. Unfortunately, however, they had only enough English to giggle on and, furthermore, he had already taken each to bed, so the novelty was gone. But they graced any room they entered, and he went to them to bring them over to Mike Kelly.

There were more young women than men of all ages. Masters had seen to that. His invitations were always honored. His parties were comets that flashed across a dreary sky and were lost if the moment was not seized. A Yugoslav young lady he remembered vaguely kissed his cheek, and he wondered who she was, he didn't remember the name, she was new, or had become new again, he must get Marco to put down the name and where she was to be found. A Swedish girl came up, unfortunately, a bit heavily fleshed; he recalled her as too easy a conquest. "So nice of you to be here tonight." She worked on a government-contracted telephone project. They had gone to bed one night when he was despairing of what his life had become. Still, he never spoke to women as he'd spoken to Ana. "I've become a machine, or maybe it's a kind of queen bee, all I do is turn out money." A wild one in the kip, he remembered as they pecked at each other's cheeks, but that Rubens, overcurved body . . . Where were the two Americans? A fantasy exploded and died quickly, one, then the other, the two together in bed with him. He looked at his wristwatch.

He went to the big windows that gave out to the courtyard where the cars were parked. He had the Rolls saloon sent to pick up the Americans, the one identical to the General's. He had had two sent by air from London for the General as a token of British gratitude, magnificent, regal machines; the General had been so moved by the gesture he insisted Masters keep one for his own use. "Brothers," Mohammed Abdullah had said. "Identical twins," he had chuckled. Masters did not use it often. It was embarrassing being taken for the President-for-Life. The black car was pulling to the *porte-cochere*. It was different, however, when one wanted to make an impression. Masters hastened to the front door.

Amanda was escorted by the lanky professor. Masters found her surprisingly attractive. The air of innocence (which he did not believe) intrigued him; shyness; a little light that spoke of timidity—fear?—that glistened in her eyes. Being drawn to a vulnerable female was a pleasant novelty. Such a lovely contrast to the fearless love goddess, Tracy, a veritable Diana the huntress, who knew and had done it all. The flash of fantasy about the three of them together lit his sky again. The huntress bringing the doe to the heights—and he would save her, take her. He put his hand on Amanda's elbow and brought her in. "Welcome, welcome."

"Tracy asked us to go on. I've sent the car back for her, is that all right?"

"Anything, my dear. As long as you both are to be here." He acknowledged Professor Carver and took her away from him.

Carver had been in the palace in the old days. He remembered the adventurer who had built it, a fascist in charge of foreign trade, as he recalled. He found himself walking among the guests to see what the new occupant had done to it. He saw Mr. Azziz, but the professor was discreet enough to offer no sign of recognition. This, after all, was the eve before the weekly holy day that the prophet brought down from the mountain as a commandment to observe.

"I'm really giving this party for you and Mrs. Boardman," Alan Masters said. They were standing in a soft light that reached the terrace from the room where most of the guests had assembled. A sinuous melody drifted over the hum of the party inside.

"We're very honored." Amanda found herself wishing she could say something more provocative, but it was clear to her whatever she said seemed to heighten his anticipation.

"I want to be your friend, your very close friend. To both of you."

"We're glad." Even that fatuity, she observed, he took as an assurance of succumbing to seduction.

"To make your stay here memorable in every way."

"I wonder," she began, and stopped quickly. She wasn't, she knew, good at these things and perhaps should leave it to Tracy Boardman. But . . .

"You wonder what?"

"If we—Tracy and I, that is—if it could be arranged for just us to spend a whole day, a whole—well, night—in the desert?"

"But of course!" He lifted her hand and put it to his mouth. "I know just the place. It's kept for a very, very few. I can arrange to have it to ourselves. Do you think Mrs. Boardman can—?"

"You're not concerned about Tracy's husband?" Amanda began as shyly as she could manage. It was all so easy she could not escape a touch of embarrassment. Tracy has certainly assessed his kind perfectly. "She and I—and you . . . Can we leave and no one will know?"

He kissed the hand once more. "A great sheikh's tent under the desert sky! It's like nothing you've ever known before. Dancing girls such as you never see in the cabarets. Do you like belly dancing? It would be marvelous for the three of us to share the excitement."

Her hand was at his lips again. The gentleman was a hundred miles ahead of her. "Are you sure you can take the time to share this silly adventure with us?" she asked demurely. "And be very discreet?"

"It will be unforgettable. We'll forget time, it won't exist for us."

"Just us, yes?" Amanda had the feeling she was standing behind herself and was hearing someone else in her body. "An important man like you, surely they'll be sending for you, needing you back here for something or other?"

"I'll leave orders—not for anything are we to be disturbed."

She felt his arms on her; the little shaking her body offered as he embraced it he must have taken as a sign of virginal helplessness. The loathing she felt rose like bile to her gorge, but she gave no sign. He held her tenderly, very gently. "I've never known anyone like you, my angel," he whispered to her ear, "so innocent, yet so daring, so daring, so bold, so adventurous." He found her mouth.

"It'll be beautiful," she heard herself say. *Couldn't he tell?*

"You won't change your mind?"

A surge of power within filled her being; hating had nothing to do with it, except to make her aware of how easy it was to manipulate the courting male. She let him put his mouth to hers again. "Never," she whispered. He felt her lips, not the loathing. "Never." She saw in the white luminescence on the marble courtyard the headlights of the stately Rolls that had brought her earlier. "Look. There's Tracy."

"Let's go and tell her."

"I'll wait here."

She had survived the worst.

Ted let Tracy go in ahead of him. He'd seen her make what he called The Entrance before. In party light the beige skin of silk over her figure made the first vision of her that of a nude goddess. It was always a shock for them to find she was in fact discreetly covered.

Ted Boardman turned his wife over to his host and moved among the furnishings, taking it all in. The few women did not interest him. He had other things on his mind. The old professor was having an animated conversation with two gentlemen in flowing gowns. He nodded and proceeded on his way. The drinks they were serving had good slugs in them. He took only one, although two was his limit when he knew he was going to fly the next day.

Through a window he saw Tracy and Amanda and the host, and he knew from the fuss they were making over him that this was the guy Roger Phillips wanted.

He saw Amanda break away from them. Tracy was doing a bit he'd seen before, the flirtatious smile, the fingers of her right hand drifting across the man's face. He left them to Tracy's game.

Ted Boardman went in search of Amanda, past a buffet set with mountains of food and a centerpiece composed of a whole lamb garnished with mountains of couscous, fruits and vegetables. When he finally reached her he found a mountainous figure had got there before him. Something he saw arrested him as abruptly as if a curtain had miraculously dropped before him. Boardman leaned almost against a wall for support. The back, that was all he had to see. *Can't be*, that was his first thought. *Had to be* was his next. The broad back going straight down all the way like a giant redwood, powerful shoulders to powerful hips to powerful thighs. He hugged the wall; the bull neck atop the body seemed to turn toward him, as if some malign instinct told the big man he was being studied. But the turn was never completed. Boardman remained against the wall, immobilized, his eyes a man's who cannot believe what they see.

At length, Boardman began to move forward, smiling wanly at two men whose conversation he briefly interrupted, using their bodies for cover. He saw the big man's face, now fully engaged in trying to make an impression on Amanda Miller. It was who Ted Boardman thought it was, beyond question.

"*I was told this was a straight contraband run down here and maybe some dope back. Nothing about taking stretcher cases.*"

"That's all it is, mister, far as you're concerned, another score."

"They don't look like something that can be put into lids for sale on the street." He pointed to two bodies on stretchers in the airport shack.

They were in a remote town in the Andes. Ted Boardman hadn't wanted to land there but when they'd stopped to refuel in Panama someone gave him the new orders. The minute he landed he could see this was not your run-of-the-mill smuggle. They were refueling the airplane as the jets whined to a stop. They wanted a turnaround in minutes and knew how to do it. Ordinarily, everything in these big-scale deals was an endless series of snafus. The refueling tanks weren't there. The trucks wouldn't start. The porters couldn't handle the load. The runway was soft. Here it all worked with professional, army-staff precision.

The big man spoke tough-guy American mixed with Spanish. It was clear he was the boss here. Hair a little too black, beard blacker than it ought to be. Voice like thunder in a mountain pass. He told the ground crew what to do in a snarl like a jaguar's. A ground crew that knew just where to unscrew plates to hide the plastic bags with the white stuff. Boardman still didn't see taking on board two near-dead people. Didn't they have hospitals down here? Suppose one of them died before he landed? He didn't fancy explaining passengers, especially when he knew there was always the possibility of a search. His eyes bugged when he saw blood dripping in stomach-churning amounts from the stretcher that held a lady's body.

"What am I supposed to do with them when I land in Uncle Sugar Able?" Boardman pleaded with the big man.

There had been no introductions. Normal enough. No small talk. Also normal. But this guy worked like he owned the country. He gave orders and Boardman could see a lot of rifles and sidearms on plainclothesmen ready to back them.

"These people are not going to the U.S.A., mister."

"I don't fly shuttles," Ted said.

"You're going back to the same airport you came from." There was a cutting edge to the words that came out of the black beard that was like a cleaver. The big man was losing patience. "And you didn't see anything here. You're bringing back four gentlemen with diplomatic papers. There are no bodies, there won't be any when you land.

Now you get back into that airplane and get started, what do you say, mister?"

"I'm not taking off with those two aboard," Boardman said flatly.

"You want to bet?" *the black beard said and showed him close to the eyes what the face end of a Magnum .357 looked like.*

There he stood, here, now, the beard as black as it was—when? *Strange how a man can forget time when he has to forget something he wants to forget, like when he was an accessory in double murder. Over the dense Amazon jungle he saw the gentlemen with diplomatic papers shove the two still-alive bodies out to an endlessly green hell five miles below, stretchers and all.*

He came to Amanda. "You've got to get me out of here."

"Your hand's shaking. Why?"

"That fellow you were talking to," he whispered hoarsely. "He'd know I'm not here for survey work for some museum. Is he connected with this Masters?"

"We can assume so. Why?"

"If he places me, we're in trouble. I once did a job he was involved in."

"I'd better warn Tracy."

"There isn't time. Get me the hell out first."

The big black Rolls designated for her use sped them to the Strand, backs of troops as well as civilians turning to it, on orders, as it passed, as if it held the General himself. Ted could not stop a chattering monologue all the way. "A dirty deal . . . real dirty. Enough for the FBI to ask questions. Some democratic opposition people they liquidated down there . . . I had to talk, do you know what I mean? The feds knew I'd chartered that plane, a year later they went over it with everything in the lab. They wanted to know about the blood on the deck. I gave them the usual story, I was ferrying, I don't ask questions. I was sure I didn't see any sick or wounded people loaded, I lied, I was busy up front. They asked me a lot about that guy you were talking to. He's a dangerous gun for hire . . . I wonder what he's doing here?"

"His name's Mike Kelly. Whatever else he's doing, far as I

could tell, he's another guy trying to make out tonight," Amanda said, to calm him.

"We've got to split—right now!"

"Take it easy," she suggested. "Get some sleep. There's no reason for him to see you."

"Roger—what in the hell is he doing?" Ted rattled nervously. "One week, that's what he said. Well, time's running out on his week. I've got a line on an airplane that I'd match against whatever they can put in the air. We've got our way out of this country."

"Tomorrow," she said, taking his hand to soothe him.

"Stay with me tonight, Mandy."

"Can't." She wiggled out of an attempted embrace. She had learned from the man's wife not to struggle, that making it a flirtation made resistance part of the mating ballet, hence acceptable.

"Remember what I told you? Stay close to me and everything will be all right," he told her.

"I'm close, Ted," she whispered. It seemed to content him.

She went downstairs to see Roger Phillips as soon as she got rid of Ted Boardman. "I may live," he greeted her wanly.

She told him about Boardman and the man in the black beard. "You did right," Roger said. "It can't be good. What about Tracy?"

"I left her with Masters. She isn't going to lose him, you can be sure of that." Amanda told him about the plans for the desert and how she had arranged for Masters not to be missed for a couple of days.

"Very bright of you."

"Oh, I've picked up on all this stuff very quickly. Mr. Alan Masters has some idea about Tracy and me playing trio with him, which I may have somehow suggested to him."

"My shy lady of the oleanders?" he said, mimicking astonishment. "She and he and she games? What an apt student you are."

"It was easy, men are so easy."

"Don't believe everything Tracy tells you about men."

"Really? Shouldn't I believe her about her and you? She tells me when this is over, you two—"

"Please," he broke in, "not now, not here."

"Funny. Masters I can understand. Ted I can understand. I can even understand Tracy. But I don't get you."

"I think I'm beginning to feel sick all over again." He put hands on her and led her, not very gently, to the door. "Tomorrow morning at eleven. I want everybody in this room. Don't let them know I've arrived." Holding her shoulders in his hands gave him pause. "I don't know what I'd've done without you, Amanda. I'm glad you're here," he said, and pushed her out the door.

TO: HONORED CHIEF, FOREIGN OFFICE, ZARPLIS,
REVOLUTION TACTICAL SECTION
FROM: AZEIRI, WASHINGTON EMBASSY

I take the liberty, Excellency, of breaking our beloved President's rule of employing only Arabic in all governmental communications in transmitting the following in its original language. I do so with some hesitation and no reflection whatsoever against the wisdom of our beloved President's decision, but only to insure that the enclosed reaches Zarplis without delay for immediate action.

Please be assured that a translation would have been prepared and transmitted but for our faithful observance of the holy day.

HENNING SECURITY CO.
111 W. 8th Street
Los Angeles, California

Reference: File 312

STATEMENT OF MRS. MARVA MILLER
214 Sunkist Road
Tempe, Arizona

I make this statement freely, willingly, and out of consideration, love and affection for my daughter, in the belief that she is not acting in her own best interest. It is also my belief that whatever she has got involved in, it is not her fault, but being a vulnerable individual, not wise in the way of the world and easily exploited by devious characters, she has allowed herself to be used.

When I last saw my daughter, Amanda Miller, she left home with a sum of money I know to be not more than three hundred dollars, everything in her savings account. Her real, born name is Mary Louise Ebersol. She is the daughter of John Edward Ebersol, whom I married when he was just beginning to climb the financial ladder.

For reasons not germane here, that marriage was dissolved, and to protect my daughter from a life of scandal and disgrace, I married Mr. Clarence Miller, an insurance man in Phoenix, Arizona, where I went to shield my daughter from any association with the infamy which my then husband was bent on visiting on her, and myself.

I worked hard, never complained, and managed to put my daughter through school. The marriage with Mr. Miller came to an end, through no fault of my own. He legally adopted my girl when she was little and gave her his name. Her present Christian name was given her at that time to protect her from any association with her natural father. My one thought was always to protect this child. As I have explained to the gentleman to whom I am dictating this statement, my daughter has always been a withdrawn and backward child (I do not mean in an intellectual sense), easily misled, always trying to achieve things beyond her natural talents. I loved her, still love her very much, although this is something she does not seem to understand. In any event, until John E. Ebersol was put on trial and convicted of so many crimes that I cannot bear to name them, this child was shielded and guarded from evil and shame and disgrace.

Despite all that I did for my daughter, she visited him while he was on trial and even insisted on continuing the association after he had been convicted by a jury of his peers!

When this man finally passed judgment on himself, needless to say, there was not a penny forthcoming to a woman who stood by his side when he entered the world of finance. Not a penny came to his daughter. Yet she chose this moment to run away from home. I do know that she withdrew her savings to go to Amsterdam, Holland, or the Netherlands, whichever is correct. We have no relatives in that country.

I have been told that she says she inherited a lot of money and that she has "funded" a society which claims to be interested in history. As her mother, I say there is no way my daughter could have come into so much money without my knowledge, unless . . .

PART FIVE

26.

THERE WAS a moment at dawn along the Sarumnan seacoast that never failed to lift Roger Phillips's spirits. The sun has just begun to make its almost perpendicular rise in this latitude against the cloudless blue sky and the haze over the sea has not yet been burned away. It is the only moment of daylight when one could shiver with cold. At this hour no cars asserted their imperial rights with horn, accelerator or steering wheel. Zarplis, the other Zarplis, decent, kind, life-accepting Zarplis, has only just begun to rise for the day's hard work and its quota of lunatic ambition and fear.

Roger Phillips stood on the sidewalk outside the Strand Hotel and once more took in the moment as he had so often in the past that it had become an insoluble part of his memory. He wore his old Adidas joggers, a sweatsuit from the other, tamed desert and a band around his forehead to keep hair and perspiration out of his eyes. Ostensibly he was about to see how well and how far he could do after the poisoning; the momentary spell of the cool of the new day held him longer than he knew.

"Ah, Roger," he heard from behind. The regius professor emeritus was garbed in a yellow jacket and jogging pants with white stripes down pant legs and sleeves. As always, he spoke as though resuming a chat terminated a few minutes earlier. "Which way do we go?"

Roger Phillips was heading east, he offered without enthusiasm, which surprised the old man; they both knew the road there curved from the sea to mudflats and a shabby area of boat-repair shops, fisherman huts and sleazy harbor buildings. "Be interesting at that," Professor Carver said brightly. "Mind if I join you?"

What Roger Phillips had in mind was to locate a spot where he might hide a car, or, lacking that, park it for a time without attracting undue attention. He shrugged, and began the run. He took it easy; he had not run for several days, and the day before had left him feeling soggy. The old man was remarkable. With his longer legs he had to shorten his stride to accommodate him, Roger Phillips observed. "Don't let me hold you back, sir," he suggested, not entirely with irony.

Carver said nothing for a time. They circled two dogs snarling and savaging each other over some foul remnant of bone or flesh. The sun was still low enough so the old buildings cast shadows across the dusty narrow streets. "I've got a gun for you." the professor murmured casually. "Handgun, that is. U.S. Army service pistol. Also the old Sten we once equipped the guard with. Never approved that sort of thing but remembered they were in the inventory and thought you could use them now, dear boy."

"Thank you very much. I can use them."

"In my room."

"Very foolhardy, professor. What if they search?"

"I left little traps to tell me if they do."

"You're marvelous, sir. I owe you an apology."

"Not at all. It's gratitude, that's all. You brought me back here, perhaps for the last time . . ."

"I lied to you."

"I've known that from the start."

"You think I'm into some glorious adventure for some gloriously patriotic cause. I now can tell you, I'm here to kidnap a man, nothing more."

"Masters," he said simply, without surprise. "So that's what it's all about. Bring him home to justice. I do read the papers, you see."

"For this I wreck your relationship with this government."

"It was wrecked on my side long before, Roger. I relish the opportunity to do whatever little against the lunatic here, you ought to know that. I would not mind if it had been an assassination."

"You shock me, professor."

"The old dilemma, you mean, Roger? Is political murder ever

justified? Academic by now, I should think. What about madmen like this one who wouldn't hesitate to make atomic war? Its usefulness, thank heavens, is occasionally, only occasionally, I concede, conceivable. You're breathing very hard."

He was out of shape. Roger Phillips stopped at a three-sided waterfront building that once must have housed some kind of machine or repair shop. A curb but no driveway. A car could make it over the curb. He leaned against a wooden wall which bore a sign in Arabic:

> MINISTRY OF PUBLIC WORKS
>
> Here will be erected installations to service harbor activities. Electricity and water will be available.
> Director, Three Year Program

"Why?" Carver asked for a moment.
"Why did I involve you?"
"Why did you involve yourself?"
"Money. I went broke. Also to escape an unsatisfactory life. Not to mention once knowing and loving this place."

The professor grinned. "My reason also, Roger. Heroic deeds are not always heroically motivated. Heroism is often in the doing as much as the purpose."

"No heroics here, sir. It's all wrapped up. I've practically got our man. Now I'm only waiting for dark."

"Today?" The professor smiled again. "Naturally. Friday. The holy day." From a tower they could not see, speakers amplified so loud they screeched were calling the faithful to another of the day's prayers. The two men stared at each other as if talk could be disrespectful. "It is a good thing you do, Roger," Carver resumed. "Anything that diminishes the swollen authority of this madman here. It will come, it must come, so every bit is important."

"Everything's working beautifully," Roger Phillips said. "It's remarkable. I'm beginning to think maybe I wasn't poisoned.' Maybe I just got sick, a touch of flu—do you agree?"

"No," Professor Carver said and resumed his morning jog alone.

179

Amanda was asleep when the tapping on her door awoke her. "It's me," the voice said. Tracy came in, dewy fresh, the hair unbrushed, uncombed, the morning after as lovely as ever, the skin-tight dress still smooth as a sheet of stainless steel.

"I told him I need to pack a few things. And of course I'd make sure you're ready."

"You think I ought to be with him, just in case?"

"He won't run away."

"You're marvelous."

"It helps when they're so starved they get themselves going on high-powered sexual fantasies. They also have a need to talk. This one spent the whole night telling me what a big man he was and what he's got. He's lonely. He misses the U.S."

"How touching. And now you're sorry for him?"

"He wants to give us the world, Mandy. Got these places all over, all the money we could need. Apartment houses he's never seen in Monte Carlo and Paris and even New York. Cap d'Antibes. Lodge in Gstaad. Town house in Belgravia. Soon, he said, he's going to be able to use them all. He's got powerful friends. He's going to outsmart all his enemies. It isn't just talk, I can spot male lies from a hundred yards."

"And what'd you say to all this?"

"Your hate vibes are showing again, Mandy. Is that why you took off with Ted? I saw you two split early. What gives?"

"And do I detect a little jealousy? I thought it was over with you two."

"I'm so confused about Ted," she broke off, "I don't know what the hell gives anymore."

"For what it's worth, my hunch is that he feels the same way." Amanda was finding the Boardmans' marital dilemma tiresome. "Know why we split so fast? This guy at the party, big fellow, black beard—apparently he and Ted had something to do with each other once."

The mention of the black beard began to put some things in place for Tracy.

"Pleaded with me to get him out fast," Amanda went on. "Told me about how this guy had bodies pushed out of an airplane."

"He wasn't making anything up. It's been a nightmare for Ted ever since. The guy's name is Mike Kelly. He's got something to do with weaponry training here."

"I don't think he saw Ted," Amanda said. "At least Ted did his best to duck him. He could be dangerous for us."

"More so for Ted, baby. What he did is called squealing in some circles."

Amanda put her hand on Tracy. "Stay with him. I'm going to want to see you both a little later."

"Poor Teddy," Tracy said.

Mike Kelly stared at himself in the mirror above his bed. He saw the reflection of the great white and gold swan, the prow at the front of his bed, once a veritable crown prince's couch of pleasure, and the half-buried head of the guest he had brought back the night before from the party.

"Wake up, chubby," he said amiably, and somewhat roughly pushed the sleeping figure.

"Hey, take it easy, man." She was the Swedish girl, Ana; her English was unaccented and almost flawlessly colloquial.

"I want to ask you something," he said, falling back on the big pillow and staring at her in the mirror. "Last night. There was this new guy. You happen to talk to him?"

"Which one?"

"American. Tall, kind of athletic looking."

"Tell me more."

"I spotted him hugging the wall. Like he didn't like what he was seeing. Or was scared."

"With one of those girls Masters was making a play for?"

"Right. What are they doing here?" he mused aloud.

"I never saw either of them before in my life."

Mike Kelly scratched his tousled beard. "I work with eyes in back of my head. Why's this guy scared of me? I kind of remember him, but from where? What's he doing? Why's he split when he spots me?"

"Mmmm," Ana murmured, not very interested, "what have we here?" Her lips brushed his chest. "Perhaps this time, darling . . ."

"If he knows who I am, why doesn't he come over and say hello? Where do I know him from?"

"It feels so *pretty*." She began climbing her companion.

He pushed her from him. "What's he doing here anyway?"

"He's on a job to make a lot of money, like everybody in this country who wasn't born here," Ana said with some irritation.

"I can't place him," Mike Kelly went on dreamily. "But I will, I will."

"It'll come to you if you don't think about it too much. Try, baby. Ana understands. Maybe this time my man will be able to ... Yes?" She found his lips.

For the moment he did not give a damn about the man, or what the hell he was doing here.

The Ministry of Foreign Affairs of the government of Sarumna is housed in a new huge rectangular building. It is four stories high and dotted with innumerable rectangular windows. Its original design called for an L-shaped wing twice its height to join the rectangle. This was in the process of being built when General Mohammed Abdullah grew furious at a political decision made by his eastern neighbor and ordered all contact to cease at that very moment. Since the whole ministry was engineered and built by contractors from that nation, it meant the ministry itself had never been completed.

But, finished or not, the ministry building did impress those who saw it from the angle that did not show the skeleton, and it was a functioning foreign office.

On holy days it was closed to the world, on the General's orders, except for its telex lines. Sarumnan missions around the world could use them only in matters of extreme urgency.

When the message from Washington began to arrive, the duty officer took note that the memo came from Azeiri, a high-ranking name he knew well although he had himself never met the man. The duty officer hesitated at receiving the English transmission which followed, not only because only one man was available to translate it, but because he did not know what to do next. The General's feelings about Arabic and its exclusive use were too well known for a mere duty officer to make himself a party to disobedience. He could not imagine the malevolent consequences his cooperation might create. The General even insisted that all proposed commercial contracts, engineering specifications, official communications as well as trivial matters like foreign passports be rendered into Arabic and all dates in those documents be reduced to their Koranic equivalents. Inside the country, whole villages had been turned out to black out any English, French, Italian or German that was meant to stand for Arabic, which included traffic signs, village designations and even corporate names on big new factory buildings along the seacoast. What might he say to being a party to all this Ingleezi on the holy day?

In his first days on assignment here the duty officer often brought messages marked "Most Urgent" to the attention of his superiors when they came from places like Cuba, Ethiopia, Uganda, Italy and Japan, but in every instance he was not praised for diligence but reminded of his sacred duty to follow strictly the rules of Arabic only and the observance of the holy days.

He had learned his lesson well. On this occasion he contented himself by leaving the Azeiri message on top of his own desk for action on the morrow.

Alan Masters slept late that morning. When he awoke, the tiniest smile creased the corners of his mouth and his eyes were bright with anticipation. He went to his bathroom, cleansed his mouth, regarded himself with approval in a full-length brass mirror the Italian decorators had installed, combed his hair and got into a dressing gown.

On his desk there were messages in Marco's fractured Ingleezi. He would have all the names, places and times wrong. It was Friday and although not at all devout, his man took his day off before he could explain. Nevertheless, Masters liked having the house to himself one day a week.

He thought of the night before. He lay down on his bed again, stared at the ceiling; the little smile grew.

He never did relish the easy conquest. For too long he had had to make do with them. Too often they were paid for, tacitly or not; he knew that even when he did his best to pretend money did not figure in the arrangements. There was always something frantic about them also, even when he could put the cash nexus out of his consciousness: He was like a starving man put before a festive table who gorged too hastily and without discrimination.

Hence, he savored this moment. He was quite serious about the offer he had made Tracy Boardman to use the residences he was arranging for himself all over Europe. He had no doubt the time would soon come when he would be able to travel. He liked her style; he liked the style of the other one too; he liked the contrast between them. It was better that they had not gone to bed; anticipation was almost as delicious as accomplishment in pleasures as evanescent as lovemaking. He had learned that very well during his stay here.

He heard his private phone. Fridays, the overseas operators here often did not reply to their counterparts across the Mediterranean, so the ringing told him whoever was on the line possessed a significant authority. It could also be the General, although being a holy day, that was highly unlikely.

It was Raskoff in London. "Thank God, I've found you in," he began.

Masters sighed. With this man, it was always a favor being sought, a rule he wanted broken or bent. And always urgent. Nevertheless, Raskoff was a man to accommodate.

"I've just come from Vienna, Alan. Do you know what your people did there? I believe your OPEC delegation has gone mad. It's spearheading another increase."

Masters knew he was not powerful when it came to discussing oil with the General. Abdullah had his own views and did not even relish comment about them from his special counselor on foreign investment.

"Can't help you there, you know that, Marcus."

"You've got to show him that with what he's got invested abroad, every time he hurts the nonproducers he reduces his own equity."

"We have an arrangement, Marcus. I don't tell him about pricing oil and he doesn't tell me where to put the money."

"What if I paid an official visit? Isn't it about time?"

"It might offend him, coming so close after the OPEC meeting. He'd know what's behind it. You know how he gets when his mind's set."

"I wouldn't discuss it. Perhaps my presence would be a sufficient message. I'll have my people weigh its merits." Raskoff ran his own State Department; he'd have a brace of differing opinions and a lot of advice before he would decide on such a visit.

"I'll keep you informed, Marcus."

"My contacts in Washington are still looking out for you, you know."

"Everything all right there?"

"You're doing fine. They need the General's good will, passive or otherwise, understand what I mean? The quiet helps you. Keep a low profile. Stay out of sight. You're not a top priority with this administration."

When he had first come here every setback was like a denial of parole to an unjust imprisonment. Now he had learned to make delay part of his own strategy. He tightened the belt of his dressing gown and went back to bed.

He did not want to look at a clock. Time would pass too slowly before the hour before sunset when he was to pick up the dear things. He actually managed to sleep again.

He awoke with a start to a heavy, booted tread on the marble outside his door. Clack-clack-clack. A pause. A knock. Before he could utter a sound, the door opened quickly to reveal a tall man in battered, sand-stained jeans and denim jacket and scuffed boots, a dirty Stetson pulled low on his forehead. It took Alan Masters a minute to see that the cigar in the mouth could not hide the face of his old, valued assistant and one-time student. Abu ben-Sadriquen did not, could not perhaps, return the grin. But he was grateful when Masters got to his feet to embrace him.

"Forgive me, Alan, I had to see you. Are we alone?"

"There's no one around. Who let you in?"

"You gave me a key once, remember? I won't stay long. The disguise has worked fine so far. Do I look like Texas?"

They went to the kitchen and found American coffee and a tin of English biscuits. "Isn't life strange?" Sad said, "I never was a traitor, but merely leaving my family village to see an old friend turns me into one."

"You can't stay long, Sad."

"I am lonely, Alan, for life here."

"It's dangerous, for you and for me."

185

"I need you, dear friend. Can't you tell him how I left you and Ebersol to return here even though I could have remained, become an American and rich? I love my land and my people."

"You know how he is once his mind's made up," Masters offered noncommittally.

"He listens to you. Everybody knows that. Talk to him. What did I do, what did I say? I'm not the only one who believes those things. There are many of us. Up and down the Mahgreb and in all the emirates, in Yemen, in Saudi, everywhere, Alan." His voice fell almost to a whisper. " 'One day,' I said, 'we will have to find a way to live together, it is not a question of to whom the land belongs, it is a matter of men living equally under One God. It will be difficult to achieve, difficult to maintain, but in the end it must be done.' Does that sound like I was a traitor betraying my faith, my people, my leader?"

"It's not what I think, Sad," Masters parried. "He's the boss, you know that. It's what he thinks. I was lucky to save your life."

"Do you know what's become of that life? I sit in my father's house in the little village of El Guettar. I have no one to talk to, nothing to read but what I left when I went away to school. Nearby, Gorbah draws tourists when there are tourists. They come to see the old Roman fortress, they come to see what was there thousands of years ago. But now? He allows few visitors into the country. Those speak no English, I have a little German, but no Polish, no Czech or Roumanian. A few English-speaking people come from the guerrilla training camp who regard me suspiciously. What am I doing there? They call themselves Sandinistas but turn out to be Americans hungry to talk English. I'm wearing one guy's clothes. My life's going down the drain. Help me, help me, Alan! Remember how much I've done for you."

There was a very long pause. "I can't help you any further with the General, Sad."

"You must! I gave *you* a new life! Give me one. At least say you'll speak for me to him."

Masters tried to be reasonable. "I could wreck my own life here if I did, can't you see that?"

"I say, for what I've done for you, it's a chance you must risk." He took a long breath. "Alan, I conspired to murder for you."

Masters sighed deeply and got to his feet slowly. "You must go now, Mr. Sadriquen." His words were stiff, as if spoken for a legal record. "Your lengthy presence here could prove very embarrassing to me when the guards return, if they haven't already."

"You are dismissing me from your home?"

"I'm afraid that's the way it has to be."

Abu ben-Sadriquen rose with great dignity and held out his hand. "Here, I'm returning the key to your house you once gave me—just in case you have to prove I got in without your consent or knowledge."

Masters received the key and put it carefully into a pocket.

"*You* are the betrayer, Masters." Abu ben-Sadriquen's voice was cold and colorless. "*You* are faithless to those who shared their lives and their eternal destiny with you."

"Get out," Masters said, "before I have you shot."

27.

ROGER PHILLIPS did not anticipate applause. On the other hand, he did not expect dissent.

"By boat?" Ted Boardman sneered. "Why not swim?"

"Boats are tricky and they take forever," Tracy Boardman added.

Even Professor Carver did not think much of the idea. "From what I read they've made the coast impenetrable."

Roger turned moodily to Amanda Miller. "And you, ma'am?" he snapped.

"Very risky."

"What gives with you people?" Roger broke in. "Has everything gone so smoothly that you've lost your heads? That seacoast's our best chance. Professor, you ought to remember that! And as for airplanes, they're fast all right, but what do you do about their Mirage and MIG interceptors? What happens when you fly over airspace you don't belong in? What happens if they stop you before you can take off?"

"I was saying, it's very risky," Amanda resumed evenly, "but in my view, the best way to get out."

"Interceptors can be outsmarted," Ted Boardman muttered. "I've done it before."

"And you're where you want to be in minutes, not slopping around on a goddam sea," Tracy appended heatedly.

"Hold it!" Roger waved a finger at all of them. The room grew quiet. He went to the door, opened it, peered down the corridor to assure himself the caretaker near the steps was still at his station. When he came to the center of the floor, he spoke quietly. "Ted," he began. "Level with me." He saw the quick exchange between the Boardmans. "You've made a score here?"

"Yes."

"Okay." Roger Phillips voiced no objection. "Where's your airplane? How do we get there?"

"Very easy. I've prepared several maps. There's a WAP shuttle. Forty minutes. I got the passes when I arranged the charter. Runs outside government red tape."

"You've filed a flight plan?"

"Of course. Coastal survey. The desert to the south. Museum stuff."

"And you'd head for?"

"Malta."

"Professor, how good is that?"

"This year they're supposedly on good terms. The General has been giving Malta a lot of money. And, I'd assume, trouble. One doesn't know the whole story, of course."

"But the Maltese could take everybody in custody and return them here?"

"A dragon could also reach up from the water and swallow us," Ted Boardman said contemptuously. "You think I've never handled a deal like this before?"

"I forget," Roger Phillips countered, "with high-class hash, you can afford expensive buy-offs."

"You bet your ass. And it also works beautifully on Customs guys who make a couple of hundred yen a year, if that."

Roger nailed him with a look and did not let him move. "You broke your word, Ted," he said coldly.

"So did you, Roger. You said we wanted this guy Masters to help get some research work started again. You're pulling a snatch. I'm running a million dollars worth of dope."

The room was still for a very long time. "Could you do this, Ted?" Roger Phillips spoke without bitterness or anger, in conciliation or surrender, none of them could be sure. "Hold the takeoff for one full day?"

"In case your boat doesn't get through?" Ted Boardman could not resist a laugh.

"It'll be there. My man has been making this run for years. The airplane's being paid for with our money, it's only fair it should play backup."

"It's a deal."

Roger said: "Who goes on the airplane?"

Hands went up slowly—Tracy and Ted Boardman.

"Professor?" Roger Phillips asked.

"You might need my help on the ground."

"Very decent of you, sir. Don't you think you'd be better off in the air?"

The old man shrugged. "A good deal less interesting. I'll stay with you, Roger. Where's our boat plan to put in? One of those little Italian islands in the south Mediteranean?"

Roger nodded and turned to Amanda. "I think you'd be better off with them, Amanda."

"Please don't pull rank. I want the boat," Amanda Miller said earnestly.

"Then it's settled." Roger Phillips sat on the bed and turned to Amanda. "When our man comes here, will we have to deal with a chauffeur?"

"We've got him thinking it's a desert rhapsody and he's promised us it's going to be a private orgy for three."

"And the car?"

"The black Rolls, the General's duplicate. Did you tell me to do that, or was that one of my bright ideas?"

"You drive after he gets here. I'll show you where to go. You pull up here." He had drawn some kind of map and put it before the women.

"Isn't he liable to say something like it's not the right road?" Amanda asked gently.

"No doubt. Tracy, you keep him occupied in back. Come back here in my car after I've got him, pick up Ted—"

"And head for the airport," Ted Boardman interceded. "Very neat game plan. Has anyone considered what happens if your guy decides to make a fight of it? What do you do then?"

"He gets calmed down—with this." A dark gray object materialized like a film effect in the hand of the regius professor emeritus of classical and Islamic history. The old man regarded it shyly. "I've oiled and cleaned it, Roger. Really quite simple, I discovered. It's got six rounds, one in the chamber, and it's on safety."

Roger Phillips did his best to resist a smile. He took the U.S. Army service pistol without comment. "Professor, remember the place the GIs used to call Eagle Rock?"

"Of course."

"Could you manage to get there by yourself without a car?"

"Dear boy, I used to walk there when the only road was a camel path. Good place to meet your boat. On the windward side, I daresay?"

"Within two hours after sunset."

"I'll be there before you."

"I still think you ought to go with the Boardmans."

"See you at Eagle Rock." Walter Evans Carver rose like an imperturbable gentleman who had found himself to be a surplus guest.

When he was gone, Ted Boardman approached Amanda. "Remember what I told you, stay close to me and you'll be all right. Come with us, Mandy."

She replied with mild irony, " No, thanks."

"This country is the pits," Ted went on. "They don't laugh, they don't smile, they catch you on the wrong side of the law, they cut the head off. They've got killers from all over the world, you saw that. Be smart. We'll be safe in Malta while they're still bucking waves."

Tracy walked to Roger Philips's side. "I've got a suggestion of my own. You got into this deal for the lady. She wants to go out on the boat, after you give her the man, you come out with us on the airplane. You earned your money." She offered Amanda a sweet smile. "Would you accept that, Mandy?"

Amanda Miller shrugged.

"There you are, Roger. Your whole package tied with pink ribbons. For once in your life, be smart," she urged. "It's a job, you did what you had to do."

"Okay with you, Amanda?" Roger Phillips asked.

Amanda Miller shrugged again.

"And do I get to keep you company when you're lonely, Tracy? When Ted goes to Lynne or whatever her name is."

"Lynne? Lynne? Who's Lynne? The terrestrial flow is in full flood. It even demands I free you from your commitment to me."

"Trace and I are getting together again," Ted Boardman announced. "We've learned here we really belong to each other."

"Congratulations," Roger said. "Wonderful what miracles a couple of tons of hash can work. I'll go out on the boat."

"We'll wait for you till the day after tomorrow, that's our deal, Roger," Boardman concluded stiffly and turned to Tracy. "We'd better get ready, darling."

Alone, Roger said: "I still think you ought to go with them. I'll have your man, I promise."

"I know that, Roger. Nevertheless—"

"It could get very hot out there on the water. The Russians have taught them how to keep people out and in."

"If the boat goes down, I want to be on it to make sure Masters goes down with it."

"You're a tough lady, Amanda Miller."

"My mother always said I was very unfeminine. Real ladies aren't iron-willed and unbending."

"She was right about you, you know," Roger Phillips said, eyeing her curiously, and added, "and very wrong."

They were seven that morning at Camptown, four men, three women, their English excellent, their attention in class intense, their experience with hardware minimal, willingness to learn, passionate. Italian. Hard. The women especially. If he looked at their tits their lips curled and they muttered some vocable he knew had to be filthy.

Mike Kelly's problem, and theirs, was simple.

A north Italian city.

Winter.

Chauffeur-driven car. Two bodyguards inside with The Object.

Four motorcycles accompany the car, front and back.

Radio communication, two ways.

The Object knows he is an assassination target.

He is well liked by the people.

He must be taken alive.

Unhurt.

Everybody else in his party can be terminated.
He is to be broken without torture.
He will, in time, be set free.
He must not know where he has been held. He must never be able to identify any of his captors or fix the location of his place of imprisonment.
Yet he must be kept alert, hopeful, able to transmit messages, letters in his own hand, read statements for radio transmission.
He is the prime minister.

Everything about Mike Kelly's teaching methods enthralled his students. He was blunt, he was unsentimental, he was as detached as an orthopedist sawing off a leg who has no interest in anything about his Object except the limb. One thing his students made plain: they liked action, not theory.

They had been working without success on the problem for weeks.

The second half was easy. They had all learned much from past mistakes. For example, how to keep The Object from ever being able to identify his place of imprisonment? In the past, The Object had been able to come pretty close by helping police specialists juxtapose routine with day and night duties; meals, music and so on with outside traffic noises and sunlight; daytime activities, with captors' voices coming on duty or leaving. At El Guettar they had devised rooms within rooms, soundproofed and artificially lit on the outside. Large enough for comfort. Even tough Red Brigaders found their breaking point approach and begged to get out when they lost touch with everything in the diabolically planned confusion.

Background music never stopped, popular tunes, bouncy rhythms filled the air with mucilaginous sweetness, blurred all other sounds, smoothed hours into a timeless blur and made all voices sound the same. Meals came at new hours; even bowel function changed.

At the training camp at El Guettar they had proved experimentally that politically mature, high ranking personalities could be broken more easily by methods other than torture or fear of personal safety.

A man of fifty has a family. He does not want them caused pain. He misses them. They learned how to intensify that.

He would have a need for rest, good rest. Sleep. This could be easily granted or taken away for reward or punishment.

His total reeducation could be managed in a short time, Mike Kelly was assured; interrogators and instructors would come armed with documents, statements, financial records. He would break.

The problem, Kelly told the pupils, still remained: how to take The Object without injuring him.

Being under no necessity to observe the holy day the class met at Camptown every Friday for high-tech instruction. For the last two weeks not one of the Brigaders had been able to come up with a suggestion that even made an approach to a solution of a proposed problem. "You call yourself revolutionaries?" Kelly taunted them. "You're schoolkids without imagination or enough brains to find the latrine," he told them.

The Brigaders loved his tough talk. Their responses betrayed their youth—comic-strip ideas, he berated them. They dreamed of laser beams and toxic gases and such.

"You've attacked the problem from one dimension," he told them. Kelly was feeling good on this day. Ana was a find. Sex was not dead in Sarumna, after all. He began to think life might become bearable. If Masters could achieve enough clout to break through the puritanical fog now and then, perhaps he could too. All problems, as he told his students from the training center, had solutions. All questions had answers, just as all situations had the proper hardware for their resolution. Of course! It came to him that sometimes the simplest is the best answer.

"Do you mean," one of the Italian young women said, "that we ought not to limit ourselves to the ground?" These women, Kelly knew, were not like the Swedish girl or those Masters had rounded up. They came to the capital to sharpen their skills, to study the new hardware; they did not flirt, they did not smile. They were hard as deckplate steel. This made the Italian girls curiously sexy to him.

"You mean a coordinated air attack?" one challenged him. This one was something. She fought hard. He was sure she put her heart into other things as passionately.

"Could you manage one?" Kelly asked sarcastically.

"No," two students yelled out.

"Buildings have roofs, haven't they?" the girl countered. "Do you mean that, *maestro*?"

"Precisely," Kelly said. "Where sharpshooters . . ."

"We stage it like a ballet!" another girl exclaimed, astonished at her own cleverness. "Rooftop snipers take care of the escort!"

A solution had come after he thought it all but impossible. You can kill a president in an open car with two or three riflemen, you could make this Object dead with a bazooka, no matter how intense the security around him, but to take him alive . . . *All questions had answers.*

Then it came to him quite suddenly and effortlessly where he had seen the man who avoided him at the party Alan Masters gave. Once there had been a problem of disposing of two Objects . . .

And that man had caved in at a simple, routine investigation.

He did not hear what his Italian revolutionaries were saying. Mike Kelly posed himself another question to which no ready answer was available, but one would, must, come:

What is that pilot from the Andes who squealed a year later doing here?

28.

LATE THAT afternoon, Amanda Miller and Tracy Boardman were waiting for Alan Masters in the shade along one wall of the terrace of the Strand Hotel. The holy day and blasts of furnace heat appeared to have stripped it of staff as well as guests. A new, brisk wind from the south whistled around corners, hot and oppressive, carrying gritty, brown sand fiercely enough to sting bare legs and arms. It had always been hot but a heat they expected and were prepared for and could manage. It was not yet fierce but it felt now like a living thing, malevolent and dangerous.

"This heat," Tracy said, waving her hand before her face like a fan.

"I studied up on it," Amanda said. "It's called the *ghibli* and one book said it's the most unpleasant wind in the world. Professor Carver says the Romans used to give names to their winds. I wonder what they called this."

"Did they have a word for hell?"

"I've no doubt."

"Then this one's the Mouth of Hell. I'm glad to be getting out of this place. I don't think I could take much more."

Amanda sought to raise her spirits. "I understand it gets a lot hotter later. But we'll all be gone."

"I'll be all right. Ted's got me a little worried, though. Never seen him like this before."

"It's called losing your nerve. Happens with advancing age. After this score, maybe you ought to get him into another line of work."

"Funny you should say that. I've been thinking the same thing." A gust whipped so hard they went to a doorway for cover. Where was Masters?

Roger Phillips saw them huddled against a doorway on the terrace as he descended the steps at the front of the Strand Hotel. He acknowledged them with a wave but did not stop his progress to the parking area. Sometimes a boy was stationed there; the desert-borne blasts had even cleared the grounds of security men, uniformed or not. Roger got into the Audi assigned the group and drove it from the hotel grounds. He would circle, backtrack, make a long detour among unpaved back streets before he finally would arrive at the abandoned shed where the Department of Public Works had promised a new building.

In his room, Walter Evans Carver was celebrating a special, if secret, occasion. It was his birthday, his eighty-first, to be exact. He had grown indifferent to enumerating his years a long time before, but on this occasion a divine afflatus, as he would have said, filled his spirit. A private rose of winds cheered him as he had not been cheered for a very long time. He had the feeling that this venture completed a lifetime for him that had embraced everything else a man could want. He loved Sarumna; he knew why people had settled along its coast for so many centuries. Whatever was to happen, he had no doubt he would not ever come here again. He had no regrets; he would complete his life in his own way. His birthday present to himself lay on the bedspread around him, a hundred bits and pieces which he was oiling and refitting like a man with a jigsaw puzzle. *Astonishing that I'm so good with a Sten gun*, he thought.

Ted Boardman was on his bed too, prone, his eyes fixed on the ceiling. He thought of New York harbor, he thought of friends he had who had friends there; figures and numbers kept careening through his head; Eddie Parker would have to understand when he said one-third he did not mean one-third of the street value, in a deal like this there were a lot of payoffs, but there would be enough, maybe more than even he had ever pulled out of one deal.

Malta will be workable. I've done that before with airplanes of this quality and the right papers.

Eddie Parker has a few names in Valletta. If they are out of the business, he says they will know where to send me.

Whoever heard of anybody staying out of the business when the payoff is this big?

The big problem is still to get out of this godforsaken country. The Mach-busting Mirages, don't forget them. You will by flying an aircraft you don't know. If you're lucky, this one won't have any tics. There are a few tricks a guy can use against high-speed jets, but . . . What if no one was looking too hard at Khorfa? What if they were busy elsewhere?

Roger's thinking it's like the old days. Backward Arabs running around in dizzy circles on the water while We Smart Guys whip through in safety. No more. These guys have got new, sophisticated gear, they are tough, mean, smart. They hate us. Roger can't make it. They catch him. Ten seconds, the computer's spitting out our names. What are we doing? We're sitting on the ground at Khorfa, waiting, playing backup, he says he doesn't need us, doesn't he?

If Roger had a chance, it'd be different. Got to lose.

Can you imagine the new stuff they've got on the water? The Mirages I've seen at the end of the airfields are so new I haven't even seen them in the journals.

They'll nail him sure.

Tracy. Christ. So she won't like it. I don't like it. She'll have to live with it. We didn't go into this to die. Roger didn't tell us everything. In a way, he brings this on himself. If Tracy says we're letting him down, what about that? Did he level with us?

Face it. Roger is totalled. Got to save your own ass now, Theodore.

At Camptown, as Friday afternoon wore down, Mike Kelly was by turns enraged and frustrated. He was calling every official number he knew. He had never had occasion to find that the holy day was so rigidly observed. At length, since he had learned the night before how close to Camptown was the residence of Hafir Azziz, he decided to visit him. For what he had in mind, he needed some high-level assurance. The two men had met for the first time at Alan's party. A minister of culture was not exactly the kind of official Kelly was accustomed to deal with, but this was, for him, a last resort.

Azziz brought Kelly in and soon confided his own doubts about the whole group.

"What do you know about them, Mr. Minister?" Kelly began. He knew, from a long time ago, how to modulate his speech for cabinet ministers.

"Professor Carver we know very well indeed. He is—was—has been an old friend, of mine, of the nation's. Phillips has been here before as a scholar, a protégé, you might say, of the professor's. Of the others we know little."

"And you let them into your country? Isn't that kind of unusual for you people?"

"It is. But they are here under Professor Carver's sponsorship."

"Then about the other three you only know what their passports tell you."

"That is correct."

"And they could be anybody?"

"You mean CIA agents, of course?" Azziz made a little smile. "We have reason to believe the professor has been approached many times. He has always said no."

"But it is possible?"

"Possible. I do not believe it likely he would be part of anything subversive."

"Forgive me, sir. Why not?"

"Too individualistic, not at all the type."

"Suppose the professor did not know, sir?" Kelly pursued. "I have had some background in this work. I can assure you it isn't always necessary for each individual in a group to know its real purpose."

Azziz hesitated for some time. "That could be," he conceded.

"Miss Miller, what about her?" Kelly resumed.

"Only routine examination, when the party entered the country; I am told it was established she is the financial support of this survey group. There is an address of a research foundation in Beverly Hills, California. She carried letters of credit, substantial money in cash and traveler's checks and so on, all in her name. So, by the way, did Mr. Phillips, but it was decided they might need such large sums to do their survey work. I understood that."

"It's possible this lady could be the mission chief," Kelly said.

"You met her at the party. You think there is someone in Washington who would give her command of so dangerous a venture?"

"Yes."

"She's so— so— well, so implausible."

"I'd say, sir, that makes my point. What about the other two?"

"Boardman is designated an air-service specialist. The lady is his wife, though I can now see how doubtful that appears after watching her and Alan on the terrace last night. In any event, she is listed as assistant air service svecialist, and papers we saw prove she is also a pilot licensed to fly jet airplanes, as is the man said to be her husband."

"I would find those qualifications of hers more interesting than whether they are married or not, which is beside the point here, right, sir?"

Azziz hesitated thoughtfully. "I would agree."

"What do you know about the man Boardman?"

"Nothing other than the information on his passport as rendered into Arabic."

"I have encountered this man before. May I respectfully suggest you message Washington for more?"

"I planned to, after a few moments with you, Mr. Kelly. This is Friday, you understand, and we observe it strictly except for a national emergency." Azziz rose to bring the meeting to a close. "Thank you for your concern. I hope it is misplaced, of course."

"I've got one interest in all this, Mr. Minister. To keep Alan Masters healthy."

"You think he could be involved somehow?" Azziz's eyes widened perceptibly.

Kelly shrugged. "Or a target, Or a means to an end. Knowing, or not knowing. Who can tell?"

"What do you suggest we do until tomorrow?"

"Surveillance, of course."

"That can be managed easily. They are driving assigned cars. Needless to say, every police station has been alerted to keep track of them if they go anywhere but to the old archeological site, or to the airport."

"That's only good as far as it goes, sir. Those cars also require protection."

"Protection? From—?"

"For," Kelly said. "For you people. I can manage that for you."

"I don't understand you, Mr. Kelly."

"Those cars could be very useful. If they tried to pull something." Mike Kelly brought his two hands together, lifted them and parted them quickly. "We have a device that would give us what we need if they were within twenty miles."

Azziz knew that indicated an explosion. "I haven't the authority for that."

"I'm not saying it's needed. I'm saying you ought to have it installed on a stand-by basis. If it's not used, no one's the wiser."

"I can see why the General prizes you, Mr. Kelly," Azziz said. "You can go ahead. I'll take the responsibility until I reach someone more directly involved in military affairs."

"Thanks, Mr. Minister."

"Do not endanger Alan Masters. The General and many others regard him as a national asset."

"I regard him as a personal asset."

"I beg you, be careful for his safety." He hesitated at the door. "If they are what you suspect, do you think Alan Masters is working with them?"

"No."

"Then that they are planning to use him somehow?"

"Damned fine-looking ladies. A lonely man. Of course we're all lonely here, but not all of us know how to do something about it." He liked ending on a casual and cheery note. He held out his hand.

"Thank you again for coming by," the minister of culture, who held $2 million worth of shares in SwisTurInt, said to his visitor, who did not know that his own $2.25 million lay in the same consortium.

201

Four hundred miles to the east, the coast of Sarumna curves into the sea to create a vast gulf. Hamaldan, the nation's second city, is, as always, recovering from death throes. A deeply quiet city, it has been sacked and ruined endless times. East and west, wars have engulfed it from earliest history until just the other year when the Africa Korps was expelled. On this day, it steamed in the heat, but no harsh wind disturbed its tranquil surface. General Mohammed Abdullah was finally meeting with his closest supporters in the Revolutionary Council after keeping them waiting for many days.

The adventure to the west had blown up in his face; the imposition of armed forces into the southern neighbor had angered the French, who still had one hundred Mirage fighters to deliver on contract; to his east one of the Arab traitors who were pawns of the loathsome Western imperialists had once again called him a war-hungry maniac.

The General had been in seclusion. He was seen only at his prayers five times a day; he saw no one at any other time. He was fasting, scourging his soul, as if preparing himself to receive a revelation, or at least a divine inspiration. It came to him that morning, so impressively he broke his own rule about observing any holy day as strictly as the holiest.

For two hours he lectured his closest friends in the council. He refused to believe that the same One who had enriched their land like none other in all the world meant for the nation to remain powerless. Sitting on the gulf, his eyes fixed westward, he said, he began to dream of Britain, *Great* Britain. A small island, a small population, it had dominated the world. Why? Whence its power? It came to him that wealth was the source. Whole continents could be bought, royal families surrendered power to rivers of sterling, thousands and thousands of mercenaries enlisted to fight under its banner. Wealth used as a weapon was its power.

"Our land is blessed, as our national song says," the General said, "but we have not been alert to use those blessings as Allah meant them to be."

He was pale and unshaven, his cheekbones were hollow from hunger and sleeplessness. His intimates had seen him like this before; it was what made this man so unique among all men. It foretold a momentous decision, religious in tone and perhaps in content as well. He had naysayers in the Revolutionary Council, although the world believed otherwise. There were a few men of power in Zarplis who felt his adventures could lead to chaos and destruction. There were holy men who wondered about his strange alliance with the Russians, who spat on every sacred prophet from Abraham to Muhammad himself. His listeners in Hamaldan knew the personal risks their leader was taking in seeing himself as the man who would create a new, a greater Britain.

"We have wealth, more than that nation of shopkeepers and foreign traders ever possessed!" the General said.

"We must learn to expand our power in ways beyond their comprehension," he went on hoarsely. "They ruined their land with filthy smoke and ugly mines. Our land remains virgin. Our blessings multiply abroad."

At least one of the listeners among the Revolutionary Council thought the General was beginning to sound materialistic, a sin he frequently inveighed against, but he kept his silence. He knew the President-for-Life was referring to his private adviser, Alan Masters.

"We must look beyond using our wealth to buy more wealth, to expand our power," the General said. "We must look beyond these shores, as that island people once did . . ."

Even the listener who thought his chief somewhat materialistic could not help being stirred by the first hints of God-given greatness. It came to him that in the past he had been only routinely friendly with Alan Masters. *I must repair that oversight*, he thought.

29.

As capriciously as it had burst into life, the *ghibli* died; or paused only to blast the scoured earth again; no one could ever predict its moods. The oven heat remained. In the long, slow sunset, the black car floated into the sand-dusted grounds of the Strand Hotel with majestic calm. All its tinted windows were up except the one at the driver's side. When the Rolls saloon circled to approach the steps, Tracy Boardman turned to Amanda Miller. "Uh-uh, you've got problems."

Alan Masters had not come alone. The driver was a bulky Sarumnan tough boy in the uniform of the Special Forces, hat dead-centered on a wood block of a head, his face chiseled into the glowering glare standard with the green uniform.

He was armed, they both saw that when he emerged from the automobile, his shoulders pulled back, hostile eyes turning from one side to another in search of an enemy. His clothes bulged with the tools of a modern bodyguard's trade. He pulled open the rear door. Out sprang Alan Masters in flawless white trousers and a blazer, wind whipping his hair and trouser legs. He could see Amanda Miller's hand on Tracy Boardman's elbow stop any move toward him. His head swiveled to the uniformed man; he understood at once the order to wait there.

"You misled us, Alan," Amanda Miller began.

"I'm terribly sorry, but—"

"Nothing to be sorry about." Amanda forced a little smile. "We won't go."

Tracy was faultless. "She's right, it'd be no fun whatsoever."

"You must understand," Alan Masters said, "I live by certain rules here. These fellows are marvelously discreet. Like our Secret Service. They don't see, they don't hear, they don't talk. I know. I've been with them before."

"They breathe, Alan," Amanda said. "Let's forget it."

"It's also insulting," Tracy said with an air of innocence that raised an eyebrow in Amanda. "As if we could be dangerous to the great Alan Masters."

"No hard feelings." Amanda hoped she sounded more convincing than she felt. "It just didn't work out. We'll be okay this weekend, Alan. Let's go inside, Trace. This wind's too much."

"Yes, darling," Tracy said.

"I'm trapped," Masters pleaded, following them.

"How sad for you," Amanda countered. "And I don't like feeling like Anglo-slave-girl-transported-under-guard-to-harem. The whole thing has become rather distasteful." She followed Tracy Boardman to the foyer of the lobby.

"I beg you to wait." A cluster of perspiration blossomed on his forehead as they silently confronted each other for a long time. He looked at his ladies, bare arms, bare shoulders in the soft, fading light, delicate, cool fabrics accenting the flow of bodies his eyes knew even better. "Please, give me just one minute."

When they were alone, Tracy said: "You are somethin', baby. Where'd you pick up all that fancy-lady shit?"

"You think maybe we could take him anyway?"

"You out of your mind? You see the armament on the guy?"

"Roger has a gun."

"Against what Soldier Boy is carrying it'd be like throwing popcorn at a tank."

Through the door, they watched Alan Masters and the bodyguard engage in what appeared to be a somber exchange. "We can't let him get away, Tracy," Amanda pleaded to her friend.

"I don't know about him. I know Ted and I have got to split soon to make the last shuttle. Soldier Boy's saying no, no, no."

"We can't lose him now." This time Amanda Miller seemed to plead to someone in an echelon higher than Tracy Boardman.

"Those are hand grenades hanging from his shoulder. Ain't

that a cute touch for a desert orgy?" Tracy offered. "Take it easy, Amanda. Never underestimate the power of a man's balls. That one wants his party a hell of a lot more than we do, remember that."

The soldier was showing his hands, whether in anger or disgust they could not tell. They saw a nervous glance-around by Masters and a fat roll of bills produced from one of his pockets. The hands seemed to grow even more positive.

"Or the power of a heavy bribe," Amanda said as the arms froze in midair. "Look." The arms descended slowly. One reached out and closed fingers around a bundle. They could see Masters talking hard to the soldier, probably promising more than money. In time, there was a sharp salute. The soldier departed with evident reluctance.

"Hurrah for our side," Tracy said when Masters returned.

"Told you." Masters embraced her, hands roaming the rise and fall of her body. Amanda threw her own arms around them both.

"I almost underestimated you, Alan," she murmured.

Tracy led him into the rear of the Rolls. Amanda took the wheel. As the car pulled out of the hotel grounds, she saw them in the mirror locked in an embrace so beautiful it warmed her heart.

URGENT!

TO: ENGLISH TRANSLATION DIVISION

Take note of accompanying transmission just received from Colonal Azeiri, Washington. This office recommends immediate translation into Arabic, despite transmission breaking the rule against use of unbeliever language in official communication.

Translate, reproduce ten copies, and bring by hand to this office for delivery to the President as quickly as possible.

Hakal, Deputy Chief, Message Center

To strict observers of the holy day, the sun had not yet fallen below the horizon. The recipient of this communication, Ahmed Memir, twenty-eight, spent five brilliant years at the University of Michigan before being forcibly convinced he and his family would be better off if he aborted his mathematical studies. Young Memir had learned one thing on being drafted for his present position: *Follow rigid rules rigidly.*

He glanced at Hakal's urgent message, had no doubt it was as importunate as claimed, but without hesitation delayed work on it until the holy day was truly gone with the sunset.

He returned to a copy of a magazine highly prized in the nation by illiterate and literate alike despite its mere possession calling for five years at hard labor. "Kim demands that the men in her life be as free and uninhibited as she is. Joy and ecstasy are all that matters, she believes, and she says her body is an instrument for her and her lovers to reach ever-greater passionate heights," the caption read under the pink gold of the skin of her thighs and the tiny rosebud which unashamedly peeked at him from its whispery bower. Memir breathed deep. He had almost an hour before the world would overtake him again.

Hafir Azziz, as Minister of Culture, lacked the access to the General he would have liked. But he had a young friend whom he had brought into the government and who had risen swiftly in the professional and personal esteem of Mohammed Abdullah.

Brigadier Hussain al-Shalhi now headed the People's Special Police. Its assignments came from the General and his own staff. Azziz told the brigadier about Mike Kelly's far-fetched story and of the possible collusion between Alan Masters and those who had been allowed into the country with the distinguished Professor Walter Evans Carver.

He had, he confessed, been generous to the old man, perhaps too much so. As for Alan Masters, his relationship to the General was special and unique. Betrayal was a possibility, unlikely as it would appear to be.

"All these people have been moving freely around the country in three cars provided them by my ministry."

"All of these people have been moving freely around the country in three cars provided them by my ministry."

"What do you want of me, dear friend?" al-Shalhi asked.

"Your authority for what I have already done. Perhaps I was too reckless."

Hussain al-Shalhi had grown restless during almost eight

months of domestic calm. The cascade of wealth pouring into the nation was greater than ever. The only man in the world from whom he took official orders had not called on him in a long time.

"I'm delighted to back you on this, Azziz."

He had spared himself at least from disgrace.

Now he could wait and let the events of the hours to come dictate his moves.

Outside, Azziz bowed his head as he heard the loudspeakers high on a minaret beckon the faithful to the last prayer of the holy day.

Laura was the name of the Italian girl whose mouth always seemed to form a dirty word every time he looked at her.

Mike Kelly grinned when he saw her turn quickly away after a class at Camptown. "Want to go on a job with me, *cara*?" he said. Long experience taught him what turned on these chicks.

"Up yours," her lips seemed to be saying, or some such equivalent.

"Blow up a car or two, a few foreign enemies."

The snarl uncurled. "You kidding?"

"Fancy new hardware. Bought it myself from the same people who supply the CIA." He knew that would grab her between the legs.

"For real, *maestro*?"

"Beautiful stuff," he said teasingly. "They've got it in Langley and I've got it in Zarplis and in all the world that's it. Radio controlled. You don't get to see the fireworks, that's the only drawback."

"I'll go," Laura said.

"Afterward, I'll show you the mirror over my bed. You ever ball on top of a swan?"

Her lips formed a dirty vocable under a smile. Still, it was a chance no committed revolutionary could properly resist. Like Tracy Boardman, at that moment rolling with Alan Masters in the back of a car, letting his hand play games under her dress, kissing him, making obscene noises into his ear, Laura never hesitated at doing what had to be done.

Amanda Miller pulled the Rolls over the curb and brought it to a stop beside the wall with the poster of the Public Works Ministry. They were engaged on the floor behind her; she could hear them; she could not see them. She flipped the switch that unlocked all the doors.

One behind her was pulled open quickly. She wheeled to see Roger thrusting the .45 into Alan Masters.

"All right, mother-fucker!" he snarled. "Get out before I blow your fucking brains all over the fucking inside of your fucking car! *Move.*"

She thought him fucking convincing. So did Alan Masters.

30.

"THIS IS your best time of day." A Toyota Land Cruiser, high off the ground from extra-heavy-duty shock absorbers and desert equipment, wheeled into the entrance of the Strand Hotel. "The sun's down but it's not yet dark," Mike Kelly went on, eyes straight ahead, certain he had transfixed the lady beside him, as older teachers infatuate a student. "Amateurs think the dark of night's td to a stop in the parking area. He did not make a move to get out. "Work slow. Always slow. If someone's watching, don't look busy or anxious." Mike Kelly turned to his passenger. "In this light everything's hazy and blurred. Besides, today Allah's with us, the *ghibli* clears out people and makes it hard to see clearly. You don't have to come out, sweetie." He reached behind for two packages, each not much larger than a shoebox.

"I want to see what you do, *maestro*," Laura said.

"Come on."

They found two of the cars he was looking for, side by side. "Stupid," he muttered. He was under each in less than four minutes and scrambling back to the Land Cruiser holding his student's hand while she was still uncertain if he had begun.

"Let's go."

"That's *all?*"

"Damned clever these Americans. *Us* Americans," he amended. Inside the car, he brushed sand from his hands and face.

"So fast?" Even in the almost-dark he could see how wide her eyes had opened. "You don't have to wire to the starter, bolt to the underframe?"

"I'll show you the brochure and the specs—specifications—later, baby." He paused briefly. "There's a third car to take care of. What would you do?"

"Wait here for it."

"Dangerous," he instructed her. "You never know who could be watching. Someone who'd see a car hang around he knows doesn't belong. Might remember it. Better to go and come back."

"You're right."

He put a hand on her knee. "I'm never wrong, baby. Say it."

"You're never wrong, *maestro*."

"Say you like me."

"I like you."

"Say, 'Take me to your room, Mike.'"

Too independent for such games, Laura put moist, parted lips to his and pushed him away after a second or two and laughed. "Will you let me connect the third car?"

"It's a deal."

She kissed him more passionately than before.

Roger Phillips had him stretched out on his stomach, his arms above his head. "What is this? Who are you? Who's doing this to me? Why?" Masters gasped into the silt of a thousand windstorms. "What do you want?"

"Turn over, Mr. Masters." He had to be kicked lightly. Roger kneeled over him as he tied his hands with a length of nylon rope. "Nothing's going to happen to you if you do what I say. This too tight?" The head shook gratefully. Roger fixed the knot. "Try to free your hands, Mr. Masters." The frightened man complied but the knot tightened. "My Boy Scout years weren't wasted after all. Try to relax."

Roger Phillips went to Tracy. "You were great in there, Trace. Thanks. You'd better get started."

"You understand about Ted and me, don't you?"

He had other things to deal with at the moment. "I'm trying." He gave it all the conviction he could muster.

"The aura over the terrestrial flow—the karma is confused."

"That makes it tough to take. Ted needs you; leave it at that."

"So you *can* find it in your heart to forgive me—despite what it means to your own karma?"

211

"It hurts, but I'm trying, Tracy." Out of the corner of his eye he saw Amanda grinning. "You'd better get going."

The farewells between the woman allowed a less florrid exchange. They exchanged a kiss on the cheek. "Thanks, Tracy. You were great, no kidding."

"You should come out with Ted and me, it'd be much safer for you."

"Everything I ever wanted is happening."

In a moment, the Audi was gone in a cloud of dust. Amanda found Roger beside her with the service pistol.

"How much does it really hurt?" she teased.

"I may not survive. Ever handle one of these?" he broke off.

"And my stepfather a devout member of the National Rifle Association? He believed firearms was up there with Motherhood and God." She took it as one must a loaded .45, carefully, made sure it was on safety, sprang the clip, pulled back the slide to make certain there was no shell in the chamber, put back the cartridges. "However, this was another thing I could do my mother didn't like."

Masters lay so still he seemed dead. Fear seemed to have rendered him immobile. "All right, Mr. Masters, you can now get up." The body did not stir. Roger kneeled to help him to his feet. "We don't want to hurt you. Do what we tell you and nothing will happen to you. Now get into the front seat of your car next to the wheel."

The figure rose, yellow desert dust falling from it. "Now go to the car, slowly, everything slowly from here on out, so there's no misunderstanding." Masters was on his feet, eyes straight ahead. "Into the car, please."

"Just don't shoot me."

"Miss Miller is going to sit right in back of you. Any shouting or gestures with your head and you're dead. Are we clear on that?"

"I'll do everything you want."

The black Rolls descended the curb to the pocked sidestreet and headed for the main road that ran into the Corniche and beyond. Life was beginning in the city after the long holy day. Street lamps were going on. Traffic was building up. Buses, passenger cars, taxis, delivery vans and semidetached trucks on their way to the off-loading pumps on the docks honked, blatted, beeped and even trumpeted the first notes of the "Colonel Bogey March." When the presidential sedan was sighted, every one of them pulled aside as if it were an ambulance. At the entrance to the Strand, Roger Phillips thought he saw the Audi turn into the hotel from the inside lane.

It was the Audi, all right.

Tracy Boardman parked the car with the others and hurried past something that looked like a big Greyhound bus that was just pulling up behind her. She took the steps to her room quickly and smiled to the hall boy in his chair, somnolent as always.

She was surprised to find Ted on the bed. "It's all set. Let's split," she announced. Before she could reach for her suitcase, Ted's hand held hers down.

"Leave everything."

There were a few things she wanted in the bathroom. When she came out she found her husband thoughtful in the middle of the floor.

"I've been thinking about Roger and Mandy and Carver. It doesn't look good, Tracy."

"You know how I feel about such negative thoughts. Please don't talk that way. So far they're doing fine."

"Beginner's luck plus amateur guts. I'm thinking about a pro like that guy with the beard. How close is he to Alan Masters?"

"This weekend he won't be. Masters is supposedly partying on the desert with Mandy and me. Now let's get started."

He had other plans. Ted Boardman had his own sense of the smell of deals that worked out and others that were doomed to flop. He'd seen it happen more than once. You never knew. Sometimes everything began well and, bang, it broke apart. Other times, it was a mess from the start. And suddenly, it worked, click, click, click, every planned move fell into place. You had to trust to the unknown instinct that told him Roger wasn't going to make it. If they got to the rendezvous, the guy wouldn't be there; if he was there, they couldn't get out of the harbor; if they got out of the harbor— The instinct kept thumping hard, They won't, they can't make it.

"We're not going to wait for them, Tracy."

"You promised."

"Not to commit suicide. If they get caught, it means we get caught. Sitting on the ground. It doesn't make sense."

"You talk as if they've been caught. They've done the tricky part, getting Masters. I really don't like the flow of your consciousness, Ted. Let's go."

"I want to save our asses, don't you see?"

"You're talking of betraying a man whose karma once ran close to mine. I don't wish to discuss it any more."

She turned from him and started for the door. *She can be handled*, he knew, *when she knows what the score is, she'll stop that cosmic shit and think straight.*

He caught up with her as she was coming into the hotel lobby, filled with freshly arrived tourists, not often seen in this city. He followed her outside. She stopped on the terrace, looking for the Audi she'd left there only to find a transcontinental-style bus blocking it. Someone dressed in Bermuda shorts, white knee-length socks, and a white yachting cap thought they were admiring the vehicle.

Behind him, the monstrous white cube astride a dozen wheels was emblazoned:

Deutsche Demokratische Republik
GRÜSSE AN UNSERE SARUMNISCHEN KAMERADEN!
    Revolutionäre Turisten-Kulturorganisation

And in Arabic, which none of them, inside or outside, could read, it proclaimed:

"All Honor to the German Guests of Our Great Revolution!"
    —General Mohammed Abdullah

"Bin ich im Wege?" the skipper asked.

"Sorry, no sprech Deutsch," Ted Boardman replied.

"You speak English!" the man responded eagerly. "I speak English! I am in charge. We are from East Germany. We go tonight for three days into the desert. That is your Audi? I am sorry, we had no alternative. Your car was left in a forbidden zone. I will move ours in a moment. Someone is checking the tires."

"Will it take long?" Tracy asked.

"We rest here for a warm wash and a hot dinner. You see, we live aboard this vehicle." Tracy's eyes went skyward. He was plainly proud of his baby. "We have twelve wheels, we—"

"Please—we're in something of a hurry, Mr.—"

"I am Heinz Puening. Dresden Workers' Tourist Confederation. The largest in the German Democratic Republic. Perhaps you would like to see the vehicle while we wait, entirely self-contained, we sleep, we bathe, we wash, we prepare meals, everything in the one vehicle. Spectacular, how you say, no?"

"Let's take one of the other cars," Tracy said to Ted.

However, even as she spoke the East German was mounting the bus and although it took another few moments, it did not seem decent to Ted to use one of the other cars when the guy had gone to all that trouble.

Five kilometers from the center of the city, the road begins to show its age. Stanchions topped by French-designed lamps come to an end; the center divider disappears. Soon even the old street lights are gone and the ancient dark envelopes the country. Wheels begin to encounter breaks in the roadway deep enough to humble the most aggressive drivers. The *ghibli* was an unseen monster, breathing black fire in the infinite dark, which had not made up its mind whether to pounce or to retreat for another time back into the deep of the Sahara. It could be seen in the swirling whirlpools of sand that blew before the car's lights. The Rolls moved forward, imperturbable as ever, over ruts, potholes and corduroy macadam. Inside, the green glow from the instrument panel lit ghostly faces.

"Are you going to kill me?" Masters asked after the road began to fall apart badly.

"I hope not," Roger said.

He was looking to his left, to a dark sea somewhat obscured by the desert dust from the landmass. Far out on the water he could make out pinpoints of lights dancing on the waiting supertankers.

"Are you CIA?" Masters pursued a little later.

"Every American in Africa is CIA, you know that," Roger Phillips said.

Masters said nothing for a long time. Finally: "You're not

CIA. I'd know. I have powerful friends in Washington. Why are you doing this to me? Whom do you represent?"

"Shut up, Mr. Masters," Roger said.

The road began to deteriorate. There had been plans for a magnificent stretch of concrete from Zarplis to Hamaldan and beyond to the border of the eastern neighbor. But Hamaldan and Zarplis have historically always been torn with mutual distrust and dislike, even before the arrival of the Prophet's armed zealots more than a thousand years ago. The subsequent deep differences between them on how strictly His Word was to be followed did not encourage communication, even now that Sarumna was a free nation.

He slowed down. The road to the promontory broke off. There had always been a marker, one of those created by idle hands during World War II had still stood when he had last been there: *Brooklyn, 4,540* miles, and all the other places homesick boys in an unfathomable land once dreamed of: *Cincinnati, 5,138* and *Manchester, 2,164* and *Des Moines, 5,124, Jacksonville, 4,918, Glasgow, 2,872, Leeds, 2,191, Fort Wayne, 5,124, Laramie, 6,129, Stockton, 7,997,* even *Melbourne, 14,191.* It was gone, at least invisible. But he knew the turnoff. Some roads were ineradicable, Professor Carver's old camel path. The Rolls traversed it with no less difficulty than it had found on the main road. They began to hear the sea through the upturned windows, and the whistle of the wind.

He brought the car to a stop. "You stay here, Masters. Remember, we won't hesitate to shoot at any move, even if it's a crazy idea in your head." A gesture of his head ordered Amanda outside.

A billion watts from the car's interior lights blinded them when he opened the door. Amanda stumbled when she came out because she had not let her eyes get used to the dark when she rushed to Roger Phillips's side.

"We made it! You did it! You did it!"

He caught her before she fell. "It worked, that's all. Everything dropped into place just as it was supposed to."

"No, no!" She clung to him. "It didn't just happen. You worked it. You're wonderful!" She pressed her head to his chest. "Thank you, thank you." He thought he felt a sob.

His hand stroked her head. "You were pretty good in there

yourself, Amanda. The isolated weekend so he won't be missed was a great idea. And so was using this car."

"I told you I'd be helpful." She held herself even closer to him.

"Am I wrong about you? Are you inconsequential, basically helpless, foolish?"

Her arms fell slowly from him. "I'm sorry."

He recognized a vestige of a woman he had almost forgotten. "Of course you're not. What an extraordinary lady you are. Or should I say, both of you are? One of you"—he took her into his arms again—"is still that mouse-girl in the oleanders and the other's a powerhouse who's not above seducing the seducer. Which one's the real Amanda Miller?"

"Which do you prefer?"

"Would the real you squeeze that trigger if you had to?"

"Yes," she said without hesitation. "Though it would make you an accessory to murder on top of everything else you've done for me, which would be rotten of me."

"They execute you here for a lot less, so don't hold back on my account." He spotted a nearby ledge from which he could keep the car in sight and led her to it.

"I have killed, you know," she said softly.

"You what?"

"Killed. Animals. I'm sentimental about them. It wasn't easy. My stepfather again. He felt it was a duty, like loving country and God. He started me with targets and weaned me on jackrabbits. I was able to graduate to coyotes. When I was twelve I refused to take a shot at a standing deer. He didn't talk to me for a week. And I never picked up a gun again, until tonight."

"And an old lady who never liked anything about you. How lucky you were."

"Knowing my father, that's where I became lucky. He was a man. He made me a woman, or start to be one anyway." There was a silence. It came to Roger Phillips that he had spoken insensitively and stupidly. "You would have liked him," she went on. "I suppose he did some things he shouldn't have. The jury and a lot of judges sure as hell thought so. He did what a lot of men were doing at a time when everybody was pushing and stretching the laws and making money to the breaking point. If it had worked out he'd still be considered the ordinary citizen's benefactor. When a financier can't produce the big bucks, no one in the world wants to think anything good about him. Anyway, my father paid the price society demanded. He served his time. He had the guts to try to come back. Perhaps you see now why I wanted to do all this, why I'm so very happy we're here this very minute."

Roger released her but took her hand and kissed it. "I'm sorry, Amanda."

"I don't know what'll happen when all this is over—I mean, they're all kinds of laws, maybe we—"

"I wouldn't worry about that now. We've got our man and an hour or two until we're picked up, so let's concentrate on that, okay?"

"Yes, of course. Sorry."

Their heads turned to the car. What was Masters thinking at this moment? Only a slight lapping against the rocks broke the quiet. The wind had become barely a whisper. They found themselves staring into the distant dark until at length the crunch of footsteps brought them to their feet. Professor Walter Evans Carver had stopped at a gathering camel market on the way, he announced. They had told him there that their own reading of the prevailing winds predicted a relatively quiet night.

Roger Phillips took his seat on the ledge again. "All we have to do now is wait."

"For whom do we wait?" the professor said idly, taking a place beside him and Amanda.

"You may have met him when we were here before. Colin Hume—"

"Remember him well. Englishman, a scoundrel—"

"No, sir. A gentleman in a long tradition of—"

"Levantine smugglers and buccaneers." The professor broke this off. "He is a good man for this moment." He turned to Amanda. "And with long experience in smuggling along this coast and in these waters. We can rest easy, my dear."

The waiting began. It was a burden they would have to share, they understood that. It would not be helped by thinking about it or talking about it. You had to put your mind to something else. A man named Colin Hume was on his way; he knew where he had to be; they were here.

"See those lights way out on the horizon?" Professor Carver, after a long time, began only to fill the emptiness. "The great new tankers. Symbols of the modern age. Destroyers and saviors of our life. Built on a small island halfway around the world by a badly defeated foe. Each is larger than any floating vessel ever built in man's long history. Sink all of them and the Western world goes cold and dark and immobile. Without them, we are back to draft animals and steam. Hence, I say, bless all ships tonight on all waters." This made him, like Roger Phillips and Amanda Miller, think of a boat heading toward them. "Sorry," the professor said.

"Are they corrupt here?" Amanda asked, to cover the old man's embarrassment.

"No more than we are," the professor began again. "We being the oil companies, bankers, spot-market dealers, ourselves as consumers and the world's largest wasters of this precious resource. The General is a religious fanatic, hence dangerous. The others are trapped by illusions about themselves, just as we are. You must understand that a mere twenty-five years ago the finest political minds in the world said that this country could not exist. The Bedus followed their sheep as they had for a thousand years. A small people barely endured on a narrow strip of green along the seacoast, this oasis in which we sit now. Others found a hard and bitter life in the desert—the toughest in the world.

"This country not only could not exist, those great minds said, it had nothing to support it. One lone American company was drilling for oil. It had been in the desert for years without success and kept saying the possibilities were nil. Well, Sarumna is one of the richest nations in the world. Are they corrupt? . . . Of course, when awesome wealth generates maniacal ambition and dreams of a pan-Islamic federation it will lead to the purchase of an atomic weapon to assure any enemy's destruction . . ." The professorial voice drifted off. "End of lecture. Sorry again. I'm trying to help pass the time."

Somewhat later, Amanda rubbed her hands briskly. "Damned wind."

"Be glad of it," Carver said. "This one's supposed to bring good luck to travelers."

"Is this the *ghibli* or does it have another name?"

Roger Phillips got to his feet suddenly, as if he saw what he was waiting for out there in the dark. But when they came up to him he turned back to the ledge. "It'll come from around there. There'll be strobe flashes every few minutes. Not in a regular pattern, of course, that would be dangerous. No running lights. But Colin knows these waters. He was never more than a little late in the old days."

"When you and he were engaged in stealing artifacts of great value, eh, Roger?" the professor chuckled.

"No, sir, for me he moved only equipment vital to the unbroken work we were engaged in."

"We had one or two other scholars who functioned in the great tradition of Napoleon, Lord Elgin and some of our finer museums, however. And for them Mr. Colin Hume worked in his tradition of the great English buccaneers, Amanda."

"Thank God for English buccaneers," Roger said.

"Amen," Amanda said.

This line of conversation petered out too. When the sea wind stiffened—later; they did not know whether one moment had passed or many—Amanda Miller said:

"It's getting cold."

"For shame," Roger Phillips teased her. "And you brought up in Arizona. Didn't they teach you the desert is frigid, it's the sun that's hot?"

"Did you not bring something warm, Amanda?" the professor asked.

"I couldn't."

"Why not?" Roger Phillips asked testily.

"I was on my way to an orgy, remember?"

He had forgotten, all that was so long ago. "I'm sorry."

The professor chose not to comment. They went back to listening to the wind and the slosh of the waves against the rocks.

"I've never been to an orgy," Amanda began again. No one seemed eager to pick up this gambit. "I wonder if I missed anything?"

There was a continued silence.

"Have you?" she pursued some moments later.

"Have I what?" Roger replied, after a pause.

"Been to an orgy?"

He did not want to look to the dark sea. "That depends on what you call an orgy."

"That's part of my problem. I don't know what happens. It was easy enough to figure out what our man in the car had in mind. A little acrobatics, and there it is, trio music. But how does everybody play when it's a quartet? Five? A quintet, with piano, so to speak? A whole orchestra of whatever they're called."

"Orgiasts," the professor volunteered.

"Thank you. Do all the orgiasts break up into smaller, more convenient groups? Do they play ensemble? Is there a leader?"

"Do shut up, Amanda, please," Roger said.

"Sorry, it's cold and I was only trying to pass the time."

"Roger, dear boy," the professor began after a pause, to revive her worthy purpose of blotting out time; they could tell that by his tone of voice, "you can surely instruct Amanda about Greek and Roman orgies. They were not so simpleminded or single-purposed as ours, judging from Ovid and Petronius, do you agree?"

"All that food and drink would ruin a modern one, that's for sure," Roger Phillips said without interest.

The professor looked over to Amanda. She caught the glance and got some encouragement from it to continue doing what she could to pass the time.

"What I'd really like to know, is who does what and to whom?"

This was too much even for so profound a classical scholar as Walter Evans Carver. "Really, Amanda," he said.

"And how," she went on, "and with what, and when."

"You're cute," Roger snapped at her. "If that isn't too patronizing a word to use at this stage of history. Is charming better? You're cute and/or charming, that okay? But cut it, huh? Say," he broke off, "your teeth are chattering. What's he doing inside while you're freezing to death? Let's put you in the car."

He got up and lifted her to her feet. They went to the car and opened the door.

The light blinded Masters. Roger reached in, grabbed his blazer and pulled him out and motioned Amanda in.

"You'll never get away with it, you know," Masters muttered, lost in the dark.

"You can save all that." Roger took his forearm like a blind man's.

"His police—the best—he's got the best—they won't let you take me."

"Yes, yes, we know all that."

"A hundred million—that's what he's spending with the Russians for sophisticated coastal patrol armament and training." Roger Phillips had him near the ledge. "We'll all be killed," he wailed. "It doesn't make sense. What do you want of me?"

"Sit down and shut up."

"Insane! It's insane. They spot you, they'll kill you! Me too!" He waved his tied hands above his head.

Professor Carver loomed over him suddenly from the dark, a figure he had never seen before. "Do be still, Masters," it uttered with professorial emphasis, and Masters was cowed. He fell to the ground, sat, elbows on his knees, head resting on his hands, the classic posture of the hopelessly captive.

The silence grew again among them, punctuated only by the patternless surge of wavelets from the dark sea.

"Is that a green light out there?" Carver rose suddenly for a better look. It turned out not to be a green light. When they sat again, they saw Masters sitting somewhat more erect, his head held a little higher. In the dark they felt his eyes peering steadily at them.

When Mike Kelly got out of bed, he said, "I'm sorry."

The Italian girl pushed her pillow higher against the swan's neck and shrugged. "It happens, *caro*." She looked around for a cigarette.

He was in his shorts before she realized he had it in mind to leave. She dropped from the swan and started to untangle her underclothes. "Where are we going?"

"You're going back to the transient quarters upstairs. I've got a little job to finish." He patted her rump.

"Hey, *maestro*, you said you'd let me wire this one, remember?"

"Another time . . ."

"Listen, we've got a big job coming up in Milano. Big industrialist. We need for this capitalist pig something special. Let me have that package if you won't take me along."

"No can do, baby—I promised the manufacturer."

"Just one." Laura did not mind begging shamelessly. "Then we'd owe you a favor. You never know when you can use us."

He stared at her deliberately enticing smile, her mouth open, the tip of her tongue glistening the lower lip, as if he had not failed her. But he said: "Nope."

"Next time you'll be better." Her thumb jutted toward the swan.

"It's still no."

"A whore's your mother," Laura said in an Italian dialect.

"What's that mean?"

"It's an insult."

"Just because I won't give you an XX-1?"

"That's what the device is called?"

"You know all about it. I saw you reading the specs on the third package when I was showering."

"See how good I can be, *caro*?" She clasped her hands around his neck and put her face very close under his. "Let me show you how to hold back. Then you will be good to the next *ragazza*." She put a kiss on his nose and went to the swan.

"I'm field-testing it for the maker, that's why he let me have them. A dry run, you might say."

"I'll send you a report on the Milano deal." Laura lay back on the rumpled sheets, staring at herself in the ceiling.

He came to the swan and sat, one foot on its platform, and looked at her nakedness for a long time. She parted her lips a little and smiled at his steady gaze. "I've got to fix the third car."

"Didn't you tell me the dark night's no good? Where are they going to go at night in this lousy town? What can they do? You know this country, on Friday, deader than the heart of a politician before a hungry peasant."

"And if I stay?"

"The mirror will blush." She held out her hands before her hips as if she held his rump in them.

"Okay. I stay."

She was sitting up at once. "You give me one for Milano? No male-pig games this time with Laura, eh? Swear on your mother."

"You bitch," he said like a compliment. "You sweet, conniving bitch." He swarmed over her. "I swear."

Too much time had passed.

They all knew it. Even Masters knew it. Now they did not try to kill the hours with idle talk. They found themselves stealing glances at their watches. It was not yet midnight; the waiting was becoming unbearable. Out on the water nothing moved; the lights on the waiting tankers had faded to nothingness. Masters stared at his captors, one at a time, his attention riveted on them in turn as if he were trying to understand each piece before he put together a puzzle. He held up his bound hands to Roger Phillips and grinned as if the joke had not yet been played out. They did their best not to look at him and to act as if his presence did not matter.

"I recall a fishing village. It's only about four kilometers." The professor got to his feet. It made no difference whether Masters heard them or not. He could not be kept from the fact that the vessel to take them away was very, very late, perhaps would never arrive. "The fishermen might be persuaded to go beyond their usual fishing grounds this morning. As a backup, you understand."

Roger gave the sigh of a man forced to confront a disagreeable alternative. "You think they could be persuaded?"

"We've no alternative, have we?"

"I can't understand it, I can't understand it!" Roger's voice rose in a crescendo of frustration. He went into the darkness to the edge of the water. "Colin!" he shouted. "Colin! You son of a bitch! You miserable rat! Where are you?"

None of the others moved. Masters started to lift himself to his feet; he turned toward Amanda and saw the service pistol clasped in two extended hands aimed dead on him. She did not have to say a word. He sat back.

Roger returned. He offered no apology. "How long would it take you?"

"Can you give me two hours?"

"And if my man arrives?"

The professor shrugged.

"I'll give you two hours."

In a moment the professor was lost in the darkness.

Again the endless waiting.

"May I say something?" Masters said softly, some time after the professor had left them.

"No," Amanda Miller said.

"Let him speak," Roger Phillips offered.

"I don't know the why of all this," Masters began softly and slowly. "Or who you people are. Whoever you're from, whatever you've planned, I give you my solemn word if you bring me back home—unhurt—I'll see to it this whole episode is—forgotten."

"Enough, Masters," Amanda broke in.

"Let's hear what kind of offer he's got in mind," Roger said.

Masters continued: "I promise you solemnly: You won't be prosecuted here. You'll be returned without harm. There'll be no trial. No publicity. As far as your superiors are concerned, it'll be a failed mission. We'll arrange things so there's no blame or disgrace. If there are any financial rewards forthcoming, we're ready to match it, whatever it is."

There was a pause. When he began again, his voice took on the power of a man who felt the tide of events running his way. "You're probably saying, 'What would stop Masters from betraying us once he brought us in?' I'll tell you. I wouldn't want anything that's happened made known. The government will want it kept quiet too. It could prejudice some business deals we've got going. Is that frank enough for you? What you've done even getting this far is embarrassing enough. The odds against it, considering the security in this country, are tremendous and you did it. We wouldn't want it known, so I'll pay you off handsomely."

"He's congratulating us," Amanda Miller interjected bitterly. A tiny seed of doubt was exploding within her. *Why should Roger necessarily resist such an offer? To him it was always a job; he could pick up the money he'd needed. Something unknown to them had happened out there in the dark waters, and it was all over.* "Don't fall for it."

Masters knew when to close a deal. "Sir, I don't know who you are, what agency you represent—listen to me. Not only do you get to go home unharmed, the money is more than you could make in a lifetime. I'm a very rich man, two, three million dollars in ransom or whatever, I make that when gold or silver moves a point or two. It's yours, wherever or however you want it—and no talk about that either. You've earned it, just in getting this far and ending even now when the boat you're waiting for isn't here."

Amanda Miller started to speak more than once but the words kept dying in her throat. Roger Phillips got to his feet, bent down for a handful of rocks. He seemed to find release in throwing them into the sea as far as he could. Finally, he turned to Masters. "I'll think about it."

"The police forces here are very ruthless," Masters urged. "Life is not held so precious when they're on the attack."

"Don't rush me. There are a few things I have to consider carefully. It's going to take a while," Roger interrupted him. "If you want to save your life from their police, I suggest you start thinking how you can help here and now. Because the plan still is if we don't make it, you don't. If they get us, you're dead. Keep that up front all the time."

"Who are you people?" Masters called out. His voice cracked as if a final appeal had been denied him. "Who? *Who?*"

"Maybe he should be told," Roger Phillips turned to Amanda Miller.

"We've met, Mr. Alan Masters," she began in a steady voice. "Some time ago."

"I don't recall."

"There is a picture. A child is on your knee, a small woolly bear is in her hands. You are laughing. Another man with you is laughing."

"I always liked children."

"The second man is John Edward Ebersol. He was my father."

In the dark they heard a groan like that of a man who has been slammed in the gut. Masters turned wildly; he began to run; he stopped, started again and fell this time, and struggled vainly to get to his feet. Roger Phillips walked to his side and took his elbow and helped him up. "Are you all right? We wouldn't want you to hurt yourself."

31.

WHEN THE WAP shuttle's engines whined to a stop at Khorfa in the desert, Ted Boardman turned to his wife and tapped her shoulder gently. All the way down she had kept her back turned to him. "We're here, Tracy."

They were the last of thirteen passengers, all men, none of whom seemed happy at arriving. At the bottom of the ramp, Ted Boardman left his wife to go up to someone he saw with a group of field personnel. They were beginning to unload the heavy equipment when Ted returned to her side.

"Fachrissake," Ted Boardman said between clenched teeth, "be nice to this guy. He's our lifeline." He took her arm and led her to Eddie Parker. "Meet my copilot. This is Eddie Parker, dear. The man I told you about."

She found a hand near her. She took it and lifted her head briefly to offer a smile. "Nice to meet you," Parker said.

"Thank you. And nice to meet you," Tracy said.

"Everything's laid on for a nice evening for you, Mrs. Boardman," Parker said hdartily. "I've got one of the suites we keep ready for when our top executives visit us. It's got everything. If you're hungry, you'll find cold roast beef, ham and such in the fridge."

The suite was a veritable desert Hilton, furnished in big-expense-account style so visiting WAP executives could be comfortable. Tracy Boardman took her leave for a bath in the gleaming white bathroom beyond the regal bedroom.

"Everything set?" Ted Boardman asked Eddie Parker when they were alone.

"Like no deal I've ever known or heard of!" Eddie Parker exploded with a grin that ran across his face like an electric sign. "You're not going to have to pull an abandon-plane number. No flying south and stealing a commercial air lane. The Jet Commander's due for a routine checkup at Valletta and the deal is now that we're chartering it to you only for Malta and you'll leave it there. Wait. It even gets better." He went to a wet-bar and poured a drink for himself. Ted waved one off. "Listen to what else. Instead of two tons, I've got three! My Bedus tell me it's the absolute finest, ready for market. On landing you're brought to the service hangar. Customs guys don't even bother to come aboard because they know the airplane and that it's strictly VIPs. They'll wait until you check in at the office. And that's not all!" He took a long swallow as if whiskey and soda could quench the fire that burned gloriously within him. "The company, *this* company's got a Liberian charter with a cargo of obsolete drilling equipment consigned to a dealer in Baltimore, Maryland. That's the pickup. Do you have any contacts there?"

Ted Boardman was grinning now too. "My people will find Baltimore a pleasure, I assure you. Maybe I will have a drink at that."

Eddie Parker made a new drink and refreshed his own. He held up his glass in a toast. "There's one small problem. You talked about taking off first thing tomorrow. I can't clear it then."

"Why not? Maybe by noon . . . .."

"It's going to Malta to stand by just in case for our big boss. The airplane gets a checkup."

"When can you clear it?"

"The day after tomorrow."

Tracy talked of fate and the irresistible flow of events. She gave it kooky names, that was her style. Now he could play it her way. The danger he was afraid of was still there, if the others got nabbed, he and Tracy still could . . . "It's a deal, Eddie," he said.

Parker took his second drink in a gulp. "I'll show you the plane in the morning. Anything else?"

"If anybody asks about us, friends, local fuzz, can you let me know right away?"

"You're okay with the security people here, aren't you?" Parker scrutinized him with narrow eyes. "We don't fool with those people. They leave us alone, we don't make waves. A little booze maybe, but—" He shook his hands.

"I was thinking of those friends who might show up. I don't know what they're into."

"I'll keep you posted."

He found Tracy in the tub, water gurgling from a golden lion-head faucet to keep the temperature hot. Western and Alliance even provided perfumed bath salts. He sat on the tub. "Tracy."

She regarded him darkly and sank lower into the water, her long hair swirling around her body.

"I was wrong about Roger and the others. We're going to wait for them, and not worry about anything. We'll give them all day just as we agreed."

"Teddy. I'm proud of you."

"We owe it to them." He told her about the arrangements Eddie Parker had made but left out the part about being given no choice but to wait another day.

"It's going to happen just the way I always knew it would. It's inevitable." Tracy stood up triumphant, Aphrodite emerging from the bathtub. "The terrestrial flow is our way, all the galactic signs point to success." Her husband held out a huge bathtowel and enfolded her into it. "You've got to trust the celestial forces, it's as simple as that." She tied the towel around herself above the breasts. A smaller towel swirled briefly and became a turban.

"I'm the luckiest man in the world," Ted Boardman said.

Ahmed Memir finished translating the transmission from Washington shortly after midnight. He found it most interesting, reminding him as it did of a girl he had once known in Ann Arbor, Michigan. He gave his rendition of the attached report from the Henning Security people somewhat more color than the dry statement Mrs. Marva Miller had dictated, as was possible in so rich a language as Arabic. Memir's American girl friend had been something of a revolutionary, at least that is how he had come to think of her, always talking about the oppression of women and asking him why he, an enlightened university graduate, did not work for what she called the liberation of Islamic women. She laughed when he insisted they were liberated in their own way; she refused to understand the very foundation of his own religious beliefs and ended their relationship by calling him an idiot who happened to be a mathematical genius. Memir did not know this Amanda Miller, but when he was finished with her mother's statement, the young lady was a very foolish and disobedient girl engaged in some nefarious and certainly dangerous enterprise. Memir was glad he was able to get back at that girl in Ann Arbor.

He ran the ordered ten copies of his translation and brought it by hand to the deputy chief of the Message Center. By the time Memir returned to his desk, the contents of the Azeiri transmission from Washington was being routed to all official Sarumnan agencies connected to American intelligence and domestic security as well as to police, the President-for-Life's special forces, Customs and to the minister concerned, Hafir Azziz.

Doraj the little village was called. It had been a Roman port, so Walter Evans Carver knew it from visits a very long time ago, although not a pebble remained from its ancient past. Old men sat inside an open doorway from which bright light flowed into the alley. Carver greeted them in Arabic and soon he was sitting with them, exchanging the usual words of an honorable guest from a far country who could speak the tongue beautifully. The professor was patient about coming to the point of his visit. He knew his people.

At length he managed to turn the talk to the weather, the sea and the fishing of its waters. "In my father's day the nets brought in more fish," an old man said.

"It is a dying sea," another said, "I have seen it fail in my own lifetime."

"Is it better in deeper waters?" the professor asked.

"It takes longer to get there and longer to return," one fisherman said. "And it is not good out there."

"How is it not good for you?" Carver asked.

"The great vessels are bad enough but the patrol vessel go so quickly, surely they disturb the fish. We believe they drive away the fish to even deeper waters."

"You have boats for those waters?"

"Some among us have new boats now. The government is very good to us."

"Can the new boats go very far into the great sea?"

"To the very coastline that protects Mecca itself. But who

could dare go far these days? Tonight monsters of steel churn the waters with propellers fierce enough to shake mountains. Their lights blind you at a hundred meters. They make the dark spark with a flood of bullets and blow the driftwood near our boats out of the water with a single shell. They can see in the dark."

"Surely they do not do all this every night?"

"They stay one night, never more. That is why we do not go out tonirht. But tomorrow we will go."

"Why Friday, the das we are enjoined to regard as holy?"

"Unbelievers lead them, perhaps. It is a small humiliation we must endure."

"Our leader is wise. On such a holy day an enemy might seek to wound us," another added.

"You will go out tomorrow night?"

They murmured agreement.

"Do any ever go to a foreign shore for trade as tey did in the old days?" the professor asked casually. Indirect, perhaps, to the Western mind, but he and they knew he was asking them for escape.

"How can we? The whole world is our enemy!"

"Even our Arab brothers are against us!" another said.

"We are alone today, here we stay, here we die," still another added.

As soon as it was polite to do so, Carver rose and took his leave.

Mike Kelly let her have the XX-1. What the hell. He was field-testing it and who knew when it might be useful to have those people owing a fat favor? When it was over this time, Laura came into his arms and said there was no reason for him to feel bad, many men were no different, all women knew that, even boastful men; she, like those women, could keep a secret too. He was strangely touched. It was after midnight when she left, reaching up to kiss him over the beard on the hairless cheek.

"We try again next week." The hall of the great house they called Camptown was dark. Student revolutionaries and teachers alike bedded down early in Sarumna.

For a time Mike Kelly thought of what had happened with Laura; he could push it out of his mind without effort. After all, what mattered were other things. He found himself wondering

231

about the third car that had not been there. By this time it had returned, he was certain.

The parking area was still as a graveyard at this late hour. He stopped before the big East German bus. Once in his company days at Langley he had occasion to assess its potentialities for some long-forgotten operation, so it distracted him momentarily in his search for the third car.

"You look for something, sir?" he was surprised to hear behind him. A man in white shorts and yachting cap pulled a pipe from his mouth. He was smiling innocently. "I take the night air. This is my boat, so to speak. May I help you?"

"How long have you been here?" Kelly asked.

"All evening. We rest here. We leave at dawn."

"I am looking for a certain car. Perhaps you have seen it. An Audi."

"It was here. Parked right there. I had to pull our bus away because I had hemmed it in. It left before we took our dinner. A young couple, Americans. You are American? I like American things very much, I hope one day, perhaps—"

"What did they look like?"

"He was an athletic man. The lady—she was, as we say in German, *fantastisch*." He kissed his fingertips.

Kelly left the skipper to go to the desk. The night clerk was busy over a ledger and a small calculator. He was slow at first but soon he did not doubt the authority in Mike Kelly's voice. The keys to the room of Mr. and Mrs. Boardman were not in the box, but that did not entirely persuade Kelly they were in the room, as the clerk suggested. The others in the party of Professor Carver sponsored by the Ministry of Culture also had possession of their room keys. Kelly insisted on master keys to all of their rooms nonetheless.

Feral instinct told him even as he walked past the sleeping corridor watchman that the Boardmans had flown the coop; when he knocked gently to no answer and opened the door, he saw the old, if artful, dodges: the radio turned on, the lights burning, the closets and drawers filled with the clothing. Even the traveling bags.

It was the same in the professor's room, except that there he found in the wastebasket an oily black rag that had once been a gentleman's handkerchief, linen, with a rolled edge. Expensive, his trained eye told him. Put to use for lack of a proper rag. It smelled of oil. Gun oil.

He was not surprised when he found that all the others in the party were not in their rooms.

The banks in California stay open until six o'clock on Friday. It is a convenience offered customers who want to make last-minute deposits or withdrawals before the weekend. R.J. Henderson, executive manager of the Bank of America, Palm Springs, was told one hour before closing that the counselor of the Embassy of the Workers Republic of Sarumna in Washington, D.C., was on the line.

Henderson glanced at his watch. It would be eight o'clock in the evening in Washington. Had he known what triggered the call, he would have also known it was well after midnight in the country of the man who wished to speak to him.

"My name is Colonel Azeiri," the caller began. "There is a matter of extreme urgency. I wonder if I may count upon your cooperation?"

There was no question the gentleman was highly distressed. He declared his official credentials and reminded the banker that his government was one of the world's greatest oil producers, a considerable factor in the banking world, and that at least two of its prime contractors were based in California. Henderson knew from his banking experience such a powerhouse opening always presaged a request if not to break then to bend a restrictive regulation.

What Colonel Azeiri appeared to be asking would be difficult to grant without the depositor's consent, without a court order, a request of a tax agency—or heaven only knows what other dispensation. He was asking nothing less than details of the bank's business with Miss Amanda Miller. He inquired where the deposits to her account originated, in what amounts, from what source, and any other information about the lady Henderson could offer.

It took a moment for Henderson to realize this was not a practical joke. Or a call totally ignorant of his own confidential and fiduciary relationship to a customer of the bank. He jollied his caller by asking if that was all the caller wanted, was he perhaps interested in the results of Miss Miller's last EKG and her school grades? Colonel Azeiri was in no mood to be played with. "I know the seriousness and perhaps technical irregularity of what I am calling about, sir," the colonel said. "I would not do so, I assure you, if the very security of my country, perhaps the lives of its leaders, are not now, at this very moment, being threatened!" His voice grew very loud. "If time were not of the essence I would not be calling you. Be assured our central bank in Zarplis has had many dealings with your head office. I am fighting time, sir!"

Henderson sought to be as measured as possible. He had no authority, he explained, to do such a thing. There were federal laws regarding disclosure, not to mention the bank's own very strict policy. The colonel was beside himself with rage. Tossing financial thunderbolts at a mere bank branch in refusing to come to the aid of a sovereign nation, the caller from Washington roared, "I assure you on Monday morning we will have everything we want to know!"

"Not through me, sir," Henderson said, and hung up on his impertinent caller.

Amanda Miller heard something move toward them in the darkness. Roger Phillips had his arms wrapped around his drawn-up legs, his head resting on the knees. She kept the .45 beside her, pointed to where Masters lay on his side, his back to them. She rose when the lanky figure of Professor Walter Evans Carver approached them.

Roger had not been sleeping. He came over to where the old man put himself down wearily. "Old age is catching up with me, the rascal," Professor Carver said with a smile. "Roger, you may want to put the gentleman there in limbo again before I report."

"The more he knows, the more he'll realize he's got to help us if he wants to survive with us, so go ahead, professor," Roger said to the reclining figure near them. "What do you have for us?"

"Nothing good."

"Tell how bad it is."

"They are sweeping the coast tonight."

"On the holy day the General insists the country observe so strictly?" Roger asked incredulously.

"They do this now and then for training purposes. Throw everything they've got into a big operation. Why Friday? A small

Russian humiliation perhaps of an ally they can't really approve of and the General's paranoia again, I suspect. He's sure an enemy would strike on a holy day."

"The one day I figured we'd be in the clear. So much for that brilliant stroke," Roger said dismally.

"They don't do it every week, of course. Bad luck that we caught it, that's all."

"When will the fishermen go out again?"

"Tomorrow night. Most of the fleet is gone by then, they tell me."

"Could they take us?"

"I'm afraid not."

"That means we're on our own, right, professor?"

"Doesn't Caesar say somewhere that the wise general knows that in battle everything goes wrong?"

"Obviously I never took that into account."

"This Hume fellow, you made no contingent plans?"

"How could we? We knew once we took our man, that was it."

Masters approached, his bound hands extended. "And it hasn't worked. I repeat my proposal. Take me back. You will be given safe conduct home. You will be rewarded for your silence. Trust me, I beg you. The matter will be closed forever."

"Why should I believe you?"

"My life is at stake. I don't believe you will get out alive. I know if you don't, I won't."

"When we turn you over, what's to stop you from double-dealing us?"

"I do not lie." He saw Roger Phillips's head turn to the daughter of Jack Ebersol. "I play hard, but I don't lie."

"Prove it."

Masters looked down to his tied hands. "How?"

"By telling us the truth—anything we want to know. If we catch you in one lie, it's no deal, now or ever."

Masters took this in, thinking furiously.

Roger looked at Amanda.

"Did you have my father murdered?" she said in a voice as dry as sand.

"I wanted him dead," Masters replied. "It may well be those who sought my favor—"

235

"You did not order him killed?"

"No, ma'am. Not directly."

"His life in prison," she went on coolly. "He always believed he was set up for trouble."

"I arranged that." His eyes closed slowly.

"You creep," she muttered through unmoving lips. "You miserable scum."

"He had made himself my enemy."

Roger put his hand on Amanda's shoulder. "At least the man isn't lying to us."

"I have a question," Carver offered.

"It may be the same one that bugs me, professor," Roger Phillips broke in. Perhaps somewhere in his head the thought persisted that he could protect the old man from too deep an involvement. "You have a good deal to do with handling government and personal investments abroad, right, Mr. Masters?"

"I'm the principal adviser, that is correct," Masters replied firmly, trying to show he would not dissemble or prevaricate.

"All movement of oil money, gold, dollars, sterling—everywhere in the world?"

"There is an Exchequer of course, but I am the General's principal adviser, as I say."

"Secret funds as well, Mr. Masters?" Roger looked over to see a faint smile on Carver's face, as if the line of questioning had indeed come to where he himself had wanted it.

"Yes, sir. Mostly private. I guess you could call it secret. You see, I am being wholly truthful with you."

"Just answer the questions, Mr. Masters. What about funding or arranging the funding for foreign terrorist groups, for subversion in neighboring countries and less hard-line Arab groups?"

"I am not always brought into political decisions outside my competence."

"Fine, I believe that. But you've arranged for transfer of money to terrorist groups, have you not—Germans, Italians, Japanese, PLO? And if you lie here, why should I believe you won't lie later?"

"I didn't like it," Masters said softly, "but I had no choice."

"You're saying you did knowingly help finance such people and operations?"

There was a long pause. "Yes." Another pause. "I'm something of a prisoner in Sarumna myself."

"All right, I believe you're serious about your proposition, Mr. Masters," Roger Phillips said. "Go get in the car and wait there."

They watched him struggle briefly with the door latch. Roger went to the car to help him and closed the door for him.

"You wouldn't?" Amanda flung at him when he returned, as if the idea was something too loathsome to hold even for a second.

"He did what he said. He didn't lie," Roger replied softly. "At least he's capable of that."

"He's corroborated what we've always suspected," Carver offered. "He is an enemy."

"You're talking big-picture politics, professor. I'm thinking of saving our skins."

"We have no other choice?" Amanda said.

Roger pointed to the dark waters. "Have we?"

"How can we even think about giving up now?" Amanda cried out. "We've got the car. It's still night. They won't know he's missing till Monday morning. Why can't we get to the border and cross?"

"Can I tell you why? " Roger Phillips told her. "First, the roads that go to the border are patrolled all the time as heavily as the coast is tonight. Second, you just don't go through at the border, you've got to have papers, which we don't have, they run an inspection of the car, which we can't take. And third, even if we crossed, what makes you think the neighbor wouldn't extradite us? They hate the General but they're also scared to death of him. They've got no outstanding indictments against Masters, so they might let him go and send us back here. Terrific, huh?"

"There must be something we can do!" Amanda pleaded. "They still don't know we've got him."

"Caesar would say it'd be wiser to assume they do know by now, right, professor?" Roger countered. "It was a good idea, Amanda, as long as we were on our way on the water. We'd better not count on that any longer."

"You talk like you've made up your mind to accept his offer," she said bitterly.

"In five or six hours someone at that desert place is going to wonder what happened to the people who were supposed to party there. He'll call Zarplis. Need I say more? There aren't many choices left."

"They haven't begun to look and we've got him. The show is still ours," she insisted.

"And when that part's over it'd be nasty enough for us, but they'd be very damned brutal to you," Roger Phillips said. "They'd gang-rape and savage your body until you'd end up pleading for them to kill you. Tell her, Professor Carver."

"It could be more terrible for you than one dare think, my dear."

"At least *he'll* be dead." Her head turned angrily to the car.

"Is his death worth it if you have to die too?" Roger said. "What he did won't be erased by your defiled body and death."

"I don't want him dead!" She broke into a sob. "I don't want to just kill him, what good would that do me? But is this what it all comes to, he gets away again?"

She was crying but there did not seem anything they could say to help her try to stop. "You haven't told me what you think about his offer," Professor Carver said quietly.

"It's a sincere one. There's even a chance he means it."

"You're not inclined to accept it?"

"I'm inclined to think about it." Roger Phillips saw Amanda turn a tear-stained face toward him. "But I'd hate myself in the morning if I made a deal now. We've still got all night." Amanda wiped her face with the back of her hand. She sniffed audibly. "We can stall a while," he told her.

"Thank you," Amanda said fervently.

"We couldn't take a chance on the main road south," Roger said almost to himself. "Or stay on the coast all the way to Hamaldan and take that road south."

"Absolutely not," the professor agreed quickly.

"There's the old road Rommel tried to rehabilitate. Across the *chott*—"

"The road that he found to his dismay his best engineers couldn't use," the professor amended. "A *chott*'s a dry salt bed, Amanda, a depression in the desert," he turned to her to explain, "the worst kind of terrain for man, animal or vehicle." He turned back to Roger Phillips. "This one's the *chott* El Jared, it even defeated the best efforts of the consul here back in the fourth century, if you recall."

"But there is some kind of a road there, professor," Roger insisted. "Straight as a ruler. My hunch is no one patrols it at night."

"No one knows how much sand has blown over it."

"This Rolls has four-wheel drive, did you know that? It surprised me when I got behind the wheel," Amanda put in eagerly.

"I noticed that too, Amanda." Roger Phillips was grinning now.

"Suppose we could make it across the *chott*? Could we count on an oasis?"

"I think there's a village, I forget the name," Carver said.

"They'd be looking for us on the roads to all the border stations. This way we'd still have a day before they started covering all the *wadis* and villages. We'd still have time—"

"Time for what, Roger?" Carver asked.

"I don't know. Whatever the hell it is you do with time when you're stuck. Of course there's no reason for you to come along, professor. You could walk back to the hotel and play the innocent dupe in all this."

"Oh, come off it, Roger," the professor interrupted irritably, "I wouldn't dream of it."

"Thank you, *magister carus*, that's very noble of you."

"Noble, my foot. All my dull life as a scholar I've read and dreamt of such enterprises, foolish, absurd, glorious, ill-fated, and could only envy those people. And here I am *in medias res*. You'd have to shoot me to get rid of me, Roger."

The professor found himself caught in another of Miss Miller's waist-circling embraces. "I love you too," she said.

"Thank you, my dear," he said, looking perplexed over her head to Roger Phillips, as if he had not quite concluded his business. "By the by, I've hidden—stashed, I believe it's called in the trade—the Sten gun I told you about down the road. Could we stop there before we head into the *chott*?"

PART SIX

32.

From minarets across the land, wherever people dwelt, the voice of the muzzein rang out at the dawn of the new day: *"La ilahah illa Allah! Muhammad Rasul Allah!"* There is no God but Allah, Muhammad is his Messenger.

In the desert near Hamaldan in the east of the country, General Mohammed Abdullah bent low in prayer with his staff, the personal advisers he had brought with him, several of his closest associates on the Revolutionary Council and many humbler men in the desert town who knew of his presence and were doubly honored to share the sacred moment with him.

In Zarplis traffic was stopped dead; it had been one of the General's first orders on assuming power. All the traffiic lights went to red on a holy day and stayed there. In the first days an attempt to enforce the same regulation at the other four times the faithful are called to prayer—noon, mid-afternoon, sunset and two hours after sunset—had been reluctantly canceled by the President-for-Life. The people of Sarumna are remarkably devout and for the most part need no temporal authority to bring them to prayer. In any case, at that hour there was not much auto traffic.

Hafir Azziz slept through the first prayer, as was his custom, except when his duties as minister of culture called upon him to play host to a stricter brother of the faith. It was not that his belief was slack, he often said. Far from it. His education in the West had subtly persuaded him that there is a difference between letter and spirit. In his mind, no system of man's relationship to his God was equal to his own. "God gave Moses the Book," Azziz often said, "He gave Jesus the Evangel; and he gave Muhammad the Koran." A fulfillment, natural and evolutionary, Azziz pointed out, not in conflict but a natural flow from the prophets of old to the man born in Nazareth to the ultimate prophet, the Messenger of Allah.

Nevertheless, faithful as he was, he slept. He would arise, as was his custom, in good time and arrive at his office after all the lesser people were at their various tasks. Then he would open the file on the people to whom he had given his stamp of approval when he opened the doors of the nation to Professor Walter Evans Carver.

The Azeiri transmission had already been received by the Wireless and Emergency Department; the Identity Investigation Department; the Central Department for Criminal Investigations; the International Criminal Police Bureau; the Electronic Computer Section of the Foreign Agent Division; Army Counter-Intelligence; the International Training Section; the People's Special Police; the Border Protection Agency; the Ministry of Cultural Affairs, as the agency responsible for the parties named in the document; and of course, the Presidential Security Section of the staff of General Mohammed Abdullah.

These policing tributaries were deliberately designed to overlap each other. Each agency was autonomously directed, owed no allegiance to any other, and frankly competed with one another. The General denied all this meant a police state; he liked to say Sarumna was a democratic, military state. But the activities of all these agencies had the effect of casting vast nets into deep and murky waters and always coming up with some catch acceptable to the government and the censored press. Six assassination attempts, three planned military coups by senior officers, and two civilian plots had been aborted since the overthrow of the old regime, it was said. In truth, the excesses were not delusional; the members of the Revolutionary Council charged with governing the nation had reason to be proud of its police work.

But government is government and a slipup or two can be expected in the best agencies as well as the worst. The Azeiri transmission was received at the desert retreat of General Mohammed Abdullah with many others after the holy day. As usual everything for him was marked "Most Urgent" and "Most Secret." His staff had been ordered to stand by for a possible return at any moment to Zarplis. The Azeiri transmission was boxed with pressing transmissions from London, Beirut and the PLO for his attention as soon as the General's plans were made known. His dreams of a greater-than-Britain remained just that; he needed allies. Where could he find them? The General hesitated to leave the desert and visions of the nation's future.

Another slipup was no one's fault or oversight. Since foreigners were involved in maritime operations, a special law had been promulgated by the council on the occasion of the $200 million order of the high-speed seacraft of which Alan Masters had spoken to Roger Phillips. It was deemed unwise to transmit sensitive messages to the Ports Security Division since the Russians were known to use them for their own purposes. The message from Washington which would most directly concern this agency, therefore, was never sent to it.

Orders for dispersal of the anti-subversion training mission concluded that morning would of course have been canceled. The fast attack craft armed with their Russian SSN-2 Styx surface-to-surface missiles would remain in place. Fourteen patrol boats, minesweepers and the guided-missile craft returned to four bases after maneuvers. Had the message been received by the Ports Security Division, the fisherman at Doraj would have seen something more stunning than the tracer bullets and cannon fire they described to Professor Carver.

So, of course, would a lone Combattante-II-class patrol boat somehow acquired by a Sicilian gentleman of considerable political power resident in the city of Catania. The boat, registered as a pleasure craft owned by a tourist hotel, carried no armament. It was, however, fitted with extra fuel tanks, elaborate radar and electronic devices of the latest design instead of the Otomat ship-to-ship missiles with which it is usually equipped. It had specifically hot-rodded engines which gave it a speed capability limited only by the strength of its hull. Its own radar, being more sensitive than its maker's NATO specifications called for, had forced a terrible decision on a reluctant skipper the night before. His screens showed

Colin Hume there was no possible way he could enter Sarumnan waters undetected or, if he was crazy enough to try and lucky enough to achieve the impossible, he could not manage to get into Italian waters before he would be blown apart by a Mirage jet fighter alerted to his presence by an outrun patrol vessel.

Mike Kelly—or Julian Christopher, and in that incarnation a canny and knowing functionary in the bureaucratic maze—had come to know the overlapping Sarumnan security agencies and he had no doubt they were by now aware of the activities he believed he was the first to uncover. Rewards for this would flow to him in good time. He had managed to get to a high-ranking official and to perform his specialties in a couple of their vehicles However, governmental experience had taught Mike Kelly that conspiracies nipped in the bud are considered hardly dangerous. Their early abortion brings no great merit. Failed conspirators are judged inept and little credit emerges from their arrest. Better to let them move about. Besides, where could these go?

What was their real purpose?

In what ways was Alan Masters connected to them?

Had Masters been promised immunity? A return to the United States?

No penalty? Or a face-saving, minor conviction?

In return for?

An overthrow of General Mohammed Abdullah?

Assassinate him?

This unlikely crew, they were bait, the flashy women, the pilot who squealed when stuck, the old prof, all would be expendable.

They would draw first fire.

The skilled operators would make the move that mattered.

Masters. Dupe or coconspirator?

My money, is it safe?

Kelly slept. All this, in his own way, he had gone through before exhaustion overwhelmed him. He tried not to think of the Italian bitch and the Polish cow—women were a drag.

Whether he was with them or not. Masters was his baby.

In the dark hours before the first call to prayer, the Rolls proceeded with imperial assurance. Every so often the pale strip that said this was the artery through the salt depression grew fuzzy with the sand blowing from the dunes around it. At such times Roger Phillips drove by touch, so to speak; he could feel the traction grow mushy. A downshift to second gear, and more than once to first, proved able to keep the car moving. Now and then a cluster of dunes rose like spectral ghost towns before the headlights only to vanish in the backwash of the surging dark. On a slight rise their hearts leaped uncertainly. Their lights cut a slash across an open plain to reveal a wall, so long, so high that they could not see the end or the top of it. A safe haven was the first thought that came to Roger Phillips, but as they came closer he turned to Professor Carver. "Fortess?" The old man nodded. "Abandoned?" he went on.

"Would think so." Carver leaned forward so his head was inches from Roger's ear. "You ought to pull up."

"Too risky. Might find someone there."

"Don't think so. The Bedu avoid these places like a curse. I'm thinking of the wind."

"Doing okay so far."

"Stiffening, Roger. I've more experience than you. This one swirls, changes direction and speed. I'd pull up, give it a half hour. I've seen it go away as unpredictably as it rises."

Roger turned to Masters beside him. He might be sleeping; perhaps he was dissembling; it did not matter. He caught sight of Amanda in his rearview mirror. The headlights revealed the old ramparts and the line of palm trees planted fifty years ago by the imperalist power. Part of the wall was crumbling but it stood against time and the corrosive wind which snarled against the windshield as if to confirm Carver's assessment.

The car came to a stop at the gaping space where once had hung the great wooden doors, long since burned in a hundred desert campfires. "I'm going to have a look," Roger said.

"I'll join you." Amanda handed the pistol to the professor, but he waved it away.

"Where would he go? He's probably frightened to death." They saw no response from Masters. "Or asleep, for a fact. I'll wait here."

Their eyes grew accustomed to the dark quickly. The high walls inside sang with the whistling of the wind against it corners and erosions. He found a door, put his shoulder to it and it fell open with a wooden sigh. "Look," he said.

Dark as it was, they could make out a large and airy room. Maybe it had once been the colonel's quarters or a staff room. Except for the layering of sand, it felt as if its occupants had vacated it the day before. The furniture was there, a table, a couch, their hands even made out a carpet over it.

"You'd think they'd have stolen everything."

Who wants these things in the desert?" Roger Phillips said. He fell down, luxuriously resting weary bones, on the couch. "Paradise," he said.

She sat, legs under her, beside him. "Are we going to stay here?"

"No."

"Where can we go? The road seems always about to die on us."

"Got to move on."

"Of course. If you say so."

He took her hand. "I have difficulty with you."

"You shouldn't. I'm easy to get along with".

"You undervalue yourself. I can't make you out. I think you're a crazy rich girl and you turn out to be an iron lady who knows what she wants. I think you're a kook who hides in bushes and you turn out to be a woman who'd trio with a man she loathes just to get what she wants."

"I'm finding out some things about myself too."

"I never thought of you as pretty," he went on. "The more I see you the better you look."

"I like that part."

"Wait, I haven't finished. We're headed for disaster. Masters is right, you know. When they spot us, they'll tear us apart with bazookas and armor-piercing shells. You seem not to mind that."

"You're telling me we've got to take Masters at his word?"

"About the bazookas, yes. I don't think we've got many alternatives."

"But you don't want to give up. Why not, Roger?"

"That's something else I'm having difficulty with. I think it has to do with you. How far did you go with Masters before you got to the let's-trio part? Why does that bother me?"

"I went skinny-dipping with him. I let him kiss me. It made my skin crawl. I'm glad it bothers you." She put her mouth to his.

"What if I say I may still have to make a deal with your man?" he said through her kiss.

"It would make a difference. But I'm also somewhat whorish; maybe this will keep you on my side."

His teeth flashed in the dark. "I'll be damned."

He reached under her dress. "No," she said.

"I'm sorry—"

"You take off your clothes, I'll do mine," she said.

He could see her fall back on the dusty carpet and arch her body to get her dress out from under her so she could pull it over her shoulders. He had to get to the edge of the couch to get his boots off and to stand up to pull his jeans away and to unbutton his shirt, and when he turned to her, her body glowed in the dark, arms above her head, little lights dancing in her eyes in the stale dark, and her mouth was parted, and naked she said, "Hello, Roger."

Masters stirred. He had been asleep. The old man, long legs stretched diagonally over a jump seat, watched him for a moment. Swirling sand hissed against the glass. "Do you want to relieve yourself, Mr. Masters? he said.

A moment later they were secure against the howling in the dark, womblike interior. "Professor," Masters began slowly. He hesitated as if sure what he had to say was not unexpected. "Why do you do this? What's in it for you?"

"A long story."

"You were loved here, a figure in history."

"History is soon buried in these parts."

"You threw it away. Or should I say, are throwing it away. Surely you didn't come to Sarumna to kidnap a man? I'm no fool. I know what a man will buy and what he won't. It's my job".

"Mr. Masters," the professor said severely, "if you're trying to subvert me, it won't work. However I came, I am now here with you, in this car, outside this old fort whose name I do not know, because I want to be here."

"So, a personal whim. Can you afford it? I've got a lot of influence with General Mohammed Abdullah. We bought into

Italia Motors, more than a billion two hundred million, at my urging. I'm teaching the man to diversify. I know what you think of him. I don't much like the way he plays footsie with certain groups, but I always think of myself. Does it hurt me? It doesn't. So I'm with him, or was, and will be again. Listen to me, I can open historical research and archaeological programs for you here and all over North Africa under his sponsorship. I can persuade him of its ultimate benefit as business. I don't deal in politics. I'll tell him it's good business. What is more important to you, professor, your lifework or helping a kidnapping for gain?"

The silence inside the car surprised them both. They peered through the glass for the swirls of sand that had been bouncing off every pane, and waited, but it seemed to have ceased. Finally, Professor Carver said: "I suppose you're sincere, Mr. Masters?"

"Phillips thinks I'd double-deal him if he let me go. Why should I? What would I have to gain? A million or two? It means nothing to me. If he let me go, we'd keep it dead quiet, I've said that before. We'd want to. If you helped me, with or without his consent, I'd give you the largest program in the history of academic research here."

"Without his consent, that would mean the General would deal with him"

"I'd have no control if he insisted playing that way. If you got Phillip's consent, we'd hush up the matter. Could I trust him to keep all this secret? I might stretch out the payments—you see, I'm serious enough about the matter to have gone into details already—I'd stretch out the payments over the years to assure his discretion. Understand, he hasn't said no to me."

"He is a realist, Mr. Masters."

"So am I. And you, sir?"

"Not a realist."

"You, a student of this world and these people for so long?"

"Is the General a realist?"

"I help pay his bills. Billions to the Russians, to the French, yes, indeed, even to our own beloved country, damned near as much as to the Russians—a man who buys hardware in such quantities has got to be a realist."

"Or a madman, Mr. Masters."

"Perhaps a bit of both, like most of us. Surely the pursuit of your work for all these years has something of a divine madness to it, professor."

The professor let out a small laugh. "You are a magnificent salesman, Mr. Masters."

"I've had to be. I don't promise more than I can deliver or go back on what I promise."

"I'm thinking of your now-silent partner, Amanda's father."

"A tragic choice, but I had no alternative."

"Like a king betrayed by his crown prince?" the professor offered bitterly.

"I was a king. I am a king. In exile."

"Yes, indeed, sir, you are a bit of a madman."

"I don't deny it. Look, give me a figure for your work here. Set it as high as you like. A foundation, headquartered in Switzerland. I like Switzerland. It's so stable. We'll fund it. I'm making the irresistible offer, professor. You'll take the gun from the girl and we'll start for home, with or without them. What do you say?"

"I do not wish to speak further to you, Mr. Masters."

"Think about it."

"Or to hear your voice, do you understand me?" His own was iced with professorial contempt. In the front seat Masters grinned to himself. Sometimes you have to make an offer and wait until the beauty of it sinks in.

The night air had grown still but the ground under them filled with sudden mushy stretches and little mounds of fresh dune-sand. Only Alan Masters seemed content to close his eyes, feet stretched as far forward as he could manage, his bound hands tucked under his head at the backrest. Carver and Amanda leaned forward, eyes attempting to pierce beyond the slow-moving headlights. An unspoken fear assailed them and they wondered if Roger was torn by it as well. The road, or what had once been or had tried to be such, seemed always on the verge of dying, or being erased. Windows down, moving slowly in the lower gears, the sound of tires against the ground they traversed told them as much as their eyes could observe. Downshifting made them hold their breath. How long? Could the road be lost in a sea of soft-driven sand so deep it could not be found again? When Roger Phillips pushed the stick to a higher gear, he could hear or sense a sigh behind him.

This desert passage had plagued and teased how many others? he thought. He tried to think without doubts or uncertainties. Rommel's engineers couldn't manage, but they had to think of moving regiments and divisions and heavy armor. He had one car, built for the caprices of the desert, four people and no baggage. Someone in Zarplis, studying the possible avenues of escape, would not come to this one until the others proved fruitless.

The car came to a jolting halt without warning. "My fault," Roger said. He charged himself silently with lack of concentration. He did not see a mound but a long mesalike rise the car had come to a stop in—as if some malevolent wind of Professor Carver's had paved what roadbed there was with six inches of the softest, airiest sand. No one said a word. Roger Phillips got out of the car; they could see him in the headlights, ten feet ahead, bending down and lifting a handful of sand and letting it sift between his fingers like powder. He got into the car. "This is what is known in the trade as strong-ass low," he muttered, found what he wanted in the gearbox, four-wheel drive and the lowest gear, gave a nervous little cough before he touched the gas pedal. The car did not move at once. He lifted his foot, looked to Masters, who seemed to be sleeping through it all, and gave the engine more power. The car lurched, sat still again. Quickly, he put his hand on the stick, pushed the gears into reverse, looked back from long habit and fed somewhat more gas than he had tried in the attempt to move forward. The wheels bit hard and the car ground backward until it was clear.

"Here we go." The car was at a stop. He shifted gears, depressed the gas pedal and the car bounced but held, the engine throbbing fast enough to fly in a top gear, but all four wheels churning with a steady rhythm under them. Roger Phillips turned the wheel from side to side, body leaning over it. How long? He did not know, nor did the two leaning over the seat before them, watching him shimmying the steering wheel as the car moved forward. Finally, his hand went to the stick, moved it once, moved it again, and they could see his body sag as he let the tension go out of it.

"What do you know? We made it."

He was back in second gear, even though the going now seemed as easy as—how long before?—it had seemed impossible. He was still afraid of another drift of sand. The very quiet of the air seemed more ominous than the dust storms that had stopped them. He felt Amanda's hand touch the skin at his neck, a finger stroking his chin. He tried to incline his head to touch her hand but it was gone when he did so.

"I would say we have traversed the very bottom of this *chott,*" Carver offered. "It was perhaps a hundred or more feet below sea level."

No one wanted to talk about it or what still lay ahead. They stared at the little pool of light the headlamps made in the iron dark before them.

In the hour before day, a total, awesome night contained them in its grip. The low-beam lights gave them all there was of the world; beyond them everything was black as pitch and full of unspoken horrors. They were glad to be encased inside any functioning machine in this unknown universe.

From the east, the first glimmer of day began to chalk the desolation; half-light revealed an endless space. The dark had limited the world to the length of the car's headlights. Now, when they saw their terrain, a small cancer of terror began to eat at them. Was there no end? They found themselves stealing too many glances at the now-visible instrument panel, particularly at the gas gauge. They were reassured by the fact that in all this time the car had not used half of its tank of gasoline. Moments later, more emerging lights revealed a cluster of sparse saltbushes, pasture for sheep, goats and camels. Roger Phillips turned to his teacher. *"Bismellahi,"* Carver muttered, the abbreviated form of the phrase that expresses gratitude to the compassionate and merciful Allah.

"Let us also thank Yahweh and Jesus, to play it safe," Roger offered.

Soft gray light sifted over the salt depression; the great waterless expanse before them stunned them more every moment, as if they had not been traversing it all night. The outcrop of saltbushes which had held a tenuous promise a kilometer or two behind them disappeared. They studied an again-merciless landscape for another sign but they could see nothing but more struggling through an endless *erg,* dune country as far as the eyes could see. The light began to brighten quickly as the sun started its climb over the eastern horizon, but everything it brought to life seemed to become even worse to those in the car. The road was narrower than they had imagined. To call it one-lane was something of an exaggeration. It stretched straight ahead of them in an endless line.

"Christ," Roger muttered. "I hope we get somewhere before we run out of gas."

Amanda turned toward Alan Masters. "And he's slept through all of this, I think."

"He's lucky," Roger said. "There'll be more gas if we get to an oasis town, won't there, professor?"

Before he could reply, they felt a sudden change of the earth beneath their wheels. It had been all rippling washboard; it became smooth as glass. Perhaps it was the contrast, but the car moved so easily, Roger was able to put it into third gear.

"What do you think that means?" he asked uncertainly.

"Not in my area of expertise," Professor Carver demurred.

In the distance the vista of despair seemed to melt in the rising sun. The sand dunes were turning gold. Far ahead of them, a sharp-rock landscape loomed, and around them they began to see saltbushes again and soon more desert scrub. A pair of dried, wind-blown palm fronds lay across the road, a sure sign that the fierce land could give way to gushing spring water, acres of shaded oases, and pastureland for goats and sheep. They would be the first to stare at these strangers from the void. Professor and student had known this experience before and treasured the anticipation. But they remained wary, as experienced travelers in this terrain, because they knew the desert is always elemental, always dangerous . . .

"I think," Roger Phillips began, but said no more.

"I think so too," Professor Carver agreed.

"Do we get to see a mirage?" Amanda Miller asked.

"Not at this hour," the professor replied. "They come late in the afternoon."

"Do people really live in places like this?" she said some time later.

"Many," Professor Carver said.

"Why?"

"Why not?" Roger Phillips said.

"That's easy for someone brought up in Phoenix. In our desert we've got Taco Bell and Baskin-Robbins ice cream, we've got man-made surf, we've got TV, and air conditioning and six-lane highways. That kind of desert man can live in."

"You're kidding, of course."

"Yes, Roger, I'm kidding. But this isn't just a desert," she went on quickly, "this is desolation, this is the world as it will be when we've burned it up."

"They live in this place because of an obstinate belief that desert ways are better than city ways," the professor put in. "When one has lived with them, it is difficult to say they are wrong."

Far ahead, the road seemed to widen somewhat and to lift itself above the horizon. Roger Phillips looked down to the stick. He was in third gear and moving so well, he put his foot on the clutch pedal and went into fourth, the first time since they had left Zarplis. He held the wheel tighter as if to make sure it was not another wheel of another car which had been magically given him. The ground lifted more and then at the far horizon something like a mirage presented itself, but, as the professor had said, there were no mirages in this light, and they saw a copse of waving palms, not shimmering as illusory trees do, but very green and very steady. "A village!" he exclaimed, and added quietly, "no people."

The professor glanced at his wristwatch. "They are at their prayers now, I would say."

Alan Masters moaned softly as he returned to them from sleep. He blinked hard to bring himself back to the world. No one made any comment when he sat up and looked out the window.

Ahead of them a surging palm-covered dune appeared. Phillips turned to his old professor and grinned. The light was slowly turning as golden as the sand around them. Before long, the road led to a long corridor of white walls, and ahead of them and to their left rose the grove of tall stately green palm trees. Roger turned his head to see how Amanda Miller was taking it. Her eyes were moist.

"Why are you crying?" he said.

"I cry at everything," she said, "basketball games, puppies, old telephone numbers, even miracles."

33.

NOT LONG after the car came to rest in the grove, Roger Phillips drew Amanda aside. "The professor and I will try to speak to the head of the *a'ila* here. That's the family. I'll take the car keys. Will you be all right alone with Masters? I'm leaving his hands tied even though he's too smart to try anything here and now."

"I can manage him."

He seemed uncertain about what else to say. "There's water near the trees. We'll find something to eat for you. Take care."

He also seemed uncertain how to leave. "Roger," she said. She wanted to tell him she understood his diffidence after their lovemaking the night before. "I'm not sorry, you know. You didn't seduce me or trick me or anything like that. It's why I insisted on taking off my own clothes. I wanted to make love to you."

He found her hand and squeezed it. "I haven't had much time to think about it. I hope I didn't exploit you or—make you think anything's changed that much."

"You mean about making up your mind about his proposition?"

"I hate to tell you this, Amanda, but we haven't come far enough to know how good it is until we get the word from the *a'ila* chief."

"And if you find it's good?"

"I'd have to ask, 'For how long?' And, 'Where do we go from there?' It's their game now. All we're doing is running away."

"We've got him. You accomplished that much. And I don't feel I own you, nor do I want to. Can you understand that?"

"I'm going to try." He pointed to where the professor had

found a spring. "They've got camels penned near the water. They don't bother you if you leave them alone."

She watched him and the professor head to the cluster of houses down the road. She felt a presence next to her and turned to Masters, also watching the two men on the way to the village.

"Who, exactly, is he?" Alan Masters asked.

She turned to look at him. He was smiling somewhat; his eyes shone with a kind of arrogance. "The professor I have heard of," Masters went on. "He was one of the very few Americans they had a good word for. Now, of course, they'll erase his name here forever. And his silly words to that song. But Phillips—how did you get him?"

"The same way you get what you need. What's it to you?"

"You don't talk to him like he's working for you."

She walked away to the spring. At its edge she kneeled and cupped the water in her hands and lifted it to her face. It was glorious, cool, sweet. She did this several times. A pair of camels came to a fence to stare at her, but soon lost interest and went back to what looked like a shoving match, yowling and braying at each other. She wanted to think of them as if they were horses, but that did not work at all. Camels were noisy and moved gracelessly. The cow began a flirtatious dance, flicking her tail under the stud's nose to display her ruby red cleft. The old boy not only wasn't enchanted, he seemed bored by the whole business.

It wasn't all that interesting to Amanda Miller either. She sat down at the water's edge where the soil was soft and somewhat damp. A shadow behind her turned out to be Alan Masters again. "I remember the day we took that picture," he began. He sat beside her.

"I don't."

"How is your mother?"

Amanda shrugged.

"She never liked me."

Amanda smiled primly.

"Your father and I were more than brothers. I've always said we could have accomplished nothing without him. Did he ever speak of me?"

"Yes. Badly."

"He should have come away with me."

"He saw no reason to run. He never felt like a thief."

"You mean I did?"

"You scrammed like one, didn't you?"

"They wanted blood, I wasn't about to pour mine for their gratification."

"They settled for his. He felt a duty to stay and teach them that there are winners and losers in any financial market and the Fund had played a winning hand and a losing hand and could have won again if they'd let it alone. But of course when you ran . . . You know the story, I'm sure."

"And I knew from the start it would never wash in court. Americans, unfortunately, are sanctimonious about losers and worshipful of winners."

"How are they about officers who steal assets and run away?"

"They forget quickly. They now leave me alone. In time, in time . . ."

In the pen, the bull bestirred himself to lift his head and roar as the female kept waving her tail before his snout and continued her little dance before him. Masters laughed aloud, whether at the awkward flirtation of the mating beasts or her own calm assurance under the present circumstances, Amanda did not know. "I'm afraid of only one thing, my dear. Not that we won't be intercepted by any one of the General's numerous police agencies, but that in the inevitable cross fire, I might get hurt."

"We'll try to spare you all that."

"You don't really still think you're going to get away, do you?"

She got up and walked toward the camels. The old bull raised his long neck briefly to look at her, snorted and turned away, the cow still in pursuit.

"What would I have to do for you to decide to let me go?" Alan Masters stood beside her, always the dealer; no situation in life was without its bargaining chips.

"You killed my father."

"I was half a world away when he died."

"No one else in the world would want him dead."

"He was a suicide."

"The papers *said* he was a suicide. I knew him during and just before they gave him his freedom. He was in love with living. We talked about it. All of it. He even told me about the kind of lady he used to dream about in prison. Quite different from any he'd ever cared for. But he accepted a new life. He never looked back. A man like that doesn't kill himself."

They were snorting and growling at each other in the pen. Amanda walked closer to them. The stud, if that was what he was supposed to be, seemed less intrigued by the cow than ever. He certainly offered no visible sign. Amanda could not resist a smile.

"I think I understand how you managed this venture." Masters did not seem to be dealing now, rather playing a game with her. "It isn't hard to figure, once I knew who was paying the bills. That's always central in any negotiation. But what I didn't know was how you could raise all the money. Shall I tell you what I've deduced?"

Without warning or much display of passion, the stud mounted the cow at last, his forelegs spread over the female's back. He grunted mightily when he sealed their bond and filled the air with rasping gasps.

"I think he's got emphysema," Amanda said, and turned away to return to the pool. Masters was scarcely a minute in following her.

"Your father was a collector. I know the government took every last thing he owned. It occurred to me they did not know of one enthusiasm that came to him rather late in life."

"I don't know what you're talking about."

The female was making remarkably anthropomorphic noises, high-pitched wails and moans so frank they caused Amanda to smile in spite of what Masters was saying. She turned to the great, awkwardly rutting beasts as if she found that a good deal more interesting than Master's discovery.

"Horses are sexier at it, I think." Masters touched her shoulder with his fingers. "Did your father ever mention a Dutchman to you?"

She shrugged away from him and pretended no interest beyond the mating beasts.

"If someone were not careful, a good thing could be lost." Alan Masters went on. "I wouldn't want to take something from you. I've no love for the IRS. The past's past, Amanda, or Mary

Louise, as I remember the name of the child in that photograph. That man in the picture adored that child. If she salvaged some little thing from a wreck, that man would be glad."

As suddenly as he had mounted, the groaning ceased, the bull fell off the cow's body, dropping on his side to the ground as if felled by surprise. He rolled on the ground, his legs over mountainous flesh quivering, flailing the air. He quit all this in a moment, got to his feet and strolled away, as if he had stumbled and could now resume an activity dearer to him, his search for something to chew. The cow arched her neck, looked about, split her haunches and let go a torrential piss.

Amanda laughed. "You bore me, Alan Masters," she said. "Especially when you think you're threatening me. I'm not frightened of you, nor anything you could do to me, because you're going to stand trial, whatever it costs, whatever I have to pay to see it's done. Now why don't you go away and leave me alone?"

Roger Phillips and the professor returned bearing obscure hunks of food of various consistencies in a palm leaf, and a jug of tea. She thought it resembled dog food and said she wasn't hungry, but at their urging, she took some things in her fingers and found herself grateful. The professor had something for Alan Masters.

"He give you any trouble?" Roger gestured toward Masters.

"He's figured out where I got the money."

"Your Dutchman, he knows about him?"

She nodded. "So when I give him to Uncle Sam, I also give away the best gem collection in the world, after the British crown's."

"It'd be easy to make that part of the deal. I really think Masters would play his part."

"I agree."

"So we'll deal?"

"So we won't."

"So you lose the second-best precious gem collection in the world?"

"So I lived without it once, I'll live without it again."

"So I find another thing about you I like. You've got guts."

"I'm the little guy who runs two bucks into a million at the gambling table and plays until he loses it all. What the hell, all I've lost is two dollars."

"You've got a lot going for you," Roger Phillips went on, "but you're a little short of common sense. Let me tell you what we're up against, straight from the family head here. If we want help, we've got to go a step higher. That's the Sarumnan way in the desert. A young man owes his allegiance to his father. The father to the head of the *a'ila,* or the family, which is the guy we just talked to. He owes allegiance to the sheikh of his *qabila,* or tribe, and that's where we have to go now. And who knows if we'll get it there? And if we get the sheikh's approval, whether we can make it out of the country, even with his help? Discouraged yet?"

"I'll never be discouraged."

"Hang on, and let me lay on you some even tougher facts about crossing the border."

"We could make the border in the car on a road between Mizdah and the El Gorbah, the man tells us. We've had the worst of it. We know Gorbah. It was once a Roman outpost. It's well preserved but sterile and used to be a tourist must. But it's got nothing for us. South and a little west of here there's Abdullah's guerrilla training center, where they teach Japanese, Italians, Germans and others to fight for freedom by shooting off kneecaps and killing accountants. Better we avoid those political crazies. There's a pretty fair road near there that runs all the way back to Zarplis. There's also a new road to the border, built recently just by way of scaring the shit out of his western neighbor. There's a town called El Guettar where the sheikh is, and, beyond that, Emgayet and then Illizi, the border town."

"Where we could cross?"

"Where they're sure to be waiting for us to try. They've got to begin to know in Zarplis we're on the lam, Amanda. Someone's asking where we are, where Masters is. We're dealing with people who are paranoid when nothing's happened. Can you imagine what hell's breaking loose there right this minute?"

"Maybe if we move fast—?"

"Thanks to a new invention called radio, we can't move fast enough."

"It's our only chance."

"I keep thinking of my pal, Colin Hume," he said dreamily, "And what the professor's fisherman told him about those patrol boats. I thought he let me down. Just didn't show. Took your gold and ran. He was there, all right. He couldn't get past the coastal patrol, that's all." He shrugged and sighed defeatedly. "A bad turn of cards for him, and sure as hell for us. I keep thinking, if I were Colin what would I be doing right now?"

"And?"

"I don't know. What the hell could one man do? He knows this country better than I. I'd be sitting up there on the hill, cursing our unlucky stars and getting stoned, as he probably is right this minute."

"What do we do here and now, Roger?"

"Alan Masters's deal sounds better every minute. You'd even have your gems to console you."

She wheeled from him and buried her face in her hands.

"Take it easy." He turned her around and raised her chin. "We'll go on and get some gasoline and talk to the sheikh. Will you accept what I decide there?"

"If I have to—what else can I do?" she said desperately.

"You're not crying. I'd think you'd be awash in tears now."

"I only cry when I'm happy."

He kissed her forehead. "That's another thing about you I like." He held her close but broke off with, "Let's get the hell out of here before it gets too hot."

34.

AFTER NOON prayers, General Mohammed Abdullah finally consented to look at the file awaiting his attention. It contained, he found, the usual basket of snarls and howls. The World Islamic League had taken violent and public exception to a recent statement he had made about the necessity for the faithful to make a *jihad* to protect Mecca. He was tired of responding to those jackals. Did not the Koran call for a holy war? The PLO was again rending itself and needed another vast sum, his own elements in it were still unable to win support for the aggressive, unrelenting tactics which could achieve victory. The vile Americans were continuing to dishonor their pledge given in a signed and paid-for contract. Dull stuff, mean and dispiritifg affairs to return to after his mind had been gloriously engaged in dreams of the new world he would help create.

He put his mark on the pages where he had to. His eyes leaped out at the transmission from Azeiri in Washington. He had a high regard for Azeiri, operating there in the very heart of the infidel's land. More than once the colonel had proved himself. *Here was another of those plots they liked to turn their filthy hands to. Clumsy. Stupid. Hopeless.*

These verminous creatures they sent to do their dirty work. Women. Whores and harlots. Corruptors of men like the professor. Cultural foundation indeed. Who else? What else? Their hand must be cut off like any thief's.

As chance would have it, he next came to the radiogram from Zarplis filed the night before and marked with the code that would assure its presence among his papers at once, a sign of the high regard with which he held its sender.

This young and daring and imaginative officer had proved himself in several difficult moments. It seemed like a sign from a power beyond him that this dispatch followed the Azeiri transmission.

"Sainted Leader," it began, "I have reason to believe a conspiracy managed and directed by Washington is already in operation inside the nation's borders. The Special Adviser for Foreign Investment may be involved, although the nature and extent of such implication cannot be measured at this moment. I have taken it as my patriotic duty to initiate certain procedures in this regard. There is no doubt that my beloved General is the target and that your Special Adviser's role in this matter must be very closely assessed. I await your word. Brigadier Hussain al-Shalhi."

The General knew conspiracy. He himself came to power as a very young man using those tools against a fat and corrupt regime. They provided his blood with a special ardor. Conspiracy and subversion were a dynamic of history. Failed or successful, they created occasions when events can take a vast leap forward.

He called for his aide.

"We leave for Zarplis immediately after prayers. I want to see Shalhi and his sources when we land."

He rubbed his hand against the heavy stubble. As one moved through history, a leader also had to contend with the grubby details of today. He went to a mirror and studied his face, the beard a little grayer than he remembered it, the fierce eyes set deep in their sockets, a face hard-boned and firm, as he liked to think of himself. He tilted his head, and though his eyes were closed, he felt his gaze penetrate the very ceiling, pierce the golden haze of morning sun outside, reach far beyond the infinite blue that vaulted his beloved desert to attain at last the very heaven itself. He knew beyond doubt that Allah was with him.

The gasoline gauge was well below the half mark, but the road was better than ever. There were signs that it was being prepared for surfacing, mounds of sand beside the soft shoulders, even recent track marks of heavy equipment that had been working there. This both cheered and gave pause to Roger Phillips and Professor Carver as their car proceeded steadily on its due west course. It was good to have an easily traversable road; they knew it would lead, however, to places where they could not hide.

Not much was known by either of them about this part of the desert. There was the General's secret training camp, of course, and that had always been off-limits. Since the ill-conceived assault on the western neighbor's border, staged and mounted at Emgayet, all the towns near the frontier would be closely guarded, both men knew that.

Then there was the car. It was fast becoming a liability. They passed a town whose name they had not known, Sinawan in Arabic; they thought it could be an old town built in the old empire days; it turned out to be larger than they expected. They would have stopped but they saw a two-story red-brick building, eight arched windows on each floor, and a large entrance that seemed to lead to a substantial courtyard where they spotted patrol and police vehicles, although the building bore no identification.

Roger Phillips turned around to see the small, knowing smile on Masters's face. The men exchanged no words. They did not have to.

"Guettar's not far down this road, I suspect," Carver said to Roger in Arabic. "Does this building signify anything?"

"Government. I would think police. Also various soldiers." He used the word *mujahidenes*, which covered all kinds of militia.

"Will they follow the car?"

"They've certainly seen it. Still, they don't know all the General's cars down here, I would think."

"What will you do after we talk to the sheikh?"

"That depends on what we learn."

"You know what he will say, of course."

"Yes. I'm afraid so."

"I say again, what will you do when we come to El Guettar?" the professor said in English.

"What would you do, esteemed professor?" Roger returned in English.

"You are doing just fine."

"You haven't replied to my question."

"I wouldn't like to lose all that I've managed so far," the professor said. He smiled at Amanda.

"Nor would I."

"I beg your pardon." Masters was addressing the professor. "Did I hear you say the name of this town was Guettar?" He pronounced it *guitar*.

"Yes, Mr. Masters."

"A lot of these names sound alike to me. Is there another place that sounds like it? Is it near the training center and some old Roman ruins?"

"It's a common name all over the north African desert, Mr. Masters. Have you been here before?"

"I've never been more than 50 miles from Zarplis, professor." A faint trace of a smile flickered on his face.

"Note, if you will, the faucets, eighteen karat." Eddie Parker gave one a turn. "This isn't your ordinary basin, swishing and hissing when you want to wash your hands. The sink's one piece of the finest Greek marble. A gift, of course. We don't charge our richer Arab friends and they in turn give us things no one can live without. This doorhandle, for instance. Those are real pearls."

Ted and Tracy Boardman were going through the Western and Alliance Petroleum plush job at the far end of the airstrip in the desert at Khorfa.

"I've got only one regret," Tracy said, as she opened the door to the pilot section.

"I know what it is," Ted Boardman added as he made way for Parker. "This is the kind of airplane to renew our membership in the Five Mile Club."

"Even though Malta's so close we'd hardly have time to get it together, right, darling?" Tracy had been elated since arising. The day was soft and glorious. They had clung to each other earlier with a fierce and new-found ecstasy, a new plateau of touch and mutual understanding.

"What's the Five Mile Club?" Eddie Parker said.

"How long you've been flying, Eddie? You've never made love airborne?"

They laughed at poor Eddie. Tracy took the copilot's chair and looked over to Ted. "It's gorgeous," she said.

"You're sitting on the finest doeskin," Eddie Parker offered.

"One of the emirs thought it'd be a nice gesture so he had someone come down from Rome and reupholster those chairs."

"I think I've fallen in love with an airplane."

Beyond the lounge, the bedroom and the galley, was a cargo section. There Eddie Parker pointed to dozens of slate-enforced cases marked SURPLUS PARTS and addressed to Terre Haute, Indiana.

"Just like that?" Ted Boardman said breathlessly.

"Just like that. And they're waiting for you in Valletta; they'll be aboard the *Norman Knight* three hours after you land."

"'God's in his heaven, all's right with the world,'" Ted Boardman said.

"Tennyson," Tracy said.

"Wrong," Eddie Parker said. "Browning. And I bet you guys thought I was dumb."

They all laughed.

El Guettar had no government buildings. It was the largest town in that part of the desert after Zarplis. It even had a modest *souk*. There was a real garage with all the gasoline they needed. For the first time, the sheer presence of Amanda Miller became a problem. When she got out of the car at the gas pumps, robed men approached her, muttering and gesturing. Roger Phillips had to convoy her to the female rest area.

The car itself drew a crowd of boys who circled and touched it. One even took it upon himself to dust it. When Roger came back he escorted Alan Masters to the rear of the place.

"Do I have to wait inside the car while you're gone? I'd like to stretch my legs. And can't we do something about my hands?"

"Miss Miller's still got the pistol, Mr. Masters. If you go too far . . ." Roger bent over the rope on the man's hands.

"I'm not crazy, not here, not now. I know what's got to happen now. You'll come back and accept my deal."

All Masters knew about the town was what Sadriquen had told him. *A Westerner walking up and down beside a car like none they'd ever seen was going to be talked about. Sad would hear; Sad would come out to see. Didn't he say life was boring here?*

He watched Roger Phillips and the professor walk to where

they'd been told the sheikh lived. Amanda, the .45 on the seat beside her, rested inside the car, all four of its doors open against the mounting heat. He noted that she had one of the jump seats in back pulled out and had stretched her legs across it. No, he decided, even if she slept he would not make a move. Where would he go? He couldn't say more than hello and good-bye in Arabic.

Sad, dear friend, Sad, whom I nurtured and trained, Sad, come out, come out, wherever you are.

An hour in the sun.

A crowd of locals gathered and dispersed on the way to or from somewhere or something. Long as he'd lived in this country, he knew nothing about these people, who they were, what they did. He told himself if he got out of this, he was going to do something about that. There was much he would do. He had taken for granted too many things. *Where was Abu ben-Sadriquen?*

It was getting too hot to walk in the naked, midday sun. There was some shade on one side of the Rolls, but he was afraid he would be hidden if curiosity finally brought Sad out.

He looked into the car. The young lady seemed to be asleep. What if he could reach in and take the gun? What then? He'd never used a weapon in his life, but, all right, it'd be in his hand and she wouldn't know he didn't know what to do with it, still what then? Where would he go? What would the garage guys do, grab him, holler, and the others would come, what then?

Sadriquen will come by. Or maybe one of those Sandinista Americans he told me about the other day, someone who understands English.

When he was notified of his orders, Brigadier Hussain al-Shalhi went to the house of Hafir Azziz. The Minister of Culture brought him to Camptown. The brigadier had not known about the activities there and, being a bureaucrat jealous of narrowing or expanding boundaries, vented irritation for a moment.

"Surely, the General knows what he is doing..." Azziz offered as they came into the big house, which closed down any further reaction.

Mike Kelly told them what he had learned the night before. Not one of the Carver group had spent the night at the hotel. One car was gone. The possibility existed, he said, that they had all gone in the Audi on an excursion of some kind, the professor and this Phillips being scholars and all that. Yes, their bags were still in their rooms. Al-Shalhi's brow wrinkled. "I hope we've not let our imaginations run away with us," he murmured.

The three of them proceeded to the home of Alan Masters nearby. Marco, the principal servant there and special agent of police, sought to put an end to their fears. Masters had gone to the desert retreat; Marco had himself made all the arrangements. Food. A trio of musicians from the south. Two belly dancers. Gifts for the ladies.

"Ladies?" the brigadier asked.

"Both," Marco giggled. "He had gold chains to give them and fine rings. I packed them myself. Just three of them. And I was not to disturb him there."

"And his bodyguard, of course he went along?" the brigadier said.

"No, just the three of them."

"But Alan Masters is under strict orders never to go anywhere without at least one bodyguard," al-Shalhi insisted.

"Thi one walks back. At the last moment dismissed him. Do you wish to talk to him?"

"The bodyguard takes his orders from the President's staff!" the brigadier exploded. "Where is he?"

On the way to the barracks house, Mike Kelly spelled out the scenario. "They trapped him just like that. What a damned fool!"

The bodyguard was in his skivvies when they found him. Yes, he understood his orders. No, sir, he did not wish to be insubordinate. Yes, sir. But, sir . . . The brigadier drew his pistol and held it against the soldier's belly. Hafir Azziz put his hand over the weapon. "We may require his testimony, Hussain," he said.

"Confined to quarters, you are under arrest, pig," the brigadier said. Everybody knew his life had been spared only to be taken at a later time.

When Abu ben-Sadriquen discovered him, he was sitting against the rear wheel of the car in the little shade the car threw with the sun so directly above them. Masters seemed to be asleep. It took a moment for Sadriquen to believe his eyes. His elation was quickly overcome by his memory of the events of the other day. His friend, his benefactor had thrown him out of the house. He did not know what he would say or do as he approached the car.

Masters was only dozing. When he saw Sadriquen, he put a finger to his lips, looked inside the car and saw that the long sleepless night had finally overcome Amanda Miller. He gestured for Sadriquen to come with him to the gas pumps.

There he put out his hand. "Sadriquen," he said.

Sadriquen did not return the gesture. "I did not know you were with the others," he began noncommittally.

"This is no time to let anger sway your judgment, Sad."

"You betrayed me. I cannot forget that."

"I did what I had to do."

"Now it is my turn."

"I ask for no more. You were my special friend, back in the United States and here."

"The others are talking to my uncle. What are you doing here with them?"

"Sad, they kidnapped me! Tricked me. The crazy thing is that they think they can get away with it. Surely your uncle isn't going to help them? He's got to know what'll happen when all the police catch up with them."

"My uncle is an honorable man. They are guests in his house."

"But he'd be guilty of helping them get out of this country."

"They want to know about roads, conditions, the special police and border patrols. Things we are accustomed to telling travelers in this part of the country since the days of the caravans."

"But don't you see what they're trying to do?" Masters looked over to the car. He thought he saw Amanda stir inside the darkness of the car. "Look, get your uncle to stall. Call for help. I promise to get the General to forgive what he considers your treason. I'll lay it on the line—if he wants me, he has to take you back."

"You could have done that before."

"I was wrong." He held his hands out in abject admission of failure. "I failed you. But we can help each other now. Sad, hate me if you like, despise me, but remember what I taught you in business. Emotion and feelings don't change facts. Right now we need each other."

"And if I refuse?"

"Insanity!"

"I prize my honor too much to offer a hand to a man who betrayed me."

"Crazy Arab thinking! Sad, you're one of us, for God's sake, I'm offering you life again. It's death for me sure if they try to run across the border—I'll be shot along with them. You know the militia. Shoot first and find out what they've killed after the gunfire stops. And what about you, isn't it as bad as death—buried in this godforsaken town? I'm giving you a chance to escape."

Sadriquen regarded him with a steady and unrelenting stare for a long enough time to make Masters want to say more, but there was nothing left to be said. He kept looking at Sadriquen, offering tentative, uncertain smiles, as if he found encouragement in the unhurried answer.

"Who are these people and why have they come to take you? Are they American agents?" Sadriquen began again.

"I'm getting along fine with Washington. They were letting me alone. In time—no, they aren't official."

"If they aren't government, who are they?"

"Ebersol's daughter. She's apparently funding the whole operation. It's illegal."

"Mr. Ebersol's daughter? And you talk of *illegal*?" He snorted bitterly. "How extraordinary. A hand from the grave reaches out to seize you."

Masters came closer to him. "If she's dangerous to me, she could be dangerous to you if you let her get away with this, Sad."

Sadriquen waved his hand at the suggestion. He walked to the open door of the Rolls. He looked inside and stood there until his presence awakened Amanda. The return to the world hit her like a blow to the head so hard that it took her a moment to fix time and place and immediate past.

"Are you all right, miss?" Sadriquen said.

Amanda reached for the pistol. "Who are you?"

"A nephew of the sheikh, miss. When he heard you were here, he offered the hospitality of his house. Mr. Phillips suggested I bring you there."

"Will they be much longer there?"

"You know how we Arabs are, miss. We never move fast. Let

me bring you to the house. The ladies would be pleased to see to your comfort. The gentleman will be quite all right in my custody."

Masters did not go with them. He watched them walk down the road and wondered what Sadriquen was up to. He gave no thought to escape. The desert terrified him; the language barrier was insurmountable; the suicidal boldness of a single-handed run for it was not his style. And he thought of Sadriquen, once his friend, a man who knew what Alan Masters meant to Mohammed Abdullah. He got into the car, put his feet on the jump seat and stretched out.

35.

THE INSCRIPTION in flowing Arabic was two hundred feet long: GENERAL MOHAMMED ABDULLAH INTERNATIONAL AIRPORT.

Unaccompanied, he strode in. Face carved to bone. His hat square across his head, the bill short, dead straight over deep, flaming eyes. Carried himself like a flagpole. No aides after him. No expression revealed it, but the sense of fury made his very presence radioactive.

He stopped before Mike Kelly, jutted a finger toward him, a demand for identification.

Kelly had been there before. "Kelly, Mr. President. Camptown."

"Ah, yes. The Redeye missiles." He nodded quick assent. He turned to offer Hafir Azziz a baleful stare. It told the Minister of Culture he bore a heavy responsibility. "You took all necessary steps, Mr. Minister?"

"Yes, Mr. President."

"He came to me the moment he discovered the deception," Brigadier Hussain al-Shalhi offered.

A faint smile flickered briefly across the granite flesh. "Alan Masters, is it possible he is one of them? That he has arranged all this?"

"We do not know, Mr. President," the brigadier said.

"We have a message from Washington. It identifies the young woman as the daughter of a former business associate of Alan Masters. She has suddenly been provided enormous sums of money. Apparently for just this job."

"We did not know that," the brigadier said.

"You, Mr. Kelly?"

"I am certain of this, General. Alan Masters did not know that either."

"So you think he is their prisoner," the General said.

"Yes, Mr. President."

"Taken by a foreign agent inside this country," he sneered.

There was no reply possible to that. Both men kept their heads high but said nothing.

"Kelly."

"Yes, General."

"You saw him at this—this party?"

"Yes, General."

"Love of women has always been my friend's weakness. I was perhaps mistaken to look the other way, to let him indulge that weakness. I knew he was lonely, used to the corrupt way of his world. What do you say to that, Kelly?"

"He was no fool, sir. He played a game with women but he would not permit himself to be used by them."

"But here he was trapped! I ask you now, is it not possible he is playing a double game? Allowing himself to be taken?"

"I did not know one of the ladies was the daughter of a business associate. He did not suspect either, General. I think he did not know he was being trapped, sir."

"Consider this, Mr. Kelly. Our man in Washington traces a penniless daughter of a former business associate who is said to be financing research here, but where does the money come from? It is apparently a vast sum. Could those clever scoundrels be only using that woman's identity—?" He left the question hanging in midair.

"As a cover for sending in agents of their own, Mr. President?"

"Yes."

"It is possible. I saw these women and the others. They seemed very inept to be professionals."

"All your agents seem very inept to us, Kelly. You think it was inept to send them here with Professor Walter Evans Carver?"

"No, sir."

The General turned from them and walked to the far end of the private military lounge. He paused before a large photograph of himself but did not glance at it. It took a long time for him to turn.

"All border stations to be alerted. Radio communication to be stopped for twenty-four hours. Cancel all nonmilitary air traffic inside and out of the country. The usual domestic procedures on all roads and border stations."

General Mohammed Abdullah came to them slowly. "My friend Alan Masters must not be abducted out of our country. Whether he has failed me or not, that is impermissible. I do not want him harmed. If it turns out he has somehow failed me, I shall deal with him. If those Satanic devils want him to get at me, we shall save him. Is there anything more you need of me?" He seemed to be addressing the question of each of them. Each in turn lifted his head and snapped, "No."

"I do not care what happens to the others, but bring my friend Masters to me as soon as you can."

He turned and strode from the lounge.

"Gorbah," Roger Phillips said when they left the sheikh's dwelling in El Guettar. "We can hide there."

"And then what, Roger?" the professor said.

"I don't know."

"You don't know?"

"I know this: Colin Hume's going to try again tonight. And if we're not there, he'll try tomorrow."

"That buccaneer? He's got his money, hasn't he?"

"He's got his honor. He never fails."

"How are you going to get into Zarplis, to Eagle Rock? You should consider viable alternatives, Roger."

"I don't like thinking about viable alternatives."

"We could try to make it to the Western and Alliance field where the Boardmans are waiting for us," the professor said.

"You think we wouldn't be stopped, professor?"

"We have a weapon, you recall."

"I ditched it. I don't need one to kill Masters, and that isn't what I came here for. Besides, I wouldn't like being caught with it."

"Thoughtful of you, my boy, but you've already committed several capital offenses under Sarumnan law."

"The point is, we'd never make it to Khorfa and the airplane. And I wouldn't count on Ted Boardman being there and waiting for us."

Amanda Miller, bathed, hair still wet, dewy fresh in a cotton frock fashionable enough to carry the logo of Hubert de Givenchy given her by the women in the harem, stood shyly before them. "What lovely, gracious people."

"We're their guests, Amanda."

She saw discouragement in Roger's eyes. "What did the sheikh tell you?"

"Bad news, I'm afraid," Carver said quickly.

"How bad?"

"There's no way out. The border stations are heavily guarded. If we got across, they'd send Masters back. Everything we've done so far would come to naught."

Amanda turned to Roger Phillips. "What do you suggest we do?"

"What *can* we do?" he replied.

"Roger believes his man will be at Eagle Rock tonight," the professor said for him. "And tomorrow night. Apparently this is a freebooter with principle."

"And a friend," Roger added.

"So let's go back there," Amanda said.

"The roads in and out of Zarplis have got to be thick with twenty kinds of police looking for us!" he exclaimed irritably. "And what do we do with Masters when they stop us?"

"Hide him in the trunk?" she suggested earnestly.

Roger grinned, "He'd be dead in an hour. If he wasn't, he'd scream his bloody head off."

"Amanda." The professor stared at her with mouth slightly open in astonishment.

"I know what Roger's thinking. Masters has given him a proposition. He always has a proposition. What's he offered you? More money?"

"He's promised me support for a research program like none that's ever been."

"And you're both tempted? You believe him?"

"He means it all right," Roger said. "At the moment," he amended after a pause. "Maybe it would be embarrassing and they'd want it kept quiet. But that's a very damned long shot. I think the son of a bitch would double-cross us the minute he could."

276

Amanda ran into his arms, felt the warmth and strength of his body. "I'm not going to let us quit now," she said firmly. "We've come too far, we've done too much. I won't, I won't."

"So let's go to Gorbah," Roger Phillips said. "They won't look for us there, not right away in any event. If I don't get some sleep soon, I'll have to find toothpicks to keep my eyes open. We can't do much for a while."

Abu ben-Sadriquen stopped them on the way to the car. He had been with other men during the audience with the sheikh, but they had taken no special notice of him. "I want to join forces with you," he began. "I know what you are doing. I am sure I can be of help."

"We could not allow that," Roger said after a moment.

"Why not, sir?"

"Frankly, your motives—"

"Are simple. I'm exiled here in this family village because I'm considered a traitor by the General. I have never had the honor to meet or to study with Professor Carver but I know and honor him. I have another reason, I once worked for the Fund headed by Mr. Alan Masters and Mr. John Edward Ebersol."

"Good God," Roger could not keep from muttering.

"I know what is happening." Sadriquen turned to Amanda. "Masters has already sought my help. But he betrayed me once. When I sought his help, he refused it. I want to pay him back."

"Perhaps this is a trick too," Roger Phillips said to him.

"You are wise to consider that," Sadriquen countered without resentment. "Masters has already offered to use all his power to get me back in the General's good graces. And I believe he might be able to manage it, for a while at least. But during my exile here I have done some hard thinking. I regret what I did to help Alan Masters. I have played a terrible part and one day Allah will judge me for it. If I can make amends, I would prove my contrition. Please have faith in me."

The professor said: "They have a saying here: 'The strings of fate are long, entwining and often tangled.' " He turned the last sentence into its original Arabic.

"And 'The ways of Allah, like the course of justice, can be foretold by no man,' " Sadriquen added, also in Arabic.

"'When tongues move quickly,'" Roger Phillips said, still in Arabic, though he chose to finish in English, "'the mind must proceed with care.' Mr. Sadriquen is looking for a way out for himself. He can't call off the police barricades, he can't stop the search, he can't get us out of the country."

"Let him speak for himself," the professor said. "What can you do to get us out of the country? Why did you not leave before?"

"I could have crossed the border with any camel train carrying contraband, believe me. However, I regarded it my duty to accept my punishment, however unjust. But now I find a heaven-sent opportunity to revenge myself on a man who became my enemy. In helping all of you after the things I did, I win some merit."

Roger Phillips grinned suddenly. "I like you. I also have to tell you, Masters has offered me and the professor damned good deals if we let him go."

"You believe his good faith?"

"I'm letting him think there's the possibility. It makes him more tractable while I keep the option open."

"He'd betray you," Sadriquen said.

"No doubt. That still leaves us with the problem of saving our own skins, not to mention getting him out of the country. What about your camel train for us?"

"They would extradite you even if you got through. They've got nothing against Masters there, so they would free him."

"Even though there's bad blood between the governments?"

"Reality demands compliance with international law," Sadriquen said. "In another few years, the General will have an atomic bomb."

"Then we're trapped here. You still wish to join us?"

"We are all in Allah's hands."

"So let's hide out in the Roman ruins. Nothing like an antiquity no one ever goes to anymore, right, professor?"

"Gorbah was always a Yale project," the professor sniffed. "I never found it interesting."

"No one goes there these days, that is certain," Sadriquen said.

They started to the car again. "Where did you go to school?" Carver asked Sadriquen in Arabic.

"What do you think of him?" Amanda asked Roger out of Sadriquen's hearing. "Do you trust him?"

"Not quite. About halfway."

"Why not all the way?"

"My father used to have a saying: 'He could sell refrigerators to the Eskimos.' Alan Masters could sell him."

"He couldn't sell you."

"Only because he couldn't find the hook. He may be working on it."

"Then you still may—"

"I say again: Compared to what, Amanda?"

Alan Masters eyed them all warily as they came up to the car, looking briefly at Sadriquen with the professor. As always, his mind began stacking minuses and pluses.

When Eddie Parker finally caught up with them at the Khorfa airfield, Tracy Boardman was kidding around with the ground crew in the shade of the Jet Commander's tail section and Ted Boardman was under the wing with a couple of Sarumnan trainees. Parker was white faced and out of breath. "We got terrible problems," he announced.

"Take it easy, Eddie." Boardman sought to soothe him. "What is it?"

"Just got a message. Close down radio communication! You know what that means?"

"You'd better tell us," Tracy urged quietly.

"Trouble! Could be anything. Maybe something political, or maybe they're on to us, maybe on to you, or the others you came with. Next they ground everything. Everything! International flights, domestic traffic, company traffic."

"How long does it usually last, Eddie?" Ted asked.

"Then they send the police—you know many police?" Parker went on breathlessly. "They find our plane, search inside, and we're dead!"

Boardman looked over to his wife. "We're not dead yet," he said. "We take off right now."

Eddie looked up at him, his eyes wide.

"You still haven't received the message to ground us, right?"

"Hold it," Tracy said. "What about the others? We said we'd wait all day for them."

"Obviously we can't."

279

"So we leave them in the lurch?"

"It's scramble time, baby. If this is designed to catch us, it's also meant to catch them."

"But they might be trying to get here right this minute."

"So?"

"We're not here when they make it. They're stuck."

"If we wait and we can't take off, what then?"

"The fighter wings must be on alert right now," Eddie Parker said. "In an hour their MIG-25 Foxbats will be scrambling, just wait and see. Their fly-boys love this stuff, any excuse to play hotshot."

"Better we blow the whole score," Tracy said.

"The best hash in the world! You know what it's worth?"

"We said we'd give them all day," Tracy insisted stubbornly.

"People say a lot of things, then they're forced to change their plans. All hell's breaking loose."

"We gave our word."

"We've done the best we can."

"You go. I'll stay."

Parker said glumly: "You'll never make it anyway."

"This plane can, can't you see, Trace? They may make a pass at us, but I've handled that before. *If* we leave right away. That's the point, don't you see?" he appealed. "We're in the middle, in the air before they order everything grounded. I'll be the hell out of Sarumnan airspace by the time that happens. Tracy, Tracy," he appealed, "didn't you yourself say everything's flowing their way and our way?"

She hesitated for a moment, put a finger between her teeth and bit it. "I did, didn't I?" she murmured.

"You accused me of having negative thoughts. What about your resisting the terrestrial tide now?"

"They *are* going to make it, aren't they?" she said aloud, but to herself. "I almost forgot."

"I don't know what you're talking about," Parker broke in. "I know these crazy fly-boys in their fancy hot MIG Foxbats."

Boardman turned wearily to Parker. "What happens if they ever get inside this airplane?"

"Why should they do that?"

"All this activity isn't to catch us, Eddie. We came in with people who were here to kidnap someone."

"You didn't tell me that."

"I sure didn't, Eddie. I just came along with them for the ride and a score. Well, my time's now and we're taking off before all hell breaks loose."

Tracy was smiling, a soft, warm and loving smile. "Ted's doing the right thing, Mr. Parker," she said. "Right for us. Right for them. Everything's going to be right for everybody because it's the universal flow."

"We better move fast, Trace," her husband urged.

For some reason, she leaned over and put a kiss on the cheek of Eddie Parker. He stared incomprehensibly at her.

She followed her husband to the Jet Commander, waving to Parker as if he were a crowd of well-wishers.

"Everything's flowing your way!" she called out.

As she boarded the airplane, she looked down the long airstrip as if she might yet catch sight of Roger and the others. She stood still on the steps when she spotted a car where the first of the oil pumps moved up and down, up and down. The car was throwing a plume of dust behind it as it raced toward them.

"Come on!" Boardman shouted.

Tracy Boardman did not move. *What if it's Roger? Wouldn't that be something?* Suddenly the car turned away from the airfield. The hot day sun was beginning to make everything in the world shimmer and glow. She heard Ted call her name. "Coming!" she shouted. But she could not be heard because the port engine whined deafeningly.

"The green of Gorbah! As far as the eye could see, twice a year all these fields were carpeted with wheat, corn and all the grains and cereals these people shipped that sustained life in faraway Rome. This was the granary of the empire." As the car approached the ancient city, brought to abandoned ruins by the winds of war, politics and the ever-encroaching desert, the regius professor emeritus's mood was epical as well as lyric. He had never before visited this city he knew as Theretrum. He now confessed to the others in the car that he had been guilty of a professional jealousy of his peers at Yale, "an occupational disease," he called it; he had always refused to be cajoled into visiting the ancient city. But he knew it well from the research and could not resist reciting its ancient glories as they approached the tall columns and arches that bestrode the cruel desert. Roger, at the wheel, could not resist a smile, yet all he thought of was not ancient Roman glories, but that he could in fact be leading them to the deadest of dead ends, a dead city in a dead world for nothing more than a few hours off the track usually beaten by police in pursuit of their quarry.

"This was no desert then, of course," the professor said. "There was water, there were springs, they were masters at irrigating the soil. All this land was indeed the granary of Rome. Rome produced no food, and when this was cut off from them by Vandal invaders, they had to wither and die.

"Soldiers founded it. The streets, as you will soon observe, are straight, at right angles to each other, laid out with military precision and unesthetic charm, everything parallel to the main road, the buildings very orderly and, as I've always said, not very interesting. We will find the mosaics worth looking at; I have seen reproductions, of course. The old city endured, became Christian when the empire did in the fourth century, and knew Byzantines as well as Vandals. The descendants of the soldiers were survivors, and there is reason to believe the city even managed to carry on after Arab armies conquered it. I shall be thrilled to see it, ladies and gentlemen, despite my personal opinion of my New Haven colleagues."

The old man lapsed into silence as the car came to the first old Roman buildings.

Roger Phillips saw the old man in the mirror, his eyes searching the sand-blown first relics, his body erect. The others said little. Amanda, her weapon in hand, sitting next to Masters and the Arab who had joined them and who had said little since getting into the car—they all seemed lost in private reveries. Only the professor could not stop talking.

"There is an interesting arch here. It is possible Marcus Aurelius spent some time here before he became emperor. Do you know that for a time it actually was a little republic with its own government?"

"Nobody seems to come here, thank God." Amanda looked around somewhat gratefully.

"In the old days it was very popular with tourists," Sadriquen said. "Tourism is not encouraged these days."

They were moving slowly on the old streets, ancient cobbles and slabs with grass growing between them. Even old Henry Royce himself would have shuddered at a machine daring so irregular a pavement. A row of pillars lined one side of what had been the forum. A wall marking a three-room temple to Minerva gave the car respite from the high, relentless sun and a position from which it could look back to the road and not be seen.

Roger was the first out of the car. "It's too hot to do anything anyway," he said. "I'm going to rest and then we'll decide what next."

There was some hesitation among the others, except Professor Walter Evans Carver. "The capitals and the pediments of a temple at the far end are worth observing," he announced and took off.

"I would like a word with you," Masters approached Roger Phillips as he found a bed of thin grass in some shade beside the temple wall on which to stretch out.

"Please," Roger began.

Alan Masters would not be stopped. "Time is running out. I want to repeat my proposal. But if you think that by playing both ends against the middle—"

"Go away," Roger Phillips said softly but firmly. "Don't try to threaten me. I told you before, I tell you now, you'll be alive so long as you don't try to escape. Right now, it's too hot to think or to move."

Masters looked up at Sadriquen and caught the steady gaze that had been unknowingly fixed on them. He walked to him slowly, as if responding to a signal, but the Arab turned and joined the professor as the old man strode joyously to his capitals and pediments, and Masters followed too.

The expected signal grounding all nonmilitary air traffic unless specifically authorized was received as the Jet Commander made its way to the end of the Khorfa airstrip. Air Control in the WAP Three Tower repeated the order:

"Tower to Jet Commander, permission to take off from Runway Two is rescinded, do you read?" There was no response to the second call. "Tower to Jet Charlie, do you read?" No response. Ted Boardman heard the radio signal but chose to ignore it as he had the other orders from the tower. He wheeled the airplane into position at the end of the runway and pushed both throttles forward as the airplane lined up. He was airborne two hundred feet before he passed the tower, the American controllers standing bolt upright to watch him speed by. They knew he had been receiving them even if he had not acknowledged.

"Holy Jesus," one said. "What do we do now?"

"Nothing. The poor bastard's got enough to worry about."

"No," the senior controller said. He went to his panel. "Tower to Jet C," he said. "Advise you return, advise you return. Condition is military alert, do not proceed." He did not want to make the usual inquiry about being read but knew he was being taped and so went through the form. "Do you read? Do you read?" he said.

Ted Boardman had the nose up, climbing at full power. His own plan was to head south keeping over Sarumnan airspace until he reached thirty thousand feet, the levels where international air carriers flew. Later he would turn and head north and west.

He was still climbing full throttle, planning to level off at thirty thousand, when Tracy Boardman saw, far to her right, three slim, bullet-shaped airplanes coming down from the sun toward them with a rush that made the Jet Commander appear to be standing still at six hundred knots. "Ted," she began, but he never did hear her warning.

36.

ROGER PHILLIPS lay on an indifferently restored mosaic on what had been the floor of a temple dedicated to Minerva. A patched wall shielded him from the sun and from the others in the party, which is why he had chosen to lie down on it rather than to absorb himself in what could be made from the faded stones of the seduction of Jupiter by the temple's namesake. Amanda hesitated, finding him so gone in sleep a stranger might think him lost forever. She kneeled beside him. His face was gentler than she had ever known it. Tousled hair covered his forehead and his hands were folded, sweetly, she thought, though she knew at once he would have detested the image, like a blissfully sleeping cherub. After a moment she carefully stretched her length along his body, so close her mouth felt the heavy breathing that issued from his lips. He did not stir from his heavy, exhausted sleep.

For a moment she reveled in the closeness and then began to speak, at first framing words without giving them sound, but finally whispering, so softly she was not aware that she was doing so.

"I don't know how to tell you this, Roger," she began, "but I'm very glad for everything so far. I know we're stuck and there isn't a lot we can do about it, but thanks for trying. You've really done remarkably. But I have to tell you flat out. He's not going to get away, even if you're forced to play ball with him. He'll double-cross you, but not me. Know what I'm saying? I've fought it since you brought up the subject. But I'm going to kill him if it comes to that. You accept his deal, fine—I'll stay behind. I know him now. Tracy taught me how to handle his kind. You get the little thing between his legs hard and his brain turns to slop. Then I'm going to figure something out. After you're in the clear. About the fee I promised, I'll see my Dutchman takes care of you. There's time for that.

"While I've got you here, there's something else. I owe you an apology. I mean, honest, when I think about it, I'm ashamed. What am I, some silly-ass virgin out of the American heartland listening to radio preachers about sin and virtue? I wasn't too bad last night on that dusty couch, was I, even if I say so myself. What I'm trying to tell you is that I'm really like all the girls I ever knew, even if I didn't used to get all the chances they did, or couldn't do it with just anybody for a hamburger, fries and a malt at McDonald's like they did. Still, I know, what's a fuck today, man? I'm hip, modern, if you can stand that awful word. Balling is just a biological thing, so what the hell, we did it. 'It's just one of those things,' like the old song says, right? I've seen you operate. Remember the other night at the Beverly Wilshire? You call a chick you haven't seen in months and hello, sure, come on over, we'll trip the light fantastic on the Wamsutta and good-bye, call again when you're in town. So we balled. I just don't want you to think that this involves you with me. You're free as ever. Don't think of me as some kind of instant glue and you're stuck with me or that's what I expect.

"So I have to tell you this. It meant nothing. Absolutely nothing. But I never knew anything like it in my whole life. It was so real I wanted to die with it then and there." She thought she heard him stir, but he was only sighing deep in his sleep. She brought her fingers to his face but did not touch it for fear it might wake him. "I might as well tell you the truth. A funny thing happened to me on the way to Zarplis. I got to like you. A funnier thing happened on the way out of Zarplis. I fell in love. Something that never happened to me in my whole life, not even a crush in high school. I told my mother about it once, she said I was frigid. I wasn't, was I? I mean, those were orgasms, darling, what I had before when I'd go hunting to catch up with my generation's sex life were spasms. I came. Three glorious times! Holy Jees, it can't be like that all the time, can it?

"Okay, don't feel obligated. I'll be around any time you want. Put my name in the book and call. Any time. That is, if I get out of here after—" She thought she heard him stir, but his eyes were closed and his face was soft with repose. "After I kill Masters. And if I don't . . ." Her voice drifted to nothingness in a mist of reverie.

"If you don't—what?" she heard, a whisper.

"I'm sorry," she exclaimed and began to move away. A hand fell across her body. "My shy lady of the oleanders. You said *fuck*. You said *come*."

"You pretended to be asleep," she said like an accusal.

"I was asleep. I thought I was dreaming."

"You were dreaming."

"Three?" He turned his body to hers. "You were fabulous, did I get to tell you? Problem is we're never alone. Did you really come three times?"

"I'm so ashamed, I could die."

"Half the female sex has trouble making it once, they tell me."

"Did you hear that part about loving you?" she said gently.

"Wouldn't miss it for the world." His hand was reaching for her under the Givenchy.

"I don't want you to feel trapped." He was kissing her before she could say more.

"Mind if I take these off?" His fingers were pulling at the elastic of her tiny panties. "You could show your appreciation by lifting your pretty tush."

She lifted. "Last time I didn't want you to think you were seducing me, didn't know what I was doing."

The panties were off. "I need help too," he said. "Zipper's loose, just down pull a little. Ever done it half-dressed?"

"I always did it half-dressed. That was one of my problems." She could feel his hardness as he turned her over and sought her between her legs.

"Bet you never did it in broad daylight in a temple to Minerva."

She held him within again, more gloriously than before. "Never, never," she moaned joyously. She opened her eyes to see him floating above her, his palms flat on the ancient temple floor so his weight was not on her, but still she felt all of him within, all of his body and his being and with him all of the world, the cloudless sky above him and the blazing sun, she contained it all.

Fingers locked, they lay side by side and watched the world come back, a row of topless columns and the wall shimmering in the molten sunlight. "Amanda, Amanda," she heard.

"Yes?"

"Amanda, Amanda," he said again.

"What?"

"Don't..."

"Don't what?"

"Don't die."

"I don't want to die."

"I may not let you..."

Staring at the sentinel columns she waited for him to finish, for his voice seemed to have been switched off in mid-sentence. She turned her head to find him lifting himself to his knees. "Let me what?"

"Good grief," he resumed without turning his own head to hers. "Look at that."

Down the ancient road, where it curved to macadam and a parking area made in other days for tourists to leave their transports, a large and stately bus rolled smoothly to a stop. They could see legends written large across it; what Roger Phillips stayed with was the Arabic:

> "*All Honor to the German Guests of Our Great Revolution!*"
> —*General Mohammed Abdullah*

No doors opened. They waited to see what would happen, but no one emerged.

"Why don't they come out?" Amanda said.

"They're afternoon-napping. Or being lectured. German tourists are highly organized. The thing's air-conditioned, so don't worry about them." He kept studying it intensely. At length, he said: "Find Carver and send him here to me. Don't let them see you from the bus. And you stay with Masters and keep him away. Got your gun?"

It lay on the ground not far from them. "*Semper fidelis*," she said, taking it up. "You see, I know Latin. Also *quid pro quo* and *habeas corpus*. Just so you don't think cultural differences separate us and all we have going for us is sex."

He grabbed an ankle as she stood up. "Be careful with Masters. He might be inquisitive. Don't shoot him."

She looked down at him on the mosaic. "I don't want to."

"We need him alive. Get going."

Still prone, he turned to study the German bus and did not move his eyes from it as she headed across the weathered marble.

In Zarplis, at that moment, the Audi was observed by a nineteen-year-old named Bashir Hamza. He walked by it several times, observing that it was not only illegally parked but that its windows were down. The young man had come from an eastern village the year before, was without family or connections in Zarplis, and had been discharged from the army after six months for some reason he did not understand. He always wanted to drive a car and seeing it apparently abandoned, he peered into it and was struck by the keys dangling from the dashboard. It never occurred to him that he was stealing, rather that he was being invited to fulfill a dream.

He found the car easy to start and after some bucking and bumping found it equally easy to get the car moving.

Fourteen minutes later, the wail of sirens confused him. As the Special Police cars approached, he panicked, ran the car off the road, smashed into a mud hut and wound up pinned behind the wheel with a badly damaged spleen. A dozen pistol barrels were inches from his bleeding face as he protested innocence of any evil design and told the angered faces that he had found the car in the foreign corporation section of the airport.

Word of the arrest reached the Special Police Force Headquarters as the young man was being extracted from the wreckage. Brigadier Hussain al-Shalhi turned to Mike Kelly. "There's your third car."

That left only the Rolls. It was still missing. They knew by now that it had never reached the desert rendezvous Alan Masters had planned. Word had already been transmitted to police stations within five hundred kilometers of the capital to be on the lookout for it. The brigadier was certain they would locate it before dark.

He was equally certain that a modest amount of routine police work would soon turn up which of them had left the Audi at the foreign corporation section and which plane they had taken.

"I believe, Mr. Kelly, we have begun to crack this case, as you people say," al-Shalhi said. "Now it is only a question of time. I have already asked for passenger lists of all arriving or departing flights."

"Do we have to wait long for something as simple as that?" Kelly asked impatiently.

"There is much rivalry in the government among the agencies, you understand. We have several overlapping but autonomous intelligence machines. We cannot transgress on other's terrain if that is the right word. We must wait for Air Command, I regret to say."

"We have the same problem, brigadier," Kelly sighed and accepted a cigarette from a pack thrust at him.

"It is only a matter of time." Brigadier Hussain al-Shalhi pulled the flame from Kelly's proferred match to the tip of his cigarette and inhaled deeply.

The brigadier was correct about jealousy and rivalry among government agencies. Air Command headquarters had already received word of a kill three hundred miles south and west of its own Central Headquarters. A young flight lieutenant sortieing for the first time in a new Foxbat with two others had spotted and discharged its missiles at twenty thousand feet. No orders to fire had been given and the flight commander believed it was possible the target was not over Sarumnan airspace when it was shot down. Also, none of the pilots could identify the fuselage silhouette. Until further study could confirm these details, Air Command decided to delay transmission of its report of the incident.

When Professor Carver reached Roger Phillips, he too saw the bus and found his eyes glued to the Arabic message it bore. "Why, it's a veritable safe conduct from the big man himself," he murmured.

"Exactly what I was thinking." There was something else, Roger confessed. He had been stupid. He had been unimaginative. He had been a damned fool. The professor soon grew tired of the litany of self-blame and insisted on specifics.

"And Colin Hume's waiting for us."

"You're still certain, Roger?"

"He's all the things you think he is, but he would never let me down. He couldn't get past all the patrol boats last night. He's going to look for me tonight."

"And you think we could make the rendezvous point?" He turned to the bus. A door was opening and the first of the tourists was descending. "And that's our transport back, you're saying?"

"With our safe conduct written across it. Now all we have to do is steal her."

"My boy, never say steal. Our Muslim brothers take that commandment very seriously indeed. Say rather, *hijack*. We have to *commandeer* that vehicle, if you will. So it isn't stealing. There is one problem." He gestured to the front of the bus, now growing somewhat crowded with a group of tourists in shorts and neck-strung cameras. "What do we do about the German comrades?"

Abu ben-Sadriquen appeared behind them. They had not heard him approach. Though he did not know what they had said, he could read their faces easily. "I know German tourists from my boyhood days. These could be given a very, very extensive tour of these magnificent ruins. They love that."

"Which I could manage," the professor said eagerly. "Thank you for the suggestion."

"And you get left behind?" Roger Phillips said. "Are you mad, professor?"

"*I* could manage," Sadriquen said. "I even speak German."

"No thanks," Roger said. "What happens to you when the police catch up with you, which they will of course?"

"By that time, I'll be with a Bedouin camel train crossing the border somewhere. They wouldn't extradite me."

"Which you could have managed before," Carver said.

"I did not want exile. Now I must go."

"Have you thought it all out?" Roger said. "The General has execution squads that kill Sarumnans all over the world."

"Muslims don't fight their destiny, they accept it. I think, also, I should like to right a terrible wrong and to repay an unforgivable obligation to John Ebersol's daughter. She may want my testimony in court."

They could see the tourists begin to scatter. The professor acted swiftly. He raised his arm and broke into his flamingo-like run. *"Meine Damen und Herren!"* he called. *"Bitte, bitte!"* Sadriquen was not far behind.

291

37.

TWENTY MINUTES later they were speeding past the last of the oases around Gorbah on the highway to Zarplis.

"How's it feel?" Roger Phillips, standing beside the driver's seat, asked Amanda.

"Like driving your house while sitting on the roof. Otherwise, it's a pussycat."

Tense as the moment had been when they saw Sadriquen lead his eager party to the farthest corner of the old Roman city, they had all burst into laughter when Roger said, "Let's go," and had piled into the vehicle only to find their leader was lost in the thicket of switches before the bus driver's wheel.

"You have with you an accredited bus driver of the Phoenix Associated School District busing program. May I?" Amanda had said, taking charge.

Masters sat glumly in a seat three behind the driver, his head bent to look out the tinted glass window. To Roger Phillips's orders he had responded with grunts. He refused to turn his head toward him. He seemed to be saying he understood all the usual warnings before and he was sick of them. His only interest was that now Roger had possession of the service pistol. This had the effect of making him hunch up against the window and close his eyes.

Professor Carver researched the interior of the big bus. It carried two gleaming white washrooms with chemical toilets, and an ingenious galley. There were four water spigots from which flowed ice water. Some of the pullman bunks were down and he even tried his length on one.

Up forward, Roger stood next to the wheel, his eyes on the

needle that showed him the graduate bus driver from Phoenix soon had no fear of pushing the monster past one hundred ten kilometers an hour.

The road stretched ahead of them, curving gently, beautifully topped all the way. "This baby probably burns twice the gas at high speeds." They could feel the bus ease down. "How's our man?"

"Sullen. Scared to death."

"But the crooked mind's working, he's trying to figure out something," she offered.

"Of course. That never stops."

"What're our chances?" Amanda turned her head briefly from the huge glass before her. "Be truthful."

"They've been worse. And better."

"Pretty soon it'll be dark and we'll be on Eagle Rock. Are you afraid your man won't be there?"

"You're taking a lot for granted before we come to that."

"Like?"

"The German comrades back in Gorbah. What do you think they'll be doing before too long?"

"Okay. Screaming and hollering about their stolen bus."

"Precisely. Which brings the police and an all points bulletin or whatever it's called here."

"You underestimate Mr. Sadriquen."

"No, he'll be good. The question is, how good? Or, how long can he keep them from asking why their bus isn't there?"

Far down the road, they could see an obstruction. Amanda relaxed her foot on the accelerator pedal. The needle fell to eighty, seventy.

"What's that?"

"A tank," Roger said without turning to her. "And another armored vehicle. And a lot of soldiers."

"What do I do now?"

"Pray. Also look innocent and drive very slowly and try to keep from stopping."

From a distance they appeared to be about twenty in number. Army green. The tank was a Russian T-55 and it sat astride the road so any vehicle would have to inch past it and would have to be carefully maneuvered not to topple off the shoulder. Another monster partially hidden by the tank turned out to be also Russian-made, a BTR-50 Armored Personnel Carrier.

"On the deck, Masters!" Roger Phillips called out. When Masters hesitated, he was shown the pistol. "Professor, you too." The old man chose a bunk. "Show 'em your teeth, Amanda, smile pretty."

The big bus inched toward the tank. Amanda waved to the first of the detachment and kept the bus moving. Its tinted windows screened the interior so completely, she pulled open the driver's window beside her so they could see her grinning face and friendly waving. Roger touched his forehead in a salute from his position behind the driver. There was adoration in their eyes—after all, these were men married to vehicles of their own, trained to worship steel monsters. He could see eyes rise to the Arabic legend across the length of the bus.

The soldiers did not smile back but as the front of the bus came within kissing distance of the T-55, an officer waved it on. "Let's go." Roger kept the grin going even after they had passed the armored detachment.

"Everybody rise and sing the hymn of praise on page 45!" he called out when he saw the T-55 disappear in the bus's rear window. He leaned over and touched his lips to the back of Amanda's neck.

There was heavy military activity on the Zarplis road.

This was not the abandoned road that cut through the *chott*. Work crews clearing it or repaving surfaces chopped up by tanks and armored artillery on constant maneuvers looked up as the big German bus sped by.

Carver came up beside them; he did not speak for a time. "I am now a stranger here." He spoke to no one in particular. "Yet I am glad I came to see it. I'm not at all depressed to find myself a stranger in a strange land. I don't like it anymore."

"You're a romantic, Walter Carver," Roger teased.

"We all are."

"Someone called me that the other day, I think. Or was it the other year? I thought it insulting."

"The old desert made romantics of us all, Roger. The new one is big oil and big-power weaponry, air conditioning, ice water and awesome monsters like this."

"Look at this road. We've conquered the Sahara."

"So the Romans thought. Read Shelley's 'Ozymandias.'"

"Too romantic for my taste."

Some time later, far down the endless strip of concrete, they could see three men in uniform astride their side of the road. A convoy of road-repair and surfacing trucks whizzed past them. Amanda slowed down but it was clear this was going to be a full stop. "Time to play again."

"You'd better hide this time, professor," Roger Phillips said. "They'd be looking for a group with an old man. Take our friend and keep him still." He gave him the pistol. He watched them enter a latrine in the bus's midsection.

Two men in fatigue greens with officer pips and gold shoulder boards knocked on the door. Amanda Miller swung it open. They mounted the steps and looked down the long corridor.

"You have papers?"

Roger Phillips pointed to a box beside the driver. Mostly maps, but he thought they surely held papers too.

"Nationality?"

"German."

The two men exchanged nods.

"Going to?"

"Zarplis."

"From?"

"Gorbah. Our people are asleep after a hard journey. Also, they are not rugged enough for desert travel. But we bring revolutionary greetings from the workers of our country to the glorious soldiers of Sarumna. Have you seen what is written outside by the General himself?"

They had not. So he dropped to the ground and pointed to it with pride. The descending sun blinded him; he had forgotten about the blast-furnace heat.

"You may proceed. You speak Arabic very well."

"Thank you. It could be improved."

"Did you see a black Rolls-Royce?" he was asked amiably as he mounted the steps.

He paused but did not turn. "We have seen very few cars. Only military since Gorbah."

After the bus started to move, Amanda said: "You're a lousy actor."

"I thought I was rather splendid."

"You overact. Study the films of Spencer Tracy."

"Interesting about our friend Masters," the professor said when he returned to them. "Utterly fearless about money and such and shaking with fear that they'd search and I'd have to shoot him first."

"Thank God for fear," Roger Phillips said.

The sun was dropping toward the western horizon when the towns outside the nation's capital began to appear. Vendors along the road, camels, kids, veiled women going about their chores. Some men paused to watch the bus roll by, their faces studiously blank. Road signs pointed arrows to neighboring towns and gave the distance to Zarplis. Once these had been in two languages, but the foreign language had been painted out and only the Arabic remained, a token of the General's commitment to wipe out alien tongues.

The big bus pounded on.

Within, all four of its riders were filled with a sense of events rushing to climax. Walter Evans Carver felt a sadness he had never known. He knew now he would never return to Sarumna and the Sahara. It had changed; he had changed. The General—perhaps the incredible wealth of oil and all its consequences—had created a world he did not know, or want to know.

Roger Phillips still wondered whether he was right to be so sure Colin would show up on this night. At one moment the hope—for that was all it was, he knew—seemed absurd; the next, logical and reasonable.

Amanda felt her foot on the huge accelerator pedal tremble nervously as the bus neared the fertile coast. They had lost the element of surprise; she was driving in an infinite darkness to a goal that might not even be there. She thought of what her mother would say. She thought of her father. Like Professor Carver, she had no regrets . . .

Masters's began to sense that a moment approached which could well be his. They had the power; he had reason and certainty. He rose and went to where Roger Phillips sat, eyes glued to the window as the Sarumnan landscape raced by.

"Even if you get me out, which I do not grant . . ." he began.

"You're telling me the deal's off?" Roger broke in bitterly. "I figured that by now."

"I'm saying that even if you get me out, there will be no satisfaction for you." He pointed to the figure behind the wheel. "Or for Jack Ebersol's daughter."

"On the contrary."

"You think Washington has really wanted me? I'd be an embarrassment. After all, they could have done what you did. They never tried. They must have known I was on the Pacific Coast not so long ago months ago. If they didn't, they're a lot less sophisticated than I give them credit for. They didn't touch me. Know why? I was spending a lot of money. And they must know in the highest circles by now, my prosecution would make a lot of people in business and government who once sucked up to me damned uncomfortable.

"But before we get to that, do you know what would happen if your crazy scheme actually works? Diplomatic protests, not only from the General but from all the OPEC oil producers. How are your people going to like being cut off from oil? How are you going to take ten cents a gallon more at the gasoline pump?

"And when you get me indicted, what then? I'll have the best lawyers in the country. They'll tangle the courts with delays and technical problems. By the time the case is finally ready to be heard everybody'll be sick and tired of it. There'll be appeals. If I serve time in the end, for how long? Maybe they'll have an exchange of prisoners. I'm important here. As for Miss Amanda Miller's fantasy about me, I had nothing to do with Jack Ebersol's death. Sure, I wished him out of my way. But that's no crime. Your best witness, that miserable ingrate Sadriquen who tried to cozy up to you—he's the guy who's supposed to nail me. And be avenged. He's going to testify against me? What do you think my million-dollar lawyers will do to his credibility?"

"Are you still offering me your deal, Mr. Masters?" he asked colorlessly.

"Yes." Anguish burned in his eyes. Masters's voice trembled. "More than ever! Be smart! For heaven's sakes! You can't win in any event! We're headed for disaster!"

Roger Phillips slid down in his chair and resumed looking out the window. After a while, Masters realized he was not going to get his answer.

In the gathering twilight, Amanda saw what appeared to be a bonfire on the road. The distant stretch of road showed no town; the emptiness could indicate five kilometers or ten. In the fading light it was hard to tell. But the fire was real. Their first thought was a burning vehicle, but as they approached, they saw it was an oil flame from the ground beside the roadway, mixing smoke and fire. Two enlisted soldiers manned the roadblock, grim, coarse-featured country boys, their rifles at the ready.

Roger Phillips signaled Carver. Masters knew what he had to do. The professor followed him to the water closet without a word. The door swung open. The men rushed in ready to fire. "Who are you? What is this vehicle?" They spoke crudely and without polish.

"We are tourists from a sister republic," Roger said in Arabic.

"You have permission to drive at night?"

"But it is not yet night."

"Do you not know there is a curfew? All vehicles must be off the road."

"We'll be off the road by dark." He was grateful for that information.

"Where are you going?"

"Zarplis."

"Sorry. You cannot proceed."

"But we are expected there."

"We have our orders. All vehicles off all roads to the city by dusk. You have papers to proceed?"

"Have you not seen what is written on the outside?"

The men exchanged puzzled looks. Roger Phillips forced a smile and took them outside. He pointed to the words of the General. Everywhere in the Muslim world an honored guest is nobly and handsomely treated, he reminded them. "There, you can see our credentials for yourselves."

The men stared. One growled. The other seemed confused. "We have our orders."

"But this shows we are guests of the General himself," Roger Phillips pleaded.

"The General?"

"Yes, of course."

"General Abdullah?" the other soldier added, slack-jawed.

These country boys can't read. "I'm sorry, men," Roger Phillips said. "It is difficult to read in this light. Let me read what the General himself has ordered for this bus." He spelled out the safe-conduct slowly.

A courtly gesture showed him the door of the bus. Their farewell wave seemed almost wistful. "Close the goddam door and let's split," he muttered under his breath to Amanda.

She accelerated so abruptly the vehicle lurched forward and sent them all looking for support to keep standing. The door to the water closet opened and the professor looked out to find them laughing at the wheel. He grinned and went out to join them. The pistol he had laid in a rack of linen towels beside the sink lay there, forgotten. How long? No matter. Masters picked it up, put it inside his shirt and came out into the aisle and took a place just ahead of the row of latrines. He sank low in the chair, eyes just above the seat ahead. His mouth went dry; the muscles in his face were taut. It was his move now. He waited. He could wait.

They raced down the highway; this was what Masters wanted, not to stop them where they would have an advantage in numbers but to let them get into the city. There, if he had to run from any of them, he would find more familiar terrain.

When the highway reached the huge new hospital whose staffing he had once managed with a $50 million loan to a Bulgarian farm-tool group and whose dedication he had attended with the General, Masters knew he had reached the outskirts of the expanding city. The long twilight was melting to darkness; lights began to appear in some of the houses along the road. He decided to make his move when the two men rose from a talk they had been having to join the woman at the front of the bus.

He rose and in a firm voice announced: "Bring this vehicle to a stop."

They all turned to see the automatic pistol held in two extended hands just as he had seen it leveled at himself. He kept it aimed at Amanda Miller.

"Stop the bus, Amanda," Roger Phillips ordered.

The bus rolled to a stop.

"Now this is what I want you to do," Masters said coolly. "First, you two men. You will open the door, Mary Louise. The men will get out. You will close the door. You will start this bus and then I will tell you where to go. You got that? Any funny stuff and I blow her head off."

Amanda looked out the windshield, as if terrified to face an executioner.

"Take it easy, Masters," Roger said. "No one wants any heads blown off. Open the door, Amanda."

"No," she said.

"You heard me. Open the door," Masters hit each word with a sledgehammer.

"Do open it, Amanda," the professor urged.

"There's no ammunition in that gun," she said softly, still facing the windshield.

"Don't give me that," Masters snapped. He cocked the hammer.

"Go ahead. Try it. See for yourself."

Roger Phillips could see the extended hands quiver a little. "You're trying to trick me." He felt under the butt of the pistol with his left hand. "The clip is still in."

Amanda turned slowly to face him. "I've grown accustomed to my face, so I wouldn't want to chance it being blown away. Do you think I'd leave a loaded gun for you? I emptied the cartridges. I don't believe in"—she smiled primly—"well, violence."

"You lie!" Masters cried out. "You lie!" He flicked off the safety. His arms stiffened, the trigger finger trembled.

"I never lie. Well, hardly ever. Or to put it another way, I sure as hell wouldn't lie now."

"Open that door! I warn you for the last time. I'm going to pull the trigger."

"Squeeze, not pull," she said and moved to get up.

Roger Phillips stared from her to the man with the gun. *Was she faking?* He couldn't be sure. He would not let her take the chance. "Do what the man says, Amanda."

"There's no bullet to stop me," she repeated.

"You asked for it!" he exclaimed. Alan Masters squeezed the trigger.

Nothing but a hollow *click*.

In that moment, Roger leaped on him and had him on the deck, slamming his fist at his head and sending the pistol down the aisle. Amanda threw herself over their sprawled bodies to retrieve the weapon. She fell on it, got to her knees and was on her feet as Roger brought Masters to the supine position.

"A little something taught me by my stepfather of blessed memory. Always keep the chamber empty, he said, it's an additional safety factor you can easily fix. But there are five rounds in the clip." She held the weapon close enough to touch the forehead of Alan Masters and jacked the slide back twice. A fat bullet tumbled out onto the floor in front of his eyes.

Masters turned to hug the deck and bury his face in his hands. "Don't kill me!" he wailed. "I'll do whatever you say."

"Then get up and relax," Roger Phillips said without rancor.

Fifteen minutes later they were near the center of busy Zarplis, pushing through the heavy traffic snarling every intersection. The bus moved slowly past the officers charged with keeping all the cars moving. Professor Carver told Amanda Miller where to turn, and soon, without touching the heart of the city, they were headed toward the Hamaldan road and the cutoff that would bring them to Eagle Rock.

The government building which Roger Phillips had observed in Sinawan earlier that day housed, among several other agencies, a Special Branch of the Presidential Security Police charged mainly with matters dealing with political opposition, called insurrection. Its report of a black Rolls-Royce spotted that morning as it moved toward El Guettar was radioed to headquarters after general orders were received by all agencies to report any movement of nonlocal vehicles in the area.

"This is the message we've been waiting for," Brigadier Hussain al-Shalhi told Mike Kelly. He translated the description of the car for his American friend and brought him to a wall map. "This is where they were this morning. I'll order every security point on every road near there to stop the car."

"Isn't that near the border, here?" Kelly pointed to the boundary line.

"They wouldn't try to cross in the car. They'd know that's impossible."

"But they're down there."

"Of that we're certain. Finding them is only a matter of routine police work now."

They left the bus on a stretch of dirt road that angled off the highway about three-quarters of a kilometer from the Eagle Rock cutoff. Night had fallen on the land and a hot desert wind was stirring the scrub and iceplant on the sandy soil. They all looked to Carver for some sign of his opinion of the gathering windstorm, but he offered none. He led the way, walking quickly and silently, and they followed.

The footing was smooth enough but the walking made Masters breathless in a very short time. "Here, I'll help you." Roger Phillips linked his arm to his. "We'll soon be there."

The wind stiffened. It was going to be something one would not like to be out in, but later, much later. Roger knew that, so did the professor. Amanda, who knew another desert, was aware of that also; they all hoped it would be hours before it burst to full life. Only Masters feared it even now. Deep instinct for any survival fought a fatigue that made him want to quit every other step of the way; some instinct persuaded him that to be abandoned even here could be death.

At the coastal road, traffic was sparse. As lookout, Roger signaled them to cross. They passed what was left of the old sign and soon were making their way to the water in the thickening dark. They began to hear the slap and hiss of the waves breaking on the rocks.

They were too far from the rendezvous point to look for lights on the sea. They did not want to begin the search of the horizon, not yet, not now. They did not want to face disappointment and the terror of a dead end when there is no other place to go.

There was a call from Gorbah.

Brigadier al-Shalhi took the call himself. Fourteen German tourists had been hoodwinked by an imposter they thought British who told them he was a guide sent to inform them about the Roman ruins. He had lectured to them for some time and then turned them over to an assistant, a young Arab who spoke German and who, after giving them a splendid tour, seemed to have simply disappeared. When they finally made their way back to their bus, it proved to be stolen.

Yes, the caller answered the brigadier, they had the Rolls-Royce in custody. Unfortunately it could not be made to run. The absconders had removed all fuses and cut many wires under the bonnet. Yes, he would see that it would not be touched. No, sir, they did not have a fingerprint man, but he would contact Sinawan.

He had of course checked the movement of the party in the Rolls-Royce. They were four in number, three men, one woman. They had conferred earlier in Guettar with the sheikh, who offered the expected politeness to all travelers who received his hospitality. They had asked him about the road conditions and the rules and regulations concerning foreigners crossing nearby borders. The sheikh had informed them of the many difficulties. He gave them tea and some refreshments, and the women of the harem gave hospitality to the woman in the party, and that was it.

The brigadier turned to Kelly and his staff after he put down the phone. "They will be trying to cross the border in that bus. You know what to do."

He had scarcely hung up when another call told him of the shooting-down of a civilian transport plane which had taken off against orders from the tower at WAP Three. Air Command had already verified that the plane had been taken without permission after an arrangement to charter it had been rescinded because of the events of the day.

"They've found the other two people in the party," al-Shalhi told Mike Kelly. "They have tried to hijack an airplane."

"And?"

"They've been shot down."

"Good." Kelly would have felt fine merely to have bested any adversary, but he had a special reason for wanting the Andes informer knocked off.

When Hussain al-Shalhi got up from behind his desk, he went to the wall map again. "Now we know just where to catch them. We won't need air support and I'll tell Coastal Command to stand by for further orders."

"Perfect, sir," Mike Kelly said.

The brigadier summoned his aide to give the necessary orders.

38.

AMANDA MILLER was the first to see them.
Far away, on the windward side of the rocks jutting out into the dark waters where wind-driven wavecaps slashed the rocks, she spotted tiny flashes of lights going on-off, on-off, on-off.

Roger Phillips came to her side; he felt in his bones they were what he wanted them to be, but it was a lifelong habit to be certain before being self-assured. "Could be," he conceded.

Nevertheless, he ordered Masters closer to the rocks that directly touched the water. The lights were wholly off for a time, then began again, on-off, on-off, on-off. *It could only be Colin Hume.* He could feel his heart thump harder. *Be there!* The vessel was heading toward them, blacked out now. That was the pattern; he remembered it from Catania. Don't flash in a regular way. On-off, on-off, on-off. The strobes pierced the darkness with tiny explosions of light, gone as quickly as they had come. *It has to be Colin. Another vessel would show running lights. Who else but Colin?*

He felt Amanda's hand touch him. He turned to her beside him. She had been there for some time, but he had not known it. Her eyes glistened with gratitude.

She did not have to say a word. "I don't know," Roger said.
"I do."

Again the strobes, flashing. On-off, on-off. As the vessel turned past the farthest outcrop, the powerful thrum of its engines was unmistakable; they could only belong to a very special vessel, Roger Phillips knew that even if he was not yet able to say it was Colin Hume.

Then its lights went wholly off. The engines were cut to idling.

Over the wind he heard something; he could not make of it more than a blur of sound, but when he heard it again it became a voice he knew. On the third repetition it was his name: "Roger!"

He cupped his hands: "Colin!"

A moment later the boat was alongside, in the old place where they had managed it so many times in the old days. He recalled how Colin used to joke that he had to hire men locally to work these rocks to make an embarkation point. It could not have been better built with concrete and wood by the best engineers.

Colin Hume's first words: "Where in the hell have you been, old boy?"

And Roger Phillips's: "Funny, I was going to ask you the same thing."

Moments later, they were moving out on the dark water. The wheel was handled by one of Colin's girls. Roger could not recognize her at once, perhaps she was not even the one he had seen up there on the hilltop. Below, a bank of glowing screens was monitored by two young ladies. "I think you've met my radar expert, Shoshana," he said. "Remember she was going back home to see a sick mother. She's stayed on for this, you know."

The woman turned from her screens: "Nothing out there, Collie," she said and acknowledged their meeting before with a grin.

"Half-speed, please," Colin said to another man, who turned out to be the lone male crew member.

"Roger," Colin went on, "you haven't introduced me to your people. The professor I remember. How do you do, sir? Nice to see you again."

The professor touched his forehead. "I am grateful to you, sir."

"This is Alan Masters," Roger began. "He's our principal passenger."

"Nice to meet you at last, sir," Colin said. "Sorry I kept you waiting."

"Collie." There was foreboding in the voice of the woman working with the radar.

"Look at this," Shoshana said in a troubled voice.

The others watched him. "Just come in, eh?" Colin Hume said.

"Haven't logged it before. North by east and moving fast."

"How far away?"

A moment later, they heard the reply. "Four thousand yards. Maybe more. Say four for safety."

"We'll go half-speed until we're clear of the banks," Colin Hume said to the woman at the wheel. "Condition red."

"Condition red," the helm repeated.

Lights went out. They began running in the dark.

"Relax," Colin Hume told them as they found places to sit. "We'll give them a run if they want to chase, but I've got to be clear of the harbor." In the dark they were grateful for the flash of his smile. He paused at Roger Phillips's side. "Nice to have you aboard, old chum. You gave me quite a turn last night. The Russkies had their students all over these waters, you know."

"We learned about it too late. It took me a while to decide you'd come back for us as soon as you could."

"Oh, ye of little faith."

Roger found Masters's eyes glued on him when Colin left his side. "May I have a word with you?" Masters said a little while later. "Alone," he added, for he saw Amanda sitting close to them.

Roger Phillips shrugged and moved to hear what Masters had to say. He almost fell as the boat picked up speed with a rocketlike thrust, but Masters caught him as he sat. The vessel shook with the thunder of its engines and the rush of air and water around it.

"I've got a deal for you. Can you hear me?" Masters began, his voice at the level of a shout.

"No." Roger patted the man's knee. "Take it easy. We're not there for some time."

Masters seemed not to understand. Every moment mattered. "Jack Ebersol's gem collection," he began but soon realized he could not even hear his own words. He slammed his fist to the deck and turned from Roger.

Colin appeared from the deck, hanging on a rail, his arm gesturing to the bow. He was also shouting, but Roger did not know what he said. Behind, him he could see a white rooster-tail over the dark sea as the boat pushed forward.

Fourteen minutes later, the roaring was throttled down. The motors ran smoothly. A switch was thrown and dim blue light enveloped the cabin. Colin walked among them, his hand supporting himself on a rail. "We're going to rest here a while. It's all over, my chickadees."

He found Roger and gestured to Masters, hunched on the deck in a fetal position. "Tired?"

"Planning."

"Escape?" Colin laughed. "Has he brought rocketproof waterwings?"

"He may try to bribe you."

"Who is he?"

"You read the papers?"

"Only for the football. Ours, not yours. Basketball, in season."

"Then you don't know Alan Masters?"

"What'd he do that made the papers?"

"A number of things. Mainly absconded with more money than all the Rockefellers combined have."

"A man I'd like to know better," Colin teased. "What was he doing in Sarumna?"

"Hiding out. Probably making more money. He's a queen bee when it comes to money."

"I think I'm beginning to fall in love with him already."

"Colin, I've got some more gold for you. Or cash. Just in case you're not kidding."

"I'm kidding, chum." Colin got to his feet to go to the radar screens. "At least I think I am."

They were at a dead stop, lights out, bobbing in the dark sea. They were startled by a hiss from a pair of speakers come to life around them. Colin's voice was easy and assured. "Evening, ladies and gentlemen. We're going to take it easy for a while. Didn't want you to think we're out of petrol or anything funny like that. We're on the lee side of one of your lovely largish oil tankers, not sure of the name. American, that we know because of the large quantity of half-consumed sirloins it keeps tossing on our deck with the rest of its high-class garbage. We'll stay here for a while, so take it easy." The speakers snapped off as quickly as they had come to life.

"I saw Masters talking to you." Amanda slid over to where he sat on the deck. She was wearing an iridescent orange covering, like the crewwomen aboard. "What's he saying?"

Roger Phillips shrugged. "I expect what he always talks about. We couldn't get into it. The noise."

"He never gives up."

"It's part of his charm."

"Put your arm around me, I'm cold," Amanda said. "That's part of *your* charm."

"I thought you loved me for my money."

"*I'm* supposed to say that. I won't have any, you know."

"You owe me a lot. Try to keep that much at least."

"When Masters starts talking about my father's gems . . . They're not my father's," she corrected herself. "Or are they? The Dutchman says they're his."

Roger brought her closer into his embrace. "The lawyers will make a fortune out of it. Think of the positive side."

"I'll try to see you get what I promised."

"Maybe you can buy five houses I happen to know are for sale in a place called Palm Springs. Before the lawyers get to work on you, I mean."

She looked about nervously. "Why are we stopping so long? What's your friend doing? Can he be trusted?"

"I promised him a bonus with money you maybe don't have. I bet Masters is thinking about him right now."

"I'm scared," Amanda said.

"Try not to think about him for a while."

He kissed her forehead lightly, as one does a child who is beginning to be boring, and left her side.

Professor Carver was clinging to a rail on the bow, looking out to the dark sea when Roger found him. The two men stood silent for a long time. There was nothing to say they had not said; there was nothing that needed saying. Besides, Roger Phillips knew, the old man wasn't thinking about Masters, the jeopardy that still surrounded them or their chances of coming through. The Mediterranean was his spiritual home, the center of the world, he used to call it, then and now, he always added. Roger could sense the feeling of loss and joy, the blending of the old man's years here gone forever with the ecstasy of study and research he had loved so dearly.

"How I wish I could believe," Carver said without warning.

"But you do, sir. Your students soon found out that beneath the professorial skepticism—"

"Believe, *really* believe. My damned generation. They trained us to look so hard, belief is impossible. I'd like to think that as I came back here with you after I thought I'd never see it, I'll return another time. I don't mean in body. These bones are not as superb as I thought them."

"My fault, sir. I shouldn't have put you through this."

"Wouldn't have missed it for the world. Told you that before. Let's not be redundant." He sighed. In the dark Roger could see the smile that meant the subject was now closed. "Where do we go? Pantelleria? One of those smaller Italian islands?"

They were asleep, all of them, Amanda on a bunk in the forward section, Professor Carver in a corner near the glowing radar screens with their pulsing lines and white and red dots he could make nothing of, Roger Phillips next to Masters, close to the engines. Colin sat between two of his crew, his feet stretched out to a rail on the bulkhead. He pulled away thoughtfully at a long, very aromatic cigar. A length of cord led to huge headphones over his ears which connected him to the boat's radio. He took a drag from the cigar and blew a plume of smoke over his head.

"Interesting," he muttered at what he heard. "What do you see, Shosh?" he asked the woman at the radar.

"Very quiet."

Colin Hume got to his feet. "Better lie low for a while longer, however."

He felt a tug at his ankle. He looked down to see Alan Masters, a beggar pleading for a glance in some old corny lithograph. It amused Colin enough to offer his hand. "Something I can do for you, Mr. Masters?"

Masters had it planned. He was brief and to the point.

"One problem," Colin said when it was all over. "Or should I say, two? The fact that he's a friend—well, the money you mention could assuage that pain. But he came up with cash, hard stuff. You happen to have a million dollars on you, sir?"

"I have twenty, fifty times that in Geneva! I have ten times that in Milan."

"But not with you. That's the problem."

"I'm fighting for my life. I wouldn't let you down."

"I wouldn't permit it if you tried, sir. But I'm too old for all that. So it comes down to cash."

When the engines came to life again, quietly, the boat turned into the wind and started moving; Roger Phillips awakened. "Where you going to put us off?" he said, shoulders hunched, hands rubbing each other, when he found Colin Hume. "Any place so long as it's Italian," he went on. "You did great, Collie."

"Your man," Colin said thoughtfully. "Offered me a million."

"He has it. He might even come through."

"So why don't *you* take the odds?"

"I'm quaint. I promised Amanda."

"You like her."

"Did it show?"

"A little. Is she really rich?"

"Queen for a day. When Masters starts to talk—poof."

"Tough."

"She's got more than money. She pulled off this whole deal. The guy Masters screwed was her father. She could've kept the money and consoled herself on various couches with all kinds of therapists, doctors and otherwise."

"Yes, indeed, you do like her. I'm glad your man didn't have the cash on him."

"I am too, you son of a bitch. I love a man I can always count on."

"About those little Italian islands. I put you off there, you'd probably have to wait for *carabinieri* or some people like that to send a launch to bring you to the proper authorities. You like that idea?"

"Not much."

"Could stay with me all the way to Catania."

"You could alert the police—"

"Heavens, no. I'd put you off. *You* could alert the police there. We have nothing to do with them, chum."

"Sorry. Catania would be better."

"You might lie with your girl, if you like. It'll take all night. We'll be there about an hour after dawn. Too bad about the money, eh?"

"Hers?" Roger said.

"His," Colin Hume said. "I never had a shot at hers."

39.

A LIGHT haze lay over a smooth Ionian Sea. In the distance they began to make out an urban shoreline, docks, moored vessels, fishing boats, even a line of sailboats and beyond them tall apartment buildings with window boxes and iron-grilled balconies. "Sorry for the delay," Colin Hume said to Roger. "Used rather more fuel than I liked so had to lower speed. We should be there rather soon."

"No problem."

"Hope no one's too hungry. There's whiskey of course."

"So it comes to this," Masters was grinning without rancor when he came topside. "You are stupid, Phillips. Stupid."

"You're not telling me what I haven't found out for myself," he replied without resentment.

"I'd've played the game if I were in your shoes. There's a good chance I'd've had no alternative but to keep my word. It really would've been better for the government to keep it quiet. I know those people. You could have been rich."

Roger Phillips stared at him briefly. "I understand you also got nowhere with my friend the skipper," he teased. "*He's* not stupid."

Masters shrugged. "I'll take care of him, the bunch of you. I'll spill the whole story about Jack Ebersol and his collection. The tax people will go after the girl and all of you who got paid off by her." He laughed, rather like a cackle, Roger thought, and not without merriment. "All the conspirators!"

"Will you laugh this way from your prison cell?"

"You'll be in prison, not me! They'll be years getting to me, I've got the money to buy the best lawyers in the world, including the ones who are prosecuting me. There'll be years of appeals, going back to the fact that I was kidnapped. There'll be screams of protests from my friends in Zarplis. I'm a citizen there. I won't spend a night in prison. And if a single one of you had brains instead of lard in your head, you'd have had everything."

Something nagged at Roger's guts, nagged and twisted them and made him feel it would be a relief to rid himself of a truth he had to swallow and couldn't. Masters was right. No matter what they did to him, Masters had the money. Hence, the power.

Also the fear. Roger Phillips could see that. Through the nausea he could see a dark web of fright entrap Masters. "So it takes ten years," he taunted. "What the hell, sometimes even the rich get thrown behind bars. I may be poor then, but think of the satisfaction."

"Fools!" Masters exploded. The bravado began to melt miserably. "I'd've come through for you, don't you see?"

The boat passed the city docks and kept a course along the coastline past Cannizzaro where the land loomed high over the water's edge and the pleasure boats were fewer.

"Everybody below, please," Colin Hume ordered the passengers. He snapped another order to the wheel, this one in Italian.

In the cabin they huddled, uncertain why they had been sequestered not far from the radio and the radar screens. The air teemed with sounds they did not remember hearing, or was it that they had paid them no attention before? Italian voices barked and snapped questions at each other.

The engines went quieter, and quieter; the bump of fender against pier; voices they heard above them told them they had come to journey's end. The radio operator cut off her switches and gathered papers in a flat leather bag. The radar was left unattended, images still on the screen, but frozen, whatever they meant. They went up without a word or a glance at the passengers. It was as if the crew had gone through this before, because when Roger Phillips rose to join the girl he knew as Shoshana, she said without a smile, "You'd better wait here."

They stared at one another, quietly wondering what was to happen next. They could hear voices, but they spoke in

Italian—Sicilian? Even Professor Walter Evans Carver, who could manage in a dozen tongues including more than one used in this nation, made nothing of what was being said. "They're doing some heavy whispering," he said. "Plainly they don't want to be overheard as well as understood. I wonder why?"

The cabin door was flung open. Colin took two steps down. "Roger," he said, and added, "the lady too, if you please."

He closed and bolted the hatch behind them. The boat was tied to a small, neatly kept pier and a man was waiting in the bow for them, flawless in every detail. He wore faultless white trousers, a narrow, double-breasted blazer with four brass buttons, a pin-striped shirt whose collar was lifted high against his neck, the points inside the jacket lapels, and a small, unobtrusive ascot tucked into the shirt. His head carried a small, authoritatively inimitable hat atop an outcropping of heavy and beautifully pushed-back gray hair that reached just below the ears. He was tall, he was composed, he was monarchical.

"Don Giorgio, my boss," Colin said. Roger thought his friend behaved somewhat like a courtier not a buccaneer, and when his and Amanda's names were given, he was not surprised that Don Giorgio did not respond to an outstretched hand but offered a nod and two rows of perfect teeth instead. "He wishes to talk to you," Colin continued.

"Does he speak English?" Roger Phillips asked.

"He knew what I was about of course." Colin chose not to answer Roger's query. "I told him about the gold bar you gave me and gave him the cash you gave me."

Phillips was glad to see the courtier was still a scoundrel; at least he did not mention the second kilo. "Tell him we are delighted at the success of the venture and there will be a bonus." He turned to Amanda. "Right, Miss Miller?"

"Right," Amanda offered over an uncertain smile.

"There is a complication," Don Giorgio said in an English accented but quick and sure of syntax. "It must be put before you. It has to do with your passenger."

"We turn him over to the police. There are several outstanding indictments here, I understand," Roger said deliberately.

"What is the complication?" Amanda asked stonily. "Is he a friend of yours?"

"No, *signora*, nothing like that. I know of him by reputation of course. I have read much about him. Colino did not mention the name to me when he left."

"I didn't know it, Don Giorgio."

"Of course. But Radio Sarumna told me. You understand we monitor many transmissions in this area. It is part, how shall I say, vital to business. To know, you understand. Even in Arabic we monitor. We do not know when they do, but we like to know what and why."

"Routine, Roger, you understand," Colin broke in.

"So when I tell them in the radio room to keep me in touch with Colino's movements, my people are quick about midnight last night to bring me Zarplis Coastal Patrol and the names. Forgive me, yours I did not know, Mr. Masters I recognized, and of course it was not difficult to see what my Combattante was up to."

"And why it was, and is, being well paid, sir," Roger added.

"Exactly. So the mission is complete."

"Thank you, sir. We would like now to call the police."

There issued a gentle, mocking laughter from between the pearly teeth. "I do not think they are aware I have a boat. Officially of course." He rubbed his hands. "I have nothing to do with them."

"Then we'll handle it ourselves."

"You are too far here."

"Then Colin can bring us—"

"No," Don Giorgio said. "I will take custody of your passenger."

It took a moment for the words to reveal motives and consequences. Roger turned toward Amanda, then to Colin and, finally, to Don Giorgio. "Sir—"

It was all he could get out before Colin stepped in front of Roger until he was sure Roger did not intend a gesture to his boss. "Sorry, old boy."

The gentleman offered a peacemaking gesture with both hands, suitable for a cardinal. "All your expenses will be returned. We are talking of frustration, personal frustration. Life is full of disappointments. I am a man who has had his share. I have a friend. Small favors I have been able to do for him. It is our style, you understand. I call him in New York last night. I find him in London. I tell him what our radio has picked up from Zarplis Coastal Patrol. My friend has been a figure in a recent very large investment of their capital here. He is grateful, more than I can tell you."

"So you'll take our man and give him back!" Roger Phillips exploded.

"Colino has brought him to these shores. That is all you contracted for," the don said coldly.

Amanda said, "You'll deal with him? You can't!"

"I told you *signora*, I know him only by reputation. My friend in London is my friend. I deal with *him*."

Roger broke from them, turned to the hatch, found it bolted and somehow managed to push back the bar with nervous fingers, misstepped on a short ladder, fell on one knee to the deck and rushed to a large nylon bag where he knew Amanda had stashed the pistol. Masters stood aside as Colin Hume came hurtling from above and fell on Roger Phillips. The men groaned and struggled; Masters attempted to go topside, but Phillips seized him at the feet and brought him down.

When Roger came back to the world, he felt a tear just below the inside of his mouth and the heavy texture of something liquid he did not know until he spat blood.

"The gun's gone," Colin said coldly. "I threw it overboard ten minutes after the girl put it away last night. Now don't be a goddam fool. Get to your feet and let my boss finish."

Imperturbable he was, as if nothing had happened. He had been joined by two men and Carver and Masters. Don Giorgio looked over his shoulder, as if receiving a cue from a servitor that it was proper to resume. "Violence will get you nothing. Do me a favor and behave gallantly and I assure you I will be very grateful."

"Fuck you," Roger said.

Don Giorgio grinned, not clerically however. He filled his lungs as if to compose himself and turned to Masters. "You will be my guest, sir."

"You fools!" Roger pulled away from a pair of huge arms. "He's worked this whole thing, don't you see? He bought us. He's got the money. He got in touch with us! The CIA! He asked them to get him out."

"He's crazy!" Masters burst out. "It's a lie! They kidnapped me."

"That's what he's got to say! Tell them the truth, Masters, you're double-dealing the General. You've promised to give us the inside dope on everything there if we brought you out and made it look like a kidnap! Tell them!"

"Not true! Not true!" Strong arms were now restraining Masters too. "It's a pack of lies. I'm a hundred percent loyal and they know it."

"Don't come looking to us for help after this." Roger Phillips said coldly.

"Lies!" Masters exclaimed, his voice cracking. Don Giorgio laid a reassuring hand on him. "Thank you, sir," he said.

"I am ashamed of your friends, Colino. A shabby trick to try to pull," the don said.

"It is not a trick," Walter Evans Carver offered. "I am the station chief. This man got in touch with us. We contrived to make it look like a kidnap. That is why we got in touch with Miss Miller. She would appear to have a strong personal motive. She was our cover."

"He's a liar too," Masters muttered.

But Don Giorgio hesitated. "Perhaps."

"Colin," Roger began. "You're my friend."

"Yes, but he's my boss, chum. Don't play against that."

"The guy's killed her father. He's stolen millions, he ran away with hundreds of millions. He's wanted in five countries."

"Talk to my boss, Roger."

Roger turned to the *bella figura*. "Sir, forgive me my bad manners, my little emotional explosion. I'm sorry. I really am. If he's got a case, let him present it in court. Let's bring him to the local police."

There was a very long pause. "Amateurs," Don Giorgio said in Sicilian, then in English. "Amateurs. Stay where you belong." He reverted to Sicilian with a heavy command under his breath and large black handguns became visible, ugly snouts gesturing for Amanda and Carver to draw closer to Roger Phillips. "Come, Mr.

Masters, you must be very fatigued. There will be a bath and a change of clothes." He put a gracious arm around his guest's shoulder. "Your friend in London says you might appreciate a companion tonight. We have luckily managed that for you as well."

Masters took a step with him, but could not resist turning for a last look. For a moment, it appeared he was going to say something, but at length he turned, silent, a little smile in the corners of his mouth. He followed Don Giorgio over the side to the pier. The last they saw of him he was walking, the don's arm linked in his, to a waiting car.

POSTSCRIPT

BY NIGHTFALL the great square was filled with fist-waving youths and green-clad soldiers with bayoneted rifles. The reviewing stand was crowded with uniforms. Even the Minister of Health and the Minister of Cultural Affairs were in uniform. The parade of armored vehicles lasted for an hour, every available camera, film, or tape requisitioned to record the awesome power General Mohammed Abdullah showed the world.

He spoke afterward for more than an hour, sending out greetings and pledges of support to a dozen countries by name and to a number of others he did not specify. He promised support, material and spiritual. He called for a new world and announced the death of the old. He called for an end to brotherly conflict, but demanded peace on his own strict terms, for, he said, he had been vouchsafed by a power larger than man's a vision of the world of the future. It would be strong; he would not shrink from his duty to lead it.

The General spoke without notes; he spent more time talking about his enemies than about his vision of the future. He named the United States of America his arch-enemy and called it the enemy of the future world and the subverter everywhere of truth, justice and self-rule. He promised to return in kind every traitorous act its spies and agents plotted against the Worker's Republic and against oppressed nations everywhere in the world.

At the end of his speech, the General called for his friend and adviser to come forward. He called him by his Arabic name. Alan Masters rose from a seat beside another adviser of the President-for-Life, known as Julian Christopher and Michael Kelly before the new name he had been lately given. The two men exchanged smiles and Masters came forward. He was embraced and hailed as a hero who had outwitted the diabolical Americans and returned to prove his love and commitment to the General. No details were spelled out.

That was the last time Alan Masters was seen. He was put to death by injection after some very exhausting sex games at Camptown. He was sleeping so soundly that his host and friend, now known as Ibn-Hariqah, was able to report that the traitor fell into his deserved hell without knowledge, or pain.

Announcement of the demise is expected any day. A medical chart is being prepared to show a long history of heart trouble. There will be a state funeral.

Mr. and Mrs. Roger Phillips were married in a ceremony in the bridegroom's house in Palm Springs. Among the guests were former friends and associates from his academic years and a number of friends in the area. Mr. and Mrs. George van Leeuwen of Amsterdam, the Netherlands, were among the guests, who did not include the bride's mother, who returned to Phoenix the day before the nuptials. Marva Miller, after giving her best motherly advice about the inappropriateness of her daughter's makeup and the cut of the simple frock she had chosen to wear, announced that her presence was unwelcome. She left after informing her daughter that detectives were asking questions about her and that she suspected her intended son-in-law of hiring those investigators. "They asked a lot of questions about money. He thinks you're rich. Won't he be disappointed!" she said on departing.